S

W

Two red-ho
passion...over and over again...

The second in the sexy
Seduce...Surrender...Satisfy trilogy,
Surrender is as sexy as they come!

CARA SUMMERS

The Dare
"A strong mystery and great sex"
—*Romantic Times*

BARBARA DALY

Kiss & Run
"Sexy and fun"
—*Romantic Times*

SEDUCE...SURRENDER...SATISFY

Surrender

Would you give in...?

sexy stories about surrendering to...

Surrender

How far will you go?

Cara Summers

Barbara Daly

M&B™ and M&B™ with the Rose Device
are trademarks of the publisher.
Harlequin Mills & Boon Limited, Eton House,
18-24 Paradise Road,
Richmond, Surrey TW9 1SR

Surrender © by Harlequin Books S.A. 2006

The publisher acknowledges the copyright holders of the
individual works as follows:
The Dare © Carolyn Hanlon 2005
Kiss & Run © Barbara Daly 2005

ISBN 0 263 85085 4

055-0906

Printed and bound in Spain
by Litografia Rosés S.A., Barcelona

The Dare

CARA SUMMERS

Dear Reader,

Writing stories about triplet sisters Natalie, Rory and Sierra Gibbs has allowed me to create three very special women who find the courage to risk it all to get what they want. As they came alive on the page, I found myself admiring each one of them. But if I had to pick a favourite, I'd lean towards Rory – perhaps because she lacks the confidence of her more focused sisters.

Wannabe magazine writer Rory Gibbs has always thought of herself as the "muddled in the middle" triplet. Her sisters are tall, beautiful and successful; she's short, still trying to figure out what she wants to be when she grows up, and as unlucky with men as she's been with jobs. However, her latest plan – to land an interview with reclusive businessman Jared Slade – will allow her to prove to herself, her boss and everyone else that she's finally found a career she's good at. Problem number one is she can't get past Hunter, Jared Slade's handsome and dangerous bodyguard. Problem number two is she doesn't want to get past him – she wants to make love with him!

I hope you'll enjoy reading about how Hunter and Rory dare to take the greatest risk of all. And I hope you'll want to read Natalie's and Sierra's adventures as well – in *The Proposition* (August) and *The Favour* (October). For excerpts, contests and news about my future books, please visit www.carasummers.com.

Happy reading,

Cara Summers

To my cousins, the Kansier women:
Jane, Kathy, Mary, Margaret, Amy and Debbie.
I admire your strength, your courage, your love of adventure – and especially your unfailing sense of humour. You inspire the kind of women I try to create.
Thanks.

Prologue

IF HE FAILED, the drop to the alley below would kill him. Harry Gibbs stood on the roof of the Hotel L'Adour Paris and glanced at the gap between the two buildings. He felt the familiar rush of adrenaline and grinned.

He didn't allow himself to look down, or to take in the picture-postcard view that the roof of the hotel offered. At 3:00 a.m., the Eiffel Tower and Notre Dame were still bathed in light, but Harry focused all his concentration on that dark narrow space—ten feet at the most. He'd paced off the distance in the alley that morning. Just in case the robbery didn't go quite as planned.

And it hadn't. He'd gotten the necklace out of the safe, but he hadn't had time to close it and replace the tapestry before Madame Cuvelier had awakened in the next room and rung for her maid. There was only one route from the maid's quarters to Madame's bedroom, and that was through the salon he'd been standing in.

Madame Cuvelier, a resident of the small hotel for the past ten years, was a restless sleeper. That information was in the dossier he'd compiled on her. That made the theft riskier.

And more fun. Instead of exiting through the door, the

way he'd come in, he'd had to hurry out onto a balcony and climb to the roof.

When the sound of sirens pierced the night air, Harry turned and strode to the far end of the roof. Then, he did what he always did when the stakes were high. He dared himself to make the leap. As he crouched down into the position of a sprinter, he thought of his daughter, Rory. He'd been thinking a lot about her lately. Tonight, he promised himself. He'd write to her.

Clearing his mind, he murmured, "You can do it, Harry. *Dare you!*" Then he ran, lengthening his stride as he raced across the roof. Fifty yards became forty, thirty, twenty, ten. He prepared for the jump, felt his right foot hit the parapet. Then he leapt.

For a prolonged second, he was arcing over the alley, his body slicing through the air. If something happened to him…

Before he could complete the thought, his foot came down hard and he tucked and rolled across the roof. Lungs burning, blood singing, Harry got to his feet and ran toward the door. It took him less than three minutes to finesse the lock. The sirens were still blocks away.

He was whistling as he stepped into the stairwell.

AN HOUR LATER, Harry stood on the balcony of his apartment in Montmartre and swirled cognac in a glass. Now that the excitement of the heist was over, his mood had turned melancholy again as he once more thought of Rory. Dammit, he missed her. He had three girls, triplets, and lately, he'd been missing all of them.

More than that, he'd been feeling an urgent need to talk to them. That was impossible, of course. They'd been ten years old when he and his wife, Amanda, had forged their agreement. She'd wanted a normal life for the girls, and so had he.

For the first ten years of their lives, he'd done his best to give them one. But he'd become bored with their "normal" life in the suburbs of D.C. He'd missed the adventure, the risk taking, the thrill of pulling off a perfect heist.

Amanda had been firm. At ten, the girls idolized him, and she didn't want them idolizing his profession. Therefore, he could leave and resume his former profession as a master jewel thief on the condition that he didn't see his girls or communicate with them until their twenty-sixth birthday.

Harry took a sip of his cognac. He'd made a mistake—the biggest one of his life—by agreeing to those terms. He and Amanda should have found another way. Two weeks ago, the girls had celebrated their twentieth birthday, and six more years had begun to seem far too long. Time could easily run out for him before that. It nearly had tonight.

Turning, he strode toward the desk in his study. On the night of their birthdays, he'd written a letter to his oldest daughter, Natalie.

But it was Rory, the second born, he'd thought of on that roof tonight. Each of his daughters had inherited something from him. Natalie had inherited his gift for picking locks and his talent for disguise. Sierra, the youngest, had inherited his curiosity and his analytical brain.

But it was Rory who'd inherited his love of taking risks and his inability to refuse a dare. Even as a toddler, she'd been the most impetuous of the three, and he'd always thought of her as his little daredevil. Natalie had worked hard to suppress any reckless streaks in her nature. And Sierra had naturally preferred to think things out, to plan.

Rory had always chosen to throw herself into situations, making things up as she went along.

Earlier he'd opened an album to his three favorite photos of his middle daughter. In one, she was running over the finish line in a race. Harry smiled. Of the three girls, she was the one who always rushed headlong through life.

In the second, she was at her senior prom. And she was beautiful. When she was a little girl, she hadn't believed that. She'd always felt that her sisters had inherited the "beauty" genes, as she'd called them. He couldn't help but wonder if the years had brought her more confidence.

In the last picture, his favorite, she was on horseback, leaping over a fence. She'd been nineteen, and no doubt she'd dared herself to do it. That was what she'd always done when she was little. Rory had always been an excellent horsewoman. He recalled the times they'd ridden together, just the two of them, and rubbed the heel of his hand against the tight little band that squeezed his heart.

He had taken those photos himself. He might have promised Amanda that he wouldn't contact them, but that hadn't kept him from being there at important events over the years.

Harry set down his glass of cognac. He might have a pictorial history of his girls' lives, but he didn't have them. Reaching for a paper and pen, he shook off the nagging feeling that his time was running out. He might have to wait six years to deliver the letter in person, but he could write to her tonight.

To Rory, my darling daredevil...

1

WHY COULDN'T SHE EVER PLAN ahead?

Rory Gibbs gave herself a mental kick as she pushed her way through the crowd in the waiting area of the Blue Pepper. When she'd made the urgent call to her sisters to join her for dinner, she'd totally forgotten that Tuesday night was singles' night at the popular Georgetown bistro. Now, as usual, she was going to have to depend on her luck to get a table. Rising to her tiptoes, she scanned the crowd trying to spot one of the owners.

George, a gentle giant of a man, would be busy at the bar, but his partner, Rad, should be somewhere near the reservation desk. Skirting a group of preppy-looking men, Rory climbed the four steps that led to the bar and once more scanned the crush of people. Or tried to. It was just hell being short.

"Excuse me." Rory smiled up at a tall man as she wedged herself a path between him and the brunette he was talking to. He didn't even glance down at her. Neither did another man whose elbow she jarred as she attempted unsuccessfully to duck beneath it. Halfway to the reservation desk, she finally bumped into Rad as they both were squeezing their way around a group of three women.

"Rory, Rory, Rory, Rory." In spite of the crush of people, Rad managed to grasp her hands and kiss the air near her left cheek. Then he stepped back to give her a critical once-over. She returned the favor, noting that tonight his hair was white-blond and spiked. Rad changed his hair color almost as frequently as he changed his ties.

Before he'd bought the Blue Pepper, Rad had studied fashion design in New York City, and he'd appointed himself fashion policeman for the Gibbs sisters. He'd convinced her older sister, Natalie, to experiment with new colors and to start wearing her hair down.

For a full minute, Rory held her breath, hoping that the outfit she'd decided on met with his approval.

Rad had insisted she develop her own signature style. But like everything else she did, she was never quite sure how she was doing. She'd gotten the idea of pairing the faded, low-slung jeans with a vintage organdy-and-lace shirt from one of the layouts in *Celebs* magazine. She'd made the look her own by tying the shirttails beneath her breasts and adding strappy, high-heeled sandals, along with cascades of thin Italian gold hoops in her ears.

Finally, Rad beamed a smile at her, then leaned in and pitched his voice to be heard above the clatter of glasses and snatches of conversation. "A very nice variation on the Sarah Jessica Parker look! And I love the little gold bar in your navel. Veerry sexy."

"Thanks." Rory tried not to think about the fact that the only men who ever used that word to describe her were gay. No negative thoughts tonight, she reminded herself as she beamed a smile at Rad. "Tell me my luck's holding and you can find me a table."

Rad's brows shot up. "On a Tuesday night? You're lucky to have two sisters who plan ahead and call for reservations. Detective Natalie paged me at noon."

That figured, Rory thought. Natalie took her responsibility as the oldest very seriously, and as a cop, she was good at thinking ahead.

"Dr. Gibbs beat her by calling this morning," Rad said.

That figured, too. Sierra was a meticulous planner. She was forever making lists on blue note cards, and it had certainly paid off. She'd recently accepted a tenure-track position in Georgetown's psychology department, and she ran her life with the same smooth efficiency that she wrote her books and taught her courses.

A little sliver of envy ran through Rory. Despite that they were triplets, she and her sisters were as different as two suns and the moon, and she wanted to be more like them. For starters, Natalie and Sierra had inherited the "planning" genes while her own approach to life so far could best be described as seat-of-the-pants.

She envied them in the looks department, too. Both Natalie and Sierra were tall like their father while she was short like their mother. Natalie was a smashing redhead; Sierra was a cool Gwyneth Paltrow–type blonde; and she was a plain brunette. But what was beginning to bother Rory most of all was that at twenty-six, her sisters were settled on their career paths and she was still trying to figure out what she wanted to be when she grew up.

Those days were history, she reminded herself. If everything went well tomorrow, she would no longer be the "muddled in the middle" triplet. She would be a reporter with a staff job at *Celebs* magazine. Nerves knotted in her stomach. If everything went well…

"Dr. Gibbs and Detective Natalie are waiting for you out on the patio," Rad continued.

Sierra and Natalie had also inherited the "title" genes. She was just plain Rory.

"I've already put in an order for the appetizer special." Rad turned her in the direction of the patio and gave her a nudge.

Food. That's what she needed to settle her nerves. Usually, she chewed bubble gum, but she'd run out—a result of bad planning, of course.

No negative thoughts, she lectured herself again. As she nudged, ducked and generally bulldozed her way through the crowd, Rory tried to organize her thoughts and screw up her courage. After all, she was about to have one of life's defining moments. She was going to open the letter her father had sent to her.

One month ago, she and her sisters had gathered here at the Blue Pepper to celebrate their twenty-sixth birthday, and Natalie had dropped a little bombshell into their lives.

After not seeing or hearing from Harry Gibbs for sixteen years, they'd each received a letter from him—a letter that had been held in trust by their father's attorney for six years after Harry had died. They'd only been twenty when they'd lost both parents within months of each other.

Even now, it was hard for Rory to let herself think about her father without feeling a few pangs of pain and resentment. She couldn't quite forgive him for walking out on them when they were ten. Neither could her sisters. Shortly after he'd left, they'd stopped calling him Dad and started referring to him as Harry.

Coming up short behind a solid wall of people who'd gathered to watch the salsa band, Rory edged her way along, looking for an opening. Just the thought of opening that letter had the nerves dancing in her stomach. Natalie had opened her letter a month ago, and the advice Harry had given her—to trust in her talents and risk everything to get what she wanted—had changed Natalie's life. Not only had her older sister decided to say yes to the adventure of a lifetime, but she'd also found love. Since Natalie had found Chance Mitchell, she'd positively glowed.

But then Natalie had always had a lot of talents to trust in. Rory couldn't imagine what Harry would say to her. Wiping damp hands on her jeans, she gave up on finding an opening in the wall of people. Instead, she ducked her head, twisted to the side and muscled her way through the crowd. After spotting her sisters, she shot across the dance floor, and finally dropped into a chair between them. Martinis were waiting, along with a platter of the Blue Pepper's famous finger food. Rory reached for a stuffed mushroom and popped it into her mouth. Then she said around it, "Thanks for coming."

"You don't have to do this if you're not ready," Natalie said.

Sierra tapped the blue note card on the table in front of her. "We only agreed that you would be the one to go second. You can take all the time you want."

Rory swallowed and drew in a deep breath. "I've waited long enough." Slipping the letter out of her pocket, she set it on the table. "I need Harry's advice." There. She'd said it, and the words eased some of the flutters in her stomach.

"What's up?" Natalie asked.

Rory glanced at Natalie. Of course, her perceptive older sister would know that something besides the letter was bothering her. She drew in a deep breath.

"I've finally chosen a career."

Natalie smiled gently. "I understand why you feel like it's important you make a decision, but you don't have to put so much pressure on yourself, you know, Rory," Natalie said.

Rory glanced down at the white envelope with her name scrawled across it. Yes, she did. Her conversation with her boss that morning clinched it. She was sick and tired of the self-doubts that had plagued her all her life. "You guys were born knowing what you wanted to do. I've changed jobs six times in four years. That must be some kind of a Guinness record."

"Who says everyone has to be like Sierra or me?" Natalie asked.

"And who says that we'll stay at our jobs forever?" Sierra peered at her over the rims of her glasses. "Research shows that most people in our age group will have to change their career paths three or four times in the course of their lifetimes. You'll be much more prepared for those changes than either Natalie or I will."

She could always depend on her sisters for unflagging support, but it didn't change the fact that she'd never felt the kind of confidence that they'd always felt about their career choices. Bottom line—she was tired of being the "muddled in the middle" sister.

Her gaze dropped to the envelope again. "I can't help thinking that if I'd only been as focused on a specific career as you both were, Harry could have come home sooner. I bet Mom was worried that I would have taken up after Dad if he'd become part of our lives again."

Natalie took one of her hands and Sierra the other. "You can't blame yourself for a decision that our parents made. And if you want to blame someone for the fact that Harry went away, blame me. I'm the one who inherited his knack for cracking safes. I'll bet that's what freaked Mom out."

Sierra squeezed Rory's hand. "Children always feel a certain amount of guilt when they're abandoned by a parent."

Rory stared at her. "You, too? What could you possibly feel guilty about?"

Sierra smiled wanly. "I was always sick. I figured that the reason Mom didn't want to go with him was because of me."

"No," Rory protested.

"Not true," Natalie said at the same time.

Then Natalie straightened her shoulders. "I think we have to come to an agreement. We aren't to blame for what they did. And we certainly aren't to blame that Harry died before he could come back and deliver his advice in person." She raised her martini. "Let's say goodbye to guilt."

Rory and Sierra raised their glasses, and then they all sipped their drinks.

"Easier said than done." Rory set down her glass.

"It's a good first step," Sierra said.

"Here goes." Rory picked up the letter from her father. After opening the flap, she pulled out a single sheet of paper.

To Rory, my darling daredevil,
Your mother and I were both twenty-six when you girls came into our lives, and we agreed that you can open this letter on your twenty-sixth birthday in the event that I'm not there to talk to you in person.

Remember when you were little and I used to warn you that you could only trust in your luck so far? Well, I was dead wrong to tell you that. That was what your mother always told me. She was afraid that some day I'd take one risk too many, and because you were always so impetuous, she worried about you,

too. I hope that you will listen to me now. Trust in
your luck all the way—and be willing to push it.
And never be afraid to take risks. You can do anything you want if you dare to take a shot at it. Most
important of all—don't be afraid to stay in the game.

If I'd followed that advice, I would never have left
you and your sisters. I will always regret that I didn't
dare to stay in the game.

Love,

Harry

Rory forgot to breathe as she reread the words. Had he
really thought of her as his darling daredevil? The thought
had her heart swelling a bit. She drew in a deep breath and
let it out. "Well."

"Look at the pictures," Sierra urged.

Rory pulled three photos out of the envelope. There'd
been three in Natalie's letter, too. Moisture pricked her eyes
again as she noted that one picture had been taken at one
of the races she'd run in high school, and another was at
her senior prom. The third was one of her on horseback
jumping a fence.

Memories stirred in her mind. When she was little,
Harry had encouraged her to ride. He'd seen to it that she'd
had lessons, and he'd never failed to be there on the side-
lines, telling her that she could do anything she dared to do.

She'd forgotten all about that. Perhaps she really had inherited a daredevil trait from him. Studying the picture
more closely, she pinned down the time to her freshman
year in college. The equestrian team had won a blue ribbon at the state finals that year, and the meet had taken
place less than a year before Harry's fatal accident.

He'd been there, just as he'd been at every other important event in their lives. An old familiar ache settled around her heart. "I miss him."

"Me, too." Natalie sighed.

"Ditto," Sierra added.

For a moment, silence stretched between them.

Finally, Natalie cleared her throat. "Okay. Now we want to know why you need Harry's advice tonight of all nights. Did you and your boss at *Celebs* come to a parting of the ways?"

"No." Rory shook her head. "This isn't about another career change. I still want to be a reporter. I think I can be good at it. But my current job hasn't turned out to be what I expected. What it boils down to is I'm really just a research assistant to Lea Roberts, one of their star reporters. I've written some pieces, but I haven't gotten a byline yet."

Even as she explained the situation to her sisters, Rory recalled the scene that had taken place in Lea Roberts's office that morning.

Lea was a tall, stunning brunette with a slender build who was always relaxed and perfectly controlled. But that morning, Rory's boss had been pacing behind her desk.

"You've been asking to do some fieldwork," Lea had said, waving her into a chair.

"Yes."

Lea circled the desk and rested a hip on its corner. "I'm going to tell you up front that I'm not sure you're ready to handle this. But I'm desperate. I can't do it myself because I have to interview Elizabeth Cavenaugh, the chief justice's wife, at her apartment in New York City tomorrow morning, and I can't postpone it. All you have to do is snap a picture. That's it."

"I can handle it," Rory said, wishing that Lea didn't sound so much like she was trying to convince herself of that fact. "Who is the person I'm supposed to take a picture of?"

Lea leaned closer. "You're not to mention this to anyone, understand?"

Rory nodded.

"I've received a tip that Jared Slade is going to be checking in to Les Printemps tomorrow morning. I want you to get a picture of him. One picture. Can you do it?"

"Sure," Rory said, a surge of excitement moving through her. She knew just about everything there was to know about the reclusive businessman who ran Slade Enterprises. She'd been researching him for Lea for two weeks, and the thought of meeting him in person…well, the man just plain fascinated her. "Is that all? Shouldn't I try to get an interview?"

Lea stared at her for a moment. Then she threw back her head and laughed. "An interview?"

Emotions tumbled through Rory. Beneath the hurt and the humiliation, she felt a little flame of anger begin to burn.

"An interview," Lea repeated as she struggled to get her laughter under control. "Slade has never granted an interview—to anyone. He loathes all reporters. You'll be lucky if you can get a picture. Just focus all your attention on that. This could be a real coup for the magazine, and I'm depending on you. If you can get the photo, I'll recommend you for a staff position."

The staff position had been her dream from the moment she'd accepted the job at *Celebs*. She should have been thrilled. But try as she might, Rory hadn't been able to forget that Lea had laughed out loud at her idea to get an interview with Jared Slade. Even now as she waited for her sister's reaction to her story, she wondered if her boss was aware that her laughter had been tantamount to a dare. Pushing the thought temporarily aside, Rory focused her full attention on her sisters.

"She offered you a staff job? That's wonderful," Sierra said.

"And it doesn't surprise me one bit," Natalie added.

When her sisters raised their glasses, Rory shook her head. "It's not a done deal yet. First I have to snap a picture of Jared Slade."

Frowning, Natalie tapped her fingers on the table. "Jared Slade…isn't he that mysterious business tycoon, the recluse?"

Rory nodded. "I've done some research on him. The *Wall Street Journal* calls him the twenty-first-century version of Howard Hughes. He's also been dubbed 'the man with the Midas touch' when it comes to business. His companies run the gamut from five-star hotels and golf courses to high-end retail clothing stores. He's absolutely fascinating."

"He's had his share of trouble lately," Natalie said. "There was a food-poisoning incident at his hotel in Atlanta and a fire at a factory of his in upstate New York."

Rory stared at Natalie. "How did you know all that?"

"He's been in D.C. twice in the past month. Part of my job is to try to keep tabs on high-profile people who might bring trouble here with them. His office always refuses to let us know where he's staying."

Rory picked up a strip of green pepper and gestured with it. "He's like a phantom. No one knows what he looks like. I'm beginning to wonder if he even exists. Maybe he's just a made-up figurehead like Betty Crocker."

When her sisters aimed two blank stares at her, she said, "You know, that was the housewife that General Mills created out of whole cloth to promote their products. She was just a picture they put on their cake mixes and stuff. It could be that 'Jared Slade' is an imaginary person that a very enterprising CEO is using to create a certain mystique about Slade Enterprises."

"You'll have to have some kind of plan if you're going to take a photo of someone who's never been seen and who might not be real at all," Sierra commented.

Rory reached for a cube of cheese and stuffed it into her mouth. Her younger sister had a steel trap of a mind that always got to the heart of the problem. Rory didn't have a plan—exactly—at least not one she could jot down on a note card.

Swallowing, she said, "It's pretty simple. Lea Roberts received a tip that Jared Slade will be checking into Les Printemps tomorrow morning. I'm going to be in the lobby waiting. I figure I'll snap the picture when Mr. Slade registers at the desk."

Natalie frowned. "It sounds risky to me. Celebrities have been known to resort to violence when their pictures are taken by the paparazzi."

Rory met her sister's eyes. "I'll be in the lobby of an exclusive hotel. And I ran hurdles in high school, remember? If worse comes to worst, I'll just make a run for it."

"I still don't like it," Natalie said.

Rory leaned forward. "I've got to do this, Nat. I want this staff job more than anything. It's my way of proving to everyone including myself that I can be successful at something."

"I think this is even more than that," Sierra said. "It's personal. You're intrigued by the man himself."

Rory turned to stare at Sierra. It never ceased to amaze her that her younger sister always saw more than anyone expected her to.

Natalie's eyes narrowed as she shot Sierra a look and then turned to study Rory. "I thought you'd decided to swear off men."

"Real men. I'm on a sabbatical from them since Paul the jerk dumped me. Jared Slade is merely a mystery I'm interested in solving. What makes a man want to hide from the world the way he does?"

Natalie held up a hand. "Let's clarify one point. I don't think that Paul the jerk qualifies as a 'real man.' He used you to help pay the rent while he made it through his last year of law school. The day he walked out was the luckiest day of your life."

"I'll drink to that," Sierra said, raising her martini.

Rory raised her glass and bemusedly toasted her good fortune. "It's not like it's the first time I've been dumped. I'm kind of getting used to it. The way I see it, I don't have good luck with men. That's why I'm not having anything to do with them until my ideal fantasy man comes along."

"A fantasy man?" Sierra grabbed a fresh note card out of her canvas bag. "I'm doing some research on female sexual fantasies. What's he like?"

Smiling, Rory drew a finger down the stem of her martini glass. "He's tall, dark and handsome, of course. And he's a little dangerous looking. He has this tough outer shell, but he's really a sweetie underneath. And when he smiles, he has a dimple—just one—in his left cheek."

Rory warmed to her theme, grateful that the conversation had veered away from the riskiness of her plan to photograph Jared Slade. "But the best part is my fantasy man thinks I'm incredibly sexy. I drive him nuts." She leaned closer to her sisters. "He has the most incredible hands."

"And you know this because…?" Natalie asked.

Thoroughly at ease, Rory selected a stuffed mushroom. "There's not much sense creating a fantasy man if you're not going to engage in some hot fantasies with him."

"Paul really did a job on you if you're reduced to having fantasy sex," Natalie said.

"Do you see me complaining?" Rory licked her thumb. "The great thing about fantasy sex is that there can be more variety than with just one real man."

Sierra glanced at Natalie, who'd grown quiet and grinned. "I don't think our big sister agrees with you. I think she's found her fantasy man. Maybe if you push your luck, you'll find yours, too."

Rory dubiously glanced down at her father's letter. "I'll be happy if I'm lucky enough to get an inter—a picture of Jared Slade."

Natalie frowned. "I'm not going to talk you out of this plan of yours, am I?"

"No, so why don't you wish me luck?" Rory grabbed another cheese cube to ease the nerves that had just returned to her stomach. She hadn't revealed the whole of her plan to her sisters. The picture was just step one.

"Well, I can't argue with following Harry's advice," Natalie said. "It got me Chance."

Rory grinned. "Maybe it will get me my fantasy man."

"Then let's drink to it." Sierra raised her glass.

"And to luck," Natalie said.

"And to Harry." Rory sipped her martini. Tomorrow, she was not only going to snap a picture of Jared Slade, she was also going to get him to agree to an interview. She could do it. She was a daredevil, wasn't she?

LEA ROBERTS STARED OUT the window of her office, but she wasn't taking in the view of the Washington Monument. She was too worried that she'd made a mistake in the way she'd handled Rory Gibbs.

The laughter might have been a bit harsh, but she didn't want Rory even to think about asking for an interview. She would be the one to do that. Jared Slade would be furious with Rory for taking his picture. That would allow Lea to step in and play good cop to Rory's bad cop. Her plan was to offer to trade the picture for an interview.

Turning from the window, Lea began to pace. She really hated to give up the reins of control, but what else could she have done? She couldn't risk taking the photo herself. If Jared Slade was really Hunter Marks, the man might recognize her.

She'd made the right decision. Rory was smart and inventive. Those qualities could work in her favor. Hell, she should be able to snap that photo and get away before Jared Slade could blink.

The problem was Rory Gibbs was also impetuous and hard to predict. She was forever doing something unexpected. Lea raised her hand and pressed two fingers against the headache that had begun to throb behind her right ear. If Jared Slade turned out to be Hunter Marks, it would be her ticket to what she'd always dreamed of: a Pulitzer and most certainly a six-figure book contract.

In her mind, it was still a big *if*. Her anonymous informant seemed certain, but Lea wasn't so sure. Was it really possible that Hunter Marks had reinvented himself as a

man who owned and ran a multimillion-dollar corporation?
It would be the scoop of a lifetime.

Oh, breaking the story about the scandal that had nearly
destroyed a town had gotten her a job with the *Boston
Globe* for a while. But the story had become old news as
soon as Hunter had disappeared. And after a few months
at the *Globe,* she'd been eased into covering the society
page and eventually she'd taken the job at *Celebs.* Had
there been a way to play her cards differently?

After moving to her desk, Lea fished out an aspirin bottle and downed two tablets without water. One snapshot.
Then she'd be able to tell if Jared Slade was the man she'd
known ten years ago as Hunter Marks. If he was, she'd
have the leverage she'd need to finally get everything she
wanted. This time she'd play her cards right.

Hunter Marks had secrets to hide, and Lea knew them all.

2

THIS WAS DEFINITELY her lucky day! Rory Gibbs barely kept herself from dancing a little jig. The sketchy plan she'd had when she'd entered the hotel had worked like a charm. The bell captain had bought her story. Now all she had to do was snap the picture. She gave her bubble gum three quick chews.

One of the two men at the registration desk *had* to be Jared Slade. She was sure of it. But which one? She needed a moment and it wouldn't do to be caught staring at a guest. Taking two quick steps to her right, she ducked behind a potted palm tree and peered through the branches at the two men.

Was it the handsome, preppy-looking blonde? Or was it the shorter, tougher-looking dark-haired man who stood next to him?

Nerves simmering, Rory blew out a small bubble, then used her teeth and tongue to draw the gum back into her mouth. The dark-haired man had given the name Jared Slade to the reception clerk, but the blonde was the one signing the registration form. Rory was betting on the blonde.

Still, it could be the shorter, darker one even though, with his horn-rimmed glasses, he looked more like an accountant than a man who ran a company. Rory blew another bubble.

The way she'd pictured him in her mind, Jared Slade had been larger and drop-dead gorgeous. And in spite of the almost picture-perfect good looks, he had an aura of danger about him. In fact, he'd looked quite a bit like her fantasy man.

Neither of the two men standing at the desk looked particularly dangerous. Rory licked another bubble off her lips. She'd lived long enough to understand the huge chasm that existed between fantasy and reality. The studious-looking accountant was probably the real Jared Slade.

As she dug in her bag for her camera, she took a quick glance around the lobby. A third man had come through the revolving doors with Jared Slade. She'd been too intent on watching the other two at the desk to pay him much heed, but she did so now. He was a large man with dark hair, wearing black jeans, a leather jacket and dark glasses. Rory blinked and stared. He definitely had fantasy-man possibilities.

At that moment, he lifted the dark glasses and shot a quick look in her direction. She felt her heart skip a beat and her mouth go dry. Then as those dark eyes locked on hers, she felt a little punch of something hot right in her gut and her mind simply emptied.

It was only when he turned back to talk to the bell captain that Rory remembered to breathe. And it was only as she drew in a second breath that the oxygen reached her brain and she began to think again.

Well. She'd never reacted that way before to any man. But then, this one was remarkably like the fantasy man she'd created in her head—tall, dark, and handsome in a rough-edged sort of way. She began to chew on her bubble gum again. Would he have a dimple in his left cheek when he smiled?

Time for a reality check, she reminded herself. Mr. Danger was probably a bodyguard with valet duties, since he seemed to be sorting out the luggage with the bell captain. When he glanced over in the direction of the registration desk, Rory scrunched herself farther down behind the palm tree. The last thing she needed was a run-in with Jared Slade's bodyguard before she snapped her picture.

She should have worn something green, camouflage fatigues. For one long moment—even through the palm fronds—Rory felt the large man's eyes on her again. It felt like a mild sort of electrical shock along her nerve endings. She averted her own gaze and willed herself invisible. Her red boots would be hidden, but not the red cap. Since she'd started to develop her signature style, her sisters had teased her about being a slave to fashion. Was she about to pay the price?

HUNTER MARKS FROWNED as he watched the woman in the red hat and boots squat behind a tall potted palm. Who was she and what in hell was she doing?

He scanned the lobby again, but she was the only person there who seemed out of place. Lately, he'd been more paranoid than ever when he checked into a hotel. Small wonder since someone was threatening his company. The procedure was that his two employees—Michael Banks and Alex Santos—checked in while he scoped the lobby for possible reporters. The system had worked well for several years. So far no one had been able to print a photo of Jared Slade. No one, aside from his most trusted employees, even knew what Jared Slade looked like. And *no one* knew that Jared Slade used to be Hunter Marks.

But the person who was sending him threatening notes knew. And more and more, Hunter was becoming convinced that the threat to Slade Enterprises was coming from within. He'd come to D.C. to get to the bottom of it.

Hunter returned his gaze to the woman behind the potted palm. His eyes had been drawn to her from the moment he'd walked into Les Printemps. One glance had him thinking of pixies and elves. And that was not the usual turn his mind took when he looked at a woman. He prided himself on being practical rather than fanciful when it came to the female of the species.

This particular specimen had been seated on one of the settees, not sipping tea or a cocktail as the other occupants of the lobby were. Instead, she'd been scanning the crowd while she blew a huge bubble. When the bubble burst, he'd watched in amusement as she pulled it off her cheeks and nose and poked it back into her mouth.

He'd taken the time to study her face then. The cherry-red lips had drawn his attention first, and he'd found himself wondering if they would carry the flavor of the bubble gum. The errant thought along with the tightening and hardening of his body surprised him.

Strange, because women never surprised him. And the pixie with the bubble gum was a far right turn from the type he usually dated. For starters, she looked too young. Of course, the slight build could account for that, along with the hair. From what he could see of it—a few wisps that peeked out from beneath the red cap—she wore her dark hair shorter than most men. He shifted his gaze down the black jean jacket and jeans to the red boots and felt his body go even harder.

Then she glanced his way and for one long moment his gaze held hers. He felt a punch of desire so strong that for a second he couldn't breathe. Then his mind filled with images of her and what he'd like to do to her.

"Here you go, sir."

With some effort, Hunter dragged his mind back to reality as the bell captain handed him three tickets. His reaction to this odd woman was unprecedented.

"The briefcase and the laptop will be taken up to the Presidential Suite for Mr. Slade," the man said. "I'll handle it personally. And the suitcases will be up shortly."

"Appreciate it," Hunter said as he slipped a folded bill across the narrow counter. Then he leaned closer to the bell captain. "Do you see that woman over there, the one behind the palm tree?"

The bell captain took a moment to scan the lobby casually. Les Printemps was a small hotel that prided itself on calling each guest by name. Hunter had researched it himself. The management catered to a very select clientele, a mix of foreign diplomats and celebrities, who paid premium prices because they valued their privacy and expected the hotel to protect it at all costs.

"That's Miss Rory Gibbs, sir," the bell captain said, a wide grin spreading across his face.

"Is she staying here?" Hunter asked.

"No."

Hunter frowned. "I thought only registered guests were allowed in the lobby."

"She's meeting her fiancé here. She said her father brought her here for high tea once, and she wanted to relive the moment with her husband-to-be. Sweet little thing. She reminds me a bit of my daughter."

Hunter returned his gaze to Rory Gibbs just as she pulled a camera out of her purse.

Shit, he said to himself as he strode toward her. Perhaps she was a reporter, after all. He prided himself on having a sixth sense where the press was concerned. But this one had fooled him.

There were only three people in his organization who'd known he was checking in to Les Printemps. Ms. Rory Gibbs was his ticket to finding out just who the traitor was.

RORY'S HEART WAS BEATING so fast that she was sure the two men at the reception desk could hear it. One at a time, she wiped her damp hands on her jeans. She couldn't afford to drop the camera. Dammit. She could still feel Jared Slade's bodyguard/valet watching her and he was having the oddest effect on her whole system.

Focus, she told herself. No one had ever taken a photo of Jared Slade. She needed this picture. Once she had it, she could negotiate step two of her plan—an exclusive interview with Jared Slade.

"We want you to enjoy your stay at Les Printemps, Mr. Slade," the neatly groomed woman behind the desk said as she pushed a key across the counter.

Rory noted that the dark-haired man picked it up. But it was the blond man who said, "Thank you."

They would turn around any minute and she would finally be looking at Jared Slade. Which one would he be?

Turn. Rory concentrated on sending out the message telepathically. But the blonde was asking about the health club facilities. Jared Slade was reputed to be a health nut.

So the blonde was Jared.

"Where's the best place to take a run?" the dark-haired man asked.

Or maybe the runner was Jared. And still they didn't turn around. So much for her telepathic powers.

Raising the camera, she pressed the button on the zoom lens and found herself viewing a close-up of a palm leaf. She pushed it out of her way, only to discover that the two men were moving away from the desk. She could see their faces in profile now. The darker haired man was tough looking and built like a boxer. The blonde had the long, rangy body of a swimmer.

If she'd had to bet money, she still would have placed it on the blonde. But this was too important to trust in her luck. She had to be sure. Edging her way out from behind the palm tree, she aimed the camera and said, "Jared Slade?"

The blond man turned first, and she had three quick shots of him before someone behind her said, "Stop right there."

Whirling, she saw the fantasy man—Mr. Danger—striding toward her. He looked every inch the bodyguard now. In fact, the combination of sunglasses, black leather jacket and black jeans had her thinking for one giddy moment of the Terminator. Rory froze.

She wasn't sure if it was the sheer size of the man that intimidated her for a moment, or perhaps that odd little punch to her system threw her off. The only thing she was certain of was that all of his attention was totally focused on her. She could feel his purpose, feel *him* in every pore of her body. He was the Terminator personified.

When he was still a few yards away, he held out his hand. "I'll take that camera."

She clutched it tight to her chest. She wanted to run. The old Rory would have chosen that option in a nanosecond. Did she dare to stay? Tucking her gum into the side of her cheek, she said, "I'll trade. You can have the pictures, but I want an interview with Jared Slade."

He took one step closer. "Not a chance. Just give me the camera."

Time to rethink her options. He was a lot bigger up close than he was from a distance, and he'd probably be able to outrun her. But if she handed over the camera…

Stay in the game. Even as the words slipped into her mind, she feinted to the right, then darted behind the palm tree. Once she'd cleared the branches, she raced for the lobby door.

HUNTER SWORE under his breath. By the time he skirted the damn potted palm, the little pixie had pushed her way through the front door.

"Stay here," he called over his shoulder to the two men who'd been at the registration desk. Then he ran toward the hotel entrance and made it out to the street just in time to see her turn the corner. By the time he reached it, she was nowhere in sight. She couldn't have reached the next corner, so she had to be in one of the shops.

Deliberately, he slowed his pace, allowing the other pedestrians on the street to flow past him. The first shop he passed had designer chocolates in the window. A quick glance inside told him that his quarry wasn't there, and there was no obvious place to hide. The second shop had lingerie displayed in the window, and he spotted her moving quickly toward the back of the store with an armful of lace and satin in tow.

Hunter glanced up at the name over the shop door and smiled slowly. This was his lucky day. Silken Fantasies was the very shop he'd come to D.C. to buy. Its location in the same block as Les Printemps was one of the reasons why he'd decided to stay at the small hotel. A quick glance at the tall, strikingly attractive woman behind the counter confirmed that she was the owner. At fifty, Irene Malinowitz was looking to retire so that she could spend time with her grandchildren. And Slade Enterprises was looking to turn Silken Fantasies into a very profitable chain.

Slowly Hunter backed out of the flow of pedestrian traffic. He had to hand it to Rory Gibbs. She had a good plan. All she had to do was hang out in one of the dressing rooms until whoever was chasing her gave up.

Except he'd never given up in his life—even before he'd become Jared Slade. Added to that, she'd had the bad luck of running into a shop where he knew the owner. When Rory had disappeared into one of the dressing rooms at the back of the shop, he moved closer to the window and considered his options. He wanted to talk to Rory Gibbs. He also wanted that camera, he reminded himself. The best way to fool her into thinking she'd taken a picture of the real Jared Slade would be to destroy the film.

Then he would ask her how she'd known that Jared Slade was going to be checking into Les Printemps. Very few people in his organization had known that. Denise Martin, the chief administrative assistant in his Dallas office, and the two men he was traveling with—Michael Banks, his executive assistant, and Alex Santos, his accountant. Up until now, he'd trusted all three of them. But now, he was sure that one of them was a traitor. Even worse, one of them knew his past and wanted revenge.

The problems at Slade Enterprises had started three months ago. There'd been an episode of stomach poisoning in his hotel in Atlanta and a fire that had caused some damage in a factory in upstate New York. He'd flown in to deal with each crisis personally. And both times he'd received notes with the same message: *No matter what you do, soon the world will know who you are and what you did ten years ago.*

Hunter was sure that the person sending the notes had to be connected in some way to the scandal that had nearly destroyed not only his family's business, but the town he'd grown up in. A scandal that he'd been blamed for. A scandal that had the power to destroy Slade Enterprises.

Ms. Rory Gibbs might very well know who the writer of those notes was.

Hunter took out his cell phone. Little did she know it, but Ms. Rory Gibbs had just walked into a trap.

RORY LEANED BACK against the closed door of the dressing room and drew in a deep breath. She'd taken a risk when she'd chosen this store. Luckily, it had a place where she could hide. For the moment.

Her last glimpse of the Terminator had been when she'd turned the corner. There'd been no sign of him when she'd ducked into the shop. When he couldn't see her on the street, he'd have to give up.

If her luck held. Crossing her fingers, she drew in another breath. The air was scented with lavender, and classical music poured out of a speaker that hung directly above her dressing room. In a minute, her heart rate would subside, she'd be able to breathe without panting, and her nerves would settle. And then she could figure out what to do next.

"I don't think you have the right sizes."

Rory jumped at the sound of the feminine, well-modulated voice behind her. "What?"

She peered through the slats in the door and made out the red suit of the woman who'd welcomed her to the shop when she'd dashed in.

"The sizes," the voice said. "In your rush, you grabbed large, and I think you'll find that petite will fit you better. I've brought you the same designs. Why don't we switch?"

As she opened the door, Rory glanced down at the bits of lace and satin she was clutching to her chest. She hadn't paid any attention to what she'd scooped up when she'd dashed in. The Terminator had been on her tail.

"Who recommended this shop to you?" the woman asked as they exchanged garments.

"No one," Rory replied. "I just came in—on impulse."

"Ah." The woman smiled at her. "I get some of my best customers that way."

Rory took a moment to look at the items for the first time. Lingerie—tiny bras and what looked to be thongs— in various shades of the rainbow.

"Wow," she said as she spread petite sizes out on a nearby bench. "These don't cover much."

"That's the whole point, isn't it?"

"I've never been able to quite figure out the point." Rory leaned down to finger the lace on one of the thongs. "I mean, no one sees this stuff."

The woman's brows rose. "A lover would see it."

Rory shot her a look. "Not for long. Mostly, they're just interested in getting me naked."

The woman's laugh was low and infectious. "You need to look for a new lover. The first step would be to wear something like this." She moved into the room, and lifted a cherry-red thong and matching bra from the bench, then handed them to Rory. "You'd be amazed at the difference something like this will make in a relationship. Wearing these next to your skin, you'll feel sexier, more attractive, and much more confident about the way you appeal to men."

"Yeah, well, finding a new lover is pretty low on my to-do list right now."

"That could change if you met the right man."

The Terminator flashed into Rory's mind and she felt her body go soft and hot as if something inside of her were melting.

"Try these on," the woman said. "What have you got to lose?"

Rory fingered the silky lace. The truth was she had nothing to lose. And this seemed to be her day for taking risks.

"Red is definitely your color."

Rory glanced up to find the woman smiling warmly at her. She smiled right back, and held out her hand. "I'm Rory Gibbs. And you're a very good saleswoman."

The woman shook Rory's hand. "Thanks. I'm Irene Malinowitz. Let me know if there's anything else I can bring in."

As Rory closed the door of the dressing room, she gave the red scraps a speculative look. She'd never worn red underwear in her life. Black, yes, when she was in the mood to feel a little "sexy" or when all of her white underwear were in the dirty-laundry hamper.

It wasn't that she didn't like to spend money on clothes. She did. Her maxed-out credit cards were a testimony to her weakness for fashion. But she preferred to part with her hard-earned plastic for what went on the outside—like the red boots or the jaunty little hat she was wearing.

She fingered the red lace of the thong—what there was of it. What would it feel like to put on? Considering, Rory chewed on her gum and blew out a bubble. What the heck. It was kind of like taking a dare. And she had some time to kill. The one thing she knew about the Terminator was that he never gave up. She could picture him walking up and down the street, peering into shops.

But first, she was going to find a place to hide the film so that he couldn't just grab it from her. Pressing a button on the camera she was still clutching to her chest, she wound the roll to the end, took it out, and glanced around the tiny room for a hiding place. The only piece of furniture in the room was the bench. Wincing at the grossness of it, she removed the gum from her mouth, and then kneeling, she stuck the film container to the bottom of the bench.

Cloak-and-dagger was not her specialty, but she could rise to the occasion—probably because she'd read so many Nancy Drew and Hardy Boys mysteries when she was a kid. And then there were all those late-night TV movies she'd watched that offered a thousand and one tips for foiling dastardly villains.

And the Terminator had *dastardly* written all over him. Just thinking about him made her feel as if a little electric current were running along her nerve endings. She pressed a hand to her stomach. There it was again—that hot, fluttery feeling. He was still stalking her. She was sure of it.

And she was going to be prepared. Fishing a new roll of film out of her purse, she reloaded her camera and took four quick shots of the lingerie. If he was waiting outside when she left the shop, and he wanted the film, at least she'd be ready. She'd run from him once. Not again.

In the meantime… Rory glanced down at the red thong

again. Standing, she slipped out of her jacket. Trying on a red thong should be no big deal. No one had to see her in it. She tugged off her jeans.

Long ago, she'd decided that the "sexy" part of the Gibbs legacy had also gone to her sisters.

Was Irene right? Could the simple act of wearing red underwear change her image of herself?

"LEA, IT'S BEEN A PLEASURE." Elizabeth Cavenaugh, wife of Supreme Court Justice Henry Cavenaugh, extended her hand. "I know you went out of your way to fly into Manhattan, but I just detest summers in D.C. Thank you."

Lea took Elizabeth's hand in hers. During the hour-long interview, the charm of Mrs. Cavenaugh's southern accent had begun to wear thin. And the glowing report she would have to write up on the woman's latest philanthropic project was the kind of article that Lea detested writing. But she managed a smile. "You'll remember to e-mail me the recipe for those scones?"

"I'll have Delia write one up for me this afternoon. But she got it from her mother. Don't be surprised if it reads a pinch of this and two dashes of that."

Lea brightened her smile. "I'll give it to my cook. That kind of recipe is right up her alley. And thank you again for the interview. I don't know when I've enjoyed one more."

As the door closed behind her, Lea pulled out her cell phone and barely kept herself from running to the elevator. One glance told her that Rory hadn't called yet.

Damn. She glanced at her watch. Noon. Not time to panic yet, she told herself. After punching the button for the lobby, she leaned against the wall and tapped her foot. The interview had been a dead bore. The piece on Elizabeth Cavenaugh's work in battling adult illiteracy would be typical of the kind of reporting she'd been doing for *Celebs* magazine for the past five years. She could write it in her sleep. It was the kind of article that made her want to scream.

No matter, she told herself. Her ticket to what she'd always dreamed of having was within reach. By this evening, Rory Gibbs was going to bring her the means to a story that would free her from ever having to write another boring article on politicians or their spouses.

Lea stepped out of the elevator and strode across the marble-floored lobby. When the doorman pushed open the glass door, a blast of moist heat struck her with enough force to have her almost wishing for the coolness of Elizabeth Cavenaugh's penthouse apartment. Almost, but not quite. Instead, she hurried to the curb and raised her arm to hail a taxi.

Two passed her by before a third pulled up.

"Kennedy Airport," she said as she climbed in. "And could you turn the air-conditioning up to high?"

With a nod, the cabdriver pulled into the busy traffic. Leaning her head back against the seat, she closed her eyes. But she couldn't relax, not until she heard from Rory Gibbs.

The air in the taxi had gone from hot to tepid when her cell phone rang.

"Rory?" she asked.

"No. It's me."

Lea's hands tightened on her phone as she recognized the voice of her anonymous informant. This was only the second call she'd received, but she still couldn't pin down whether the voice belonged to a man or a woman. The two things she was sure of were that she'd never heard it before and it was cold. Bone-chilling cold. "Yes?"

"Do you have the pictures?"

"Not yet. It's only noon."

"He's checked in to his suite."

Lea's heart stilled. If that was true, she should have heard something from Rory. "The photographer I sent hasn't reported back yet."

"I trusted you to get those pictures. I won't be happy if you failed."

Lea couldn't repress a shudder even though her temper flared. "Look. I told you I had another commitment. Besides, he might have recognized me. So I sent someone who's as hungry to get those pictures as we are. I can guarantee I'll have them for you by the end of the day."

"You'd better."

"Look, I don't like to be…" She knew that her caller had clicked off, but she said the word anyway. "Threatened. I don't like to be threatened." But even in the still-hot taxicab, she shivered. She couldn't shake off the feeling that whoever was feeding her information on Jared Slade was dangerous.

Pushing the feeling away, she reminded herself there might be one hell of a story here. Besides, she'd dealt with all kinds of anonymous tipsters before. It was ridiculous to let this one frighten her.

And if Jared Slade turned out to be Hunter Marks as the anonymous caller had promised, she'd break the story of the year. Lea managed a smile. Who better to write it than the reporter who'd broken the original story that had caused Hunter Marks to disappear off the face of the earth?

3

HUNTER STEPPED THROUGH THE DOOR of Silken Fantasies. A little bell jangled over his head, and the woman behind the counter glanced up with a smile.

"Welcome to Silken Fantasies."

"Irene Malinowitz?" he asked, taking out a card as he moved toward the counter. The shop was small, but elegant. He noted with approval the plush carpeting, the accents of glass and chrome, and the merchandise displayed gracefully on mannequins and arranged artfully on tables. He'd seen photos, but this was his first trip to the store itself. There was a scent in the air and the muted tones of Chopin floated out of the speakers. He also knew that Irene Malinowitz had built her clientele mostly by word of mouth, and that since she'd launched her catalog, her net profits had risen to just over five million dollars a year.

"Yes?"

Hunter handed her the card. "I'm Mark Hunter, one of Jared Slade's executive assistants." Mark Hunter was the name he used when he traveled and when he dealt personally with clients.

Irene glanced at the card and then met his eyes. "I don't believe we've met."

"No." Hunter seldom spoke with clients directly. Voice

prints were as individual as fingerprints. The more successful Slade Enterprises had become, the more effort he'd put
into protecting his anonymity.

"What can I do for you, Mr. Hunter?"

"Mr. Slade has just checked in to Les Printemps, and he
would like to have you sign the contracts now in his suite,
if that's convenient. He'll want to review them personally
and there's something else that demands his attention this
afternoon."

A flicker of a frown passed over Irene's face. "I'm sorry,
but I have a customer in the dressing room right now, and
my assistant is at lunch. Perhaps in a half hour or so?"

Hunter smiled at her. "That's why Mr. Slade sent me in
person. I'll be happy to cover for you."

A phone rang on the counter behind Irene.

"That will be Mr. Banks now. He'll verify who I am."

Irene picked up the phone. "Hello?"

Hunter counted five beats until the smile appeared on
her face.

"Yes, Mr. Banks."

His executive assistant, Michael Banks, had handled all
of the negotiations with Silken Fantasies, so Irene would
be familiar with his voice. Michael was bright, and he was
good with clients, especially the female ones. Being a
man's man, Alex Santos was better with males, and he
was a whiz at crunching figures.

Irene was still smiling when she hung up the phone.
"My customer is in the dressing room. I should—"

"She'll be fine," Hunter said. "I'll take good care of her."

THE FIRST THOUGHT THAT CROSSED Rory's mind as she studied herself in the three-way mirror was that she had to get

to the gym more often and do some of those exercises that promised to lift her rear end. Then she shifted her position and backed away two steps so that she could study herself from the front only.

The image staring back at her from the mirror nearly had her laughing out loud. She'd left only her boots on, and now she wore nothing else but the lacy red thong and the merest excuse for a bra. It seemed that this was her day for really being daring.

And it felt good.

She picked up her jean jacket from the floor and slipped it on over the red bra. Then she walked back and forth in front of the mirror. No one looking at her would know what she was wearing beneath the jacket. But she would know. And the secret knowledge made her feel sexy. Really sexy. As if she could have any man she wanted.

She took off her jacket and then traced her finger along the waistband of the thong. She sighed. There was no way that she could afford this pricey little number, but she really had to add it to her fantasy life. An image of the Terminator tumbled into her mind. What if he saw her in this? Closing her eyes, she let herself imagine just how he might look at her—those dark eyes filling with hunger. And those hands. Oh, he definitely had her fantasy man's hands. The one that had reached out to take her film had a wide palm and strong-looking fingers. They wouldn't be gentle when they touched her. No, they would be hard, calloused, demanding, as they moved over her breasts. Her insides clenched as she imagined those hands trailing down her skin to the thin strap of lace at her hips and then lower—

When she heard the bell on the shop door ring, she jumped. Then with a hand pressed to her heart, she made herself breathe. It was a customer. This was, after all, a store.

Her heartbeat had just returned to normal when above the piano music drifting out of the overhead speaker, she heard a deep voice. A man's voice. With a sinking feeling in her stomach, Rory whirled away from the mirror and dropped to her knees. Then she jiggled the slats in the door to get a look. Black boots, black jeans and the bottom of a black leather jacket. The Terminator.

He'd come for her.

Her mind racing as fast as her heart, she rose and pressed her back against the door. A plan. That's what she needed. Maybe there was a back way out of the shop. She opened the door and took a quick look. He was facing Irene across a glass-and-chrome counter, and she was talking on the phone.

Just looking at him in profile had that strange little zing of awareness shooting along her nerve endings again. *Escape,* she reminded herself. *You're looking for a way out.*

A quick look in the other direction dashed any hope she had of getting away. The back of the shop was a solid wall. Ducking back into her dressing room, she leaned against the door.

And then it struck her. She was thinking of running away, and that wasn't what she wanted to do. This was her chance to negotiate that interview.

To calm her nerves, she focused once more on her image in the mirror. To her surprise she looked even sexier. Her skin was flushed. Somehow, she looked taller, her legs appeared to be longer, her breasts fuller.

In short, she looked like a woman who could get what she wanted.

And she wanted more than the interview. She wanted the Terminator. The awareness that she'd felt the moment she'd looked into his eyes was back—and it was growing. Her insides had begun to melt the moment she'd seen him again. And there was a growing ache right in her center. Rory pressed her hand against her stomach.

Get a grip, she told herself. This was no time to let some pricey undergarments turn her into a nymphomaniac. Nor was it time to become muddled about her objective. The interview. She had to talk to the Terminator and convince him to set up the interview with Jared Slade.

She grabbed her jeans—but first she had to get dressed.

The bell over the shop rang.

Dropping the jeans, Rory tensed, holding her breath.

He was leaving. She had to stop him. She moved to the door, opened it and stepped out.

But it wasn't Irene Malinowitz's back that she saw at the door to the shop. It was the Terminator's.

"I'll take care of everything, Irene," he said.

She heard the door close, the lock click. Then he turned to face her.

For the second time in one morning—perhaps in her life—Rory felt her mind go perfectly blank. She couldn't identify one thought—there were too many sensations cartwheeling through her. Heat. Cold. Nerves. And an electric spark of lust. He was walking toward the dressing room with the same purposefulness in his stride he'd had when he'd moved across the lobby.

He was coming after her.

This time she wasn't going to run.

THE MOMENT HE TURNED AWAY from locking the door to Silken Fantasies, Hunter Marks felt his body go absolutely still. She was standing right outside the dressing-room door, and as his gaze raked over that creamy, porcelain-smooth skin, those wispy bits of red lace, and the incredibly long legs, he felt his head begin to spin. He moved then, almost as if he were being drawn by a magnet.

There was something about her. He'd thought of her as an elf or a pixie. But standing there right now, she looked like an exotic dancer in a high-priced strip club. Was it the elf or the sex goddess who was drawing him?

Or was it something else? She wasn't trying to escape; she hadn't even made a move to cover herself. And there'd been that moment in the lobby of Les Printemps—just before she'd bolted—when her gaze had met his and he hadn't seen a trace of fear in her eyes.

Courage was a rare commodity, and Hunter had always admired it when he saw it. Was that why she pulled at him? As he drew closer, he ran his eyes over her again. Or was his attraction to her merely an incredible trick of chemistry? Whatever caused it, he couldn't look at her without wondering what it would be like to touch her—to taste her and touch her until she was slick and wet and hot for him.

His body heated, hardened, as he imagined what it might be like to slip inside of her and feel her close around him like a moist, tight fist.

Hunter stopped short when he was still a few feet away from her. For one chilling moment, he realized that if he allowed himself to get any closer, he would touch her. Kiss her. Pull her to the floor of the shop and—

Ruthlessly, he shoved the images out of his mind and tried to replace them with some semblance of rational thought. Even as a voice at the back of his mind whispered, *Take her,* he struggled to recall why he'd followed her in here. What did he want from Rory Gibbs?

"I'll give you the film on one condition," she said.

The film. Hunter's eyes narrowed. His brain was starving for blood while hers was clicking along at full speed. He watched her chew on her bottom lip.

Nerves. It gave him some satisfaction to realize that the sex goddess wasn't quite as cool and pulled together as she appeared to be. This close, he could see that her eyes were a deep, golden amber, the color of well-aged whiskey. He could see the flicker of nerves there, too. And he could smell the faint scent of cherry-flavored bubble gum. He managed to keep his gaze from returning to her lips.

"Don't you want to know what the condition is?" she asked.

The condition. Once more, Hunter found himself admiring her for keeping her mind on business. She didn't even seem to be conscious of the fact that she was conducting negotiations while wearing next to nothing. But she wasn't indifferent to him. Through the sheer red fabric covering her breasts, he could see that her nipples were hard little berries. And a pulse was beating at her throat. Thoroughly intrigued, he let himself wonder for a moment—what might it take to taste her right there?

But that wasn't what he'd followed her into Silken Fantasies to do. Annoyance flared—not with her but with himself. He'd dealt with a lot of women in his life—family members, business acquaintances, lovers, and even some enemies—but he'd never met one who could cloud his mind the way this particular one could.

"What's your condition?" he asked.

She briefly chewed her bottom lip again, then said, "I work for *Celebs* magazine, and I want an exclusive interview with Jared Slade."

Not going to happen. And nothing she could have said would have more quickly catapulted him out of the fantasies he was building. She was a reporter, Hunter reminded himself, and he felt his body and his mind finally begin to cool.

He extended his hand, palm upward. "I'll take the camera."

She hesitated. "He hasn't agreed to the interview yet."

"First, I'll develop the film and see what you've got to negotiate with," he said.

She frowned at him. "If you take the film, I won't have anything to negotiate with. You'll have the pictures."

He shot a dry smile at her and saw her eyes widen suddenly in surprise...or fear? "What is it?"

She licked her lips. "You have a dimple."

"Yeah." No, it wasn't fear that was in her eyes. "Now that we've settled that, give me the film. We both know that all I have to do is walk over to the bench, dump your purse and take the camera. You won't be able to stop me."

The pulse fluttered at her throat again, and it took all of his concentration to keep himself from reaching for her. To his surprise, he found himself saying, "I'll give you my word that I'll talk to Mr. Slade and put in a good word for you. Under one condition."

When she licked her lips, Hunter dropped his hand, fisted it at his side, and reminded himself that he was dealing with a reporter.

"What's the condition?" she asked.

"Who told you that Jared Slade would be checking in to Les Printemps this morning? And don't give me any crap about protecting your sources. I want a name."

There was a trace of a frown in her eyes when they met his. "I don't have a name. My boss received a tip and she sent me to take it because she had an interview she had to do in Manhattan today. I told her I could get it. That's all I know."

"Your job was just to snap a picture?"

"Yes."

"What about the interview?"

"That was my idea."

Despite that he considered the words *reporter* and *liar* to be synonymous, his gut instinct told him that she was telling the truth. There was an innocence in those amber-colored eyes that contrasted sharply, irresistibly with what she was wearing. Or wasn't wearing.

She ran a hand through that short dark hair, and his fingers itched to do the same thing. He could anticipate what the silky texture would feel like beneath his hands.

"Look, getting an interview with Jared Slade will get me a staff job at *Celebs*. And I need the job. I need to prove myself. Can you understand that?"

Hunter said nothing, but he did understand. Perfectly.

"Tell him he can do a Wizard of Oz thing and sit behind a curtain. I only took the pictures because I thought they would give me some sort of leverage to get the interview. You can have them."

She moved to the bench and extracted the camera from a gigantic purse. When she turned back to him, his gaze shifted for a moment to the image of her backside in the three-way mirror. His mouth went suddenly dry. Except for two pieces of red lace, she was nude. The only sign of the thong from the angle was the thin red fabric that dipped low from her waist.

"Here," she said.

As he dragged his gaze back to hers, he was vaguely aware that she'd handed him the camera and he slipped it into his pocket. He could also see her mouth was moving. She was obviously saying something. But he couldn't hear her. He wasn't sure he could even think.

"One kiss," he said.

Rory glanced up. Her throat dried, and her body seemed to be experiencing a meltdown. She couldn't possibly have heard him correctly. But his eyes were so hot that she could feel them on her skin. She licked her lips. "What did you say?"

"One kiss. I want to taste you." He took a step toward her. "One kiss and I'll do everything I can to get you the interview."

One kiss. Rory thought that her heart might just beat out of her chest. One part of her mind—the daredevil part—was thinking yes. What could it matter? But there was another part of her that knew it would matter a lot. Kissing this man might be the biggest risk she'd ever take.

He wasn't moving. In spite of what she could see in his eyes, the decision was going to be hers.

She wanted the kiss. Desperately. She wanted him. But… She felt her old fears swamping her. Where was the confidence that she'd felt just moments ago when she'd looked in the mirror?

Never be afraid to take risks. As the words from Harry's letter streamed through her mind, she suddenly remembered the first jump she'd ever taken on a horse. Her father had given her a little pep talk before she'd ridden out into the ring. "Just dare yourself to do it, kiddo. That's all you need to do. It works like magic."

She'd made the jump. And she was going to kiss this man.

"One kiss," she agreed.

Hunter wasn't sure how long he'd waited to hear her answer, but it had seemed way too long. In the interim, he'd tried to tell himself he was making a mistake. It had been years since he'd done anything this impulsive, this rash. Oh, he'd been plenty reckless before he'd changed himself into Jared Slade. And he'd paid the price. Even in his incarnation as Jared Slade, he'd played some long shots—but only in business and only when he felt confident that his luck would hold.

Right now luck didn't matter to him. Nothing seemed to matter except this hunger that demanded to be quenched. He wasn't even aware that he'd moved until her back was against the mirror, and he was close enough to feel the heat from her body. He touched her, drawing one finger over the pulse that was beating at her throat. Her breath hitched, her skin heated, and the pulse beneath his finger quickened.

"Last chance to change your mind," he managed to say.

"I'm not going to change it."

He placed his hands on either side of her head, noting that her hair felt every bit as soft as he'd anticipated. Then lowering his head, he drew her up on her toes and covered her mouth with his.

It was the heat that hit him first. In that split second before his lips had touched hers, he'd seen the flame light in her eyes. But the shock of it as it shot through his body in an explosive rush surprised him. He thought of the wildfires he'd seen as a child—the kind that devoured everything in their path. Only this one left a hard, unrelenting need in its wake.

The second surprise was her taste. Oh, it was sweet at first, but that was only the first layer of flavor. Beneath that, he tasted heat and spice. What other flavors would he find?

When she nipped at his bottom lip, another arrow of heat

shot through him. He ran his hands down her body and drove his tongue deeper. And all the time he marveled that her mouth, her tongue, her teeth were every bit as aggressive as his. He'd never been so aware of a woman before. Of those small sounds she made when he nipped at her bottom lip, or rubbed his thumb over her nipple.

Her skin was smooth and hot and growing damp beneath his hands. He wanted to taste every inch of it. Her body was small and supple and strong. He wanted it beneath his, bucking and straining.

And he could have her. She didn't seem to believe in holding anything back. Her hands were racing over him— over his shoulders, down his arms—just as his were exploring her. He felt them slide beneath his jacket and move down his back to knead the muscles at the base of his spine. It wasn't enough, not nearly. He wanted the pressure of those fingers, the scrape of those nails, on his bare skin.

He wanted her. One kiss was not going to be enough. He wasn't sure that anything would be enough to stop the ache inside of him. He had to have her. Images flashed through his mind, of driving himself into her on some moonlit beach while waves pounded on the shore. Of carrying her to the nearby bench and letting her ride him. Or merely opening his zipper, then lifting her and taking her against the mirror where they stood. His hands moved down to cup her buttocks and pull her up. He said her name, which turned into a groan, when she wrapped her legs around him. Then he very nearly sank to his knees when she pressed her heat against his and began to rub against him.

Slamming one hand against the mirror to steady himself, he dragged his mouth free and tried to think. First he had to breathe. The sudden rush of air burned his lungs. There were reasons why he shouldn't do this. Couldn't do this. Then he made the mistake of looking at her. Her lips were moist and parted, still swollen from his kisses. Her eyes were huge and the deep golden color was misted. He wanted—no, he needed—to see what those eyes would look like when he entered her and filled her. He leaned forward and took her mouth with his again.

Rory sank into the kiss, eager to drown herself in it, in him again. There was a greed in him that matched her own. Never had her fantasies been this sharp, this real. Never in her wildest imaginings could she have conjured up the sensations shooting through her. There was such heat—glorious waves of it. And each movement of his hands, of his tongue, seemed to throw fuel on the fire. She'd known hunger before but never one this desperate, this enormous.

His taste—she couldn't get enough of it. There were so many flavors, each one more unique, more secret, more dangerous than the last. She dragged her mouth from his and sank her teeth into his shoulder. His moan sent little explosions of pleasure through her. She was torn between twin desires—she wanted to devour him whole and she wanted to savor one delicious body part at a time.

His hands. Everywhere they pressed and molded, her skin burned, then itched to be burned again. She felt the pressure of each finger and that hard, wide palm as he ran his hands down her sides and slipped his fingers beneath the lacy band at her waist. Then he was gripping her buttocks with both hands, kneading her flesh and pressing her closer until the hard length of him was pushed flush against her. She arched her body, straining against him as everything tightened inside of her. She arched again, but it wasn't enough. She had to—

"I want you." His voice was a rough whisper in her ear.

"Yes." She wasn't sure she could survive without him.

"Right now. I want to be inside of you. Are you protected?"

"Hmm?" She tried to shake her head to clear it.

"Are you on the pill?"

"Yes," she said as the words finally penetrated. "Yes. Hurry."

Listening to the three words, Hunter felt something inside of him snap. He let her down so that he could free himself from his jeans. Then he pushed aside the lacy triangle of the thong and pulled her close again as he guided himself into her. But it wasn't enough. Gripping her hips, he drew her even closer, and then with a hard thrust of his hips, he sank deeper. He could feel her stretch, as he made a place for himself in her slick, hot core. His climax immediately began to build inside of him.

Drawing in a quick breath, he tried to maintain some control, but it was no use once she began to move. Digging his fingers into her hips, he thrust into her, harder and faster, driving her, driving himself until he surrendered to the hot, dark pleasure.

When he could think again and breathe again, he was lying beside her on the floor of the dressing room. He wasn't quite sure how they'd gotten there, nor was he sure how long they might have been lying there when his cell phone rang.

Swearing, he unfastened her arms from around his neck and levered himself up so that he could take the call. "What is it?"

"There's been…sir…"

"What is it, Michael?" Hunter frowned. Michael Banks was usually cool and unflappable, but he barely recognized his executive assistant's voice.

"A bomb."

"What?"

"A bomb was delivered to your suite."

RORY STILL WASN'T SURE she could move. Her body had never felt so free, so relaxed, so pleasured. But the Terminator was already getting to his feet and moving away from her. She wanted him back down beside her. Without him, she suddenly felt cold. The chill grew worse when he scowled at whatever news he was getting. She couldn't yet separate what he was saying into words, but when she sat up, she could feel the hard floor of the dressing room under her bottom. She figured her brain cells were beginning to function again because the analytical side of her mind was beginning to realize what had just happened.

She'd just made love with a complete stranger in a dressing room of a ritzy lingerie shop. Well, maybe he wasn't a complete stranger. But when she'd made up her fantasy man, she certainly hadn't expected him to walk right into her life.

It was the kind of thing that happened in movies—or in hot, steamy romance novels. In real life, people didn't really make love to strangers in the dressing rooms of fancy lingerie shops.

But she had. And she wanted to do it again. Astonishment warred with the hot lick of desire that was fanning itself to life again. She had dared to do something she'd never done before.

And she'd liked it very much.

"Are you and Alex and Ms. Malinowitz all right?"

Rory felt a little ribbon of relief roll through her system.

She could make out what he was saying now. And she knew who Ms. Malinowitz was. In another minute she'd be back to her old self. And then she'd figure out what to do next.

Chemistry, a little voice at the back of her mind told her. Hadn't she read that the chemistry between two people could be very powerful. Irresistible. As the Terminator paced back and forth in the small space, Rory caught a glimpse of herself in the mirror. She was still wearing the red bra and thong. She recalled Irene's prediction that the thong would make her feel different about herself.

Oh, yeah. She'd definitely felt different ever since she'd put it on. She narrowed her eyes. Was the red thong the cause of what had happened? Or was it Harry's advice?

"A note?" he asked.

Rory tore her gaze away from the mirror and shoved the thoughts out of her mind. The here and now were what she had to concentrate on. The complete stranger was standing just outside the dressing room door, and he wasn't happy.

"What did the note say?" he asked. "I'll be right there."

Rory used all of her concentration to gather her thoughts as he shifted his gaze to her again.

"Are you all right?" he asked.

"Yes," she said, crossing her fingers to protect her nose from growing at the lie. She was certain she would be all right…soon.

"I have to go."

She nodded. Obviously, the red thong hadn't changed her that much after all. He'd bounced back from the chemistry overload a lot faster than she had. Her knees were still weak. But her brain cells were definitely perking up. "About the interview…?"

There was a brief flash of puzzlement in his eyes before they narrowed and turned into lasers. "Interview."

If she could have scooted any farther away, she might have, but she was sitting with her back against the mirrors. "With Jared Slade," she said. "That was the deal."

"So it was." He inclined his head slightly and patted his pocket. "Just as soon as I get these developed, I'll be in touch."

Rory watched as he turned and moved away from the dressing room. He'd be in *touch.* He'd only had to *say* the word to melt her insides. Pressing her hand to her heart, she began to rise awkwardly to her feet. When she heard the bell ring over the door of the shop, she remembered— she'd given him the wrong film. "Wait!" she yelled. "Just a minute!"

She crawled to the bench and tore the container of film off the bottom of it, leaving the gum behind. Then she managed to stand and race out of the dressing room. He was still there in the doorway, and with the sunlight behind him, he looked more formidable than ever.

"Here!" She held the film out. "These are the real pictures that I took. Take them."

He plucked the film from her hand and slipped it into his pocket. "You could have let me walk away without these."

Rory drew in a deep breath. "Yes, but my whole future at *Celebs* depends on my getting that interview with your boss. I want you to know that he can trust me to paint an honest and fair picture."

He nodded at her. "I'll tell him."

Rory watched him walk out and close the door behind him. Only then did she sink to her knees. It had to be the red thong. She'd just made a deal with the Terminator to get the interview of a lifetime.

Maybe she truly was a daredevil.

LEA WAS GOING through the drawers of Rory's temporary desk again when her cell phone rang. She willed it to be Rory, but this time she read the caller ID before she answered.

Private.

Ignoring the little sliver of fear that slid up her spine, she said, "Yes?"

"Do you have the film yet?"

"No. It's only been an hour since you called the last time."

"I want the name of the person you sent in your place."

Lea hesitated for a moment, hating that this disembodied voice could frighten her.

"The name."

What did it matter? she thought. "Rory Gibbs. I'm expecting her at any moment."

"You'd better get those pictures."

4

HUNTER STOOD in the French doors that opened onto a patio and offered a view of rolling lawns and tennis courts. He spotted a pool beyond a low row of hedges. A woman sat in a lounge chair, sipping something from a tall glass. He assumed she was Lucas Wainwright's wife since he recalled that his old friend had married a little over a year ago.

Looking at the scene, he couldn't help but think that Lucas was a very lucky man—he had a home and someone to share it with. Long ago, he'd accepted that he would never have either of those. It was too much of a risk for someone who had to hide his true identity. Pushing the thought aside, he turned to face Lucas. "Nice spot."

"Thanks." Lucas removed three bottles of beer from a small refrigerator. "It's private, and Tracker here can attest to the security."

Hunter took the bottle when Lucas handed it to him. Though he hadn't seen his old friend face-to-face since they'd been in college together, they'd kept in contact. When Lucas had taken his phone call today, he'd agreed to meet with Hunter immediately once he'd explained that a bomb had been delivered to his suite at Les Printemps.

A bomb.

Hunter had been trying to get his mind around that reality ever since Michael Banks had told him about it on the phone. Thank heavens Michael and Alex had been meeting with Irene Malinowitz in a different suite.

While he took a long swallow of his beer, Hunter studied the tall, quiet man Lucas had introduced as Tracker McBride. He felt perfectly comfortable with Lucas. He felt less comfortable with the man who handled Lucas's security arrangements.

As if sensing his reservations, Lucas said, "Tracker and I served in a special-forces unit together seven years ago shortly after I left college. He handles all my security, and he's the best. You can trust him."

Hunter wasn't so sure he could trust anyone anymore, but he was willing to take Lucas at his word. Moving to the desk, he extended his hand to Tracker. "Okay."

"I thought it would save time if you explained to both of us what happened," Lucas said.

"First, I need to know how confident you are that you weren't followed," Tracker said.

Hunter had to give the man points for asking. "I wasn't followed." He'd made damn sure of that once he'd had his meeting with Michael and Alex. The small bomb had been delivered to the suite assigned to Jared Slade, a suite he would have been working in if he hadn't followed Rory Gibbs into Silken Fantasies. And then there was the note. He'd still been rattled about what had happened in that dressing room when Michael Banks had given it to him.

Hell, he was still rattled now. He'd taken a woman he didn't know—a reporter—in the dressing room of a lingerie shop. Acting on impulse was a luxury he hadn't allowed himself in years—not since he'd transformed himself into Jared Slade.

And then he'd just left her there. Not that he'd had a choice. Hell, someone had delivered a bomb to his suite. And she'd said that she was all right, though he knew he couldn't be sure about that.

"Are you sure?" Tracker asked.

Hunter dragged his thoughts back to the question. McBride obviously wanted details. Lucas had picked a good man to head up his security. "Once I read the note, I decided to make myself scarce by escorting Irene Malinowitz back to her shop." He'd insisted on escorting her back so that he could make sure that Rory really was okay. But she hadn't been there.

"Then I went back to Les Printemps, left the lobby by the side door and hailed my own taxi. I had the driver drop me off at the Four Seasons where I called Lucas from a pay phone. Then I walked through the lobby, exited by another side door and hailed another cab. This time I went to the airport, rented a car, and followed your directions out here. Not even my two assistants know where I am."

"Good." Tracker gestured to one of the chairs in front of Lucas's desk. "We can talk now."

Almost amused, Hunter sat down in the chair. "Glad I passed the test. What would you have done if I'd been stupid enough to bring a tail with me?"

Tracker smiled. "We'd have gone somewhere else for our meeting. I don't like to lose clients."

"Fair enough," Hunter said as he reached into his pocket and pulled out the note. "My assistant Michael Banks found the package with the bomb and the note when he went to my suite to get some papers. It was on a table in the sitting room."

"What do the police think?" Tracker asked.

Hunter's brows shot up. "I didn't ask them. And I didn't show them the note. When I left, I heard that they had disassembled the bomb, and they were waiting to question Jared Slade."

Tracker took the note from Hunter and read it out loud.

"Slade
Ticktock. Ticktock. The bomb is ticking. No matter what you do, soon the world will know who you are and what you did ten years ago. Then you'll die."

Tracker met Hunter's eyes. "Succinct. Lucas mentioned this wasn't the first note."

"There've been three in all. The other two said the same thing—*No matter what you do, soon the world will know who you are and what you did ten years ago.* They're in my safe in my office in Dallas. The first one came right after there was an incident of food poisoning at my hotel in Atlanta. I flew there personally, and even though I'm always careful to keep my whereabouts a secret, the note was delivered to my hotel room. The next note was delivered to my private plane after another incident—a fire in a factory I own in upstate New York. I'm very careful about protecting my privacy, my anonymity. Someone at the very top levels of my organization has to be either behind this or at the very least feeding information to the person or persons who are behind this."

"Any ideas about who's after you?" Tracker asked.

Hunter shook his head. "I'm traveling with my chief accountant and my executive assistant, Alex Santos and Michael Banks. I made the reservations at Les Printemps myself, but I informed them where we were staying yesterday. My chief administrative assistant in Dallas, Denise Martin, also knew. There was a woman in the lobby of Les Printemps when we arrived this morning—from *Celebs* magazine. She took some pictures, and I chased her from the lobby. She says that she got the information from an anonymous tip that was delivered by special messenger to her boss yesterday."

"Her name?" Tracker asked.

"The name she gave the bellman was Rory Gibbs, and she told me she works for *Celebs* magazine."

Tracker and Lucas exchanged glances.

"You know her?" Hunter asked.

"Yeah, we've met," Tracker said. "One of her sisters is a good friend of mine. She's a detective in the D.C. Police Department. Her other sister works with Lucas's wife at Georgetown. They're triplets."

Without warning, Hunter found his mind wandering back to those few moments when Rory's legs had been wrapped around him and he'd been deep inside of her.

"Hunter?"

It was Lucas's voice that drew him back. "Sorry."

"I was just saying that I can talk to her and see if she'll give me more information," Tracker said. "I'll also see what I can find out about the magazine. It's interesting that the informant chose *Celebs*. Why not the *Post* or something?" Tracker wondered.

"Ms. Gibbs may have been in contact with my office. She's done research on Jared Slade, and she's very intent on getting an interview. Denise or Michael may have spoken with her."

Tracker glanced at Lucas. "If she's anything like her cop

sister, odds are she'll keep after you." He looked back at Hunter. "Did she get your picture?"

Hunter shook his head. "No. The pictures she snapped were of Alex and Michael. I took them with me."

Tracker grinned at him. "Good work. If you ever get tired of running Slade Enterprises, I can offer you a job working security for Wainwright Enterprises."

Hunter's answering smile was grim. "If we don't get to the bottom of this, I might have to take you up on your offer."

Tracker's grin faded. "We'll get to the bottom of it."

Lucas circled around his desk and sat on one of the corners. "You've already narrowed the suspects down to Denise Martin, Alex Santos or Michael Banks. That's why you let only those three know where you were staying here in D.C. Have you picked a favorite?"

Hunter took a swallow of his beer. Lucas had always been smart. That was what had drawn them together in college. That and the fact that they had family problems in common. Before the notes had started coming, Hunter would have sworn that Lucas was the only person in the world who knew he'd changed himself into Jared Slade.

Now he was afraid that someone else knew, too. But who?

"Denise has worked with me from the beginning of Slade Enterprises. Over the years—six now—she's become vital to me. I'd have to hire three or four people to replace her. Alex has been with me for four years and Michael for three. They each came to Slade Enterprises right out of business school. For the past year, I've worked closely with both of them. Alex is thorough, but not that great with people. But he's the best number cruncher I've got in the company. Michael is a quick study and his instincts are excellent. And he's good with people. Today, I felt perfectly comfortable letting them handle the final paperwork with Irene Malinowitz."

Pausing, he sighed. "I don't want to pick a favorite. "But if I had to narrow the list, I would lean toward Alex or Michael. Either of them would have had easy access to the suite where the bomb was left. However, I'm not sure I see any of them objectively. They're like family."

But he'd been betrayed by family before.

"Where were you when you learned about the bomb?" Tracker asked.

"I was in Silken Fantasies. I'd offered to stay there while Michael and Alex had Ms. Malinowitz sign the papers. They used Michael's suite, thank heavens."

"When you went back to the hotel, tell me exactly what happened," Tracker said.

Hunter replayed the scene in his mind, trying to capture every detail. "Michael answered the door when I knocked. The police and hotel security were closeted in my suite. Michael's hand shook when he handed me the note. I only caught a brief glimpse of Alex over Michael's shoulder, but he seemed to be calmer. Irene was smiling at something he'd just said when I asked Michael to step into the hall so that he could report."

"What did he say?"

"He told me that he'd had to go to my suite to get a copy of something that Irene had requested. When he saw the note and the package, he was immediately suspicious because of the other two incidents, so he read it. He left the suite immediately and called me. Then he called hotel security and the police. He kept the note out of sight until I got there."

"So Michael had ample opportunity to plant the bomb," Lucas said.

"Yes. But he and Alex hadn't been together the whole time. So Alex also could have left it there. Denise could have hired someone to plant it. All of which leaves me with no clear suspect. That's why I need your help."

"You've come to the right place," Lucas said with a smile. "Tracker's the best. He's managed to save my sister's life twice, so you're in good hands." He turned to Tracker then. "Any preliminary thoughts?"

Tracker looked at Hunter. "I'd say someone knows your past—who you really are—and they have an old score to settle. Any idea who that might be?"

Hunter shook his head. "I've been racking my brain since I received the first note."

"Could it be someone in your family?" When Hunter said nothing, Tracker continued, "You know, in a homicide, the prime suspects are either lovers or close relatives."

"No one in my family cares whether I'm dead or alive."

"Any other enemies from that time?" Tracker pressed.

Hunter thought briefly about the woman who'd been his lover and who'd betrayed him. He doubted that she ever gave him a thought. "No. I've been through it over and over."

Tracker glanced at Lucas. "I'm going to have to pay a visit to your hometown and dig around a little bit there."

Hunter opened his mouth, but Lucas spoke first. "Tracker can be very discreet. He's also good. No one will know that he's even interested in you."

Hunter didn't like it, but he couldn't see any way around it. "Okay. But I don't think the death threat is imminent. I think whoever this is—he or she—wants to expose me first, perhaps do more damage to Slade Enterprises. The important thing is to prevent my past from coming out. It's very important that Slade Enterprises never be connected to my family."

"Yeah, I figured that," Tracker said. "That's why I'm recommending that we try to flush this person out before he or she is ready. Is that okay with you?"

Hunter nodded. "The sooner the better."

Tracker paused to grin at Lucas. "He's a lot like you." Then he turned back to Hunter. "Here's the plan. Lucas has a place down in the Keys, an island where his grandfather built a fishing shack. You're going to let Denise, Alex and Michael know that you're going down there for a few days for a little R & R. I'll put tails on them, taps on their phones, the whole deal."

"And I'll wait for them down in the Keys," Hunter said.

"Oh, no. One of my men will wait down in the Keys. You'll be right here where I know I can keep you safe."

Hunter frowned, but it didn't keep Tracker from continuing.

"I told you before. I don't like to lose clients. Maybe this person wants to make you suffer by exposing you first. But maybe not. There was a bomb delivered to your suite. And it was discovered and disassembled. But who's to say it wouldn't have killed you if you'd been close enough to it when it went off? I'd rather err on the side of caution. Plus, we'll be working at the problem from both ends. I'll be trying to find out who from your past has a connection with one of the three top people in your organization, and we'll see if the trap set down in the Keys nails our suspect down. That should mean faster results."

Hunter turned the plan over in his mind. It made sense. "The only thing I don't like is not being personally involved."

"The farther away I keep you, the less chance there is of any of this leaking to the press," Tracker pointed out. "And Lucas's estate has a lot to keep you occupied. Tennis courts, horses, sauna, pool. To my way of thinking it beats the hell out of that old fishing cabin in the Keys for a little R & R."

Hunter turned to face his friend. "I don't want to intrude on you and your wife."

"Not at all," Lucas assured him. "Mac has an apartment in Georgetown and we'll be driving back there tonight because she starts the second summer session at the college tomorrow."

"There's just one thing I ought to mention," Hunter said, glancing from one man to the other. "I promised the Gibbs woman I would get back to her about the interview."

"Why don't I take care of that?" Tracker said. "When I talk to her, I'll tell her that Jared Slade was called out of town suddenly and you'll be in touch about the interview as soon as possible."

"Good," Hunter said. That was the best plan. Hadn't he already decided that it wouldn't be wise to see Rory Gibbs again?

"If we're done with business, I think we ought to go out to the pool so that Hunter can meet Mac," Lucas said.

"It's not necessary," Hunter said. "It's probably better that I keep a low profile until you leave."

"I insist," Lucas said, exchanging a look with Tracker. "See, my wife has just published a book on male sexual fantasies—part of a research project she did." He cleared his throat. "She's presently on her cell phone sharing the best parts with my sister, Sophie—Tracker's significant other. If we don't interrupt them soon, Tracker and I are going to have a very strenuous night ahead of us."

Tracker laughed then. "I'm not complaining."

As he followed the two men out to the pool, Hunter found himself envying them. His mind once more slipped back to those few moments that he'd shared in the dressing room with Rory Gibbs.

It was on impulse that he'd escorted Irene Malinowitz back to the shop, and he hadn't been able to stop himself from going into the dressing room again. He could still smell Rory. And she'd left the red bra and thong. He'd acted on impulse again when he'd bought them and had Irene send them to her at the magazine.

He wouldn't see Rory Gibbs again, and there was no way he could give her that interview. It was too risky. Acting on impulse wasn't something that he could afford to do again.

RORY SPOTTED NATALIE at the bar the moment she walked into the Blue Pepper. At five-thirty, the dinner crush hadn't started yet, but there was a good crowd enjoying the cocktail hour. Tightening her grip on the bag she was carrying, Rory pushed and nudged her way to the upper level to join her sister. Natalie's message on her voice mail had been cryptic. "Meet me at the Blue Pepper at five-thirty. I have some info on your mystery man."

She was sure that Natalie was referring to Jared Slade, but Rory had begun to think of Slade's bodyguard as her current mystery man. Even now when she thought about what had happened in that dressing room, she had to pinch herself to make sure the whole thing hadn't been a dream. Of course, the red thong she was carrying in the pink Silken Fantasies bag was proof positive of that.

No man had ever made her feel so wanted, so needy, so

sexy, so…everything. The Terminator, as she called him, was her fantasy man made flesh, right down to the dimple. But even in her fantasies, she hadn't imagined that clever mouth and those incredible hands. And she didn't even know his name. He hadn't signed it to the message he'd sent with the red thong and bra.

I've never enjoyed a kiss so much. That's what the message had said. The one sentence had been playing itself over and over in her mind since the pink bag bearing the logo of Silken Fantasies had been delivered an hour ago to her temporary desk at *Celebs.*

The message had set off a string of questions. Did it mean he wanted to see her again? Did it mean he was going to get the interview for her? When she'd stopped by Les Printemps, all she'd been able to discover was that Jared Slade had checked out.

But the question foremost in her mind was would she feel the same way if he kissed her again? In her fantasies, Rory had explored that particular scenario several times. But the more logical side of her mind understood that fantasies and reality were worlds apart. And the logical side of her mind suspected the lingerie was a "dumping gift." Paul had bequeathed her his toaster when he'd moved out of her apartment. His note had said, *No hard feelings.*

How many such gifts could she accumulate over a lifetime?

As Rory crossed the floor to the bar, she rubbed her left temple where a little headache was beginning to throb. Well, a red thong was a much classier "dumping gift" than a used toaster. And she hadn't given up yet on tracking down the Terminator.

It was only when she reached Natalie that she recognized the man on the stool next to her sister.

"Hi, Chance," she said and tried not to giggle when he took her free hand and kissed it. "I didn't know you were back from London."

"Always a pleasure, Rory," Chance said. "I can't stay away from your sister for very long."

Rory wrinkled her nose. "You make it tough on a plain Jane like me. She's even prettier when you're around."

Surprise flashed into Chance's eyes. "Where'd you get the idea that you were a plain Jane?"

"Her ex planted that in her mind," Natalie said. "He was a class-A jerk."

"Want me to beat him up for you?" Chance offered.

"He's history," Rory assured him.

"Sierra and I have it covered," Natalie said. "We have a voodoo doll in his image, and we take turns sticking pins into it."

He pretended to look alarmed. "Remind me not to cross you." As Chance slipped off the stool, he turned to Rory and winked. "Let me know if you change your mind. Right now, I have orders to disappear for a few minutes so that I won't intrude on the girl talk."

Rory climbed onto the stool and set her bag on the bar. "You know, I like him more each time I see him. You really hit the jackpot, Nat."

Nat's eyes were glowing as she watched Chance walk away. "Yeah, I did."

"What'll it be, Rory?"

"Hi, George." Rory shot the tall, bronze-skinned man a smile. "A glass of white wine would be nice."

"You got it," he said as he pulled a glass from an overhead rack. When he set it down in front of her, his gaze fell on the pink bag, and his brows lifted. "What's in the Silken Fantasies bag? Inquiring minds want to know."

Natalie stared at the bag. "I thought only the rich and the famous could afford to shop there."

Rory could feel the heat rise in her cheeks. "I didn't shop there. Not exactly. I just ran in to try some things on, and— it's a gift. Not for someone else. For me." She was stuttering. "Someone gave it to me. I'm deciding if I should give it back."

George winked at her. "Never give back expensive lingerie. But you'll have to model it before I can give you an informed opinion."

"Not a chance," Rory said.

"Who gave you something from Silken Fantasies?" Natalie asked when George had moved down to the far end of the bar. "Did you get that from Jared Slade?"

"No." Then she sighed. "It's a long story."

Natalie's brows shot up. "Can I at least have the *Reader's Digest* version?"

Rory took a sip of her wine and then gave her sister a modified version of her morning's adventure. Since Natalie was a natural-born worrier, she left out the part about actually making love to a complete stranger and played up the kiss part.

"You didn't get your interview, but you kissed Jared Slade's bodyguard. And now you have a five-hundred-dollar red thong and matching bra and a note that says *I never enjoyed a kiss so much*," Natalie summarized.

"In a nutshell."

Natalie's eyes narrowed. "And I thought Harry's letter had changed *me*. How was the kiss?"

Rory ran her finger down the condensation on her wineglass. "On a scale of one to ten, it was about a thirty."

Natalie grinned at her. "Good."

Rory shook her head. "It was the kind of kiss that makes you want it to happen again. And that's not good. I'll probably never see him again. I probably won't get that interview, either. I gave up any leverage I had when I gave him the pictures. Not that I could tell which one of the two men was the real Jared Slade anyway."

"Hey, where's that devil-may-care attitude? You're sounding far too negative."

Rory stared at her sister. She was right. "Negative's the old Rory. The new Rory doesn't want to be like that."

Natalie smiled. "Sierra and I liked you just fine. But I think that you're having more fun as the new Rory. And I have some news that may help you to nurture your inner daredevil."

"What?"

Natalie leaned closer. "This is all off the record."

"Of course."

"I told you my partner and I were trying to keep tabs on Jared Slade. Right around noon, there was a call put in to the police. Someone delivered a bomb to his suite at Les Printemps. No one was hurt, but Matt and I were called to the scene."

"Did you see Jared Slade?"

Natalie shook her head. "He wasn't in the suite when it happened, and he took off before the uniforms arrived. But I do have a lead for you. Chance and I stopped by Sophie Wainwright's shop this afternoon, and from something she said, I think this Jared Slade might be staying out at the Wainwright estate in Virginia."

"What did she say?"

"Rory. Rory Gibbs, is that you?"

Recognizing the voice of her boss at *Celebs,* Rory placed a hand on Natalie's arm and turned to smile at Lea Roberts who was striding toward them. Lea was looking very put together in a beige linen suit, and wore her dark hair long and straight in an attempt to carry off a maturing Demi Moore look.

"Lea," Rory said, "this is my sister, Detective Natalie Gibbs."

As the two women nodded at each other, Rory continued, "Lea has been my boss and mentor at *Celebs.* She's done a lot to help me there."

"I pick my protégées very carefully," Lea said to Natalie. Then she turned to Rory. The smile on her face didn't reach her eyes. "I've been trying to reach you all day. When I missed you at the office, I went over to the hotel, but I was told that Jared Slade had already checked out. Tell me you got the picture."

"Yes, but—" Rory began.

"Wonderful. Let me see." Lea held out her hand, her fingers wiggling.

Rory felt the heat rise in her cheeks. "I don't have them with me. I—"

"You left them on my desk then." Lea glanced at her watch. "I have time to—"

"No." Rory swallowed. "By the time I got them developed, I knew it would be too late to give them to you at the office, so I left them at home. I'm sorry. I had no idea I would be running into you."

Lea's smile didn't waver, but her eyes heated several degrees and her foot started to tap. "You're sure you got a picture of Slade?"

"Absolutely."

Lea hesitated, and Rory was sure she would have said more if Natalie hadn't been present.

"I was counting on having them today. Please have them on my desk at eight-thirty tomorrow morning."

"Sure."

Lea gave a brief nod to Natalie. "Detective." Then she whirled and strode away.

"She's not a happy camper," Natalie said.

"She's been very good to me."

"She reminds me of the villain in those *101 Dalmatians* movies. All she'd need is a white streak in her hair."

Rory grinned. "Cruella DeVil. They are a bit alike, I guess. Lea's always on goal. She doesn't let much stand in her way. I've learned a lot from her."

Natalie studied her sister. "And you just lied through your teeth to her."

Rory shrugged. "I couldn't very well tell her that I'd given the pictures back. If I can still get that interview, she'll be happy."

"And if you don't?"

Rory beamed a smile at her. "I have a sister with connections who's about to tell me where I can find Jared Slade. How can I fail?"

Natalie was still studying her. "This is really important to you."

"Yes," Rory said. But even as she said it, she realized that her quest to interview Jared Slade wasn't the only reason she wanted to track him down. Jared Slade was her ticket to seeing the Terminator again.

"Tracker McBride—that's Sophie's significant other— is spending the entire day on the Wainwright estate because some rich businessman who keeps a low profile with the press had an attempt made on his life today."

"Interesting coincidence," Rory commented.

"Tracker heads up security for Wainwright Enterprises. Chance and he go back to the days when they worked in a special-forces unit. I asked Sophie if she was talking about Jared Slade, the rich mystery tycoon, and she couldn't confirm that because Tracker didn't mention a name. He just said that this mystery man and Lucas had gone to college together. But how many rich, media-shy businessmen could there be visiting D.C. this week? I figured you might want to check it out."

Rory's mind was racing. A bomb had been delivered to Jared Slade's suite. Why? By whom?

"I have to admit that I feel a lot better about you going after this interview now that I know Slade's connection to the Wainwrights. They're solid people."

"If this person *is* Jared Slade. Did Sophie say how long this mystery man would be staying at the Wainwright estate?"

Natalie nodded. "At least until tomorrow. She doesn't expect Tracker back until late tonight."

"You don't by any chance have directions to the estate?"

Nat grinned at her as she took a folded paper out of her purse. "Yeah. I figured you might want them. I went to a party there last winter. Good luck."

Rory pressed a hand against the nerves jumping in her stomach. "Thanks."

She had a hunch that she was really going to need her inner daredevil to come out now.

IT WAS MIDNIGHT when Lea's cell phone woke her out of a half sleep.

"Well, is Jared Slade the man you knew as Hunter Marks?"

Lea resented the way the voice on the other end of the line could chill her. "I haven't seen the photo yet. But I'll have the pictures first thing in the morning. She definitely got one of Slade, but we kept missing each other all day long."

"This is not going well."

Tell me about it, Lea said to herself. She'd come within an inch of firing Rory in that bar. But that wouldn't have gotten her what she wanted. She needed those photos first. What she said out loud was, "I talked to her and she definitely got the picture. We'll both have what we want in the morning."

"Where are the pictures right now?"

"She said she left them in her apartment. I'll have them at eight-thirty."

"I'll be in touch."

I sincerely hope not, Lea thought as she ended the call. Once she had the pictures, she wouldn't have to have anything more to do with her anonymous informant.

RORY STIRRED, WHACKED HER ELBOW hard against something, and came abruptly awake. Before the bubble of panic could even fully form in her stomach at the bewildering surroundings, she remembered where she was—in her car a short distance from the Wainwright estate.

The streaks of pink in the east told her that it was close to sunrise. The moon had shone full and bright in the pitch-black sky when she'd parked her car at the side of the road shortly after one o'clock, and now, finally, she was going to make her move.

Leaning back in the seat, she crossed her fingers and prayed for all of her luck to be up and running. No more backsliding. She was not going to slip into the pattern of

self-doubt the way she had when she'd been talking to
Natalie in the Blue Pepper. Just as a little extra precaution,
she'd put on the red bra and thong. Irene had told her that
it would make her feel more confident about herself—and
she was going to need every shred of confidence she had—
or could borrow—to get the interview with Jared Slade.

She wasn't even going to think about what she would
do if she met the Terminator again, let alone what would
happen if he kissed her again.

After stepping out of the car, she hurried across the road
and used the grasses growing in the ditch for cover as she
approached the drive that led to the Wainwright mansion.

As far as she could see there wasn't a guard. Just a wide
wrought-iron gate between two twelve-foot brick walls.
Thanks to a full moon, she'd gotten a good view of the
main house and grounds when she'd crested the last hill,
and she'd noted that a brick wall bordered the rambling estate on all four sides. She'd counted two other buildings
besides the house—a pool house and what she guessed to
be a stable. Lucas Wainwright had some pretty nice digs.

Pushing her way through the grass, she climbed out of
the ditch and crossed the road. The gate held when she
pushed against it. Moving to the right, the direction she'd
come from, she studied the wall. The bricks looked fairly
new—the mortar that held them was smooth. Not a chink
in sight. But she'd passed a tree. Breaking into a jog, she
headed toward it.

The limb was just out of her reach, so she jumped for
it. When her hands slipped the first time, she landed on her
butt. Making a mental note that she had to start going to
her gym on a more regular basis, she scrambled to her feet
and leapt for the lowest branch.

This time her grip held, but it took her three tries before she managed to swing her legs up and hook them around the branch. For a moment, she hung there and just concentrated on breathing. Upper-body strength was what she needed. Along with that fanny lift. She'd start first thing tomorrow.

For now, she wiggled, swore, wiggled and swore again until she sat upright on the branch. The ground looked far away and, up close and personal, the branch looked a lot less sturdy. It bobbed and swayed in perfect rhythm with the way her stomach was pitching around as she inched her way along its length. Once she reached the wall, she crawled carefully onto it, then made herself take slow, calming breaths.

A quick assessing look around didn't make her stomach feel any better. There was no tree in sight on this side, and the ground still looked far away. All she had to do was dare herself, then wiggle to the edge and drop. Twelve feet wasn't that far. She'd just count to three and take the plunge. Eyes closed, she'd counted to two when she heard the dogs barking. She opened her eyes and spotted two large black Labs barreling toward her. Any thought of sweet-talking them evaporated when she saw the man following them. Her Terminator.

She felt that same punch to her system she'd felt the first time she'd spotted him in the lobby. He was walking toward her with that same ground-eating stride, that same focused purpose. Each step he took increased the sensations racing through her—the tingling in her palms, the race of her heart. And she was suddenly very aware of the way her nipples had hardened against the sheer fabric of her bra.

This time, he was wearing gray sweats and a sleeveless gray tank top. As he drew closer, Rory could see the muscles that she'd only felt in the dressing room. She'd also become very aware of the way the red thong circled her hips and dipped low at the small of her back and she could feel the thin piece of lace that lay dampening at the center of her heat.

Questions tumbled through her mind. Why was she reacting this way to this man? And why couldn't she seem to control it?

She still had time to climb back down the tree and run. The moment the idea slipped into her mind, she shoved it out. This man was her best chance of getting an interview with Jared Slade.

The dogs reached the wall and were barking and leaping as high as they could. But Rory couldn't take her eyes off the Terminator. Fear, anticipation and excitement tumbled through her, nearly making her dizzy. She pressed her hands hard into the top of the brick wall to steady herself.

When he reached her, he settled the dogs with one quick gesture. Then he met her eyes and said, "What the hell are you doing here?"

5

"YOU DON'T LOOK HAPPY to see me," Rory said.

He wasn't. He'd been just about to take a run when a security guard had pointed her out on one of the monitors, and Hunter hadn't been able to prevent the quick flash of pleasure that had shot through him.

As she'd tested the front gate, he'd made a list of the reasons he shouldn't be happy to see her. For starters, her presence meant someone knew where he was, and the trap Tracker was setting might be totally useless.

Secondly, he didn't need the distraction. Just in the short time that it had taken him to reach her, his body had hardened painfully, and he was very much aware of his arousal pressing tight against his sweatpants. His reaction to this woman seemed to be completely out of his control.

There had to be a reason for that. Studying her, he took in the black T-shirt she was wearing and the faded jeans that had worn thin at the knees. The red boots had been replaced by serviceable-looking sneakers. There was nothing at all about the outfit that should be remotely sexy. Nothing that should make him wonder how fast he could get her out of it and what she was wearing beneath it.

She wasn't his type. How many times had he reminded himself of that in the past twenty-four hours? He preferred women who were sophisticated, who knew the score, who were beautiful.

Rory Gibbs wasn't beautiful. He raked his glance over the pixie features, the slim, strong-looking body. Cute was the most he could grant her. She looked small, defenseless and strangely defiant sitting there looking down at him. That shouldn't appeal to him, either—but it did.

When she licked her lips, he fisted his hands at his sides and stifled the urge to reach up, grab her ankles and pull her off that wall. He wanted her thousands of miles away from him. But even more than that, he wanted that small, compact body bucking beneath his as he thrust into her.

Tightening his grip on the control that had never deserted him before, Hunter said, "I asked you what in hell you're doing here."

When she lifted her chin and met his eyes squarely, he couldn't help but admire her.

"You've had time to develop the pictures I gave you. So I've come for the interview you promised."

His eyes narrowed. "I didn't promise you an interview."

"Close enough. You promised to talk to Jared Slade, and you look like a pretty persuasive man to me. Did you talk to him?" Her tone was quiet and her gaze never wavered.

"He left before we could discuss it."

"He left? I missed him?"

There was such shock, such disappointment on her face that Hunter wondered how there could be a dishonest bone in her body. If she tried to lie, surely her face, her body language would give her away. "How did you know he was here?"

She raised a hand. "No. Wait a minute. You're here. He wouldn't go away without his bodyguard."

Hunter's brows shot up. "Bodyguard?"

Rory pointed a finger at him. "Don't try to deny it. You chased me out of Les Printemps to get the film. You're obviously Mr. Slade's bodyguard. And you're still here, so I don't believe he's gone."

"I'm not Jared Slade's bodyguard. I'm his executive vice president in charge of retail acquisitions. He left me behind to finish up a deal we're working on."

"With Irene Malinowitz at Silken Fantasies?"

"No comment." She *was* sharp. Either that or someone in his organization was keeping her well-informed. His eyes narrowed as her face suddenly flushed.

"I—I want to thank you for the…red…under things. You really shouldn't have, but…I mean…"

A very vivid image slipped into Hunter's mind of that moment when he'd first seen her wearing the red thong and bra—the way she'd looked wearing nothing but those thin wisps of lace and those red boots. Whatever cooling off his body had done stopped and went into an abrupt reverse. Shoving the image out of his mind, he said, "You haven't answered my question. Who told you my boss was here?"

She hesitated and he could almost hear the wheels inside her head start to turn.

"You can't lie to me. So don't even try."

RORY GRIPPED THE EDGE of the wall and wished that she hadn't left her bubble gum in the car. He had the Terminator look back on his face, and there was a part of her that wanted to do a Humpty Dumpty into his arms and just see where she would fall.

But she'd come here to get an interview. "If I tell you, will you call Mr. Slade and set up the interview?"

"I'll call him and ask him about it. That's all I can promise."

She nodded. "Okay. It's a little complicated. My sister Natalie is a friend of Sophie Wainwright and Sophie told Natalie that a reclusive tycoon who was worried about his safety was consulting with her brother's chief of security." She paused to take a breath. "And Lucas Wainwright's chief of security happens to be Sophie's main squeeze. No names were mentioned—but Natalie works for a special D.C. police task force, and her office was called about the bomb scare in Mr. Slade's suite. She told me about that—strictly off the record. But how many media-shy tycoons with security problems could be in Washington at one time?"

Hunter wasn't sure whether he wanted to laugh or to swear. The story was way too convoluted and way too plausible for him to doubt it. Unless Rory Gibbs was a very talented liar.

"Did you let anyone at your magazine know that you were coming out here?" he asked.

"No. If it didn't pan out, I'd look like a fool, wouldn't I?"

Another convincing answer. Whether she was lying or not, he'd have to let Tracker know she was here—and he'd have to at least pretend to make a phone call to Jared Slade.

"Come with me. We'll talk inside," he said.

"What about the dogs?"

"They're friendly." He moved closer to the wall. "Jump and I'll catch you."

Rory saw those hands reaching for her and her whole system began to have a meltdown again. Images slipped into her mind of what she'd seen them do to her in the mirror in that dressing room. Whatever else happened, she wanted those hands on her again.

Scooting to the edge of the wall, she didn't even count to three before she took the plunge. And then he was holding her tightly against that body again. For one scorching moment, she was aware of nothing but hard angles and rock-hard muscles pressing into her. An instant later, he set her on her feet with an abruptness that had her taking a quick step back to the wall for support. Before she could even be sure of her balance, he turned away and started toward the drive with the dogs loping along happily at his side.

Rory frowned at him. Then she took several quick steps to catch up. She'd come here to get an interview with Jared Slade. The one she'd been promised. And she wasn't going to give up.

But as she followed him up the curved driveway, she found her focus slipping again. Even from the back, he radiated a kind of raw energy that was both primitive and sexual. If she'd inherited just a portion of her sisters' planning genes, perhaps she could have stopped staring at the damp hair that curled low at the back of his neck. Or she might have kept her gaze from drifting down the length of his back and lower.

His sweats were made of some thin material that fit snugly over his backside. Her eyes lingered there as her stomach clenched and she started to lose the feeling in her legs. She knew what it would feel like to slip her hands beneath the waistband and explore that taut, smooth skin. Would it be as hot as it had been the last time—as hot as hers was beginning to feel? Rory's eyes widened as she watched her hands reach out of their own accord. Snatching them back, she stumbled.

In a move so quick, it sent whatever breath she had left backing up into her lungs, he turned and grabbed both of her arms to steady her. "You all right?"

No, she was anything but all right. She was turning into one big puddle of lust. And it was clear that he wasn't. At least not anymore. His eyes were almost clinical as they searched her face. "I'll get you something to drink when we get to the house."

She didn't need anything to drink—except perhaps a long swallow of him, but he didn't seem to be on the same wavelength anymore.

Wasn't that just the story of her life when it came to men? Try as she might, she just didn't have the equipment to turn men into lust puddles. At least not for very long. Otherwise, he would have pulled her to him and that gorgeous mouth would be feasting on hers again.

But it wasn't. And she was *not* going to think about what that mouth had felt like on hers. She couldn't afford to go there. One thing at a time, she told herself. Getting the interview required all of her concentration. Drawing in a deep breath, she met his eyes and said, "I'm…fine."

His gaze remained locked on hers for one more moment, and Rory held her breath, hoping that nothing he saw would betray her.

Finally, he nodded. "Watch your step on the gravel." Then dropping his hands, he turned and led the way along a path to a patio. Just as they passed through open French doors into what looked like a study, the phone rang. She lingered in the doorway as he strode to the desk and picked it up. Grateful for a slight reprieve, she pulled her eyes away from him and looked around the room. Three of the walls were lined with books that looked like they'd been read.

"Yes?" He spoke the word into the phone as if he'd been expecting the call. "We need to talk. Just hang on a minute, will you?" He set the phone down, then moved toward her. "I have some business to discuss. Would you mind waiting out on the patio for a bit?"

"No." She stepped back through the French doors.

"There's a housekeeper—a man named McGee. The Wainwrights left him in charge when they went back to D.C. I'll have him bring you something to drink. Would you prefer coffee? Iced tea? A soft drink?"

"There's no need. Really."

His brows lifted. "I'm going to tell him to bring you something, so you might as well take your choice."

She raised her hands, palms out. "Okay. Coffee would be fine."

"Good. Why don't you go over and sit by the pool? It's cooler there. I'll join you as soon as I'm finished on the phone."

When he stepped back into the study and closed the French doors in her face, Rory had the distinct feeling she'd been handled and dismissed. Through the glass, she watched as he circled the desk, then met her eyes again and waited. For five long beats, she stayed right where she was. But it was the wrong battle to draw a line in the sand for. Turning away, she started toward the pool. As Jared Slade's vice president in charge of retail acquisitions, he was probably used to giving orders and having them obeyed.

She'd never been good at taking orders or following someone else's agenda, but she'd do what he wanted for now. She had a feeling she'd need all the energy she could muster up to get that interview.

FOR A LONG MINUTE, Hunter didn't pick up the phone. Instead he let himself recall just what she'd felt like pressed against him for that moment after she'd jumped off the wall. He hadn't wanted to let her go. For an instant, every bit of the desire he'd felt for her in that dressing room had returned. And it wasn't going to go away.

Not seeing her again might have solved the problem. But avoiding her wasn't going to be possible now. Frowning, he picked up the phone and said, "Tracker?"

"I'm still here. I take it you have a visitor?"

"Yeah. Rory Gibbs. Seems she got wind of the possibility that Jared Slade was here to consult Lucas Wainwright's chief of security. She knew about the bomb scare, too, but she assured me that part was off the record."

Tracker swore, then said, "Do you know her source?"

"Sources. And you're not going to like it," Hunter said. Then he repeated Rory's explanation.

"Damn," Tracker said. "Sophie is usually more discreet than that."

"Don't blame her," Hunter said. "She was talking to friends. One of them just happened to be the sister of a woman who's determined to interview Jared Slade. My bad luck and Rory Gibbs's good fortune."

"Look, I just put my man on Lucas's private plane. I'll come out to the estate and have a talk with her."

"I don't think that's a good idea," Hunter said.

There was a beat of silence on the other end of the line. "I'm listening."

"She seems to always be at the right place at the right time, but I don't think she's being fed information. She's just got brains and good luck. And a reporter's curiosity— which could mean trouble."

"What are you going to do?"

"I wish the hell I knew." But talking to Tracker was helping him work through it. And it wasn't hurting that Rory Gibbs wasn't in the same room. His brain cells were beginning to function again. Through the window, he could see her reaching the gate of the pool. The dogs were romping around her, but they didn't seem to scare her. She stooped down, picked up a stick and shot it away. The dogs tore after it. "She's…"

"Yes?" Tracker asked.

A constant surprise, Hunter thought. But what he said was, "She's a loose cannon."

"Meaning?"

"I'm afraid if you talk to her, warn her off, it's only going to make her more curious. She'll start digging, probing." He started to pace back and forth in the space behind the desk. "It's like she's got a sixth sense or something. I'm afraid that she may even come up with the theory that *I'm* Jared Slade."

"And if she does?" Tracker asked.

"I'm trying to prevent that. I told her that Slade's gone, that I'm his vice president in charge of retail acquisitions. That's when she guessed I was acquiring Silken Fantasies."

Tracker couldn't prevent a laugh. "She's as smart as her sisters."

"I wonder if she knows that," Hunter mused.

"How's that?"

"Nothing." He watched the huge black Labs race toward her, topple her over on the grass. When she sat up and looped her arms around their necks and let them lick her face, he was abruptly and totally charmed.

"I'm going to keep her here until we sort this out," Hunter said.

"And just how do you plan to do that?"

The plan was beginning to take shape in his mind. "Jared Slade doesn't give interviews. I'll offer her the next best thing—an interview with his vice president in charge of retail acquisitions, Mark Hunter. I use that name when I travel," he explained. "There's even a personnel file on Mark Hunter in the Dallas office." Then he thought to ask, "I assume there won't be any problem with her staying here on the estate?"

For five beats there was dead silence on the other end of the line. "She's the sister of a friend of mine. I don't want to see her hurt. Her sister wouldn't want to see her hurt. Neither would Lucas."

Hunter's brows rose. There was a clear warning in Tracker's voice. "Let's look at it this way. The interview will be legit, and it will be the next best thing to interviewing Jared Slade. She'll have the scoop she needs to get her a full-time staff position at *Celebs*. And I'll have the certainty that she's here where I can keep an eye on her while you're springing the trap we've set."

"I don't know," Tracker said.

"There's something else to consider. What if she's not just lucky and smart? Someone sent an anonymous tip about my hotel to *Celebs* and not to the *Post,* as you mentioned earlier today. What if the bastard who set the bomb is using her as a pawn in the game he's playing? Until we know what's going on and who the players are, she'll be safer here with me than she'd be trying to get a lead on Jared Slade's whereabouts."

As he watched Rory throw a stick for the dogs, he waited out the silence again.

"Why do I think that there's a more personal side to this than you're telling me?" Tracker finally asked.

"Because your nature is to be suspicious. But neither one of us wants her stumbling onto something that will lead her down to the Keys," Hunter said.

"Yeah." He sighed. "You're right. I'll be in touch when I have something."

After hanging up the phone, Hunter walked to the French doors. Whatever he'd said to Tracker, he wouldn't lie to himself. He wanted Rory Gibbs with him for very personal reasons that had nothing to do with her safety or protecting his anonymity.

He didn't kid himself, either. Keeping her here was every bit as risky as letting her go. But he hadn't built Slade Enterprises by running away from risks. He would just have to be careful. He watched her race across the lawn with the dogs chasing her and felt his body begin to harden again. Would she be that reckless, that abandoned when they made love again? He wanted to find out. He would find out, Hunter decided. Soon. That decision made, he began to plot a strategy for handling Rory Gibbs.

6

RORY WAS OUT OF BREATH by the time she reached to open the gate to the pool. The dogs pushed through it, jumped at her, licked her face, and finally sent her tumbling into one of the lounge chairs. Laughing, she patted one head then the other. "Down," she ordered, then watched in amazement as they settled, tongues hanging out, one on each side of her chair.

"How do you like your coffee, miss?"

She glanced up from the dogs to see an older, distinguished-looking man in navy blue shorts and a crisp white short-sleeved shirt set a tray on the table next to her chair.

"Black, thank you," she said. "I'm sorry for the trouble. I told him that I really didn't need anything. Oh, my... cookies." She beamed a smile at him as she reached for one and took a bite. "You've saved my life. Food always settles my nerves. Plus, chewing makes me think, and I left my bubble gum in the car." She took another cookie. "These are delicious, Mr...."

"You can call me McGee. And the cookies are no trouble. Mr. Lucas likes to know that his guests are well cared for."

"You shouldn't have brought so many. I'll probably eat them all."

When he handed her a mug of coffee, Rory took a sip

and then closed her eyes and sighed. "Perfect. This is French-pressed, isn't it?"

"Indeed." McGee smiled at her. "You have a discerning taste. Mr. Lucas prefers French-pressed coffee."

Rory smiled at the man over the rim of her mug. "I do, too. Could you pour yourself a mug and join me? Is that allowed?"

The corners of his mouth twitched. "Strictly speaking, no. But it's kind of you to ask."

"What about the coffee beans? You must grind them yourself?"

"Yes, miss. The beans are grown in Kenya. Mr. Lucas has them flown in."

She nodded. "Heavenly. And please call me Rory. Can you at least sit?"

When he did, she took another cookie. "You've been with Mr. Wainwright for a time?"

"Ever since he came back to take over the company. My son, Tim, works in the stables. If you want to ride, let him pick your mount. He's a good judge."

"Thanks. I won't be staying long." She took another sip of the coffee. "Mr. Lucas's guest—do you happen to know his name?"

"Mark Hunter," said a voice that she recognized. Turning, she watched him enter through the gate and approach her in that long-legged Terminator stride.

"Will that be all, miss?" McGee asked as he rose.

"Yes. Thank you," she replied as nerves sprung to life again and twisted into a knot in her stomach. Mark Hunter. The last name suited him, she thought. Hadn't she seen the hunter in him from the first? He had that look about him now as he sat down on the foot of the lounge adjacent to hers.

He was prepared, his quarry in sight. And she'd spent the time playing with the dogs and talking to Lucas Wainwright's butler. She could have kicked herself. As usual, she was going to have to develop a plan by the seat of her pants. Once McGee had let himself out the gate, she reached for another cookie. "These are delicious."

Mark Hunter filled a mug from the carafe. "You eat when you're nervous, don't you?"

"What makes you think I'm nervous?" she asked around a mouthful of chocolate crumbs.

He took her hand as she reached for another cookie. "Because your hand is trembling."

"Did you talk to Jared Slade?" she said quickly, changing the subject.

He met her eyes. "Yes. He won't agree to an interview."

She straightened, swinging her legs off the side of the lounge so that her knees brushed briefly against his. "Mr. Hunter, there's got to be some arrangement we can make."

"You can call me Hunter. That's what my associates call me."

"Hunter, then. Mr. Slade doesn't have to see me or even talk to me. I could give you some questions to ask him. You could tell me the answers."

Hunter shook his head. "He hates the press. He's not going to change his mind."

Her eyes narrowed suddenly. "You knew that from the beginning. You conned me out of those pictures, knowing that I'd never get an interview. I could have published them. I should have turned them over to my boss. But I stalled her."

He studied her as she spoke, watching temper darken her eyes and emanate from her in little sparks he could almost feel on his skin. Here was the passion that he'd only begun to explore in that dressing room. He wanted to taste it again. He wanted to push it, push her until she exploded in his arms.

Rising, she paced away toward the pool. He rose and moved toward her.

"I never should have given you those pictures." When she whirled back to face him, she walked smack into him, then took a quick step back. He grabbed her arms to keep her from falling into the water. It might have worked if those excitable dogs hadn't gotten involved. Two strong paws hit him right in the small of his back. He stumbled forward, then twisted and took her with him as he fell back-first into the pool.

When they came up for air, she was sputtering and coughing. Then to his surprise and delight she began to laugh.

Treading water, he stared at her. Any other woman would have been angry. Her eyes were light now, liquid gold with darker flecks. And with her hair plastered to her head, she looked like some kind of water sprite. And that mouth. He had to taste it again. Soon.

But first they had business to settle between them. He moved toward her and urged her to the side of the pool where the dogs were barking and hoping for more horseplay.

"Down," he said, and they moved back to settle themselves on either side of a lounge chair.

He returned his gaze to Rory. The depth was shallow enough that he could stand, but he noted that she secured herself by placing a hand on the ledge that ran around the side of the pool. Her legs tangled with his before she pulled hers back.

"I'm still angry with you," she said.

"But not for pushing you into the pool."

Her brows shot up. "You didn't. The dogs did." She leveled her gaze on him. "I try to be a fair person. But you weren't fair with me."

"Strong words," he murmured.

"If the shoe fits…"

He raised a hand, palm out. "Okay. You're right. I did know from the beginning that Jared Slade was not going to give you that interview."

"So, you negotiated a kiss on a lie."

"Okay. But maybe you dazzled me so much that I shouldn't be held responsible for that."

She snorted. "Yeah. Right. I go through life dazzling men. Wherever I go, they fall at my feet."

He studied her for a moment. Was it possible that she didn't know how attractive she was? That might explain the innocence he kept sensing in her. Hunter ran a finger down her cheek to her throat and felt her pulse scramble. "Before I become dazzled again, I have a compromise I want to offer you." He traced his finger along her collarbone, and then he saw it—the thin red strap. His mouth went dry, and the water surrounding them in the pool suddenly seemed warmer.

"Compromise?" she asked.

He dragged his thoughts back from the red bra and the red… "Yes." He swallowed hard as he forced himself to meet her eyes. Every time he got this close to her, she sent every rational thought he had flying away.

Yet she didn't think that she had any power over men.

He'd come out here with a plan, a strategy all worked out. And he simply didn't care about it anymore. Hunter held her gaze. "Are you wearing the thong?"

Her eyes darkened from amber to dark, rich cognac in a heartbeat. "Yes."

"Show me," he said as he backed a few steps away. Then he watched as she dropped her hand from the edge of the pool and tugged the snap of her jeans open. Impeded by the wetness of the fabric and the water, she had to tug and wiggle, then tug and wiggle some more as she slid the jeans down those slender, strong legs and kicked them off. It seemed to take forever, and the water surrounding them grew steadily hotter and hotter until the sun beating down on his shoulders felt cool in comparison.

Still, he didn't rush as he moved his gaze slowly up her legs to where the little triangle of red lace beckoned to him. His hand felt heavy as he moved it to her and traced the lace edge with one finger. She was wearing a silver bar in her navel, and when he touched it, desire curled within him, tangling with an ache that was unexpected and raw.

More than anything, he wanted to push that sheer red fabric aside and watch what happened to her eyes when he slid into her heat. He let his gaze move higher up that slim waist to linger on her breasts. The nipples were hard and he could see them through the wet fabric. He was going to touch them, too.

His original plan had been to wait—to give her part of the interview, wine and dine her…then succumb to his need for her. But he'd never been pulled so strongly by a woman before. And he'd waited long enough.

Meeting her eyes, he said, "I want to kiss you again. And I want to make love to you. If you have a problem with that, now would be a good time to say so."

She met his gaze steadily, keeping her head above water by merely kicking her feet. It was happening again—just as it had in the dressing room. He wanted her. She could read the desire in his eyes, feel it in the heat of his body.

She'd come here for this as much as for the interview, and there wasn't a chance for her to fall back into the old indecisive Rory when he looked at her the way he was right now. But there was one thing she had to clear up first.

"I'm not going to kiss you again for an interview or a compromise. Let's just get that straight. This time I'm going to kiss you because I want to."

Hunter nodded. "Agreed. Now, take off your shirt."

The ache inside of her only twisted tighter as she did what he asked, bobbing gently in the water as she struggled to get the damp T-shirt over her head. Then she was naked except for the red lace.

"We shouldn't do this here." His voice was hoarse as he closed the small distance between them.

"No. I should be asking you about the compromise. But I can't seem to keep my mind on task when I'm with you." She looped her arms around his neck and brushed her legs up against his.

With a groan, Hunter trapped one of her legs between his. "We'll get to the compromise. Later." He wasn't sure whether it was her words or the way she looked in the water—part sex goddess, part mermaid, but he felt the same urgency that he'd felt in the lingerie shop. All that mattered was having her. Now.

"Hurry."

Hearing her say that one breathless word had an arrow of heat shooting through him. His head was spinning. The restless, wanton movements of her body against his had him swaying. To steady himself, to steady both of them, he pushed forward until her back was against the side of the pool.

"Kiss me."

He wasn't sure who'd spoken the words or if he'd just thought them, but he took her mouth with his.

OH, YES, RORY THOUGHT as his flavor exploded on her tongue and poured into her. Yes, yes, yes, yes. Her mind took up the chant as his tongue moved in a slow, steady rhythm over hers, and his hand stroked down her body possessively. His flavor was just as she remembered—dark and rich like some exotic kind of chocolate. Forbidden and addictive.

Her breath caught in her throat and her body arched toward his as his fingers began to toy with the waistband of her thong. Her skin trembled and arrows of heat shot through her as they moved along her waist to her back. But he didn't linger. Instead, he moved his hands, those long fingers, those wide palms, to caress her buttocks. She felt each individual finger burn into her skin like a brand before the pressure increased and they drew her cheeks apart.

Pleasure and anticipation streaked through her, and heat built in her center. Then he began to trace the thong along her bottom, spreading her cheeks even farther to give his fingers more access until he was pressing them just where she wanted.

"Harder," she whimpered as she arched and wiggled herself against them. "Please."

He lifted her then and she wrapped her legs around him, pressing herself against the hard length of him.

She moaned when he slowly retraced the path his fingers had just taken along the lace strap of the thong between her cheeks.

Tightening her legs around him, she said, "I want you inside of me, now."

He had no choice. After shoving his sweats down, Hunter found her opening and pressed himself against it. Then he pushed himself into her and felt her heat grip him tightly. After withdrawing a little, he drove in even farther.

"Yes," she whimpered against his ear.

He withdrew and thrust in even deeper. Just this one more time. Hadn't he told himself that if he could have her this way again, that would be enough? But as her heat burned him, and her muscles fastened around him like a clamp, he wasn't sure that his hunger for her would ever be sated.

He withdrew and thrust in again, this time to the hilt.

"More."

Every muscle in his body sang with the need to obey her command, but he was aware that the lawn mower that he'd heard earlier had moved closer. Above the hedge that bordered the pool, he could see the straw hat of the driver. This time when he withdrew, she clamped her legs around him tightly.

"Don't you dare stop."

He leaned closer and whispered, "Shh. We're not alone." Though he was confident that the man on the mower wouldn't be able to hear them, he couldn't be sure that the man wouldn't glance over the hedge and see them.

"I can't wait."

Even though he was gripping her hips firmly, she managed to thrust herself against him. Suddenly, he couldn't wait, either. Very slowly, he withdrew and then pushed into her again. When she stiffened and murmured his name, he heard something inside of him snap just as clearly as he heard the sound of the lawn mower fade.

He slapped his hands against the tiles and then thrust

into her again—faster, harder, again and again. Each time he pushed into her, she seemed to grow hotter, and her grip on him—inside and out—tightened.

No, this was not going to be enough. He would need this again and again. Even as the realization poured through him, he felt the water around him churning, heard little waves slapping against the sides of the pool. She was moving with him, thrust for thrust. Just as the heat became searing, unbearable, he felt her stiffen. Then he surrendered to her climax and to his.

RORY WAS AWARE that on some level, her body had gone as limp as her mind. If Hunter's body hadn't been pressing hers so firmly against the wall of the pool, she would have slid right down to the bottom and drowned. She could still feel him embedded inside of her, and though she wouldn't have thought it possible, the knowledge, the pressure had something inside of her warming again. She drew in a breath, and when her lungs burned, she wondered just how long her body had been without oxygen.

"Are you okay?"

She managed a weak nod. "But I can't move yet."

She felt his lips curve against her shoulder. "I'm having a bit of a problem with that myself."

When she felt him pull out of her, she nearly cried out in protest. She might have tightened her legs to keep him there, but they still felt like soft, runny butter. A minute later, she found herself sitting beside him on the steps leading out of the pool.

"Wow," she said, snuggling her head against his shoulder because she simply didn't have the strength to hold it upright.

"Ditto."

"Next time, I vote we do this on dry land."

"I can vote for that, too," he said. "And to hurry that process along, why don't I get you a towel?"

For a moment after he pulled away, Rory felt cold and a bit bereft. The ringing of a phone caught him halfway to the pool house, and he strode quickly back to the table near the lounge chairs to pick up the extension.

"Yeah?"

She saw the frown come to his face a second before she swept her gaze down the length of him. The wet sweats were clinging to his body, revealing every hard angle and plane. And he was still wearing his running shoes. A short distance away, her sneakers lay on the bottom of the pool, peeking out from beneath her jeans. He was still fully clothed and she was wearing only a red bra and thong.

And she'd just been ravished at the side of a pool. Well, not ravished really. Technically, to be truly ravished, she suspected that the ravishee had to put up at least a token resistance.

She hadn't. The only thing she'd done was make it very clear that making love with him was not going to be some quid pro quo thing. What they'd just done had nothing to do with the interview. Leaning back against her hands, she extended her legs and examined her body. Was it the red thong that was giving her the confidence to do things she'd never done before?

Her gaze returned to Hunter. Or was it the man who'd made her feel so daring? Slowly a smile curved her lips as she thought of the way Sierra would answer that question. The only way to find out would be to do some further research.

"LOOKS LIKE YOU WERE right," Tracker said on the other end of the line.

"About what?" Hunter asked.

"About Rory Gibbs. I stopped by her apartment on a hunch."

"A hunch?" Hunter shifted his gaze to Rory.

"I've been known to have them. Perhaps it was your characterization of her as a pawn. But it occurred to me that if she was stumbling into information that you didn't particularly want her to have, someone else might not want her to have it, either. Anyway, her place just happened to be on my route from the airport to the Wainwright offices."

"And you knew the address because…?"

"Hey, I'm a top-notch security expert. We know these things—or can find out."

As Tracker continued to talk, Hunter's eyes narrowed. Rory shivered a little as she drew up her knees and wrapped her arms around them. She was cold, and he'd promised her a towel.

"Hunter, are you still there?"

He dragged his thoughts back. "What?"

"The door of her apartment had been forced, and the place had been trashed. I suppose it could be a random break-in."

"I don't think so."

"Neither do I. That means that someone was probably watching her place. And they were looking for something."

"What?"

"Answer that and you, too, can become a security specialist. You can pass along any theories you have when I get there in an hour or so."

Hunter lowered his voice. "I think we should keep this

under wraps for now. She might want to leave—and for the time being she's safer here."

"I can't argue with the logic of that."

Hunter kept his eyes on Rory as he hung up the phone. How much danger was she in?

7

"So you drove out here last night and slept in your car?"
Hunter sat at the head of the table in a dining room that was
as large as her whole apartment.

"More chicken salad, Miss Rory?" McGee asked, offering her the bowl.

"Yes…I mean no, thanks." She glanced down at her
plate to find that it was empty. She'd had two helpings already in hopes that the nerves in her stomach would settle. "Well, maybe," she said, sending McGee a smile. "It's
delicious." She piled another spoonful onto her plate. "And
the answer to your question is yes, too," she added as she
met Hunter's eyes.

She tore off a piece of croissant and popped it into her
mouth. Perhaps the nerves were due to the fact that Hunter
had slipped back into Terminator mode from the moment
he'd hung up the phone at the pool. Oh, he'd been perfectly
polite. He'd found her some dry clothes in the pool house,
and he'd even had McGee show her to a guest room where
she could shower. But since they'd sat down to lunch, he'd
been treating her like a perfect stranger.

Exactly the way he'd treated her after the phone call that
he'd taken in the dressing room at Silken Fantasies.

"Did you have any reason to suspect that you were followed out here?" he asked.

"Followed?" The thought had her frowning. "Why would anyone follow me?"

"Mr. Wainwright's security team would like to know if they should expect any more visitors to climb over the wall."

"Ah." She busied herself, scooping up another forkful of chicken salad as she thought about it. Could she have been followed? She hadn't even gone home after she'd spoken to Natalie at the Blue Pepper. Instead, she'd had something to eat, talked with Rad and George and then decided on the spur of the moment to drive out to the estate that night.

It had been late when she'd crossed the bridge into Virginia. Glancing up, she met Hunter's eyes. "I wasn't followed. Once I got off the main highway, I didn't notice any headlights behind me. And out here in the country, I think I would have." She gestured with her fork. "I read a lot of Nancy Drew mystery stories when I was growing up."

"Nancy Drew mysteries?" he asked.

"Yeah. Nancy Drew, girl detective. You probably read the Hardy Boys. But I liked Nancy. She had great girlfriends, drove a great car, had a steady, faithful boyfriend, and she had a great father."

He was looking at her curiously. "You read stories as a child and so you're sure you would have noticed headlights following you on a country road."

She nodded. "You try reading thirty or so books where a girl detective is looking for clues and being chased by bad guys. You'll notice all kinds of odd things. Didn't you ever read the Hardy Boys?"

He shook his head. "Can't say that I did. Should I consider my education lacking?"

She tilted her head to one side. "Only if you wanted to

grow up to be a supersleuth. You probably had other goals in mind." After setting down her fork, she pushed her plate aside and crossed her arms on the table. "Why are you asking me all these questions? Does this have something to do with the bomb scare at Les Printemps?"

Hunter had known that the question would come sooner or later, and he thought he had a plausible strategy for handling it. "I mentioned at the pool that Mr. Slade is prepared to offer you something in lieu of an interview with him. Part of the compromise I'm prepared to offer you requires your assurance that there will be no mention of the bomb scare in any article you might write. Mr. Slade is disturbed enough that you're here. However, he's aware that you gave back the pictures you snapped in the lobby. So he's willing to offer you something in place of an interview with him."

Her eyes narrowed. "What?"

Hunter wiped his mouth with his napkin and set it at the side of his plate. "If you're finished, why don't we take a walk while I explain?"

Without a word, she rose and followed him down the hall to the study and then through the French doors. He didn't cross the lawn to the pool, but instead guided her down a path that wound its way past the tennis courts toward the stables.

They walked in silence for a few minutes while Hunter reviewed his plan. It should provide both of them with what they wanted, and that was the key to any successful negotiation. In his mind, he pictured the plus columns on each side. An interview with "Mark Hunter," someone high up in Slade Enterprises, should be enough to get Rory Gibbs the staff job she wanted at *Celebs* magazine. And keeping her occupied on the estate while Tracker sprang a trap on whomever was behind the threats would ensure her safety.

Of course, there was the possibility that she would figure out that he was "Jared Slade." But he'd decided to risk that.

Hunter glanced down at the top of her head as she walked by his side. Who was he kidding? He wasn't really offering her the interview because of the advantages to either one of them. He was going to offer her the interview with "Mark Hunter" because he wanted to make love to her again. Dammit. He wanted her right now.

Desire had always been something he could handle, something he understood. But he had a hunch that desire was only a part of what he was feeling for this curious woman. He wanted to get to know her. He wanted to figure out how that agile mind of hers worked.

He hadn't allowed himself to really get to know a woman in years. He'd never intended to. It wasn't fair to them or to him. But he wanted to be as fair as possible to Rory. So he would clarify the parameters of their relationship. He would let her know exactly what to expect and what not to—

She stopped suddenly and pointed up into a tree. "Look. A tree house."

He glanced up and spotted the wooden floor wedged in a circle around the tree trunk and the small roofed structure that sat on two sturdy limbs.

"I always wanted one as a kid." Rory grabbed the rope ladder and began to climb, talking as she went. "My dad was going to build me one, too. He would have if he hadn't left. Of course, it probably would have freaked my mother out. She was always so afraid we would get hurt, break an arm or a leg. I take after her in height and coloring, but I'm glad I didn't inherit all of her fraidy-cat genes."

When she scrambled onto the ledge, the branch swayed, and the tree house tilted.

"Grab the railing," Hunter said as he climbed up the rope ladder to join her. Together, they gingerly settled themselves on the wooden platform outside the little house itself. Below them the lawns rolled away on all sides. To the left there were tennis courts, and beyond the pool, he could see the white fences that surrounded the stables.

"Do you ride?" he asked.

She wrapped her arms around her knees the way she had on the steps of the pool. "Yes, but I haven't had the opportunity in years." She angled her head to face him. "Do you ride?"

"I used to play polo," he said. Then he could have kicked himself. Where in the world had that come from? His polo days had ended when he'd stopped being Hunter Marks.

"Very cool. The closest I've come to a polo match is watching clips in a movie or on TV. I just love it, though. It's the same feeling I get when I watch the Kentucky Derby on TV. For the five or six minutes while the horses are being led to the starting gate and the race is run, I always feel like I'm one of the rich and the famous. Then it's over, and I'm back to being plain Rory Gibbs again."

"Why do you think of yourself as plain?" he asked.

"Because I am. No." She raised a hand to stop him. "You're a nice man. But I'm twenty-six, I'm short, and I'm sandwiched between two sisters who are truly beautiful. You should see them. Sierra's a blonde—not the dumb kind. She's the smartest one in the family, with two Ph.D.s. You know what they say about blondes having more fun? In Sierra's case, her work is what she considers 'fun.' Natalie's a redhead, and she's a cop. They say redheads get into more trouble, and she does. But she loves it. I'm a brunette. You never hear anything about brunettes. We're just ordinary."

He tamped down his anger as he studied her. Going with an impulse that he didn't quite understand, he put his arm around her. When she snuggled her head into his shoulder just as she'd done in the pool, he had an odd feeling, as if his heart had turned a little somersault. "Someone did a job on you."

"Ancient history. I have a talent for attracting men who are eventually going to dump me, starting with my father who walked out when I was ten."

"Your father must have been a fool."

She sighed. "You *are* a nice man. But there were extenuating circumstances—he was an international jewel thief and my mother wanted to raise us in a stable home."

"Your father was a jewel thief?" he asked incredulously.

Rory nodded. "A very good one. He couldn't seem to give up his profession and my mother didn't want us following in his footsteps. So they made this deal that he had to leave. Now that I'm older I can see it from their perspective. They did it because they loved us."

He ran a hand over her hair. It couldn't have been easy to understand it at ten. He'd had to separate himself from his family when he was nineteen—and he hadn't fully understood it even at that age.

"So?" She lifted her head and met his eyes. "We could spend the whole day sitting in a tree house. Or you could tell me about the compromise."

Hunter turned to study her. She looked strangely at

home in a tree house with dappled sunlight highlighting her features.

With some effort, he pulled his mind back to business. "First off, you should know that I'm not a nice man."

To his surprise, she grinned at him. "Of course, you're probably not nice when it comes to Slade Enterprises. The first time I looked at you, all I could think of was the Terminator."

Baffled, he stared at her. "The Terminator?"

She waved a hand. "Only in the first movie—you know, Arnold Schwarzenegger, when he was the bad guy, before he transformed himself into a superhero and eventually ran for governor."

"Oh." Mentally, Hunter dragged up an image of the mechanical robot fixated on destroying the woman and her future son in the first *Terminator* movie.

Rory laid a hand on his cheek. "I know that you can be a ruthless negotiator. Jared Slade would never have hired you otherwise, and you did talk me out of those pictures. But you can't expect me to forget how sweet you are."

"Sweet?"

"You sent me that lingerie. And now you're letting me ramble on and on about my family."

Hunter's mind was swimming. How in the world was he supposed to deal with a woman like this? "Do you always say what you're thinking?"

"Yeah. Mostly. I know it's not a good thing. My most recent ex-boyfriend found it quite annoying."

He gripped her chin in his hand. "It's fine. You're fine, and you should stop beating up on yourself."

"Okay." She smiled at him. "Didn't I tell you that you were sweet?"

Hunter gave up. There wasn't anyone who'd ever dealt with him who would have called him that. Ruthless, yes. And usually fair. But never *sweet*. Maybe it was time that he proved that to her. He dropped his hand from her face. "This is the compromise, Rory. You get to interview me instead of Jared Slade. I'll be here for a day or two until I finish my business, and I'll give you what time I can—under certain conditions."

RORY'S HEART BEGAN TO SKIP and race. She was almost used to the feelings that he could stir in her when he looked at her in that intent way—as if he could see right into her soul. First there was a pulse of fear, then a sliver of anticipation, followed by a hot clutching sensation in her stomach—the lust. She licked her lips. "What conditions?"

"First, you have to stay here a day or two. I'll sandwich the interview in between the work I have to do."

"And?"

His eyes narrowed. "You can't imagine that we can stay in close proximity and not have a repeat of what happened in the dressing room and the pool."

Somewhere in the vicinity of her heart, she felt a stutter of relief. But her throat had become so dry that she had to swallow. "No. I mean…you mean…?"

"I can't be around you and not want to have you again."

"Oh."

He studied her for a moment and said, "One doesn't have anything to do with the other. Mr. Slade was agreeable to having you interview me. My wanting to make love to you again is an entirely separate matter."

"Okay. I couldn't agree more. I wouldn't sleep with you to get an interview. The two matters are completely separate." She was rambling, mostly because of the melting sensation that seemed to be turning her insides into liquid.

"And this day or two. It's all we'll have. I want you to understand that. As soon as my business is finished, I'll go back to Dallas."

Rory studied him. It was the first time that she'd ever had a man set up the dumping ahead of time. And he didn't look anything like the Terminator right now. No, the man facing her now was cool and collected, his mind focused on business.

Perhaps that's why the idea popped into her mind. Or maybe it was her father's advice. She drew in a deep breath. "Okay. But I might have some conditions of my own."

She saw the surprise glimmer for a moment in his eyes, but it was masked as quickly as it appeared.

"State your terms," he said.

"It's…" Secretly, she wished for her bubble gum. Anything that would settle her nerves and give her courage. But the idea had sprung full-blown into her mind. Well, maybe not full-blown. Perhaps the seed had been planted that very first time she'd seen him in the lobby of Les Printemps, and it had certainly been nurtured by their encounter in the dressing room at Silken Fantasies. The whole thing about taking risks and trusting in your luck was that you weren't sure exactly how you came to decisions—they just happened.

"Yes?" he prompted.

"I'll accept your terms for the interview. Thanks. I mean, interviewing you will be the next best thing to interviewing Jared Slade. I guess."

"But…"

She shook her head. "No *buts*. My terms have to do with

the sex part. And the whole thing is a little delicate. I'm not sure…exactly how to put this."

"When in doubt, just say it."

Rory let out a sigh of relief. "Okay. Here's the deal. You say you want to continue our…relationship."

He met her eyes steadily. "I do."

She tried to ignore the heat that shot through her again. "It's not that I didn't like what happened in the pool—or in the dressing room."

His eyes narrowed. *"But…?"*

She drew in a deep breath. "It was all a little fast."

"Fast."

She reached over to put her hand on his. "It was incredible. Really. The best sex I've ever had. Only…"

"Yes?"

She met his eyes then. "It's hard to say this."

"Shoot from the hip, Rory."

She drew in a breath and let it out. "I haven't had much experience…sexually, I mean. I've had three lovers—four if you count the frat boy in my freshman year in college. He was the first boy to really pay any attention to me, but we only had one date and we did it in the back of his car. I've tried very hard to have amnesia when it comes to him and the whole experience."

"Good plan," he murmured as he turned her hand over and linked his fingers with hers.

"You're a good listener. But I won't bore you with all the details of lovers two, three and four. Not that they're worth describing. In summary, most of the men that I've had sex with have the wham-bam-thank-you-ma'am technique down pat."

"And you'd like more variety this time," he said.

"Partly." She squeezed his hand. "And I want you to know that the wham-bam in the pool was the best that I've ever had."

He cleared his throat. "Thank you."

She sighed. "I'm not doing this right. I tend to speak first and think things through later."

He squeezed her fingers. "You're doing fine."

"It's not just variety that I want. I'm sure that you could be very good at…making love to a woman in a number of ways. But what I'd like is for you to let me experiment a bit and take control. I'd like to try some things I've only fantasized about. I've never been able to do that before. Would that be all right?"

HUNTER STARED AT HER. She was every man's fantasy come to life and she didn't have a clue. "I can handle that."

She beamed a smile at him that had his heart stuttering again. "You really are sweet."

He met her gaze squarely. "I'm not sweet. I want you to remember that."

"Okay. When do you want to get started?"

Right now, he thought. But if he touched her, he was sure that what would happen would be of the wham-bam variety. So he said, "You'll need to tell your sisters where you are, but I'd appreciate it if you'd swear them to secrecy. Tracker will talk to them, assure them that you're safe."

"Sure. And I'll need some clothes."

"I'll arrange for that." The sweats she was wearing were too big. She'd had to roll up the legs and sleeves, and the end result was that she looked a little like one of the seven dwarfs. Not that the outfit had dampened his desire or his intentions. In his personal opinion, she would have looked sexy in anything, but she didn't believe that. Not yet. He was going to change that.

"And I'll need a place to work—a computer. I left my notebook and pen in the car."

"I'll have McGee handle that."

"Then we have a deal." She held out her hand.

He looked at her hand, then at her. "One question."

"What?"

"You don't have to always be in control, right?"

"No. Just sometimes."

"Good." He took her hand. "Because I want to make love to you right now."

Her eyes widened. "But I haven't even thought about what I want to do."

"I like spontaneous, don't you?"

"Sure, I—" She broke off when he lifted her onto his lap.

"You don't mean right here. In a tree house?"

"Afraid so." He moved a finger along her collarbone and watched the little pulse at her throat scramble.

"We could fall."

He dipped his head and brushed his lips over hers. "Funny. I didn't peg you for someone who was afraid of taking risks."

"Really?"

"Really." He nipped her lower lip and then soothed the small hurt with his tongue. "And I'm a man who can never resist a challenge."

And she had challenged him, whether she knew it or not. This time he'd go slowly, make sure they took their time. His mouth made a lazy journey to her ear and then back again to her mouth. But he didn't kiss her, not yet.

"I wasn't gentle with you before?"

"I liked it."

He smiled against her lips. "So did I. But let's try this." He kissed her then and kissed her again. And again.

Rory felt as if she were falling under a spell. He'd never kissed her this way before, as if he had all the time in the world and intended to take it. His mouth was so soft, so warm. And so skilled. She'd never been kissed like this before by anyone. Each time he withdrew, it was only to change the way his mouth fit against hers, and then he would take her deeper. Even his flavor was different, richer, sweeter.

She wanted more, but she couldn't seem to move. Her arms felt so heavy, and her head was spinning. When he moved his hand beneath her sweatshirt and skimmed those clever fingers up her ribs to her breast, she trembled.

She…should…do something. Pull back to clear her head—or draw him closer. Something. She'd had a plan. She wanted to seduce him. But her mind began to float and then her body. Oh, she knew that she was still sitting on his lap. She could feel the hardness of his erection pressing against her thigh, but it felt like floating.

When he moved his mouth to her throat, those teeth nipping, that tongue soothing, her skin began to burn. He was running the pad of his thumb over her nipple, and suddenly the need inside of her grew edgy. "Hunter, I—"

"Mmm?" His voice was just a vibration on her skin, but it sent twin sensations of fire and ice dancing along her nerve endings. "If you don't like what I'm doing, I could stop."

"No." She raised her hand then to grip his shoulder and arched against him. "I want—"

The branch of the tree dipped slightly, and they both suddenly slid toward the edge of the platform they were on.

"Whoa…" Hunter gripped her tight as he grabbed onto the railing and shifted back toward the door of the tree house.

"Maybe we should postpone this," she said. But she didn't pull away.

"Is that what you'd like to do?"

She shook her head.

He smiled at her. "Then I think we can rise to the challenge." He moved some more until they were inside the tree house.

"There's not a lot of room in here," he commented but he didn't hesitate to draw her shirt off and toss it aside. When he reached for the waistband to her sweats, she batted his hands away and grabbed the bottom of his T-shirt instead.

"I haven't seen you naked yet."

Together, they got him out of the shirt and his sweatpants and then she wiggled out of her own, a bit awkwardly considering the place was not more than five by six feet.

"This is going to be some challenge to rise to," she said. "I think I already have a sliver in my knee."

"I don't even want to think where I might get one," Hunter said.

She gestured with a hand. "There's a fifty-room mansion right over there and we're naked in a tree house."

When her laugh bubbled up and filled the tree house, Hunter found himself joining her. He felt like a teenager. Surely he'd been an adolescent the last time he'd done something this foolish. But somehow he wanted her even more—and he didn't want to wait.

Just as he reached for her, she said, "I have an idea."

"Me, too." He eased her down onto some of their discarded clothes, then positioned her so that he was kneeling between her legs.

"Whatever happened to ladies first?"

"I'll let you go first down the rope ladder," he said as he lowered his mouth until it hovered over her breast. "I'm a man who likes to finish what I start, and I started this. First, I'm going to taste you all over. And I'm going to take my time."

And he did—starting with her breasts. It was as if she were a meal that he'd been starving for. Using teeth and tongue, he circled the top and underside of her breast before he closed his teeth on the nipple and then took it into his mouth to suck. Arrows of heat shot through her, and she was sure that she felt the pull of his mouth right down to her toes. When he turned his attention to the other breast, she threaded her fingers through his hair and simply held on as the air around her seemed to grow hotter, thicker.

He moved his mouth lower, whispering kisses down the valley between her breasts, and then down her stomach. He lingered at her waist as if there were some taste there that he favored and then he went lower.

He drew her legs farther apart and held them down. And then she could feel his breath right there where she burned for him.

"I'm going to kiss you here—in a moment. But first…" He trailed kisses up and down one thigh and then the other, at times coming close to where she wanted him…but not close enough.

Sensations swamped her, each one growing more intense than the last—the scrape of his teeth at the back of her knee, the texture of his tongue on her thigh and the terrible aching emptiness that seemed to fill her. When she thought she couldn't stand it one more minute, he was there close to where she wanted him again.

"Now, Rory. I'm going to taste you now."

Then his mouth was exactly where she wanted it, his lips brushing little kisses—not nearly hard enough. But when she tried to arch closer, he tightened his grip on her legs.

Finally, he pressed his mouth fully against her and used his teeth and his tongue. Heat shot through her, scorching her. She tried to move, but he wouldn't allow it. She was trapped—she could barely breathe as he used his tongue to penetrate her again and again. She couldn't lift her hips.

"Hunter!"

As if he had been waiting for her to say his name, he used one thumb to rub her hard and plunged the other one into her. She erupted, pleasure careening through her in one wave after another.

He gathered her to him, holding her tightly against him until the last echo of her climax died away.

"A little improvement on the 'wham-bam' in the pool?" he finally asked.

Although she wouldn't have thought it possible in her present state, she laughed. "It was wonderful. But I would never complain about the pool. You may be turning me into a sex maniac."

"My good luck."

She lifted her head and met his eyes. "No, it's my good luck. And I think it's my turn now."

Using both hands and all of her strength, she rolled him on his back and straddled him. Then she took his erection into her hands. "Another time, I'll return the favor, but right now I want you inside me."

As if her wish were his command, he gripped her hips, lifted her and penetrated her. She wanted to laugh with the joy of it, but the hunger was building too quickly. His first two thrusts sent her spinning back to the world of sensations he'd trapped her in only minutes ago. Her skin burned where those long fingers pressed into her hips. And those eyes—they were focused on her with that intentness that heightened the pleasure of each thrust. Grasping his shoulders so that she wouldn't fall, she kept her gaze steady on his. The instant his features tightened, her own pleasure exploded again. "Come with me, Hunter. Come with me now."

Then she began to move faster and faster until she heard his cry of satisfaction.

8

"LEA ROBERTS IS RORY'S EDITOR at *Celebs?*" Hunter turned from the French doors in Lucas Wainwright's office to face Tracker.

Tracker's gaze narrowed. "Sounds like you know her."

Hunter's mind was racing. "I know the name. If it's the same Lea Roberts I used to know, we go back a long way." He stopped then, wondering how much he would have to tell Tracker.

"You'd better tell me everything," Tracker said after a beat. "I'll find most of it out anyway, and it might speed up the solution to your problem."

Though his respect for the man seated behind the desk was growing each time they met or talked, there were some things that Tracker would not discover. Hunter intended to keep it that way.

He walked forward and took one of the two chairs in front of the desk. "I haven't seen the Lea Roberts I used to know in ten years. She worked for the local newspaper in the town where I grew up, the *Oakwood Sentinel*. She was twenty-eight, bright, beautiful and skilled in many ways that would appeal to a nineteen-year-old boy."

Tracker's gaze narrowed. "You were lovers?"

Hunter nodded. "For about six months. It started out as

a summer romance during my last summer before college, and then it continued when I came home on breaks that first semester. She even visited me on campus once. My family owned the paper as well as the bank. She was beautiful, smart, and though I didn't see it at the time, she was ambitious. She probably figured that having an affair with one of the Marks sons would eventually pay off career wise. And it did."

"How did you feel about her at the time?"

Hunter met Tracker's eyes. "I thought I was in love with her."

"Did your family know about the affair?" Tracker asked.

Hunter thought for a minute. "I never considered that before—but they might have."

"And they didn't object?"

Hunter paused again to consider the question. This was a period of his life that he rarely reflected on. "They might have even approved. I was pretty wild my last year in high school. Driving under the influence, minor vandalism. Classic behavior for a kid in rebellion. That changed some when I went off to college. Meeting Lucas was good for me. My family problems at the time seemed to fade when he talked about his. But I had the well-established reputation in Oakwood of being the black sheep of the Marks family. My older brother was the model child, groomed to take over the company, and perhaps even to go into politics. Looking back, I can see that my parents might have thought Lea was a good influence on me."

Tracker leaned back in his chair. "I'm planning on making a trip to Oakwood this afternoon to see what I can dig up on whatever your anonymous enemy is going to reveal about you. You could save me some time."

Hunter spread his palms wide. "My life is an open book in Oakwood. I was still seeing Lea when I came home from college over Christmas break. And that's when the scandal broke."

"The scandal?"

"You can access the whole story in the *Sentinel*. It spread to other major newspapers, too. In a nutshell, while I was away at college, my family, namely my brother and my father and mother, discovered that there were millions missing from investment accounts that they'd been managing at the bank, and that was due to the fact that I'd been doing a little embezzling. Of course, I'd intended to pay it back, but my gambling habits made that impossible. If the news had leaked out, there would have been a run on the bank. Luckily, my family discovered it in time and forced me to liquidate my trust fund to cover the amount. I left town in disgrace. The bank, the townspeople and my family lived happily ever after."

Tracker studied him for a moment. "No one pressed charges?"

"I didn't stick around. And my father and mother got off easy. They had a lot of friends. Plus, the way the story was handled played up the fact that the Marks family saved the bank in spite of my unfortunate gambling and embezzling habits. The day that I left town was the last day that Hunter Marks existed."

Tracker studied him for a moment. "How much would it hurt Slade Enterprises if your past came out?"

"Enough. I've built a good reputation, but some people would hesitate to do business with an embezzler."

"You're not telling me everything."

Hunter merely held the other man's gaze.

"Okay. We'll leave it at that for now. But I still have a couple of questions. Does this Lea Roberts know what you're still keeping from me? And does she know that Jared Slade and Hunter Marks are one and the same?"

"Good questions," Hunter said. He couldn't have phrased them any better himself. "There are several possibilities. I can't believe she's behind the threats. And she doesn't necessarily know who I used to be. So she could just be after an exclusive with Jared Slade. Or she could be working with whomever is making the threats. Or she could be a pawn, someone that's being fed information."

"You think it's just a coincidence that *Celebs* got the anonymous message?" Tracker asked.

"No. But it could be that whoever is behind this has an ironic turn of mind. Writing about the downfall of Hunter Marks was Lea Roberts's ticket out of Oakwood. Exposing the true identity of Jared Slade could give another big boost to her career."

"But she didn't come in person to the hotel. She sent Rory Gibbs," Tracker mused.

"Lucky for me."

"Maybe she didn't want to be anywhere near the hotel in case the bomb went off. I'll find out where Lea Roberts was when the incidents in New York and Atlanta occurred. I'm also still checking the whereabouts and phone records of Denise Martin, Michael Banks and Alex Santos for those dates." Tracker paused and leaned back in his chair. "One more question—though I hate to ask. Could someone in your family be behind this?"

Hunter shook his head. "No. They don't know who I've become. Hunter Marks has been dead to them for a long time."

Tracker sighed. "This would be a lot easier if you told me everything."

Hunter avoided that topic and instead said, "There's another question—one you haven't asked," Hunter said. "Is Rory Gibbs a pawn or is she involved right up to her pretty little neck?"

Tracker met his eyes. "I figure that's an answer you've decided to get for yourself."

RORY STARED DOWN at the array of clothes that McGee had delivered to her room.

"Just a few things Mr. Hunter wanted you to have since you didn't have time to pack," McGee had said.

Hunter had said that he'd get her some clothes, but…she hadn't expected him to send McGee shopping at a nearby mall. She'd seen the names of the stores on the boxes—high-end places that she wouldn't have the courage even to walk into.

No, scratch that, she thought as she reached out to finger the lace on an oyster-white camisole. This had come from Silken Fantasies, and she'd been in that shop—at least in the flagship store. A smile curved the corners of her mouth. That had been her lucky day. Would any of this have happened if she hadn't ducked into that store to escape the Terminator? Or if she hadn't tried on that red bra and thong?

Rory pressed a hand to her stomach, then lowered it to where the red triangle fit snugly beneath her jeans. When she'd returned to her room to shower, she'd put it on again for luck.

She let her gaze sweep the room. During the course of the afternoon, McGee had delivered more than clothes. A laptop computer sat on an antique mahogany desk. She also had Internet access and a printer. Plus, McGee had informed her she had an appointment to meet with Mr. Hunter at five o'clock for the first part of the interview. Hunter had even sent up a little schedule of the evening's events: *Interview—5–6; Dinner—7–8; Interview Cont'd—8–10.*

She had to hand it to him. Hunter was a ruthlessly organized man. A quick glance at her watch told her that she still had half an hour to prepare for the interview. And that was what she should be doing rather than gazing at a wardrobe fit for royalty.

With a sigh, she ran a hand down a silky red sundress. Next to it was a pair of matching sandals. The ivory-colored suit was pretty, too—slim-legged pants with a short double-breasted jacket and tank top. There were strappy sandals to match that outfit, too. There was even a strand of pearls with matching earrings. Unable to help herself, she picked up the earrings and put them in her ears. She moved to the mirror and smiled at the way the small pearls dangled from thin gold chains. Then she walked back to the bed. Looking at the clothes, she felt a little like Julia Roberts in *Pretty Woman*—way out of her league.

Then her gaze fell on the last thing that McGee had unpacked and set on the bed—a small brown bag filled with bubble gum. Her heart did a slow tumble in her chest just as it had when she'd first peeked inside.

Hunter had asked McGee to bring her bubble gum. She picked up the bag and held it close.

HUNTER LOST TRACK of the time as he stood there in the open doorway watching her. But when she lifted the bag of bubble gum and clutched it to her chest, the doubts seemed to slip away again. True, he'd been led down the garden path by a woman reporter when he was nineteen. But he wasn't a naive nineteen-year-old anymore, and Rory wasn't Lea Roberts.

Still, he wasn't so sure that he fully trusted his instincts where she was concerned. From the first moment he'd seen her in that lobby, she'd clouded both his senses and his mind.

But she wasn't sleeping with him to get a story. Hadn't she made that clear? And he noted with a slight frown that she was wearing the faded jeans and T-shirt she'd arrived in that morning. Plus, she was barefoot.

"You don't like the clothes?" he asked.

She whirled to face him and he watched the heat rise in her cheeks.

"I didn't hear you come in."

"You're not wearing any of them."

"They're beautiful. They're just not me."

No, she wouldn't think they were right for her. Hunter tamped down on a quick spurt of anger. It wasn't the first time that he would have liked to get his hands on her four ex-boyfriends.

"What kind of clothes *are* you?" he asked.

She glanced down at what she was wearing. "Blue jeans, T-shirts. When I get dressed up, I usually go for modern and funky things that make a statement—rather than classic and elegant."

He moved closer to the bed. "You don't see yourself as elegant?"

"I'm barely five foot two. Elegant is more like my sisters."

He frowned. "Why are you always comparing yourself to them?"

She raised her eyebrows. "Do you have any siblings?"

He thought of his brother. "Point taken."

"Did your parents favor your sisters?" he asked. Then he wondered how in the world the question had popped out. Until his recent conversation with Tracker McBride, he hadn't let himself think about his family in years.

"No. They were great. My dad especially was always pointing out my talents to me and encouraging me to nurture them." She shrugged. "He did that with all of us. Natalie inherited my father's knack for cracking safes and his gift for disguise. Sierra got his brains."

"What did you inherit?"

"I just got his luck."

"Don't knock luck. I'll take it any day in a pinch." He reached out and brushed a finger against her earring. "Some people see pearls as elegant. I'm glad that you're wearing them."

"I couldn't resist. But I'm going to give them back. And you should be able to get your money back for the dresses. We're hardly going to need them. I'm going to be interviewing you here. It's not like we're dating or anything."

He regarded her steadily. "We're not dating?"

"No…we're…that is, I'm…I'm interviewing you, and that's business. And in an entirely separate arrangement, we're also enjoying a temporary, mutually enjoyable… adult relationship." She paused to frown a bit. "Not that I'm trying to put words in your mouth when I say it's mutually enjoyable."

"Not at all. In fact, you took the words right out of my mouth." The nerves and concern in her eyes had him reaching out to place a hand on her cheek. "Did you think I had the clothes delivered as a sort of payment for sexual favors?"

"No. That's not…I really didn't." She paused to gather her thoughts. "I didn't mean to imply that at all. It's just that they're clearly expensive and unnecessary. And if I don't wear them, you can get your money back."

He'd never met a woman quite like her, Hunter decided. Studying her for a moment, he wondered what tack to take. Finally, he said, "Why don't you think of them as costumes?"

"Costumes?"

"You did say that you wanted to experiment a bit at being in control? Dresses, jewelry, shoes—aren't they just part of the arsenal a woman uses to seduce a man?"

Rory glanced down at the clothes. "I suppose."

"I've always found that elegant can be quite sexy."

She met his eyes then. "Really?"

"Uh-huh. Right now, I'm picturing you sitting across the table from me in the main dining room wearing that red dress. McGee is serving us, and all I'm thinking of is how quickly I can get you out of it."

She glanced at the dress and back at him. "I don't think it would pose much of a problem."

"And I'll be wondering if you're wearing the red thong underneath it. Or nothing at all."

He could see her bite back a grin, but all she said was, "For a man so successful in business, all you think about is sex."

He flicked the pearl dangling from her ear again. "In the right company, it's pretty much all I can manage. Right now, I'm imagining you wearing nothing but pearls."

She took a step back from him, but she was smiling now, and he sensed that the battle had been won.

"All right, I'll wear them."

"Good." He gave her a satisfied nod.

She cocked her head at him. "You're one smooth negotiator, aren't you?"

"I do my best."

"Well…" She glanced at the bed. "Before I fulfill any of your adolescent fantasies, we're going to start that interview—and we're going to do it in the downstairs office."

"Damn," he said amiably as he led the way out of the room. "If I were really a smooth negotiator, I would have convinced you to postpone the interview, and we'd be doing something much more interesting on that bed."

Her laughter filled the air as they walked companionably down the stairs together.

RORY BLEW A BUBBLE as she studied the sheets of paper—three in all—that Hunter had handed her the moment that they'd entered the office. They reminded her of Sierra's note cards. Everything was perfectly clear, concise and prioritized with numbers. Nerves had knotted in her stomach the moment she'd seen them. She should have anticipated that he'd be fully prepared for the interview. For a moment, she allowed herself to feel a pang of envy. He was as organized as her sisters, maybe more so. Then she remembered what he'd said about not comparing herself to others, and she blew another bubble.

She could handle this interview. So what if she didn't have three pages of questions or a clue as to what angle to take yet? She'd find it.

"You should find everything you need right there," Hunter said.

The papers she held contained a brief profile of Mark Hunter, along with a résumé. Donald Trump would probably find the information impressive. But as she skimmed through it, Rory discovered that it gave very little away about the man she'd talked to at the pool or in the tree house.

Finally, on the third page, something caught her eye. He'd lost his entire family—his parents and a brother—when he was barely nineteen. A tight band settled around her heart as she glanced up at him. "I'm so sorry. That must have been horrible—to lose your whole family when you were so young. My sisters and I were orphaned when we were twenty, but we still had each other. Did you have any other relatives?"

"No," Hunter said.

When he didn't elaborate, she asked, "How on earth did you manage?"

"I don't see how that's pertinent."

"It's part of what made you who you are."

"I'd rather stick to what's on those papers."

Rory didn't doubt for a moment that he'd have preferred to control the interview just as much as he wanted to manage what she wore and what they did when they made love. She was going to have to find a way to change that, so she took a moment to study him.

He looked confident and thoroughly at ease, his hands folded in front of him on the desk. This was a man who'd be perfectly at home in a boardroom. But behind that facade was someone who'd also be perfectly at home in a street fight. Hunter was both those men. Even now, there was a leashed energy radiating from him that hadn't been acquired in an Ivy League school. And there was no explanation for that on the three sheets he'd given her.

What was it going to take to get him to open up to her? And what was it going to take to get him to hand over control later tonight when they made love again?

She skimmed through the information again. He'd attended Harvard and he'd played polo—so there must have been money or connections. Looking up at the wall behind his head, she spotted something she'd noticed when he'd first ushered her into the room. "Harvard. Lucas Wainwright graduated from Harvard, too. Is that where you met him?"

There was just the slightest hesitation before he said, "Yes. We were classmates."

She rose and moved closer to the photo. "Which one are you?"

"I'm not in it. I dropped out right after my parents died. You're very observant."

Her brows shot up. "I wouldn't make a very good reporter if I weren't. Why did you drop out?"

"Financial reasons."

A partial truth, she decided as she studied him. "I wanted so much to drop out of college after my parents passed away, but my sisters wouldn't hear of it. I started to call them the school police."

"What would you have done if your sisters hadn't pressured you to stay in school?"

Rory moved to perch on the edge of the chair again. "I would have traveled. Is that what you did?"

"A bit."

"Where?"

"Here and there. Everything that's pertinent to my work at Slade Enterprises is right there on those papers."

And everything else is a big secret, Rory thought. Well, she'd always been fascinated by secrets. But the man sitting in front of her didn't look to be someone who would part with them easily. She skimmed down his work history and blew another bubble. What she needed was a question that would take him off guard and make him open up.

"You're nervous," he said as she licked the bubble gum back into her mouth.

"A little," she said. "I want to do this right, and you're not cooperating."

He gestured to the papers. "I've laid everything out for you. You should be able to write a good article from that."

She set the sheets on the desk. "It's not that this won't be helpful, but the problem is this tells me only about your success in business."

He raised his eyebrows. "I'm a businessman. I thought that would be the angle you'd take."

She smiled at him. "Have you ever read *Celebs?*"

He shook his head. "No, I can't say that I have. But I've seen it on the newsstands."

"You should be able to tell by the headlines and the cover pictures that it's not the *New York Times* or the *Wall Street Journal.* The people who read it are looking for the story behind the story."

"Gossip?"

She laughed. "It's number two on the list right after love for making the world go round. But we're a cut above the tabloids. And we prefer to say that we take a more personal slant on a celebrity's life."

Hunter frowned a little. "What if I told you that my work is the whole story?"

She shook her head as she moved forward to sit on the very edge of her chair. "It's not. Oh, it explains part of who you are—the person who went to Harvard for a year and got snapped up by Jared Slade when he was just building his business. But that's just the tip of the iceberg. When I look at you right now, that's what I see, just the surface stuff—a very self-contained man who prefers to be in control, someone who weighs every decision he makes very carefully." She lifted the papers and set them on the edge of his desk. "I'm really not going to be able to use much of what you've given me here."

Hunter studied her for a moment. "Just what is it that you're after?"

She met his eyes steadily. "The secrets. What lies below the surface. I want to know why you dropped out of Harvard, what you did after that. I want to know what kind of books you read, what kind of sports you play besides polo, what it's like to work for a man like Jared Slade." Acting on instinct, she decided that she might as well go for broke. "I want to know if Jared Slade really exists and why someone set a bomb off in his suite at Les Printemps."

9

CAREFULLY MASKING HIS SURPRISE, Hunter studied Rory. He hadn't expected either question, and she'd fired them off like a pro. That should have bothered him. Instead, he couldn't help but admire her technique. Clearly, this wasn't going the way he'd planned, but that seemed to be par for the course with Rory Gibbs. Was her unpredictability why she fascinated him so?

She'd been in almost constant motion from the moment that he'd led her into the room. She'd fidgeted her way through the papers he'd prepared for her, blowing bubbles and tapping her feet. Even now, she was perched on the edge of her chair like a butterfly that might take flight at any moment. Was that why he was constantly tempted to reach out and grab her? For a moment, he let himself imagine what it might be like to do just that—to pull her across the desk and onto his lap.

"Well?" she asked. "Who wants to hurt Jared Slade?" Then she frowned. "Or is it you they want to hurt?"

"Me?" Startled by the question, he narrowed his eyes. But it wasn't just curiosity he saw in hers. No, it was a flood of concern, and he couldn't help but be moved by it. "Why would you think someone would want to hurt me?"

She waved a hand. "Because you're here, isolated."

"I'm enjoying Lucas Wainwright's hospitality while I finish up the business that brought Jared Slade to D.C. That's all. Why do you think that my boss doesn't exist?"

Leaning back in the chair, she rested her elbows on the arms and steepled her fingers. "I have this theory that he's just a figurehead like Betty Crocker, and that people like you really run his businesses."

Hunter smiled and hoped that it reached his eyes. "Jared Slade is every bit as real as I am." Her mind was as sharp as a razor, and if he wasn't careful...

"Why all the secrecy then?" she asked.

Hunter met her eyes very steadily. He couldn't recall the last time anyone had made him feel as if he were walking along the edge of a cliff. "Mr. Slade prefers his privacy."

She tapped her fingers on one arm of the chair. "He's hiding something, isn't he? And it must have something to do with the person who planted the bomb."

Hunter raised both hands and made a T. "Time out. I agreed to give you an interview, but I'm not at liberty to discuss Mr. Slade, and there won't be any mention of the bomb in your article."

"Okay." Rory moved to the edge of her chair again. "Why don't we just get back to those questions that I originally asked? Why did you drop out of Harvard and what did you do in those five years before you joined Slade Enterprises?"

Hunter couldn't help but admire the way she'd manipulated him. She wouldn't press on the bomb issue if he answered the more personal questions. She was good. He should have foreseen that and prepared for it. The information on the three sheets he'd given her would check out, but if she wanted personal information on Mark Hunter, he would have to create it out of whole cloth. It wouldn't be the first time that he'd created a personal background story for himself. But he'd never before done it off the cuff and for a reporter.

Was it the fact that she posed a risk for him that intrigued him? If he could figure out exactly why she appealed to him so, he could control it.

"I won't promise to answer every question you ask," he said finally.

"Fair enough."

"And I want to read the story before you send it to your boss."

"You want to censor it?"

He shrugged. "Take it or leave it."

"Are you going to answer the questions that I've posed so far?"

"I think I can agree to that."

"Then you've got a deal." Rory plucked a pen out of a container on the desk and turned over the three sheets of paper. Then she edged her chair closer to the desk.

"One other stipulation," Hunter said. "For every question you ask, I get to ask you one."

Surprise flooded into her eyes. "Why?"

"I'm curious about Rory Gibbs."

She shrugged. "Okay. Sure." Then she shot him a quick grin. "But if you write it up and decide to sell it, I get to okay it first."

He couldn't help smiling back. "You've got a deal."

"Okay. Tell me about Mark Hunter."

"That's not a question."

"Okay. First, what made you drop out of Harvard?"

"I already told you that I dropped out of Harvard for financial reasons."

"You couldn't afford to go there after your parents died?"

"That was part of it."

She waited, tapping her pen on the desk.

Hunter thought of several stories he could make up, but he'd learned a long time ago that when you were lying through your teeth, it was better to stick as closely as possible to the truth. "I wanted a change, a new start." That was partially true. By the time his family had laid out the little scenario they'd wanted him to play a part in, he'd very much wanted a whole new life as far away from the Marks family as he could get.

"So you were running away from your old life?" Rory asked.

"I'd rather look at it as running toward a new one."

"Why did you need a new life?"

"Isn't it my turn for a question?" Hunter asked.

Rory shook her head. "You have to finish answering this one first. Why did you need a new start?"

Persistence was something else about her he had to admire. Because he hadn't prepared the answer, Hunter chose his words carefully. "My family always thought of me as a black sheep. My older brother was one of those people who did everything right. Since in my parents' eyes, I never quite measured up to him, I fell into a habit of proving to everyone that I never would." He paused with a frown. "I'm not sure I'm explaining it right."

"You're explaining it perfectly. I had the same problem with my sisters. After my father left, I even went through a period when I thought it was my fault that our father had left us. So I started—I think the term the school psychologist used was *acting out.* Basically, I skipped classes at school and got into fights."

Hunter studied her. She spoke so matter-of-factly about her insecurities. He wanted to change that. "So you thought of yourself as a black sheep, too?"

She shot him a smile. "I thought of myself more as an ugly duckling."

"You're not ugly at all," he said impatiently. "The first time I saw you, I thought you were incredibly cute."

Rory snorted. "Cute? You mean like a puppy?"

This time Hunter pushed down the impatience. "A cute lady wearing sexy red boots and a cap. The contrast intrigued me. And when I saw you again in Silken Fantasies, I thought you were some kind of sex goddess."

"Really?"

Hunter raised a brow. "I've never followed another woman into a dressing room and made love to her. I had no business doing that with you. I don't have any business wanting you right now. But I can't seem to stop myself. Every time I look at you, there seems to be a total disparity between what I know I should do and what I want to do."

She was listening to him now, really listening. He could tell by the way her eyes had become totally focused on his.

"A few minutes ago, I wanted to reach across this desk and drag you onto my lap. Then I would have kissed you and touched you until you could think of nothing but how it feels when I make you come."

Her pulse was fluttering at her throat. Hunter wanted to taste her right there, but he wanted something else even more. "Promise me something."

"What?" Rory asked.

"When you dress for dinner tonight, put on that red

dress and the pearls. Then you take a good look at yourself in the mirror and think *princess.*"

She snorted. "Princess?"

"No. I mean it. And see if I'm not right."

Rory's eyes narrowed. "You're trying to build up my self-confidence."

"You don't do enough of that for yourself. So what if you're different from your sisters? You have your own unique qualities. You need to believe in them more and push them to work to your advantage."

Rory blinked. "That's what my father advised me to do. Is that what you did to compete with your brother?"

Hunter frowned as she scribbled something on a sheet of paper. "No."

Rory glanced up, then reached out to lay a hand over his. "I'm sorry. Of course, you couldn't do that. There wouldn't have been time, not when he was snatched away so suddenly."

Hunter saw the quick rush of sympathy in her eyes and felt it in her touch. Once again, he was moved by her concern. They'd both lost family, he realized. He wasn't even fully aware that he'd turned over his hand and linked his fingers with hers, but suddenly, he was tempted to tell her what had really happened that summer when he was nineteen. Not the edited version he'd given Tracker, but the real story.

He couldn't afford to do that, he reminded himself. Rory Gibbs was a reporter. If he told her the real story, she would be that much more likely to connect the dots between Mark Hunter and Hunter Marks.

Still, it bothered him that she felt bad about something he'd fabricated.

"I never should have asked that question," Rory said. "It

was clumsy of me. I'm sorry. I'm a beginner at this inter-viewing thing."

"For a beginner, you're very good at it," Hunter said. She'd only begun and she'd already steered him in directions he'd didn't want to go.

"Thanks. I've never done anything this important before."

"And your question was a good one. I was too hasty in saying no." Releasing her hand, he leaned back in his chair. "Before the…accident, I was acting out, too—drinking, coming home late, letting my grades slip. After I reached a certain age, I gave up on competing with my older brother." It hadn't done any good. Sports had been an area where he could outshine Carter, but his parents had always gone to Carter's games and not his. Carter Marks III had been born with a silver spoon in his mouth, and he'd been raised to take over the family business. Hunter's mother had made it clear to him that the only reason he'd been conceived was that she was hoping for a daughter.

"What happened after the accident?" Rory asked.

Hunter gathered his thoughts. It had been years since he'd allowed himself to remember this part of his life. "I wanted to create a new life and prove to myself that I could be better than anyone could have dreamed." Even as he spoke the words, Hunter realized that there was a lot of truth in them. Beneath the anger and disillusionment, he'd been driven by a desire to prove something to himself. And to his family.

"How did you go about doing that?"

Hunter narrowed his eyes. "Oh, no, you don't. It's definitely my turn for a question…or two or three."

Rory wrinkled her nose. "You can't blame a girl for try-ing." Then she leaned back in her chair. "What do you want to know?"

Are you wearing the red thong? That was the question that popped into Hunter's mind and he barely kept it from popping out of his mouth. He had an agenda here, too, he reminded himself—and he'd better stick to it. "Tell me about your boss at *Celebs* and what it's like to work for him or her."

Rory grinned. "That's not a question."

He nodded. "Okay. Who is your boss, and what is it like to work for him or her?"

"It's a her. Lea Roberts." Rory's fingers tightened on the pen she was holding and she chewed on her bubble gum.

"She makes you nervous."

"A little. She's very good at what she does. I was lucky to be assigned to her. She's demanding. But she's been very encouraging. Most of the time."

"She can't be happy that you gave me the pictures."

Heat stained her cheeks. "Well, I didn't tell her about that. When I ran into her at the Blue Pepper yesterday, I lied and told her they were in my apartment and I'd get them to her today. I'm hoping that when I turn in this interview, she'll overlook the fact that I had to buy it with the pictures."

For a moment, Hunter said nothing. His mind was too busy sorting through possibilities. Lea Roberts had thought that the pictures were in Rory's apartment. Was she behind the break-in? And why was she using Rory? Had she known about the bomb ahead of time? Was Tracker right about that being the reason why she hadn't come herself to Les Printemps?

"My turn again," Rory said. "I want to know how you spent the five years between leaving Harvard and taking a job with Slade Enterprises."

Hunter dragged his thoughts back to the question. For this part he was on much safer ground. He could stick close to the truth because he'd used several different names, and none of them could be connected with Hunter Marks or Mark Hunter. Leaning back in his chair, he said, "The first job I took was with a cruise line. I started out in the kitchen and ended up dealing blackjack in the casino."

"Really? I'm so jealous. How did you get the job? What was it like?" Rory rattled off the questions as she reached for the sheets of paper. "Tell me everything."

For the next two hours, Hunter found himself doing just that.

RORY CHECKED THE BEDROOM one last time. McGee had provided the candles, and they flickered on the nightstand and dresser. But it had been Hunter who'd sent up the champagne. That probably meant that he had a plan, too.

Well, she'd just have to figure out a way to handle him. She had during the interview.

The whole dinner was a blur. McGee had served it on the patio, and she'd worn the red dress and the pearls. Hunter hadn't taken his eyes off her once. She couldn't even remember what she'd eaten or what they'd talked about.

Rory stopped at the window and looked at the last streaks of color in the western sky. She was waiting for her lover to come to her. Two phone calls. That's what he'd said he had to make before he joined her.

Turning, she glanced around the room again. Everything was in place—the red thong was on the nightstand next to the champagne. Moving to the full-length mirror on the closet door, she checked herself one more time. She was wearing the lace chemise that McGee had brought to the room that afternoon. The thin creamy color was a perfect match for the pearls. Raising a hand, she fingered the double strand of small, perfectly shaped beads at her throat.

She'd done just as Hunter had suggested before she'd gone down to the dining room. She'd stood here looking at her image and thinking *princess*. Cool, confident. Grace Kelly. Diana. But as she studied herself in the mirror now, she felt more like the princess Audrey Hepburn had played in *Roman Holiday*—not quite sure of herself, still sort of experimenting with life and prone to making mistakes.

Lifting her chin, she straightened her shoulders and reminded herself that Audrey Hepburn managed to carry everything off at the end of the movie. Rory Gibbs would, too. Tonight might be her last night with Hunter.

So she was just going to push her luck to the limit. And if she didn't quite pull it off? Well, there just wasn't a downside to making love with the Terminator.

Now, where was he?

THROUGH THE FRENCH DOORS in Lucas Wainwright's office, Hunter looked at the darkening sky. Night was falling and he was here waiting for Tracker's call when he wanted to be upstairs with Rory. This might be the only night that he could spend with her.

He'd had McGee take up the champagne. And he'd planned all during dinner exactly how he was going to seduce her. Once Tracker had a line on who was behind the threats, he would return to Dallas and he wouldn't see Rory again, so he wanted to make the most of what could be their only night together. Something tightened around his heart.

Recognizing the feeling, Hunter lifted his hand to rub his

chest and frowned. Loss. He hadn't allowed himself to feel
that in years. If you didn't allow yourself to get too attached
to something or someone, loss was never an issue. Hell, he'd
only known her—what? Less than forty-eight hours. And
he was going to miss her. He missed her right now.

When the phone rang, Hunter picked it up. "Yeah?"

"We picked someone up in the Keys," Tracker said.

"Who?"

"A guy by the name of Robert Saldano. He has a fairly
extensive rap sheet with the Miami police, mostly assault.
He was indicted once for murder, but it didn't stick. He
claims he doesn't know who hired him."

"Any chance he's telling the truth?" Hunter asked.

"Sure, if you believe pigs fly. But he's a pro and he's
not likely to give away a name."

"Lea Roberts may have broken in to Rory's apartment,"
Hunter said and then filled Tracker in on what Rory had
told him. "If she did break in, she's not going to be happy
that she didn't find the film."

"Somebody's not going to be happy that Robert Saldano
didn't finish his job in the Keys. We make enough people
unhappy and someone might get careless."

"Have you turned up anything on Denise, Alex or
Michael?" Hunter asked.

"Not yet. Tomorrow, I'm going to fly into Oakwood and
see if I can find some kind of connection between one of
them and your hometown."

"I'd like to come with you," Hunter said. Then he was
stunned that he'd not only said the words, but that he'd
meant them. When he'd left Oakwood, he'd vowed to himself that he'd never return.

"No. You stay right where you are. That was our deal."

"Yeah." That *was* the deal. What had come over him that he would even think of going back there?

"And keep Rory with you. I don't like the idea that Lea Roberts might have broken in to her apartment."

"I don't like it much myself."

"I'll check in as soon as I have news," Tracker said and ended the call.

Hunter hung up his receiver slowly. He hadn't been back to Oakwood since he'd left on that Christmas eve ten years ago. Not once had he ever thought of seeing his family again. He hadn't wanted to. Had revisiting his past with Rory today changed all that?

Hunter gazed out the window again. The sky was dark gray now, and he could see several stars and a thin sliver of moon. The problem with digging up the past and looking at it was that at twenty-nine you were bound to have a slightly different perspective than you did at nineteen.

Objectively speaking, his mother and the other board members had come up with a solution to the embezzlement problem that had minimized the effect on Marks Banking and Investments and the town. His services as a scapegoat had saved the company. From a business standpoint, he could even admire the scenario that his mother had created. But none of that changed the way he felt about what they'd done to him.

And he was wasting time thinking about the past when Rory was waiting for him. There were so many things he wanted to show her, and this might be his only chance. Turning, he strode from the room and climbed the stairs.

10

THE DOOR TO HER ROOM was closed, so Hunter knocked.

"Come in."

The room was dark except for the candles that burned on every surface and the moonlight that flowed into the room through the open balcony doors. But the moment he looked at her, his senses were swamped. Music—something soft and bluesy—thrummed, and he smelled the citrus scent of the candles, but those sensations were muted. What overwhelmed him was her.

She stood halfway between the balcony and the bed wearing nothing but pearls and a swatch of creamy-colored lace. He felt his breath back up in his lungs and begin to burn. Bathed in moonlight, she made him think of a porcelain statue. Fragile and untouchable. But she was very much alive. Even now, he could tell that every muscle in her body was tensed for movement. And the fear shot through him that if he moved toward her she might take flight like some will-o'-the-wisp, and he would never find her again.

Nonsense, he told himself as he drew close. He knew she was real, and he knew how her flesh would heat when he touched her and tasted her. He knew how that body would come to life beneath his. Even as the thoughts swirled through his mind, desire sharpened inside of him until it turned into a deep, aching need.

He took one step, and she raised a hand. "I have a plan."

He didn't stop moving toward her. He wasn't sure he could. "A plan?" His had nearly evaporated the moment he'd seen her. The long, slow seduction he'd mapped out during dinner was threatening to disappear somewhere in the mist that was now fogging his brain.

"Well, maybe not a plan." She clasped her hands together and twisted her fingers. "Exactly. I didn't write it out. It's more some things that I'd like to try out."

He freed one of her hands and raised it to his lips. "So it's flexible?" With his other hand, he traced his finger along the edge of the silk that rode over her breasts.

"I guess you could say that. But we did agree that you would give up control."

He trailed a finger down to where her nipples had hardened into dark berries beneath the thin lace of the chemise. "We did. But we didn't say when. And I have a plan, too. Don't you want to know what it is?"

She grabbed his wrist with her free hand. "No. I mean, yes. Eventually. It's not that I think it wouldn't be enjoyable. Because I do. You're the most incredible lover I've ever had."

He leaned down and brushed his lips over hers. "A point in my favor. My plan starts with champagne."

"So does mine." Rory concentrated very hard. His mouth was so close, so tempting. Already her bones were melting.

"Plus, I think I still need some more practice on slowing down my wham-bam technique. Why don't I show you?"

"I—umm." She broke off when his lips brushed against

hers again. It took all her concentration to focus on her plan and to take two steps back from him. "I know that you want to make love to me, and I want you to. But…" She paused for a moment to search for the right words. They never came easily to her when he was this close. "I know that you like to be in control. But I just want to return the favor."

He held out a hand. "It isn't necessary. Do you have any idea of how much pleasure you give me each time you come in my arms?"

"No," she replied, shaking her head. "That's just it. I don't. And I want to. I've never had a lover like you. I don't think I ever will again. I'd also like to know what you're feeling when you make me come. I want to experience that kind of power. Just once. Is that so hard to understand?"

"No."

Rory drew in a breath and let it out. "Then you'll let me do whatever I want to you?"

The corners of his mouth twitched. "You want me to agree to that without any more information?"

"Yes."

"If you worked for Slade Enterprises, you'd have to submit a three-page proposal."

She felt some of her tension ease. He was going to go along with her. "But I don't work for Slade Enterprises."

Hunter's eyes narrowed. "Maybe you should. You're a pretty good negotiator."

She smiled then as a little thrill moved through her. "Thanks. Shall we get started?"

"It's a shame to waste that champagne."

She led the way to the bed and climbed onto it. "Who says we're going to waste it? But first, you have to take off your clothes."

HUNTER STUDIED HER as he began to unbutton his shirt. The idea of being seduced by her was appealing. But even if it hadn't been, he wouldn't have been able to resist her argument. She wanted to experience a feeling of power, and what better way could he help her gain more self-confidence than to let her experience that? At least for a short amount of time. Years in business had taught him that there was more than one way to negotiate a deal. So he'd merely take another tack.

Keeping his eyes on hers, he shrugged out of the shirt and dropped it to the floor. Then he tackled his belt. Her eyes shifted to watch just what his hands were doing as he unfastened the button of his slacks. "What if I can convince you to let me take over?"

"Take over?" She was still watching as he slowly pulled down his zipper. Then he eased his slacks down over his hips and let them drop to the floor.

"Okay?" he asked.

"No. You're not going to convince me. And you still have too many clothes on."

"Why don't you help me get them off?"

She shook her head, but her eyes never left the spot where his penis was pressing against his briefs. "You do it."

Obligingly, he slipped his fingers beneath the waistband, pushed his briefs to the floor and then he clasped his shaft in his hand. "You can have this right now, if you want."

"I'm going to touch it in a minute." Her voice was husky, but she didn't move. "First, lie down on the bed."

"You'd like what I have in mind," he said as he moved toward the bed, then climbed onto the mattress. He still held his erection in his hand, and he was so close that she could reach out and touch it.

She didn't. But he saw the effort it took for her to tear

her gaze away from it, and this close, he could see the rapid rise and fall of her chest. "You want to touch it," he said.

"Oh, yeah." The words were expelled on a breath. But she merely clasped her hands more tightly together.

Suddenly, he wanted those hands on him. He wanted to feel her fingers gripping him, pumping him. "Touch me."

She met his eyes and he could feel himself sinking into those deep, warm golden pools. "You have to lie down first."

He did because the teasing he was doing was backfiring. He wanted her hands on him. Now. Then he'd convince her to let him take over.

"Give me your hands," she said.

He saw that she was holding the red thong.

"If you want me to touch you, you have to give me your hands."

The moment he did, she captured both of his wrists in the lacy straps and then drew them over his head and tied them to the headboard.

"What are you doing?"

"Something I wanted to try." She shrugged. "You could get yourself loose, but I want you to pretend that you can't, that you're my captive."

Hunter frowned. "Why would I do that?"

"For several reasons," she said as she threw one leg over him to straddle him at his waist. "First, because you've agreed to let me be in control—at least until you convince me otherwise. Second, because you're going to like what I'm going to do to you. If you don't, you can just suggest an alternative. Third, because if you touch me while I'm touching you, we'll both be distracted, and I want you to just feel. Fourth, because if you lose control, you can get yourself free. Fifth, because—"

"I don't lose control," Hunter said.

"Shh," she said, leaning down to brush her lips over his. "I know. It's going to be all right." She ran her hands experimentally down his chest. "Just relax."

Relax? It was hardly an option when her fingers were running so softly over his skin, leaving little ripples of static electricity in their wake. "You're not touching me where I want you to."

"Soon." She wiggled up his body to brush her lips against his again. He tried to capture them. If he could kiss her, really kiss her, he could convince her to put an end to this game. But she wiggled out of reach of his mouth.

This time, as she slid down his body, the shock wave of heat nearly melted his bones. He could feel exactly how hot and wet she was. When he caught his breath, he said, "You're not wearing any panties."

"No. I needed my thong for something else tonight."

She moved again to reach for the bottle of champagne, and the dampness of her heat sent another shot of fire through him. His hips rose off the bed of their own accord. "Move lower. I want to be inside of you."

Rory tipped champagne into a glass. "I thought you wanted me to touch you first."

"I did, but—" His thought was cut off when he felt the icy drops of champagne on his face, his lips, his neck. "What are you doing?"

"I'm going to find out what you taste like mixed with champagne."

"That was my plan."

"Too bad." She used her tongue on his forehead, his eyelids and cheeks, then lingered at his lips to trace the fullness from one corner of his mouth to the other. The little tremors that rippled over his skin sent explosions of pleasure rocketing through him.

"Rory—" When she used her teeth on his shoulder and shifted lower on his body, he lost the rest of the sentence. Each lick of her tongue, each scrape of her teeth created sensations so sharp, so intense that they left no room for thought.

And the heat. It wasn't just the fiery dampness of her tongue—it was that hot, moist heat at her center, pressing, and then sliding over his skin as she shimmied lower. It seared him until he was sure his body would melt and merge into hers.

He sucked in a breath when she sprinkled icy pellets of champagne over his chest, and the throaty sound of her laugh made his blood begin to pound.

He could stop her. He could easily twist his hands free. Then he could grab her, lift her and pierce her. She would take him in and tighten around him like a tight wet fist. But he couldn't seem to move.

"I want—"

"I know what you want." Her hand closed around him for one second. "But I'm not through tasting you yet. Mmm. Your flavor is even better here," she murmured as she closed her teeth around one nipple.

"Rory—" He moaned her name as she flicked her tongue hard into his navel.

"Delicious. But I'm not sure which flavor I like best. Let me see…" She moved up to brush her lips over his. "There are so many flavors in your mouth—dark and forbidden— better than the best chocolate I've ever had." She slid her tongue along his. "When you kiss me, I can never seem to get enough."

He couldn't, either. He'd felt hunger for a woman before, but not like this. And he wasn't sure how much longer he could wait for more. Her mouth was only inches from his. He could free his hands now and put an end to the torture. But his arms felt weak. No woman had ever made him feel weak before.

She tangled her tongue with his again, then said, "Before I decide if I like your mouth best, there's a part of you that I haven't sampled yet. I wouldn't want to rush to judgment."

Her breath against his lips along with the image that was forming in his mind set his body aflame.

"First, I'm going to sample some of this champagne."

He watched her sip from the bottle, replace it on the table. Then as if she were moving in slow motion, she shifted so that she was straddling his legs.

He waited, watching her through narrowed eyes as she closed her hands around him and lowered her head. The first lick of her tongue on the tip of his shaft had him moaning her name. It was cold from the champagne and the shock sent a shudder moving through him. Then she licked him again…and again.

"Rory—" He barely recognized the raspy sound of his own voice. He couldn't for the life of him figure out what he wanted to say. Did he want her to stop? To go on? Each lick of her tongue as she moved her mouth lower and lower on his shaft sent a knife-sharp arrow of pleasure shooting through his system. She was devouring him as if he were some treat she'd been starving for. The sensations were agonizing. Incredible. He closed his fingers around the posts of the bed and held on tightly. Then when he was sure he couldn't take it anymore, she took him into her mouth.

"Mmm."

The soft murmurs of pleasure she made vibrated

through him and drummed their way into his brain. His heart was beating so fast that he was sure it would burst through his chest.

Her mouth was hot now, almost as hot as the fire raging inside of him. Each time she moved those lips down and then up, she pulled one emotion after another from him—things that he'd buried deep. And he was powerless to stop her.

His climax was building. He could feel it the same way he could feel a storm building when thunder rumbled and lightning flashed. No one had ever made him feel helpless like this. The sensation shuddered through his stomach and burned through his brain. He shouldn't, he couldn't let her do this to him.

Twisting his hands free, he reached for her and pulled her on top of him. The moment he entered her, it was too late to regain control. The storm that she'd been building inside of him from the moment that he'd walked into the room suddenly broke free, and he began to move inside her, matching her rhythm until with one last thrust, he gave himself to her.

RORY COULDN'T HAVE NAMED the feelings swirling through her when Hunter finally drew her to him. Should she have known that making love to a man like that would bring such a variety of pleasures? Should she not have been amazed that a sigh could make her burn or that the raspy sound of her name on Hunter's lips could make her almost forget what she was doing?

Each time she'd touched him, each time she'd tasted him, the thrill of his response had only increased her hunger for him. Even now, his scent tantalized her, and the damp heat of his flesh beckoned to her. There were flavors that she hadn't discovered yet. She was sure of it.

When she angled her head and licked his neck, he tightened his hold on her. "Give me…a moment."

She could do that. His heart still thundered under hers, and he was holding her as if he never intended to let her go. That brought its own very separate kind of feeling. Because he would go. They'd laid the ground rules.

Even as a little pang of loss stung her heart, she pushed the thought out of her mind. She wasn't going to think of what it would be like not to have him like this. Not to be able to touch him or taste him again.

"That was…incredible."

He was still short of breath. How amazing to learn that making a man breathless, making him shudder, could bring such a pleasure-filled power. She couldn't wait to experience it again.

She nipped his shoulder. "I'm up for seconds. How about you?"

The next thing she knew, she was beneath him on the bed. And he was amazingly ready. She could feel the hard length of him probing her. Wrapping her arms and legs around him, she said, "I guess all you really needed was a moment."

"I want you again right now."

She thought she heard a hint of anger in his tone, but what she saw in his eyes was vulnerability. Whatever power she'd felt before changed to wonder. She wanted him even more than she had a second ago. Tightening her hold on him, she struggled to pull him in even deeper. But it was like trying to move a rock. "You can have me. What's the problem?"

He framed her face with his hands. "I'll tell you what the problem is. I want to do to you what you just did to me. I want to touch you and taste you and torture you until you can't think of anything but wanting me inside of you."

"That's all I can think of right now." That was nothing less than the truth. She wiggled, tried to thrust against him, but he stayed right where he was. Her insides were melting, but he wasn't where she needed him to be. "Please."

He withdrew and then pushed himself a little farther into her. Still not far enough.

"Every time I'm near you, the same feeling comes over me that came over me in that damn dressing room," he said. "I have to be inside of you."

She arched against him, trying again to take all of him. "You know, if torture was what you had in mind, you're on the right track."

She felt him smile as he pressed his lips against hers. But when he lifted his head and met her gaze again, his eyes were serious. "It's never been this way for me before. I've never wanted anyone this much."

"Same goes for me," she said.

"That's a problem."

There was that hint of vulnerability in his eyes again, and she wanted to soothe it away. "Can we solve it tomorrow? I have a much bigger problem for you to take care of right now. I'm think I'm going to explode if you don't make me come."

"I can take care of that," Hunter said as he pushed himself a little deeper.

Her breath caught in her throat, but she managed to say, "More. Kiss me and come all the way inside. Now."

THE MOMENT THAT HIS MOUTH took hers, Hunter felt himself sinking into her. Would it always be like this? He'd never had this temptation—no, this *need*—to lose himself in a woman before. On one level it terrified him, but on another, it drew him like a magnet. He caught her bottom lip between his teeth and pushed into her all the way.

She tightened around him, trapping him with arms, legs and with that slick, hot core. He lifted his mouth from hers, then held himself perfectly still as he met her eyes. He could see himself trapped there, too—by everything that was Rory. Slowly, trembling with the effort, he withdrew and pushed into her again, withdrew…and pushed in.

"Please—" She arched against him.

He wanted to keep the pace slow—to spin out the pleasure for both of them. But he was losing that battle, too. Each time he withdrew from her, he left parts of himself behind. Each time he pushed in, he felt as if he were coming home. Needs, emotions and pleasure entwined to drag at his control.

"Faster. I need you."

Hunter wasn't sure if she'd said the words or if it was his own inner voice speaking. Suddenly all he knew was that he had to bring her to that peak again where she would shatter around him. He thrust into her faster now, and she matched him move for move. She was his now. He wanted to keep her this way, remember her always with her cheeks flushed, her eyes clouded but fastened on him. Then she stiffened, her fingers dug into his hips and he was helpless to do anything but pour himself into her.

RORY WASN'T SURE HOW LONG she let herself drift, savoring the pleasure of lying beside her Terminator. She wasn't even sure when he'd shifted her so that they were lying side by side on the bed. But her head was resting on his arm and the fingers of her left hand still clasped his. Finally opening her eyes, she saw that he was studying her, his gaze dark and intent.

"No one has ever looked at me that way," she said.

"What way?"

"As if you could see all my secrets. And I feel as if I don't know *you* at all."

He lifted their joined hands and pressed a kiss on her knuckles. "You know me."

"I know parts of you. But there's so much I don't know."

"Like?"

"Your favorite food, your favorite color, what you like to do when you're not working for Jared Slade." She felt his fingers tighten slightly on hers when she spoke the name, and instantly she regretted it. "This isn't the reporter talking. It's me."

He said nothing for a moment. "It's important that you know those things?"

She nodded her head. "I want to know everything."

"I don't think I have a favorite food, but I'm partial to anything Italian. And my favorite restaurants are all in New Orleans."

"I've never been there."

"I'd like to show it to you."

For a moment, there was silence in the room. Then he said, "As for my favorite color, I don't think I ever had one. But recently I've developed a fondness for red, as long as you're wearing it."

Pleasure streamed through her, not so much triggered by the comment as by the intimacy of the moment. She felt so comfortable lying here like this, talking to him. "What about your favorite thing to do?"

"That's easy. This." He ran a hand up her inner thigh.

"Besides that," she said. But her heart was already beginning to beat faster.

"Well, let me see." He opened her cleft and ran his finger slowly down it. "There's this."

Her hips shifted involuntarily. "I'm serious. What do you do when you're not working—besides have sex?"

For a moment, he didn't say anything. But he didn't remove his hand, and she didn't ask him to. She was so aware that his fingers were right there, almost entering her.

"I like to ride," he said finally.

"Me, too. My father used to take my sisters and me for riding lessons every Saturday when we were little. Nat never took to it, and Sierra was always afraid. It was the one thing that I could do better than either of my sisters. My dad was really proud of me."

"We'll go for a ride tomorrow morning."

"Really? You'll have the time?"

"I'll make the time. But, right now I have a different kind of ride in mind." He levered himself up and positioned himself between her legs.

"Yes," she murmured as she arched up to take him in.

They began to move together, but it wasn't long before Rory said, "Faster."

"You're so demanding," Hunter teased, keeping the rhythm slow and steady. "As a rider, you must know that it's never good to rush your fences."

"Please." Her breath was coming in the short pants that always made him burn. It took all his control not to rush.

"Why don't I tell you what I eventually intend to do with that red thong and the champagne?"

Leaning down, he began to whisper his plans in her ear. And it wasn't long until they were rushing the fence together.

LEA ROBERTS BARELY MANAGED a smile for the guard as she pulled up to the booth and flashed her parking permit.

"Working late, weren't you, Ms. Roberts?" he asked as he gave the permit a cursory glance.

"Yes." She was careful not to let her frustration show in her voice. Long ago, she'd found that being nice to security guards, secretaries and receptionists made her life run more smoothly. But she couldn't prevent her fingers from tapping on the steering wheel as she waited for the guard to open the gate.

It was nearly four in the morning, and she'd spent the entire day and most of the night trying to locate Rory Gibbs. Not even her sisters had been able to help. But they knew where she was all right. The cop had been cool and polite, but she'd been lying through her teeth when she'd claimed not to know where Rory was.

Lea hadn't had any better luck with the academic. Dr. Sierra Gibbs had peered at her through glasses that made her eyes look owlish and acted as though she could barely remember she had a sister named Rory. But the twit had known where Rory was. Lea would have bet her next paycheck on it.

But she didn't need them. It had taken her a while, but she was pretty sure she knew exactly where Rory was. And she owed it all to a hunch. A good, old-fashioned reporter's hunch. How long had it been since she'd had one?

Years. Ironically enough, the last time she'd had a good one had been back in Oakwood, Connecticut, when she'd broken the embezzlement story at Marks Banking and Investments.

She'd known from the moment that she'd started a relationship with Hunter Marks that the family was her ticket out of Oakwood. And she'd been right.

She hoped to hell she was right this time, too. After pulling out of the garage, she headed up Fourteenth Street. When the light at the corner turned red, Lea swore under her breath, then began to tap her fingers on the steering wheel again. If her hunch was right and Rory was where she suspected, she needed to hurry.

She felt the press of cold metal at the back of her ear at the same time that she heard the voice.

"Don't move."

Lea didn't think she could, not with the blood freezing in her veins. The voice was even more frightening in person than it was over the phone.

"You're not answering your phone. Why not?"

Keep calm, she told herself as she cleared her throat. "I've been busy."

"The pictures weren't in Rory Gibbs's apartment."

Lea moistened her lips. "I don't have them. I've been working all day trying to locate her. I'll have them for you soon."

"I don't like people who fail. Those pictures should have been on the front page of the *Washington Post* by now."

Lea shuddered when she felt the cold metal trace a path to the back of her neck. "I think I know where Rory Gibbs is."

"Why should I believe you?" The metal pressed harder into her neck.

Despite that she was cold to the core, Lea felt beads of sweat form on her forehead. "Look, we want the same thing. We both want a story that exposes the true identity of Jared Slade. If I'm right, Rory Gibbs is with Jared Slade right now, and I can tell you exactly how to get there."

There was a pause. It couldn't have been long because the traffic light hadn't yet changed. But to Lea, the stretch of silence in her car felt like an eternity.

"Tell me."

Fingers gripping the steering wheel and sweat dripping down her face, Lea said, "They're on the Lucas Wainwright estate in Virginia."

11

As they rode across the first field, Rory couldn't prevent an envious glance at Hunter's horse. It was large and black, a real beauty named Lucky, and she was sure it could outrun the lady's mount that McGee's son and Hunter had chosen for her. Not that she was unhappy with the pretty filly she was riding. She leaned forward and patted Priscilla's neck and then glanced at Lucky again. She was developing a definite preference for dark, slightly dangerous males.

Hunter hadn't been in her bed when she'd awakened that morning. But McGee had brought a note with her coffee and told her that Hunter was in the stables, seeing to the horses. There'd been a flower, too—a red rose from the gardens. The note had read simply, *Wear the red thong.* She had.

"Why don't we head up that hill over there and get the lay of the land?" he asked.

"Sure." Eager to see what Priscilla could do, Rory urged her into a trot, then a canter. Hunter rode at her side as they crossed the field and crested the hill. Though it hadn't looked to be steep, Rory discovered that it offered a breathtaking view. Ahead were rolling fields and a stream that snaked its way through them and into woods. Over her shoulder she could see the entire Wainwright estate—the pool, the tennis courts and the stables.

There was a security guard at the gate watching them now through binoculars. He hadn't been happy when they'd announced their intention to go for a ride, but he hadn't argued with Hunter. Suddenly, Rory recalled the bomb scare at Les Printemps. How could she have forgotten that? She'd agreed not to ask questions about it, but how could it have completely slipped her mind?

"A penny for your thoughts," Hunter said.

Turning, she met his eyes. "Have they found out any more about the bomb scare in Mr. Slade's suite?"

When he hesitated, she held up a hand. "Off the record."

"What makes you ask?"

"The security guard down there wasn't happy." She studied him as a sudden thought occurred to her. "They're guarding you, too, aren't they? You're in danger." She reined in her horse. "We should go back. I mean, this is wonderful, but you have to put your safety first."

He reached out a hand to cover hers before she could turn the horse. "They're just being careful. Mr. Slade was concerned. That's why Lucas Wainwright offered to let me stay here. We're perfectly safe, and I didn't suggest you go for a ride with me to make you worry."

She glanced around at the empty fields. "You're sure you'll be safe?"

"I'm positive, and so will you. You see that stream down there?" he asked. "Are you up to a race?"

He saw the excitement leap into her eyes, and for a moment he was so distracted that he simply sat there as she shot past him. She was halfway down the hill before he dug his heels into Lucky. She was good. More than good, he amended after a few moments. The only reason he was gaining on her was that he had the faster mount.

It wasn't until they were halfway across the next field that Hunter drew even with her, and for several moments, they galloped side by side. There was nothing but the sun beating down, the scent of the fields, the wind rushing past, and the feel and the sound of the powerful horses beneath them. This was how he'd always centered himself and found his strength. And he'd never shared the experience with another person before.

Except for his brother.

The hedge came up fast. He barely had time to worry if she could make it when they were sailing over it. Then heads down, knees hugging their horses, they raced neck and neck toward the stream. Lucky surged ahead. Seconds later, Hunter reined the horse in at the stream. Then she pulled up beside him.

"You're very good," he said.

Laughing, she said, "Did I mention that the equestrian club at my college made it to the state finals in steeple chasing?"

He shot her a grin. "No, but I can believe it. How did you do?"

"Second place. I took a personal blue ribbon."

He studied her for a moment. Her face was flushed, her eyes laughing. Why hadn't he noticed before that she made his world a brighter place? That he was… He felt his heart stumble.

"Rory, I—" He caught himself, a sliver of panic moving through him. What words would he have blurted out if he hadn't stopped? Would he have told her what he was feeling—that he might be falling in love with her?

"What?"

No. Another needle of panic raced up his spine. Love?

That couldn't be true. It was ridiculous. He'd known her for two days. Still, the urge to reach out to her was so strong that he tightened his grip on the reins. Lucky began to dance. He had to think, make a plan. One thing he did know—once words were spoken, they couldn't be taken back.

"Let's ride along the stream for a while," he said.

"Sure." She eased her mount to his side as he steered Lucky along the water's edge.

Hunter searched for a topic of conversation, something, anything, that would stop the words that he couldn't seem to get out of his head.

But it was Rory who asked the first question. "Why did you decide to go into business?"

"It was a family tradition."

"What kind of business was your family in?"

"Banking and investments. I'd always thought I'd become part of it." Even when he'd been heavily into rebellion. At nineteen, he'd thought he had a knack for investing. At the end of that first semester of college when he'd come home, he'd intended to sit down and talk to his father about working in the investment section of the bank.

"I'm so sorry. Forget I asked that. I mean…you lost so much when you lost your family."

When he looked at her, he saw nothing but pure distress on her face. Impatience and guilt streamed through him. "You don't have to be sorry. It was a long time ago." He hesitated for a moment, then said, "There's a story I'd like to tell you. I'd like your take on it." The words had poured out, surprising him.

"Sure. Go ahead," she said.

"I told you part of it yesterday. There was a young man—he had parents, a brother, and a family business that he figured he'd go into eventually, although it had always been made clear to him that his older brother was slated to step into his father's and grandfather's shoes and run the business. He felt resentful and since he wasn't destined for the role of crown prince, he decided to assume the role of black sheep."

"Understandable."

Hunter wondered why it was so important that he tell her the whole story. Perhaps he needed to lay it all out for himself again. Perhaps he needed an objective opinion. Whatever the reason, he couldn't seem to prevent himself from continuing. "The last summer before he went away to college, he didn't stifle any of his rebellious urges. He had an affair with an older woman, he partied, he drove fast. He reported in late to work at the family bank and he left early. No one was happy with him, except for the woman he was having an affair with. She seemed to be highly amused by his behavior."

When he paused this time, she said nothing, but as the horses continued to walk, she reached out a hand and covered one of his.

"Then he went away to college and began to see things a little differently. He could continue to play the role of black sheep, or he could find a way to carve out a niche for himself in the family business and prove everyone wrong. Then something happened when he went home for the holidays."

Rory tightened her grip on his hand. "He lost the family that he wanted to make amends to."

"Yes," Hunter said. The horses stopped, and they loosened the reins. "He lost them—but not in an accident. On the night he came home, the family was having a meeting. They were all seated at the dining room table."

As he spoke, Hunter could picture it in his mind as if it had only just happened. "One of the bank's attorneys was there, too. It seems that his father and brother had piled up some gambling debts at a nearby casino, and they'd 'borrowed' quite heavily from the investment accounts at the bank."

"They'd embezzled investors' money?" Rory asked.

"In plain terms, yes. Of course, they'd expected to be able to pay it all back before the quarterly audit, but they never quite managed to win that jackpot in the sky at the casino. The news of the embezzlement was going to hit the papers within the week. They'd called in some favors and had managed to delay the story, but they couldn't bury it forever."

"And once the story hit the newspapers, there would be a run on the bank's funds, and thousands of people could be hurt."

He turned his hand and linked his fingers with hers. "Exactly. But the attorney and the family had a solution. All they needed to pull it off was a scapegoat. The key element of the plan was to make sure that investors didn't lose their faith in the bank or in the people running it."

"So the black sheep became the scapegoat?"

The anger in her voice softened something deep inside of him. "Yes. Since he'd never been associated with the running of the bank, he was the perfect choice. All he had to do was confess, sign over a trust fund he'd inherited from his grandmother to cover the losses, and promise that he would never work for the family business."

"What about the crown prince? Did he have to sign over a trust fund, too?"

Hunter nodded, almost amused by the fury in her voice.

"Oh, yes. There was a lot of money to replace. But the attorney had the papers all drawn up. The trust-fund money would eventually be replaced with legitimate bank profits. And there would be an advisory board appointed by the board of directors to see that no one was able to do any more 'borrowing.' The solution had been carefully thought out."

"Except that no one was thinking about the scapegoat."

"No. Everyone at the table seemed to think that he'd be perfectly willing to go along with it."

"What about the older woman he was having the affair with? Didn't she stick by him?" Rory asked.

Hunter shook his head. "She was a reporter and the family gave her an exclusive on the story."

"She couldn't have believed it."

The conviction in her voice had him staring at her. "Why do you say that?"

"She should have known him better than that."

Hunter wondered for a moment what difference that simple kind of faith might have made in his life ten years ago.

"Did you…did the scapegoat go to jail?"

"No. The family and the bank's attorney had connections that extended to the prosecutor's office."

"What happened to him?" Rory asked.

"The day that the story broke, he made all the required public apologies. Then he left town and never went back."

She threw her arms around him then and held tight.

Hunter couldn't have described the emotions swirling around inside of him. First faith and now understanding. He'd lived without them for so long. If someone, any member of his family, had shown him either ten years ago, everything might have been different.

When she finally lifted her head, he saw that her lashes

were wet, but her eyes were still angry. This time he felt his heart take a long, slow tumble.

"Why did you tell me this?" she asked.

Using his thumb, he wiped away one of her tears. "I'm not sure. I guess I've been thinking about going back there."

Priscilla raised her head and gave it a shake. Taking it as a signal, Lucky took a step forward, and Rory tightened her grip on the reins as her horse followed. "I think they want to get going."

For a few moments they rode in silence. Then Hunter asked, "What would you do?"

She glanced at him in surprise. "I'm not sure that I can advise you. I can only tell you that family stuff can really haunt you. I was so angry with my father for years. I thought he'd abandoned us. Then out of the blue, my sisters and I got a letter for our birthdays a few weeks ago. From him. He'd left them with his attorney. For the first time, I saw things from his point of view."

"Did it help?"

She smiled at him. "Some. It didn't change the fact that he left us. But I learned that he loved us and he regretted leaving. I think if he'd had it to do over again, he would have stayed."

Hunter wasn't so sure that if he went back to his hometown, he'd find such a happy ending. "I swore I'd never go back."

"Maybe that was the best decision back then. But I think that being older and looking back can sometimes shift your perspective. You can change your mind about going back."

Yes, he could, Hunter thought, and he wondered if he'd been moving toward the decision ever since the first threatening note had been delivered to his hotel room. When he glanced at Rory, their eyes met and held for a moment. "Rory, I—"

Whatever else he might have said was interrupted by the ringing of his cell phone. After lifting it to his ear, he said, "Yeah?"

"You weren't supposed to go off of the estate," Tracker said.

"Good morning to you, too," Hunter said.

"You're not going to think it's so good when you get back here. I just arrived a few minutes ago and I ran into Lea Roberts at the front gate."

Hunter swore under his breath, then said to Rory, "Lea Roberts is at the front gate."

"There's no telling who she might have told or who might have followed her. Where exactly are you?" Tracker asked.

"We're on the other side of the hill across from the estate. We've been following the stream toward the woods." On the other end of the line, he could hear Tracker talking to someone. Then he came back on the line. "Follow the stream through the woods. McGee's son and I will bring the horse trailer, but it's going to take us a half hour or so. We'll take the long route to avoid being followed."

"Got it," Hunter said.

"Do me a favor and get into those woods. I don't like the idea of you riding around out there in the open."

"Yeah." Tucking his phone back into his pocket, Hunter said, "Tracker wants us to get into the woods ASAP. They'll be picking us up on the other side in half an hour."

Rory nodded and then urged her horse into a canter. Hunter followed suit, but he was on the alert now, scanning the surrounding fields and the hills. It wasn't until they entered the woods and slowed the horses that Rory turned and spoke. "I know Lea wants those pictures, but how could she know about this place? I didn't tell her."

"Good question." He'd been thinking about the same question, and the most probable answer didn't make him happy. Lea had remembered that Hunter Marks had gone to college with Lucas Wainwright. That meant that she suspected his true identity.

They rode in silence until Rory said, "I can see the road ahead."

Through the trees, Hunter saw an SUV drive past. A glance at his watch told him that they still had another twenty-five minutes before Tracker would pick them up. "We might as well circle back and rest the horses in that clearing back there."

Once they'd dismounted and tethered the horses, Hunter began to pace. There was only one solution. He was going to have to go back to Oakwood and find a connection between one of his employees and what had happened ten years ago. As good as Tracker McBride was, the man hadn't been there. He didn't know the players.

"I know it's hard to wait," Rory said. "According to my sister, Tracker McBride's about the best there is when it comes to security."

"Yes," he said, stopping to turn to her. She was leaning against a tree, and in the dappled sunlight, she reminded him of a wood sprite. Feelings moved through him again, and each time they did, they grew stronger.

She extended a hand to him, and he found himself moving toward her before the thought had even entered his mind. Would she always have this kind of pull on him?

"I have an idea of how we could pass the time," she said as she grasped his hand.

"By blowing bubbles?" He dug into his pocket and pulled out two pieces.

Laughing, she said, "Not exactly. I have a better idea."

"Me, too." He shoved the gum back into his pocket.

"Tell me your idea. You know how I hate waiting."

He brushed her lips with his. "I noticed that last night." Then he was delighted when heat flooded her cheeks.

"Thank you for last night, by the way," she said. "For letting me try all those…things. And the stuff you tried, that was good, too."

He raised her fingers to his lips. "My pleasure."

"I want you to know I'll remember last night forever. I'll remember you forever."

Hunter felt his heart turn over again as a new realization streamed through him. He wanted more than memories of Rory. Barely understanding his feelings, he couldn't tell her yet what he was thinking, but he could show her. "Why don't we create some new memories for both of us?"

"You're reading my mind."

He leaned down and nipped her earlobe, then whispered, "Are you wearing the thong?"

"Maybe." She pressed two hands against his chest and looked up at him. "Since we're creating another memory, there's something that I didn't get to try last night."

His eyes narrowed. "Does it involve tying me up again?"

"No, unless you'd prefer that."

"I'd like to keep my hands free."

She touched the pearls she was wearing around her neck. "It involves this necklace you gave me. I read about it once, and I'd like to try it."

Hunter wondered if he could have refused her anything. "We've only got about twenty-five minutes."

She smiled at him. "I'll have to make you come very fast, won't I?" Then she reached down and touched the swollen length of him.

He sucked in his breath, and Rory felt that same ripple of power that she'd felt last night when she'd been in control. Moving her fingers up and down his length, she said, "I don't think there'll be a problem. Just put your back against this tree."

While they were shifting positions, she said, "Since we're pressed for time, I won't ask you to strip, although I enjoyed watching you do that last night." Talking helped her keep her mind on her plan, she discovered. While she opened his belt and pulled down the zipper, she continued, "Sierra, that's my academic sister, says that power is a potent aphrodisiac, and…" Once she had him free of his briefs, her breath backed up and she lost her train of thought for a moment. But her body seemed to know what it was doing. Her hand enclosed him and she felt his erection hard yet velvet smooth against the palm of her hand.

"You better get on with whatever you're going to do, or this will be very fast indeed," Hunter rasped.

"Yes." Rory licked her lips and nearly bent down to taste him, but then she remembered. "The pearls." After releasing him, she fumbled with the clasp, then freed the necklace. Fighting against the trembling in her hands, she finally managed to get the strand of pearls wrapped three times around the base of his shaft.

At his raspy groan, Rory glanced up at him. His eyes were dark, Terminator eyes, her fantasy man's eyes. But now she knew the real man—and he was kinder, gentler, and much better than anything she could have imagined. Keeping her eyes fixed on his, she closed both hands over the "bracelet" of pearls and slowly drew them up the length of his aroused penis.

"Rory—" His voice was raw, and she was sure she could feel the heat in his eyes sear her skin.

"You like that," she murmured as she managed to reposition the pearls.

"Like? I—" He broke off as she drew the pearls up his length again.

"I like it, too," she said. "I like to hold you like this. I like knowing that I can give you pleasure." His breath was coming in pants now, and the power she felt brought a fresh wave of pleasure. "You asked me earlier if I was wearing the thong. I am."

"That's it." He gripped her hips and shifted her so that her back was against the tree. Then he all but tore her jeans and boots off.

She heard a low moan when he fingered the waistband of the thong, and then his hands were pressed like a brand against her naked buttocks, and he was lifting her.

"Wrap your legs around me," he ordered.

And then at last he was inside of her. When he withdrew and thrust in again, she felt the scrape of the bark against her back and the hard length of him filling her completely. She was tender down there from the ride, but that only seemed to add to the pleasure.

"Hold tight. This is going to be a very rough ride." Then he began to move and each thrust brought a sharper wave of sensations.

"It's just like it was the first time," she said.

"It's nothing like it was the first time."

He was right. That first time, he'd been a stranger. The Terminator. Her fantasy man. But Hunter was real. And for the moment, he was hers.

"Say my name. Tell me you want me," he said.

"I want you, Hunter."

He increased the pace. "Say it again."

"Hunter," she said as she felt her climax begin. Even as the waves of it began to roll over her, catching her up in its power, the realization moved through her again—this was nothing like the first time. Because she'd fallen in love with Hunter.

"Mine."

She was barely aware of him crying out the word. All she could see was his face, all she could feel was him as he drove her, drove them both, over an airless peak.

12

"ARE YOU ALL RIGHT?" Hunter asked.

"Mmm. Perfect." She sat on his lap, her head resting against his shoulder. She loved this man. She felt as though she'd been sitting, letting him hold her, for a very long time. "I don't ever want to move."

"Tracker will be here soon," he said.

Maybe not so perfect. The moments were ticking away, and the time that they had together was fading fast. As long as they were here in the woods, he was hers. Deep inside she knew that when they got back to the house, everything would change. Lifting her head, she met his eyes. "I wish there was a way to stop time."

"Me, too."

Was she imagining it or did she see in his eyes some of the confusion and the wonder that she was feeling? "Hunter, I—"

Behind them, Lucky snorted impatiently, and Priscilla gave a ladylike whinny. A cell phone rang.

"This will be Tracker," he said as he shifted her off his lap and tugged out his cell phone out. "You'd better get your clothes on."

Rory grabbed her jeans and pulled them on. If the phone hadn't rung just then, would she have blurted out to him that she loved him? She jammed her foot into a boot and steeled herself to look at him again. He was totally focused on the call, frowning at something Tracker was saying. She had to get a grip. His boss was being threatened. He might be in danger. He certainly wouldn't want to hear some babbled profession of love. She didn't want to hear it herself. Great sex, fun and a story. That's what they'd agreed to, hadn't they?

"Right," he said.

Right, she told herself as she jammed her foot into her other boot. When she glanced down, she saw that they were on the wrong feet and she tugged them off again. Life was just never perfect. She was standing ready, her boots on the right feet, by the time he finished his call.

"Tracker's waiting for us at the bridge where the stream intersects the road."

With a brief nod, Rory walked over to mount Priscilla. When he was seated on Lucky, he reached over to put a hand on hers. "You were about to say something when the phone rang."

Rory managed a smile. "It was nothing." She placed a hand on his cheek. "Just thank you. I enjoyed the ride. Both rides."

His grip on her hand tightened. "Rory, I—"

Lucky took two steps back, forcing him to let her go.

"We'll talk when we get back to the house." He tightened his grip on the reins and urged Lucky forward. Neither of them spoke again as they followed the stream out of the woods.

Tracker and McGee's son, Tim, were leaning up against the side of a large SUV that was pulling a horse trailer. Neither one looked very happy.

The moment she dismounted, Tim McGee took Priscilla's reins. "Ladies first. Lucky has an aversion to trailers. It'll be better if she's on board before he puts up a fuss."

As if on cue, Lucky whinnied and rose on his back legs.

"Easy, boy." Tim and Hunter spoke the words in unison, and Tracker moved to help Hunter handle the black stallion. Rory stepped out of the way and waited on the grass verge as Priscilla walked like an angel into the trailer, and then all three men turned their attention to Lucky.

They had him halfway up the ramp when a tractor trailer whipped by, sending enough wind and vibrations to have Lucky backing quickly down the ramp and rearing again.

"Sure. You had to ride the stubborn one," Tracker complained to Hunter, but Rory noted that his hands were gentle on the horse.

Hunter patted the horse's neck and crooned softly, "Don't listen to him, boy. You're a beauty."

"Ms. Gibbs," Tim called from the mouth of the trailer, "if you see another truck, let us know."

"Sure." She moved out far enough into the road behind the trailer that she could see approaching vehicles from either direction. "Everything's clear right now."

The moment they had Lucky settled down, the three men started urging him up the ramp again. It was slow going. Tim was at the front, keeping the reins taut while Hunter walked beside Lucky, his hand spread on the horse's neck, talking to him softly the whole while. Tracker joined her as he waited for the horse to get all four feet on the ramp.

Rory glanced at him and saw that his eyes were scanning the road and the fields. "You're really worried about Hunter, aren't you?"

"I don't like to lose a client," Tracker said.

Rory frowned. "I thought your client was Jared Slade."

Tracker glanced down at her. "Mr. Slade and his associates. Right now that includes both Hunter and you."

Lucky chose that moment to stall halfway up the ramp.

Tracker grinned and called, "Maybe you'd like a pro to show you how it's done."

"The more the merrier," Hunter said.

As the three men continued to chide one another and coax the horse, Rory glanced between the road and Hunter while her mind raced. If Tracker McBride had been hired to protect Jared Slade, why wasn't he with Jared Slade right now? He had security people stationed at the Wainwright estate who could guard Mark Hunter. Yet he'd been here yesterday and today in person. Why? And why would he go to all this trouble to make sure they got back onto the estate safely unless…?

Could Hunter be Jared Slade? The moment the question completed itself in her mind, it began to make sense. Hadn't she had a hunch all along that Jared Slade was merely a figurehead? What better way to keep Jared Slade's identity a secret than to travel under a different name like Mark Hunter?

The scene in the lobby of Les Printemps replayed itself in her mind. Two men had gone to the registration desk, one had stayed with the luggage. No one—not even the bell captain in the lobby, would be able to say they'd seen or met Jared Slade for sure. The reception clerk would have been as confused as she'd been. And in the meantime, Hunter would simply slip into the elevator with the luggage and go up to the suite. Anyone would assume what she had—that the Terminator was some kind of manservant/bodyguard.

And if Jared Slade hadn't chased her out of the lobby and tracked her down in Silken Fantasies, would he have been injured by that bomb?

The chilling thought was still spinning around in her mind when Rory heard the car approaching. Shading her eyes, she tried to gauge the distance. "There's a car coming," she called out. "But you should still have time to get Lucky in."

As if he'd understood what she'd said and wanted to protest, Lucky whinnied and pawed the end of the ramp where it intersected with the trailer bed.

Hunter laughed softly. "Easy, boy. It's going to be all right. I promise."

Rory looked at Hunter again, studying him as he used both his hands and his voice to gentle the horse. The more she thought about it, the more logical it seemed that this man really was Jared Slade. Why hadn't she seen it sooner?

The answer to that was as simple and uncomplicated as it got, she thought as the three men and the horse finally made it into the trailer. She'd been totally blindsided by lust.

And then she'd taken that long, slow tumble into love.

From inside the trailer, Lucky whinnied, this time as if in agreement and Rory glanced back at the road. The car was still about a hundred feet away, but it was slowing. She barely had time to absorb that before Hunter/Jared started down the ramp. He was halfway down when the car pulled to an abrupt stop right beside her.

She shifted her gaze to the driver. He wore mirrored sunglasses, and he had the window down and the sunroof open—in spite of the heat. Then she saw a man with a gun push himself through the open sunroof. After that, everything happened at once.

Hunter stepped off the ramp.

"Jared!" She had time to scream that one word before she launched herself at him.

The shot rang out, loud enough and close enough to make her ears ring, and her shoulder burned as if it had been stung by a giant killer bee. She absorbed those two sensations as she smashed into him. Then they fell, hitting the ground hard enough to knock the breath out of her. With the pain still singing right through to her bones, they began to roll.

HUNTER STOOD IN THE STUDY of the Wainwright house in much the same position as he had on his arrival—was it only two days ago? He ran a hand through his hair and shoved down hard on his emotions as he listened to Tracker making arrangements on the phone.

He couldn't afford feelings right now. A cool head had always served him well, and it was his only solution now. Rory was all right. Banged up, a bit bruised. The bullet had only creased the skin of her upper arm. But the blood…

Turning away from the window, he shoved the image ruthlessly out of his mind. He'd been able to stop the bleeding right away, and McGee was seeing to first aid. She would be well taken care of by him. She'd gotten to the Wainwright's butler just as surely as she'd gotten to him.

Shoving his hands into his pockets, he stifled the urge to pace. He was going to be cool and logical. He knew what to do when he wanted something. And he wanted the person who was responsible for hurting Rory Gibbs.

Tracker set down the phone. "The helicopter will be touching down in a few minutes."

"Her sisters will be on it?" he demanded.

Tracker's brows lifted. "Yes, sir, as ordered."

"Sorry. I just—I know I've been snapping out orders ever since we got back."

"Forget it. She's important to me, too. Natalie Gibbs is a very good friend, and she's not going to be happy that her sister got hurt. At least it wasn't more serious."

"Dammit, she tried to take a bullet for me!" Hunter whirled and paced back to the window as all the emotions he'd been suppressing bubbled to the surface. "She could have been killed."

"She wasn't," Tracker pointed out. "She's fine. McGee served in a medical unit when he was in the military. He says she likely won't even have a scar."

Hunter ran a hand through his hair. "I just keep thinking of what could have happened."

"Don't. Believe me, I've been in your shoes. If you keep letting your emotions rule, they'll cloud your thinking."

"Don't you think I know that?" Hunter said. Then he sighed, strapping down his control as he ran a hand through his hair again. "Sorry. You're right."

"Let's concentrate on getting the bastard who's behind this," Tracker said. "I got a license plate. My men are checking out the owners as we speak. My guess is that they'll find the car was reported stolen. Those men were pros."

"Alex, Michael and Denise—I pay them well enough that any one of them could afford to hire someone. But how did they know I was here? What did you get out of Lea Roberts?"

"Not a whole damn lot," Tracker said, disgust clear in his voice. "When I asked her where she got the information that Jared Slade was here on the estate, she said that Rory Gibbs had told her that in a phone conversation yesterday."

"That's a lie."

"Maybe."

"No. Not maybe. She's lying. Rory doesn't know that I'm Jared Slade."

Tracker studied him for a moment. "I'm afraid you're wrong there. Just before the shooter drove up in that car, she was interrogating me about why I was here and why I was so concerned with your safety when I was supposed to be protecting Jared Slade. Then do you recall that she called you Jared just as she shoved you out of the path of that bullet?"

Stunned, Hunter replayed the scene in his mind, but he couldn't remember what she'd called out. The whole scene was a series of flashing images and sensations—the man pointing the gun, the sound of the shot, the impact of Rory's body against his, and the fear that had iced him through to the bone.

He began to pace. "No, I don't remember. But if she did call me that, she'd only just put it together." He turned to face Tracker. "I have to see her. I have to explain…" What? That he'd lied to her, that he'd given her an interview with a man who didn't exist? How in hell was he supposed to explain that?

Tracker's cell phone rang just as Hunter heard the sound of the approaching helicopter.

"Yeah," Tracker said into the phone. "We're ready." When he hung up, he said to Hunter, "Your conversation with Rory will have to wait. I'd like to get you out of here as soon as that helicopter lands."

"I want to take her with me."

"I can understand that," Tracker said. "But I'm voting against it." He held up a hand when Hunter opened his mouth. "Hear me out. If we're going to get to the bottom of this, I could use your full attention on the problem. And Rory is safer here. I've called in extra men to protect her. Besides, you're the target. If you're not here…" He shrugged and he let the sentence trail off.

Hunter paced to the French doors and watched as the helicopter landed on the grass near the stables. Dammit. Tracker was right. Rory would be safer here with her sisters, and the best thing he could do for her right now was to figure out who had shot at her.

"If Rory didn't tip off Lea Roberts, do you have any idea why she showed up outside the gates?"

"Yeah," Hunter said. "She knew that Hunter Marks went to college with Lucas Wainwright."

"There you go," Tracker said, nodding.

"Can you confront her? Get her to admit what part she's playing in all of this?"

Tracker shook his head. "I'm not the police—and you don't want them involved. When I went out to the gate to speak with her, I kept it very friendly. All I had to do was ask her a few questions and she was making excuses about going back to D.C. We have no solid evidence that she's connected to either the shooting or the bomb."

"There's no solid evidence connecting anyone to the shooting or the bomb," Hunter said. The moment he heard the frustration in his own voice, he shoved it down. He'd built Slade Enterprises by being cool and logical. He was going to have to use those same skills now if he wanted to save it.

"It's possible Lea told someone about the connection between you and Lucas. Or it's possible that the person behind the threats is very smart and dug up the connection on his own."

"All three of our prime suspects—Denise, Michael and Alex—are very smart."

"We'll just have to be smarter. C'mon," Tracker said, leading the way out onto the patio. "Once we get to the Wainwright Building, I'll show you everything I've dug up. And I can protect you there until we can figure this out."

Hunter met Tracker's eyes. "I'm going to Oakwood. Whatever the hell is going on, it started there, and I'm going to end it."

Tracker sighed. "You're just not going to make this easy for me, are you?"

Hunter met his eyes steadily. "I know that you went there, looked at the stories in the local paper, talked to some people. But there must be something you've missed. Maybe I'll see it."

Tracker studied Hunter for a moment as they walked toward the waiting helicopter. "Okay, this is the way it will be. My men and her sisters will protect Rory. We'll stop at the Wainwright Building and take a look at my file. If we're lucky, you'll see something there and we won't have to go to Oakwood. If we have to make the trip, I'll be going with you." He raised a hand to stop whatever objection Hunter might have made. "It'll cause less notice if you cooperate, but either way I'm going."

RORY SAT AS CLOSE as she could get to the edge of the couch, concentrating hard on the patterns in the kitchen floor. She didn't dare look at the mark the bullet had left on her arm. The first time she'd looked at it in the ditch where she and Hunter had landed, she'd passed out.

"This is going to sting a bit, Miss Rory," McGee said. "But I have a pot of tea brewing. I know that you prefer coffee, but tea has medicinal benefits, and I made another batch of chocolate-fudge cookies this morning."

"I know the drill," Rory said, tensing. "A spoonful of sugar makes the medicine go down. The one thing that I always used to do better than my sisters was get hurt, so I'm used to it. Just do it. I want to see Hunter." Or whoever he is.

She hadn't seen him since they'd gotten back to the estate. She had a vague memory of him holding her in the truck, but she'd been drifting in and out. And the next thing she knew, McGee was bending over her holding smelling salts under her nose.

The kitchen was huge with a sitting area that boasted an overstuffed couch, a fireplace, and a patterned floor with white and black tiles marching along together.

"Ouch," she said as McGee swabbed her shoulder with something nasty. "That really hurt."

"Sorry. I promised both Mr. Tracker and Mr. Hunter that I could take care of this. But if you'd prefer, I could drive you to the emergency room in town."

"No. Swab away." She winced as he did just that. Mr. Hunter. Then she remembered. Not Mr. Hunter at all, but Mr. Jared Slade. That's what she'd been thinking about when the shooter had risen out of the sunroof. Hunter had to be Jared Slade. That would certainly explain why Tracker had been so upset that they'd left the estate to ride the horses, why he'd told them to take to the woods, why he'd come for them in a trailer.

And why someone had shot at Hunter.

A bomb had been planted in his hotel suite, and Mark Hunter, alias Jared Slade, had gone into hiding at his friend's estate. It all made horribly perfect sense.

"This will feel cool, Miss Rory," McGee said as he rubbed something onto her shoulder.

McGee was right. It did feel blessedly and deliciously cool. She just wished it could do something for the sick feeling in her stomach. For a moment, she closed her eyes and tried to think. "I need to talk to Hunter. Can you tell me where he is?"

"Mr. Hunter and Mr. Tracker are in the study, I believe. They're waiting for Mr. Lucas to arrive."

Mr. Tracker, Mr. Lucas and Mr. Hunter, she thought. Odd that everyone called Mark Hunter by his last name.

"I'm going to put a bandage on this now," he said. "And then I'm going to pour you some tea, and you'll eat some of the cookies you like."

Rory's stomach gave a lurch. Then there was a sudden noise that sounded as if a tornado had just touched down. "What on earth—?"

"It's just Mr. Lucas's helicopter. Sometimes, it's the most convenient way for him and Dr. Mac or Miss Sophie to get here."

As the noise suddenly stopped, Rory imagined how it was going to be. Mr. Hunter or whoever he was would be closeted with his friend Lucas forever. "Are you finished?"

"Just a moment," McGee promised as he smoothed down a bit of tape. "If you're very careful and massage the salve in every day, you won't have a scar. And now you can have some of those cookies."

"Thanks." Rory rose from the couch. "First, I need to talk to Mr. Hunter or whoever he is. I'll be right back." She made it to the door, but when she opened it, Natalie and Sierra rushed in.

"Are you all right?" Natalie asked, taking her hands.

"Is she all right?" Sierra asked.

"I'm fine."

"She'll be fine," McGee assured them. "I've treated the wound. The bullet just grazed her skin. Would you like tea? I've prepared some of Miss Rory's favorite cookies."

Sierra studied him for a moment, then smiled. "Yes. Tea and cookies would be perfect."

"We were so worried," Natalie said, studying Rory closely. "Tracker said you were all right. But we had to see for ourselves. He arranged for Lucas to bring us."

"I need to see Hunter," Rory explained. "Or Jared. Or whoever he is."

"Jared? Jared Slade is here? Tracker said you were interviewing this Hunter person," Natalie said.

"I was," Rory said. "But I'm pretty sure he's really Jared Slade, and I have to—"

The deafening noise of the helicopter starting up drowned out her words and suddenly her stomach lurched again. She turned, rushed to the kitchen window and saw her worst fears confirmed. Hunter, alias Jared Slade, head bent low, was running across the lawn with Tracker at his side. He hadn't even said goodbye. As she watched them climb in, she felt the same stream of sensations she'd felt years before when she and her sisters and mother had gone to the airport to say goodbye to their father.

Oh, Harry had said that he'd only be gone for a while, but it had been a lie, and she'd somehow known it. Men always lied to her when they were never coming back.

Behind her, Rory heard a cell phone ring. Then it rang again. Still, Rory ignored it.

"It's not mine," Sierra said. "Mine plays Chopin."

"Don't look at me," Natalie said. "Mine's on vibrate."

Rory whirled then and dashed to the table where McGee had set her purse. Hunter was calling her. "Hello?"

"I'll give you one hour. If you don't deliver those pictures to me, you're fired."

"Lea?"

"Yes, this is Lea—Lea Roberts, your boss, the one who sent you on a very simple mission—to get a picture of Jared Slade. Do you have the photos?"

Rory drew in a deep breath. "No. I traded them for—"

"Sex. Don't think I don't know what you've been doing. You've been holed up there with the man who now calls himself Jared Slade, and you've been sleeping with him. For your sake, I hope that he was as good in bed as he used to be because your little dalliance has cost you any hope of a job at *Celebs*. You're fired."

When the call went dead, Rory merely stared down at her cell phone. Whatever luck she'd once had—it had just run out.

13

"TRACKER SAID HE WANTS YOU to stay here until this is all cleared up," Natalie said.

"I can't," Rory said as she led the way up the stairs to the room where she'd been staying.

"You'll be safer here," Natalie said. "They don't know who's behind these incidents yet. Your apartment was searched, you know."

Rory turned to her sister. "No one told me about that."

"Tracker thinks whoever it was might have been after the photos. Please. Someone's already taken a shot at you. I'd like you to stay here where Tracker can protect you until this is over."

Rory lifted her chin. "I can't."

McGee knocked on the doorjamb. "I thought you might like tea up here while I pack your things."

"Yes…I mean no. I won't be taking any of these things with me." Rory took the pearls that she'd stuffed in her jeans pocket and dropped them on the dresser. She didn't ever again want to see any of the things that Hunter had given her. She certainly didn't need another dumping gift from Jared Slade, alias Mark Hunter.

McGee set a tray down on a glass-topped table near the windows and pulled up three chairs. "Things always seem a bit better after a cup of hot tea." Then he left.

"I totally agree." Sierra wrapped her arm around Rory's waist and lead her to the table. "And look at those cookies."

Rory sat down and let Sierra pour her a cup of tea. "I'm fine. Really."

Natalie took one of her hands. "No, you're not. I know just how you feel. I felt the same way when I came home from Florida last month and I learned that Chance had flown to England without saying goodbye. I wanted to kill him. But even more, I wanted to bury myself in a hole and never come out again. Men can be such jerks sometimes."

Sierra passed Rory the plate of cookies. "Chocolate helps. There's a lot of research supporting the fact that dark chocolate is a mood enhancer, especially for women."

"No, thanks," Rory said.

Sierra and Natalie exchanged a look.

"If you're not eating, you must be in love," Sierra said.

"No, I—" To her horror, Rory felt her eyes fill with tears. She rubbed away the one that escaped and blinked back the others. She never cried. Never. "I'm just not lucky that way. Even if I were, I just don't have… I'm going to be fine. I'll find another job and I'll…" What? Find another man? Not likely. Jared Slade had even ruined any relationship she could have with a fantasy man—because her fantasy man was him. "I'll…go home and just…"

Rory lifted her teacup and then set it down. She was thinking of doing what she'd always done. She was giving up and running away.

Suddenly, the advice her father had given her in his letter came back to her, almost as if he were sitting beside her, whispering in her ear. *Trust in your luck…stay in the game.*

Rory glanced around the room. This was the room where she'd seduced her Terminator—whatever his real name was. She'd driven him crazy. And she could do it again. She wanted to do it again.

"No." Straightening her shoulders and lifting her chin, she faced her sisters again. "I'm not going home."

"Good," Natalie said with a sigh. "I'll feel so much better if you stay here."

"I'm not staying here, either. But I'm not going to run away and start over—looking for a new career and a new man. That's what I always do. Lea Roberts isn't the only boss in the world, and *Celebs* is not the only magazine."

"Here! Here!" Sierra said, raising her cup again.

Rory was out of her chair and pacing. "And I'm not going to go looking for another man, either. Hunter—or whoever he is—is the only man for me."

Natalie and Sierra exchanged another look.

"You're right. She is in love with him," Natalie said.

Rory raised a hand. "Maybe. I'm not sure. I—"

"She's definitely in love with him," Sierra said. "The confusion, the fear, the fact that she's passing up food. Classic symptoms across cultures."

Rory clapped her hands over her ears. "I'm not listening. I'm not even going to think about that right now." Then moving to the door, she called out, "McGee?"

"Yes, miss," he said, stepping out of a nearby room with a suitcase in his hand.

"I changed my mind. I'd like you to pack everything, please."

Nodding, McGee followed her back into her bedroom. "I thought you might. Shall I pack the bubble gum, too?"

"No, I'll put that in my purse. And the cookies, too. Can you wrap them up, please? And one other thing. Why do you call Hunter Mr. Hunter?"

"Because that's what Mr. Lucas has always called him—even back in the days when they went to college together."

"Hunter might be his first name then," Rory said, turning to Natalie. "I'm going to need your help."

Natalie frowned.

Rory fisted her hands on her hips. "Don't give me that look. If Chance hadn't come back from London a few weeks ago, what would you have done?"

"She would have gone after him," Sierra said when Natalie hesitated. "You know you would have, Nat."

"You followed Dad's advice," Rory said. "Now it's my turn. If I don't take a risk, I may lose him."

Natalie threw up her hands. "Okay. What do you need?"

"I need all of your research skills and the equipment at D.C. Metro. I want to know the hometown of a man—first name of Hunter, I think. He went to Harvard with Lucas Wainwright and he was accused of embezzling from his family's bank about ten years ago. Can you get me that?"

Natalie smiled. "I'll try. But you'll have to help me out. You're the one who inherited the luck genes."

THE APARTMENT THAT TRACKER kept at Wainwright Enterprises offered a view of the Washington Monument and the Mall. But Hunter wasn't seeing it as he gazed out of the window. He couldn't get images of Rory out of his mind. Rory laughing in the sunlight as they rode. Rory, her eyes misted and locked on his, saying his name. Rory rushing toward him as the man standing in the sunroof pointed the gun at him.

He wanted her with him right now. His body was hard just thinking about her. And he was beginning to regret that he'd left without talking to her, seeing her. Touching her.

"Earth to Hunter."

He whirled from the window to find Tracker standing in the doorway to his office. "I've called your name twice."

"I never should have let you talk me into coming here without her."

Brows lifted, Tracker studied him for a moment. "You've got it bad, pal."

"What are you talking about?" Hunter asked.

Tracker grinned. "You've fallen in love with her. As a recent victim, I can spot the signs."

Hunter frowned. "What signs?"

"For starters, you've been staring out that window for the past ten minutes. You can't hear your name when it's called and you can't clear images of her out of your mind. Plus, you want her with you pretty much all the time."

Since Hunter realized he was presently experiencing everything Tracker had just described, he didn't comment.

"And even though you've spent your life doing just fine on your own, you're beginning to see that a future without her in it would be empty."

Was that true? No. Hunter sank down on the arm of a nearby chair. But hadn't that been the very direction his thoughts had been taking in the woods right after they'd made love? Hadn't he felt what it might be like to have her with him when they were old? And it had felt right somehow.

Tracker moved behind a sleek stainless-steel counter, pulled two beers out of a tall refrigerator, and handed him one.

Hunter twisted the cap off and took a long swallow. "Suppose all that's true. It doesn't mean I'm in love. I just never should have left without talking to her." He rose and began to pace. "She doesn't have a lot of self-confidence where men are concerned. She's probably already convinced herself that I've dumped her, that I won't come back. Hell, maybe she doesn't even want me back. I've lied to her right from the start. She'll think everything—everything we shared—was a lie." Turning, he found Tracker regarding him steadily, a sympathetic look on his face.

"I'm not…" Hunter began. "I don't…I never wanted to be this responsible for another person. I—"

Tracker lifted his beer in a toast. "Ain't love grand?"

"It isn't…" Hunter began. He wanted to deny that he'd fallen in love, but he was beginning to be very afraid that he had.

"I was in denial at first, too. I just didn't think that people as different as Sophie and I were could ever make a go of it."

"What happened to change your mind?" Hunter asked.

Tracker grinned. "She made me an offer I couldn't refuse. And you can make Rory Gibbs one just as soon as we figure out who's trying to kill you."

"Right." First things first, Hunter thought as he strode to the large oak table where Tracker had spread out the contents of a file.

"This is what I've got so far," Tracker said. "Michael Banks, Denise Martin and Alex Santos—our three prime suspects. I've run background checks on each one of them and I can't connect them to Hunter Marks. Plus, everything on their résumés checks out."

Hunter studied the faces of his three most trusted business associates. If he wanted to get back to Rory, he had to solve this problem first. "Okay. We've run into a dead end with who. Maybe we'll have more luck with why. This has to go back to the embezzlement scandal in Oakwood. He or she knows what I did and wants to expose me and perhaps destroy Slade Enterprises, probably for revenge."

"That may well have been plan A, in Atlanta and New York, but the threats got more personal once you arrived in D.C.," Tracker said. "The question is, why?"

"Lea Roberts was here. With her help, Jared Slade could be exposed in the press as Hunter Marks—because she was the one who originally broke the old embezzlement story."

"Why the bomb?" Tracker asked.

"A message to me along with the note that the exposure is only step one of the master plan."

"And if the bomb in your suite had killed you?" Tracker asked.

Hunter shook his head. "It wasn't meant to. It was set by someone who knew I was definitely out of the suite." Reaching down, he turned Denise Martin's picture facedown. "Which eliminates Denise. Now there are only two suspects."

"Okay. The note and the bomb are delivered to let you know that the threat is personal and serious. Next in the plan you see Slade Enterprises ruined because it's suddenly revealed that Jared Slade is none other than the embezzler who used to be known as Hunter Marks. Then you die."

"But the plan goes awry. Rory doesn't turn over the pictures on schedule, and her apartment is searched without success, and I go into hiding."

"Panic sets in," Tracker said. "And he goes to plan B— just shoot you. Which one of them is more capable of coming up with a complicated plan like that?"

"They both are."

"Pick a favorite," Tracker said.

Hunter stared down at the photos and finally shook his head. "I still can't see either of them doing this."

"Then we'll have to find something that links one of them with your past as Hunter Marks."

"You've checked places of birth?"

Tracker nodded. "Alex was born in New York City. I'm still checking on Michael."

"Maybe we're coming at this from the wrong perspective," Hunter said. "Assuming it is one of these two, they've been working for me for some time. I covered my tracks well, but one of them somehow made the connection between Hunter Marks and Jared Slade and applied for a job with Slade Enterprises. Why wait three or four years to get revenge?"

"You're wondering what happened to trigger the notes and the incidents in Atlanta and New York?"

"Yes." Then Hunter suddenly sank into a chair. "Of course. That has to be it. I don't know why I didn't see it before. Three months ago, I made plans to take over Marks Banking and Investments, my family's company. Both of them worked on the research."

Tracker nodded. "It started one of them thinking and they connected you with Hunter Marks."

Hunter met Tracker's eyes. "That's why I have to go back there. There's something that I'm not seeing, something that I don't know about. No one was supposed to get hurt or lose any money. That's why I let them make me the scapegoat."

"Ah, the deep, dark secret at last. You're not really an embezzler."

"I'm going back there," Hunter said.

"We'll be there when the bank opens in the morning."

"Damn!" Lea Roberts slammed on the brakes as she hit the bumper-to-bumper traffic that she'd have to battle all the way into D.C. She needed to get to her office and clear her calendar for the next few days. Her trip to the Wainwright estate had been a bust in all but one respect. She now knew that Jared Slade had been there. From the looks of the security, he'd been hiding out there. So there had to be some truth to the tip she'd received about the bomb in his suite at Les Printemps.

Frowning, she tapped her fingers on the steering wheel. So Jared Slade, alias Hunter Marks, was under siege. By whom, was the question. Of course, it had to be her anonymous tipster. But who in the hell was that?

As if to join in on the little discussion she was having with herself, her cell phone rang. She nudged her car into a faster-moving lane, and then pushed the button on her speaker phone. "What is it?"

"I want you to run the story proving who Jared Slade really is."

It was the same androgynous voice, and there was more than a trace of anger in it. Lea bit back her own temper. "No."

"Why not?"

"I still don't have the pictures."

The voice swore. "You always were incompetent. Even years ago, you didn't cover the story well. You covered up the harm that the Marks family did. You were on their payroll just like everyone else in town."

Even as Lea blinked in surprise, the call ended. So it all went back to the original embezzlement. And there'd been a cover-up? Suddenly, she knew where she might find Hunter Marks. If she was right, the story was even bigger than she'd originally thought.

OAKWOOD HADN'T CHANGED MUCH in the ten years since Hunter had last seen it. As Tracker drove the rental car down Main Street, he noted that most of the family-owned stores were still in operation—Maisie's Diner, Bob's Barbershop, the Law Offices of Thorne and Grayson. It had been Marshall Thorne Sr. who'd sat on the bank's board and advised his family.

The only new business he saw was an antique shop where Dennison's Jewelers used to be. When they pulled to a stop at the traffic light, Hunter glanced at the library first. The large redbrick building stood in the center of the block, flanked by parking lots on two sides. He wondered if Daisy Brinkman still patrolled her building, breaking up necking sessions in the stacks.

Even when the light turned green, he waited until the last moment to shift his gaze across the street to Marks Banking and Investments. The three-story structure stood at the intersection of Main and First streets. The solid look of gray stone and the clean lines of the Federal-style architecture projected security. How often had he stood in front of it as a boy and known that one day he would work there?

As they pulled into the curb in front of it, Hunter noted that the sign on the door was just the same. Come In and Bank with People You Trust.

Right. The last time he'd seen those words had been the night he'd left town, and he'd hurled a rock through the window, breaking the glass. One last hurrah to assuage the mix of fury and disillusionment that had been burning inside of him.

Odd, but he felt none of those things now. And yet nothing had changed, neither the building nor the reasons why he'd given up all ties to his family ten years ago. Still, just looking at the building had some of his tension easing.

Perhaps he'd changed. If he had, he owed it to Rory.

Firmly, he pushed her out of his mind. She was safe, and he'd see to it personally just as soon as he finished what he'd come back to Oakwood to do.

"I'll go in alone," Hunter said.

"No way." Tracker let himself out the driver's side and caught up to Hunter as he pushed through the glass doors. "Until we catch whoever's out to get you, just think of me as your guardian angel. You won't even know I'm here."

"I need to talk to my brother alone," Hunter said, and he was surprised to find it was true. He did need to talk to Carter and not just about who might be threatening him.

The building smelled just the same, a mix of lemon wax and old leather. The tellers still worked in little cubicles behind a row of brass bars. Miss Tolley, his father's secretary, still had a vase of fresh flowers from her garden on her desk. But when he shifted his gaze, he saw there was young a woman in a neat black business suit sitting at the desk that used to belong to his brother.

"Miss Tolley," he said as he reached the secretary's desk. He saw recognition flash into her eyes the moment she glanced up at him.

"Hunter?"

He grinned at her. "Still sharp as ever." His smile faded. "I want to see my brother."

She lifted the phone. "I'll tell him you're here."

Hunter strode toward the door behind Miss Tolley's desk, the door that now had his brother's name on it.

"I'll be right here," Tracker murmured.

For a moment, Hunter continued to stare at his brother's name on the door. Why hadn't Michael or Alex mentioned that it was Carter Marks III who was now running the bank? With his hand on the knob, he hesitated another moment, and then he walked into the office.

Carter rose from behind the desk, but he didn't move. As Hunter walked toward him, he saw a flood of emotions flash over his brother's features—shock, apprehension. And was there some guilt? He'd imagined this scene so many times in the first few years after he'd left home.

And then he saw in his brother's eyes what he'd never seen in his dreams—pleasure.

"Hunter." Carter circled his desk. "I'd given up. I never thought I'd see you again—or that you'd want to see me. Welcome back." He held out his hand.

Was it just that simple? When Hunter grasped his brother's hand, he felt his tension ease. "How are you?"

"A bit harried. Mandy, that's my wife—your sister-in-law—she's expecting twins in a week or so. The doctor says it could be anytime." He ran a hand through his hair. "There's other stuff—business. Someone's trying to buy us out, but we've been able to prevent it so far."

Not much longer, Hunter thought. Not with the sweetened deal that he was going to offer the board and the town council. "Where's Dad?" he asked.

"Dad hasn't been here at the bank for almost ten years."

Once again, Hunter wondered how this information hadn't been in the reports he'd been presented with. "What happened?"

Carter flushed a little. "He couldn't get the gambling thing under control, and so the board forced him into retirement."

Hunter studied his brother and saw what he wasn't saying. "You caught him with his hand in the till again?"

Carter nodded. "About six months after you left, Mother moved him to a nice retirement community in North Carolina. He still has his horses, but she holds on to the purse strings and sits on the town council. They visit up here twice a year, and she doesn't let him near the bank or any casinos."

"How about you?" Hunter asked. "Do you ever get the urge to gamble?"

Carter met his eyes steadily. "If you're asking if I visit casinos, no. The only gambling I've done in the last ten years was to marry Mandy. So far it's paid off."

"You're lucky."

"Yes, I am. Hunter, I—I'm glad you're here."

Hunter felt something inside of himself loosen. And although he never would have predicted it, he found that he was glad, too. But he wasn't ready to say it, wasn't ready to trust completely.

"I came because I have some questions."

"Sure. Sit down. I'll have Miss Tolley bring us coffee."

Hunter waited, happy for the reprieve as the coffee was served. Finally, when Carter was seated in the chair beside him, he said, "I need some information about what happened after I left. Did anyone in town lose money because of the embezzlement?"

"Absolutely not. I made sure of that."

Hunter studied his brother. Carter had been less than a year out of college when he'd taken over the bank. "You must have put in a lot of hours."

Carter shrugged. "I'd do it again."

"Why did you ever get mixed up in gambling and embezzlement in the first place?"

Carter shrugged. "In those days I did everything that Dad did. I figured it was the only way to really fill his shoes. And I didn't know about the embezzlement until you did."

For a moment, Hunter let the silence stretch between them. Then finally, he said, "Someone told me recently that the thing about revisiting the past is that you see it in a different perspective." Then taking a sip of his coffee, he refocused his thoughts on the problem at hand. "Are you sure that no one in town was hurt by the embezzlement?"

Carter hesitated for a moment, then said, "Well, there was Mike Dennison, the jeweler. He committed suicide the night before the story hit the papers."

"I was still here. Why didn't anyone tell me?"

"No one knew. The body wasn't discovered for three days or so. His wife claimed that he learned about the embezzlement and panicked. She always blamed us for his death. We never accepted the responsibility, of course."

"I thought the board and our attorney had the news sewn up tight. They were so afraid of a run on the bank. Who would have leaked the information?"

Carter shook his head. "We never found out."

"Would you still have a list of employees from that time?"

"Sure." Carter studied him for a moment. "This is important?"

"Yes."

Carter reached for the phone and instructed Miss Tolley to gather the information. When he finished, he glanced around the office again. "It'll be tight for a bit. There won't be as much money as you might expect, but there's room for you here. You can have a desk in here if you want. We'll move mine. There should be room."

Hunter frowned. "What are you talking about?"

"You coming on board. I've been trying to track you down for years. To tell you the truth we could use some help in handling investments. If we can strengthen that department, we can discourage any future attempts at a buyout."

Hunter's brows shot up. "You're offering me a job? You don't even know what I've been doing for the past ten years."

Carter met his eyes steadily. "You're my brother, and you took a fall for Dad and me ten years ago. I never should have let you do it. I wouldn't have if I could have figured out a better way to save the bank. I certainly wouldn't have let you do it if I'd known I wouldn't see you again. But what you did—it saved Marks Banking and Investments. This place is here because of you, so you have a job here anytime you want."

Carter held out his hand.

Perhaps it *was* just that simple, Hunter thought as he took his brother's hand and then pulled him into his arms.

When he drew back, he said, "There are some things I need to tell you first."

"About what you've been doing for the past ten years?"

Hunter smiled. "That, too." And Hunter began to fill him in.

14

IT WAS AFTER TEN when Rory pulled into the driveway next to the Oakwood Public Library. During the drive from D.C., she'd had plenty of time to debate where to start—the newspaper office or the library. When she spotted the latter first, she went with it.

At least she had a name. Natalie had found the name Hunter Marks and the small town of Oakwood for her within an hour. But it had taken Rory another three hours to gather all the information about the embezzling scandal she could find online. Then, since her sister hadn't been keen on her visiting Oakwood, she'd had to be sure that Nat was asleep before she'd sneaked out of her sister's apartment.

After parking her car at the back of the brick building, Rory climbed up the short flight of wooden steps to the back entrance. The moment she walked through the door, she found herself in a small room where a group of children, either sitting or stretched out flat on the floor, were listening to a young woman reading aloud. They paid her no heed as she moved quietly into the next room. Here, sun poured through immaculately clean windows, and she had to shade her eyes to see the woman behind the information desk.

As she drew closer, Rory saw that the woman was a perfect fit to the image she carried in her mind of a small-town librarian—tall and thin, wearing Victorian-style clothes, with gray hair pulled back neatly into a bun. At first, Rory guessed her age to be about seventy, but up close, she could see that the dark eyes held both intelligence and humor, and the welcoming smile softened the older woman's features in ways that shaved years away. Daisy Brinkman was the name on the little brass plate on her desk. It suited her to a T.

"Well, this is Oakwood's day for visitors. What can I do for you?" Daisy asked.

"My name is Rory Gibbs." She handed the woman a card and drew in a deep breath. "I work freelance for *Celebs* magazine, and I'm researching an article on Hunter Marks and the scandal that drove him out of town ten years ago."

Daisy studied her for a moment. "Hogwash."

Rory just stared at her. "What?"

"I said hogwash. You're lying. And you don't have the eyes for it. Plus, I read *Celebs* magazine. The Marks embezzlement is an old story, not at all the kind of piece your magazine would run. The editorial staff there likes its scandals current." Her eyes narrowed. "Unless Hunter Marks has resurfaced as some sort of celebrity in his own right?"

When Rory continued to stare, Daisy tapped a pencil on her desk. "That might explain why he's come back to town to talk to his brother after all these years. The return of the prodigal—now rich and famous, is he?"

Rory swallowed. "He's with his brother?"

Daisy nodded, her eyes sparkling. "Leona Tolley over at the bank called me not half an hour ago. And Lea Roberts, the reporter who broke the embezzlement story, is hanging out at Maisie's Diner. Add that to the mix and there's got to be a good story. She hasn't been back here in ten years. You working for her?"

"No." Rory studied the woman for a moment and then went with her instincts. "What I just said *was* hogwash. I don't work for Lea Roberts or *Celebs* anymore. She fired me. But I am here to find out everything I can about that old scandal."

"Why?"

Rory was beginning to think the tiny woman in front of her had picked the wrong profession entirely. She'd have made a good cop or P.I. And Rory didn't think she was going to get much information unless she came clean. "What if I told you that I'm trying to prove that years ago Hunter Marks took the blame for someone else?"

"Hmmph. Wouldn't surprise me a bit. The story that Lea Roberts printed in the papers had cover-up written all over it. But it saved the bank and the town. Why do you want to dig up that old scandal after all these years? Young Carter has done a fine job of running the bank."

"Because the truth might save someone's life," Rory said. "Hunter Marks's life. Someone is trying to kill him, and I'm pretty sure it's connected to that old embezzlement scandal. Can you help me?"

Daisy studied Rory for a long moment, then said, "What exactly do you want to know?"

"Who was hurt enough by the embezzlement to want to kill Hunter Marks?"

"Come with me," Daisy said, stepping out from behind the circulation desk and leading the way to a staircase. "I store files on the third floor. Now mind the railing. It needs tightening."

The narrow room that she led Rory into was dim and

almost airless. The light filtering through one low dormer window was thick with dust motes. One wall of shelves was lined with books, the other filled with storage boxes. Daisy threw a light switch and began to scan the boxes. "Here it is."

Rory helped her set the box on the floor and opened it.

"I kept a folder with all the stories. But you won't find much about the one tragedy that was linked to the rumors of embezzlement at the bank."

"A tragedy?"

"Yes. Ah, here it is." Daisy pulled out a file and flipped through it. "Very unfortunate. Mike Dennison who ran Dennison's Jewelers—the store used to be right on the corner where the antique shop is—he killed himself. His wife maintained that he got wind of the scandal and knew that he would be wiped out if there was a run on the bank. The Marks family was able to keep the suicide from getting much news coverage. Mrs. Dennison did file a civil suit against the family on behalf of her son and herself. It was settled." Daisy fished out another clipping.

Rory looked down at a yellowed picture of a stocky woman and a thin boy. "How old was the boy?"

Daisy thought for a moment. "Twelve or thirteen."

"Where are they now?"

Daisy's eyebrows shot up. "I can keep pretty good track of people while they're in town, but Michael and his mom moved out of town right after he graduated from high school. Rumor was young Mike got a free trip to the college of his choice as part of the settlement. When he left for his freshman year, she moved out of town, too. I heard she got married again."

Rory was still studying the picture. The story was interesting, but it didn't sound like the Dennisons had been hell-bent on revenge. "You don't happen to have a more recent picture of young Mike, do you?"

Daisy shot her a smile. "I keep copies of all the high-school yearbooks. Wait right here."

Rory knelt down to inspect the file again. All there was on the Dennison family was an obituary. She'd been so sure that she could help, but she had the feeling that she was following a dead end. No. She started through the files again. There had to be something here. All of her instincts told her that what was happening now had to be tied to this old tragedy.

"Here it is," Daisy said as she hurried into the room. "Michael was the valedictorian of his class, a very bright boy. Word was he was going to major in business."

As Rory studied the picture, she saw a blond young man, very preppy looking, and a little flutter of recognition moved through her. In her mind, she attempted to add on ten years, and the flutter grew stronger.

"You're sure that no one else was hurt by the possible collapse of the bank?" Hunter asked.

Frowning, Carter shook his head. "You of all people know what the family did to keep anyone from being hurt, how quickly we acted. Dennison panicked."

Dennison. Hunter had only been able to come up with a vague image of the jeweler in his mind. The store he could picture, but at nineteen, he hadn't had any reason to go in or get to know the family. "How did he learn about the embezzlement? I didn't even know until the night before the press release. And that was the night he hung himself."

Carter nodded. "The widow claimed that it was her son who brought the news home."

"So the son brings home a rumor, and his dad kills himself before the truth comes out." Hunter shook his head. "That's a huge burden to carry around with you for the rest of your life."

"When we made the settlement, we urged Mrs. Dennison to move out of town and make a new start. But she wanted her son to remain in Oakwood." Carter sent him a troubled look. "I can't see any connection between Mike Dennison's suicide and these threats on your life."

Hunter couldn't, either. Tracker was having his men trace the mother and the son, but that would take time. A fresh wave of frustration rolled through him along with a feeling deep in his gut that time was running out.

There was a knock at the door. *Tracker,* he thought as he turned. But it was Rory who rushed into the office. Tracker followed, talking on his cell, but Hunter couldn't take his eyes off Rory. His first thought was that he'd conjured her up because he'd been wanting her with him ever since he'd left her at the Wainwright estate. She looked hot and sweaty and there was dust on her face and arms. Just seeing her made his mouth go dry.

"I think I know who's threatening you," she said as she placed an open book on the desk and pointed to a photo.

He didn't glance down right away because he couldn't stop looking at her. His heart took a long, slow tumble as he faced what he hadn't been able to accept before. He was in love with Rory Gibbs.

"Look," she said impatiently. "You have to imagine him with ten years added on. Do you recognize him?"

Hunter looked at the photo for a moment. Then, eyes narrowing, he leaned closer to study it more thoroughly. Finally, he straightened and turned to Tracker. "Mike

Dennison's son is my executive assistant, Michael Banks."

Tracker conveyed that information to whomever he was talking to.

"Where did you find this?" Hunter asked.

"The library. Daisy Brinkman was very helpful."

Carter's intercom buzzed, and he pressed the button and picked up the receiver.

"I have a question, too," Tracker said. "Just how did you manage to get away from both your sister and the man I had following you?"

Rory looked at him and shrugged. "I climbed out a window and cut through an alley to where I'd parked my car."

Hunter couldn't prevent a smile, but it faded when he saw the expression on his brother's face.

"Miss Tolley says that there's a reporter here asking to see you, Hunter. Lea Roberts."

"I don't like this," Tracker said. "If she's here and Rory's here, can Michael Banks or one of his hired killers be far behind?" He glanced at Carter. "Is there a back way out of here?"

"Right through that door over there." Carter dug in his desk and pulled out a set of keys. "Take my car. It's a beige SUV right outside the back entrance. I'll stall Lea Roberts."

"I don't want her to know that Jared Slade is really Hunter Marks," Tracker said.

Carter grinned. "Don't worry. I can handle her. I never did like her much."

"C'mon." Tracker urged them toward the door.

"I have a plan we can use to trap him," Rory said.

"Good. You can tell us all about it once we're safely out of town."

HUNTER SHOVED A BASEBALL CAP down low on his forehead and scanned the dining room of the Blue Pepper again. He didn't like Rory's plan one bit, not even with the revisions that Tracker and Natalie Gibbs had insisted on making. And he hated the onlooker role he'd been assigned in the little charade they were going to play out.

Of course, he had to admit that the others were right. If he got too close, Michael could recognize him, and that would spoil everything. Plus, it might put Rory in even more danger.

So he was stuck sitting at the bar while Rad, one of the owners of the Blue Pepper, escorted Rory to a table in the upper-level dining area. After a glance at his watch, he took a sip of the beer in front of him. Rory had called Michael, inviting him to meet with her because she had proof that he was trying to kill Jared Slade. She was wired, so they could hear and record everything, and if she could get Michael to admit what he'd done, then everything would be over.

Tracker had explained to him what they needed on the ride back to D.C. Even though they'd discovered that Michael might have motivation, they still had no proof tying him to either the bomb or the shooting. Hunter shifted his gaze to the dining room again as Rory took her seat. She was wearing the red sundress that McGee had purchased for her. And she'd told him that she was wearing the red thong just for extra luck.

He wished to hell that he had some of her confidence that this was going to go well. The fact that Chance Mitchell and Natalie Gibbs were stationed at the table next to Rory's eased his fears somewhat. But there were things that could still go wrong.

Tracker climbed onto the stool next to Hunter. "One of

my men just spotted our friend walking toward the restaurant. He's about a block away."

Instead of easing the knot in Hunter's stomach, the news only tightened it. Michael had taken the bait, but now the danger for Rory was real instead of theoretical.

"I still don't have a good feeling about this," he said.

"Chance Mitchell is the best. And the two other men I have stationed up there are top-notch, too. Ah, here's our boy now."

Hunter didn't move his head, only his eyes, but he kept them steady on Michael Dennison Banks as he walked up the stairs and sat down at Rory's table.

"HI," RORY SAID as Michael Dennison avoided the chair that Rad was holding for him and sat in the one next to her.

He said nothing until Rad was out of earshot. Then he pitched his voice low. "What kind of game are you playing? I had nothing to do with the bomb at Les Printemps. I don't even know anything about a shooting."

Her nerves were jumping so much that Rory barely kept herself from blowing a bubble. She knew what she was supposed to say. Tracker and Natalie had taken her through the script over and over. She kept the bubble gum tucked in her cheek while she said, "I went to Oakwood, Connecticut, and did a little research. I know about your father's suicide, but I haven't told anyone yet."

"So?"

The voice and the eyes were so cold that Rory barely kept herself from shivering. "So my sister Natalie is a cop with the D.C. police. There was a fingerprint recovered from the bomb. Once they discover it belongs to Michael Dennison, alias Michael Banks, how long do you think you can continue to play dumb?"

For a moment he didn't say anything. Once more, she had to stifle the urge to blow a bubble. He was thinking, weighing the truth of what she was saying. Rory remembered Daisy Brinkman saying that she didn't have the eyes for telling a lie. Could those cold blue eyes staring at her now see that?

She leaned toward him. "I can either tell them or keep your identity a secret. It's up to you."

"Tell anyone you want. I don't know what you're talking about."

"HE'S NOT ADMITTING ANYTHING," Hunter murmured. "He's going to stonewall her."

Tracker laid a hand on his arm when he would have moved. "Give her a few more minutes."

Hunter took another drink of his beer as he watched Rory reach out a hand to keep Michael from rising.

"I can understand why you did it," she said. "You blame him for what happened, don't you? Everyone in town knew that he was reckless, the black sheep of the Marks family. And he'd certainly lived up to his name—gambling and then stealing money to cover his losses. Stealing your father's money. Your money."

"She's off script," Tracker murmured. "But she's keeping him there."

Yeah, Hunter thought. But the bad feeling he had wasn't getting any better.

"You know nothing," Michael said.

"I know you lost your father. I lost mine, too, when I was ten. He died in a car crash. The driver of the other car was drunk. He never even went to jail. If I could have, I would have gone after him and made him suffer for taking my father from me."

Hunter stiffened then. "She's lying. She can't tell a lie to save her life."

"Wait." Tracker tightened his grip on Hunter's arm.

"Hunter Marks deserves to die," Michael said.

"See? She's playing him just right," Tracker said.

"I know just how you feel," Rory murmured. "How did you ever find him?"

"Luck. I had no idea when I went to work for Jared Slade that he was really Hunter Marks. I only put it together when he told me to do the research on buying out Marks Banking and Investments. He was actually going to buy them out. I've seen what he can do when he takes over a business. Within a year, he would have doubled their profits. And my father wouldn't be there to benefit from any of it. I knew then what I had to do."

Rory tried to suppress a shiver. She couldn't take her eyes off Michael's, and she was beginning to glimpse the madness just beneath all that ice.

"Oh, I would have found him eventually. I was saving every cent I made for that purpose. It was my mother's idea. She always told me that I would have to track him down and make him pay. That's why we stayed in town for so long. She was waiting for him to come back. And when I finally left for college, I promised her that I would carry out her wishes."

Rory licked her lips. "Your mother wanted you to kill Hunter Marks?"

"He destroyed her one true love. The two men she married after that never loved her the way my father did. She depended on me to get her justice."

"You changed your name."

"My mother wanted me to use the name of her second

husband. That way no one could ever connect me with the Marks family."

When he paused to smile at her, Rory did shiver. But she made herself ask, "What is Lea Roberts's connection to all of this?"

Michael shrugged. "She wrote the original story that told the truth about Hunter Marks. I thought she deserved to be able to write the final chapter in Marks's life. But she proved to be incompetent. I'll handle that, just as I'm going to handle you."

Rory felt something hard poke into her side.

"I've got a gun. Get up slowly and smile at me. Then we're going to leave the restaurant. If you try to signal anyone or give me any trouble at all, I'll shoot some of the other customers."

"Don't use the gun," Rory said as she rose. "You haven't killed anyone yet. And Hunter Marks isn't the monster you think he is. He'll help you."

"Shut up." He took her hand and pulled her closer, pressing the gun in his pocket against her side. "Don't you think I know that you're his girlfriend? He'll come after you, and then I'll finish this."

"EVERYONE STAY BACK." Tracker spoke into his mouthpiece. "That includes you," he added to Hunter.

"To hell with that," Hunter said as he got off his stool. "I warned you that he was smart. He wants me, so he's going to get me."

Tracker grabbed his arm. "Let him get out of the building. If he's that smart, he'll know that he can hurt you by killing her."

An icy knot of fear twisted even tighter in Hunter's

stomach as he edged his way through the crowd. It seemed forever before Tracker said, "He's out and moving up the street."

They began to move more quickly then.

"Can you keep your cool?" Tracker asked as they pushed out onto the street.

Hunter nodded. "I'm going to try to reason with him."

Michael and Rory were halfway down the block. Salsa music blared from the patio, so Hunter didn't bother to call out. He just broke into a run. He knew that Tracker had moved into the street on the other side of the parked cars, but Hunter kept his eyes on Rory. He was going to get her back safely.

When he was close enough to be heard, he called out, "Michael, it's me you want."

Michael turned then, but he kept his grip tight on Rory, and Hunter saw that the hand gripping the gun didn't waver. "I want you both."

Hunter raised his hands, palms out and prayed that the reasonable side of Michael Banks's brain was still functioning. "You can't have us both. The man in the street to my right will take you out before you can get a second shot off. It's either me or Rory. Which one would your mother want you to shoot?"

When Michael took his hand out of his pocket and pointed the gun at him, Hunter began to let out the breath he was holding. It caught in his throat when Rory threw all of her weight at Michael Banks and two shots rang out simultaneously.

"IT'S A DAMN MIRACLE you didn't get yourself shot," Hunter said.

"It was luck," Rory corrected. They were seated on the curb down the street from the Blue Pepper with a blanket wrapped around them. She hadn't been able to stop shaking after the shots were fired, so one of the policemen had dug a blanket out of his trunk. It was only after Hunter had joined her beneath the warm folds of cloth that she'd begun to get warm again.

Michael Banks was being loaded into an ambulance. Tracker and Natalie were talking with the detectives who'd arrived on the scene. Two uniformed policemen were encouraging the Blue Pepper patrons to go back inside and enjoy the evening.

Rory blew out a bubble, then sucked it back into her mouth. "My knees are like jelly now. I'm not sure I can walk."

"Yeah. I've got the same feeling in mine. Maybe we'll have to stay here all night. Are you warm enough?" He slid his hand up her side and drew her closer.

"I'm warmer now."

The doors of the ambulance swung shut and Rory said, "I feel sorry for him. He lost his dad, and he had a wacko for a mother."

"Seems that way," Hunter said. "I'm going to hire him a good defense attorney."

She turned to stare at him then. "You're the sweetest man I've ever met. You took the blame for your brother and your father all those years ago because you didn't want anyone to be hurt. Never mind that you lost everything."

Hunter smiled. "I haven't done so badly for myself. And my brother's done a good job with the bank. He told me today that the merchants in the town have rallied behind him to prevent Slade Enterprises's hostile takeover."

"Maybe it's time for the whole story to come out," Rory said.

"That's what Carter would like. But he stonewalled Lea

Roberts because I told him I happen to have this other reporter in mind," Hunter said. "She has good instincts, and I think she'll tell the story well." He lowered his mouth to hers, and then he said against her lips, "I'm going to offer her an exclusive interview if she'll give me just one kiss."

She wanted to laugh, but she was already sinking into the kiss, and his hands became very busy under the blanket. When one of them parted her thighs, she started to protest. "Hunter…"

"Shh," he whispered. "You're wearing the thong." He traced his finger down the little red lace triangle that covered her cleft, and she shuddered.

"I can never look at you without wondering if you're wearing this."

"You have to…" Stop. That was the word she should say, but he was moving his finger over her again, and she could feel her insides heating and melting.

"Do you know how long I've been thinking of doing this? That whole long drive back to D.C. with Tracker." He stroked his finger down her again, and Rory bit down hard on her lip. "And all the time that he and Natalie were prepping you, I was thinking that I just wanted to hold you in my arms like this and make you come."

She had to fight the moan back when he slipped two fingers into her, then curved them and began to rub them on the spot he'd found before.

"You…can't," she whispered.

"Yes, I can," he murmured against her ear. "And I can do this, too." He continued to move his fingers inside of her, while he found her clitoris with his thumb and began to rub that also.

Blending with the murmur of nearby voices and the

sounds of the salsa band at the Blue Pepper, Rory could hear her own breath coming in pants.

"I love to hear you breathe like that. You have no idea what it does to me," Hunter whispered.

A flood of sensations moved through Rory. She had a feeling that they were heightened by the fact that they were seated in the shadows between two parked cars. At any moment, someone could turn and look at them. "We're…on a public street."

She could feel his lips curve against her ear.

"That means you have to be very quiet when you have your orgasm," he said. "And you can't move, either."

She should stop him. But her body had become swamped by the pleasure he was giving her. The fact that she couldn't move, couldn't make a sound sharpened each response that was streaming through her.

As if he could sense the moment that the first wave of the orgasm moved through her, he took her mouth with his while she rode it out. Then he continued to hold her tight even after the last little shock wave passed.

It might have been minutes or hours before Tracker came over and said, "Hey, I've been sent over to break this up. They don't allow necking on one of the main streets of Georgetown."

RORY BLEW OUT A BUBBLE as she stepped off the elevator into the reception area of the offices of *Celebs* magazine. Hattie Miller, a perky blond receptionist who'd always been nice to her, beamed her a smile. "Ms. Gibbs, congratulations on your story."

"Thanks, Hattie." Her story on Hunter Marks, alias Jared Slade, had appeared in an edition of *Vanity Fair* that had hit the newsstands the day before. As she neared the desk, Hattie winked and pitched her voice low. "It's caused quite a stir around here. Some of the suits flew down yesterday from the New York office. Word is that heads are going to roll and you can name your price if you'll come back to work."

"I think Ms. Roberts is expecting me," Rory said.

Hattie nodded. "Yes, sirree. You can go right on back."

Rory walked down the short hallway to Lea's office. On the way, she passed her temporary desk. It looked the same as it had the last time she'd been here—as if it were just waiting for her to return to work.

The phone call from Lea had come that morning shortly after Hunter had left for Dallas on business. It had been thirteen days since Michael Banks had been arrested, and ten days since she'd sold her story to *Vanity Fair*. But the time had flown by, and Hunter had spent more time in Dallas and Oakwood than he'd spent in D.C.

That was beginning to worry her a little. Pausing before the door to Lea's office, Rory drew in a deep breath. She hadn't wanted to agree to meet with Lea. The old Rory never would have. But the new Rory had questions and something to say to her old boss that had to be said in person.

She raised her hand and knocked on the door, and the moment she heard Lea's muffled "Come in," she entered and closed it behind her.

Lea rose from behind her desk, and even though she was impeccably dressed and groomed, she looked older. And tired.

"Congratulations on your story," Lea said stiffly.

"Thank you."

"I don't imagine that my call surprised you."

"As a matter of fact, it did. I can't imagine what you want to talk to me about."

Lea's brows shot up. "You might as well can the act. I know that you're not nearly as naive as you make yourself out to be. The shit pretty much hit the fan yesterday when your story came out. My boss learned that you used to work for me, and he was unhappy that you didn't bring the story to us. When they asked why you weren't working here anymore, I told them you quit."

"I see."

"If you deny that, it will be your word against mine."

"That's why you wanted to talk to me? To tell me that?"

Lea circled her desk and propped a hip on one of the corners. "For starters. I also wanted to see what it was that I'd missed. I'm usually a good judge of people. But you really fooled me. I didn't expect you to double-cross me, and I certainly didn't expect you to sleep with Hunter Marks just to get a story."

Rory lifted her chin. "I'm not surprised that you believe that because that's what you did, didn't you? You had an affair with him in the hopes that it would help your career. And it did."

Lea smiled, but it didn't reach her eyes. "Touché. I guess we're even more alike than I thought."

"No." Rory took a step toward Lea. "I don't think we're alike at all. I would never have written that story ten years ago."

Lea's brows shot up. "It was news. The public had a right to know."

"He was in love with you, and you believed what you wrote, didn't you? You believed that he'd embezzled the money?"

Lea folded her arms across her chest. "Of course, I did. Everyone did."

"Did you even ask him if he was guilty?"

"No. He confessed."

"He needed someone to believe in him."

Lea stared at her for a minute. "Good Lord. Don't tell me. You're in love with him, aren't you?"

Rory felt the heat rise in her cheeks.

Lea started to laugh. "You little fool. Sleeping with him is one thing. But falling in love?" She shook her head. "Maybe I wasn't so wrong about you after all. You can't think that Hunter Marks is going to settle down with someone like you."

Rory said nothing. There was nothing she could say about what Lea was implying. She and Hunter hadn't had time to talk about the future. Or they hadn't made the time. Pushing the nagging worry out of her head, she said, "Why don't you ask me why I agreed to see you?"

Lea's smile faded. "That's easy. You have to know or at least suspect that *Celebs* wants to make you a job offer. I'm authorized to make it a very generous one."

Rory shook her head. "That's not why I came."

"No? Well, if you've come to gloat because you got the story and I didn't, forget it. I may not have broken the Hunter Marks story, but my bosses are pleased that I've landed an exclusive interview with Michael Dennison Banks. My agent is already shopping around for a book deal."

"Congratulations." Rory knew for a fact that Lea was lying through her teeth. Michael Banks's lawyer wasn't letting Michael speak to anyone until the trial was over, and she had the inside track for an interview once the verdict was in. For the first time since she'd walked into the room, she felt a little sorry for Lea Roberts.

"That's not why I agreed to see you, either. I came because I wanted to thank you for hiring me. None of this would have happened if you hadn't had faith in me and given me a chance here at *Celebs*."

Lea merely stared at her. Rory knew as she turned and left the room, she wouldn't forget the stupefied expression on Lea's face for a long time.

Nor would she forget the laughter. It was the second time that Lea Roberts had laughed at her.

So she was a fool if she believed that Hunter Marks would settle down with someone like her, was she?

Ha. She'd just have to see about that.

15

"GOOD LUCK." Irene Malinowitz took one last look around Silken Fantasies and Rory followed her gaze. Natalie was lighting the tall pillar candles that rested on nearly every surface in the store, and Sierra was unpacking the contents of a small picnic hamper and checking each item against a list she held in her hand.

"Not that I think you'll need luck," Irene added as she turned back to smile at Rory. "I think you and your sisters have the plan completely under control. When is he due?"

Rory glanced at her watch, then at her sisters. "Soon. You're sure you don't mind my using your shop?"

Irene smiled. "It's not my shop anymore. I'm just managing it during the transition period. Jared—I mean, Hunter—convinced me to stay on for a while. Besides—" Irene paused to wink at Rory "—you can't spend a large part of your life in the lingerie business unless you're a true romantic at heart. Have fun." She leaned closer. "And I hope you're planning on making good use of some of the merchandise."

Rory smiled at her. "Thanks. I've already picked up several of your red thongs. You were right that first time I came here. I've been getting pretty good mileage out of them."

"Good," Irene said. "I'll just let myself out the back way."

Rory watched as Irene slipped through a curtain behind the sales counter. Then she gave her gum two quick chews and blew out a bubble.

"Everything is here," Sierra said as she tucked her list back into her canvas bag.

Natalie lit the last candle. "When exactly is Hunter due to arrive?"

Rory glanced at her watch. "Any minute."

Sierra put the final touch on a tray of chocolate-covered strawberries, then turned to survey the rest of the room. "I think this is so romantic—to return here."

"Desperate times call for desperate measures."

Natalie frowned. "Desperate? I thought everything was going well between the two of you."

"Everything is just…" Rory blew out another bubble, then licked the burst bits of gum off her bottom lip. "It's just that… Things have been… For the past two weeks, since Michael Banks was arrested, we've both been so…"

"You've been busy," Sierra said.

"Yes." They had been busy. When she'd sold her story to *Vanity Fair,* the magazine had wanted a follow-up on the whole Marks family in Oakwood. And Hunter had been swamped, too, flying back and forth from D.C. to Dallas. They'd both gone to Oakwood when Carter's wife had delivered the twins. Rory shrugged and took the bubble gum out of her mouth. "We just haven't spent much time…" She waved a hand. "You know…"

"Alone together," Natalie finished for her. "In other words, you're sex starved."

Rory smiled. "Well, there's that. He's been gone for two days. Although we usually manage to fit in making love—sometimes in the oddest…" She thought of sitting on the street in Georgetown between those two parked cars.

"Places." Sierra finished the sentence this time as she stepped forward to take Rory's hands. "Have you told him yet that you love him?"

Rory felt a familiar jolt of panic and wished that she hadn't gotten rid of her gum. "No."

"Tell him," Sierra suggested.

"I'm planning on doing that tonight. But he has a way of distracting me."

"You'll do just fine," Natalie said.

Rory swallowed hard. "What if he doesn't want to hear it?" The panic had morphed from a jolt to an earthquake in her stomach. "What if he…?"

Natalie patted her shoulder when her sentence once more trailed off. "I'm in thorough agreement with Sierra on this one. Just tell him."

There was a knock at the door.

"Speak of the devil," Natalie said as she leaned down to kiss Rory's cheek. "We'll exit through the back door the way Irene did."

Sierra hugged her and whispered, "Remember Harry's advice. You can do anything you want if you just dare to take a shot at it."

There was another knock as her sisters disappeared through the curtain. Rory straightened her shoulders, turned toward the front door and reviewed her game plan. Two simple steps. First tell him and then seduce him.

She took one last look around the room as she walked to the door of the shop. Pushing her luck had never seemed this important before.

The moment she opened the door and saw Hunter, her

.

plan began to fade from her mind. He was dressed just as he'd been the first time she'd seen him in that lobby—sunglasses, black leather jacket, black boots, black jeans. Her Terminator and fantasy man all rolled into one.

HE'D HAD A PLAN. When she'd left him the voice-mail message to meet her at Silken Fantasies, the idea had sprung full-blown into his mind, and on the three-hour plane trip from Dallas he'd had plenty of time to hammer out the details. He'd even stopped at a jewelry store on the way from the airport.

But seeing her now, wearing the same clothes she'd worn in the lobby of Les Printemps…those damn red boots had his throat going dry. And he knew she was wearing the thong. Would it always be this way? Hunter wondered. Would she always stir up needs in him until his whole body pounded with them?

"Hi," he said.

"You brought me flowers."

He glanced down at the bunch of daffodils he'd picked up on impulse from the stand at the end of the street. He'd completely forgotten about them. "Here."

She took the flowers and looked at them as if they were dozens of red roses. Stepping into the shop, he shut the door behind himself and locked it. "I had this plan. I worked it out on the airplane." Perhaps if he stopped looking at her for a moment, his brain cells would resuscitate and he'd be able to remember it.

"Me, too," she said. "I mean about the plan. I had one."

He managed to tear his gaze away from her long enough to take in the candles, the champagne and the tray of food, and his heart took another tumble. "I think I'm going to like it."

"You are. But I'm already thinking it needs revision."

She moved to him, placed her hands on his cheeks and drew his mouth to hers. "Because right now I want to make love to you in that dressing room."

"Yeah," he managed to say as he gripped her hips and raised her so that she could wrap her legs around him. "We can do that." When she began to rain kisses on his eyelids, his cheeks, his neck, his mouth, he stumbled and wondered if he was going to make it. But he did.

"Clothes," he said as he pushed her through the door. She was already unbuttoning his shirt. "Let's lose them."

"Right." She allowed him to pry her legs loose. Then they went to work on what still separated them. Flesh to flesh was what he had to have. Her skin, already hot and damp, made his mouth water and his fingers fumble. Shirts, jeans, boots fell to the floor until finally, he was naked and she was wearing only the red thong. He could see all of her in the three-way mirror. Images of the first time they'd made love flooded his mind, and desire hardened every muscle in his body.

"One kiss." He barely recognized his own voice. "One kiss." That's what had started it all. But when he reached for her, she placed a hand on his chest.

"Time for another revision. Lie down on that bench."

He glanced at it in the mirror. "It's small."

"It'll be fine, but we have to move it first," she said, grabbing the end and angling it in front of the three-way glass. "Now, sit down on it."

He was never going to be able to predict her, Hunter thought as he sat down on the bench. His own plan had involved making love to her slowly, thoroughly, building the pleasure, layer by layer. Then when she was fresh from his loving, he would take out the jeweler's box.

"No. You have to sit back farther." When he complied, she straddled him on the bench, placing one knee on either side of his hips. His breath backed up and burned in his lungs when she rubbed her damp heat against his erection, and his fantasy of how the evening was going to go evaporated in the wake of the desperate need she was creating. All the urgency that had exploded in him when he'd first stepped into the shop bubbled up again.

"Now," he said as twin urges battled inside of him. He wanted to drag her mouth to his for that kiss. But his hands went to her hips instead. He couldn't get a handle on his hunger. He had to be inside of her.

"Look in the mirror," she urged as he dug his fingers in and lifted her. "Watch me take you in."

Hunter's head began to spin as he did what she demanded. He could see everything. As he lifted her a bit higher, he saw her reach down to move the thong aside and then he watched the two people in the mirror as he pushed himself into her and felt that wet searing heat grip him. He had to close his eyes then as bright explosions of pleasure ripped through him.

"Watch. Keep watching," she said as they both began to move.

And he did. The two figures in the mirror seemed to be two other people there in the room with them, matching their movements stroke for stroke. The woman had thrown her head back, and her nails were digging into the man's shoulders as she raised and then lowered herself to take him in again and again. He felt like a voyeur at the same time that he was experiencing everything he was seeing. The added thrill brought a dark, erotic edge to the feelings streaming through him.

"Hurry," she said.

He managed to drag in a breath as he turned his gaze back to Rory. Her slim, strong body moving faster now.

"Hurry. Hurry."

She filled his vision as his body responded to her commands. He thrust himself into her, feeling helpless and powerful at the same time. She obsessed him. Possessed him.

His mind and vision had begun to blur when she raised her head and gripped his in her hands. Then her eyes fastened on his.

"Come with me, Hunter. I love you."

Something snapped inside of him then, and he allowed everything that was him to pour into her.

WHEN RORY OPENED HER EYES, she saw that they weren't on the bench anymore. She was sitting on Hunter's lap in much the same position they'd ended up in the first time that they'd made love. She didn't want to move. She wasn't even sure she could.

But the seconds turned into minutes. She could feel his heartbeat slow under her ear, and he still wasn't saying anything. She'd told him she loved him. Not the way she'd planned, but she'd said the words.

When she couldn't bear the suspense of the silence any longer, she said, "Wow."

He ran a hand down her back. "I can second that. That was some revision. And it's all your fault that it was wham-bam."

"Sometimes I like wham-bam."

"Me, too. What was your original plan?"

Raising her head, she met his eyes. "I was going to strip for you, very slowly, all the time luring you back into this dressing room."

"Well, we sort of did that, just in fast-forward, and I helped with the stripping."

"The bench was something I thought up on the spur of the moment," she said. *But before I did all that I was going to tell you that I love you,* she thought. He hadn't said anything about that. Maybe he hadn't heard her.

"The bench was a very nice touch. You're beginning to convince me that even the best plans are meant to be revised."

Distracted by the compliment, she said, "No kidding?"

"I had a plan, too," he murmured as he leaned down to drop a kiss on her bare shoulder. "I was going to seduce you slowly—very slowly. And then when you were still weak and thinking only of me, I was going to show you something."

"What?"

"Are you weak and thinking only of me?"

She pretended to consider that for a moment. "Close enough."

He reached for his jeans and dug something out of his pocket.

Rory felt a tightness around her heart when she saw the small velvet box. A jeweler's box.

"Aren't you going to take it and open it?" he asked.

Her hand trembled when she did, and she nearly dropped the box when she saw the ring. "Wow…I mean…I didn't expect…" She met his eyes and then hurriedly glanced back down at the ring—a diamond surrounded by tiny rubies. "I…I need some bubble gum."

It wasn't the reaction he'd expected, but then when had she ever reacted the way he'd expected? He dug into his jeans again and pulled out two pieces of bubble gum and unwrapped them. The suspense, the uncertainty, had tied his own stomach into knots. Together, they chewed in silence for a while.

Rory blew the first bubble and licked it off her lips. "A ring. I wasn't expecting it." Rory pressed a hand against her stomach. "The gum isn't working."

Hunter tried a bubble. No, it wasn't, he thought as the knot of nerves in his stomach tightened. He turned her then on his lap and drew her chin up so that her eyes met his. "Look. I know you might feel that it's sudden. And I know we haven't talked about the future. But we've been spending so much time apart lately, and I don't like it. I want you with me. I want to start something with you. I—" For the first time in years, Hunter felt at a complete loss. He had to find the words and he wasn't sure he could. "Did you mean what you said while we were making love?"

Rory drew in a deep breath and let it out. "Yes. I love you."

The knot began to loosen. "Look, for years I didn't have a family. I didn't think I'd ever want one. But you helped me find them again." He paused again to search for the right words. "I want you with me when I'm old."

Her gaze remained steady on his. "Why?"

His lips curved into a smile, despite his jangled emotions. "A tough question."

"Uh-huh."

"Because I love you, too."

Rory took the ring out of the box, handed it to him and extended her hand. When he slipped it on, she said, "I want to be with you when we're old, too. I'll bet that by then you'll have no problem making love to me very slowly."

They were both laughing as he rolled her beneath him on the floor.

"Complaints. Always complaints," Hunter said as he made a place for himself between her legs. "I think I'll just have to work on my technique."

"For a very, very long time," Rory said as she took him in.

*Natalie and Rory have both found
their happily-ever-afters.
Now it's Sierra's turn.
Don't miss* Risking It All *by Cara Summers,
part of the irresistible* Satisfy *anthology.
Available next month.*

Kiss & Run

BARBARA DALY

Dear Reader,

Speaking as one who has an out-the-car-window relationship with cows, I can easily see how life as a big-animal veterinary surgeon in rural Vermont could have its limitations, even if you had eleven cats to keep you company. So I understood why Cecily Connaught would view an obligatory wedding weekend in Dallas as her time to break out, have a fling with a stranger. Nor was it difficult to imagine that Will Murchison, no matter how much he wants to be Cecily's weekend fling, could get a little distracted by the missing groom, his client, whom he suspects of tax evasion.

But how can these two encounter a host of problems, conflicting life goals and continual interruption and still manage to fall in love, all in twenty-four hours? Read on...

Cheers!

Barbara Daly

PS Share your twenty-four-hour romance story with me at bdalybooks@aol.com.

In loving memory for my own Cecily, who gave her family sixteen years of pure pleasure and unconditional love.

1

"KEEP THE CHANGE."

"But lady, it's a—"

"Smallest the ATM had." Cecily Connaught got a grip on her luggage, leaped out of the taxi and ran hell-for-leather into the church foyer, narrowly avoiding collision with a person hauling a chicken-wire structure out of a florist's van. Once inside, she halted for a moment, dizzied by the whirlwind of activity that surrounded her.

"Cecily, is that you?" Elaine Shipley's eyes were wide as she darted toward Cecily.

"Now is not the time for chit-chat," said a woman wearing peach who followed closely behind Elaine. "You're late," she told Cecily.

"At least she's here," said Elaine, "which is more than I can say for—"

"Now is not the time for gossip," said the woman in peach. "Get out of those shoes and put these on."

"But—" Apparently now was also not the time for protests. Someone took the bags out of her hands, sat her down, stripped off her comfortable, clunky sandals and slid her feet into a pair of mother-of-pearl satin stilettos—instant Misery by Manolo.

"You must rehearse in the shoes," Miss Peach said firmly, hauling Cecily to her feet. "We don't want any klutziness going down the aisle tomorrow. Now that you're here we have to get started," she muttered. "I don't give a damn who else is missing."

She got a tourniquet-strength hold on Cecily's arm and rushed her over to a group of women. Cecily took one look at them and segued from dazed to fashion-panicked. They were perfectly made up and coiffed and were wearing cute little skirts, short but not too short, that showed off endless, thin, tanned legs and were topped with belly shirts that revealed flat, tanned tummies. In the long, droopy bachelor's-button-printed sundress she'd bought at the Blue Hill Thrift Shop when Vermont had an unprecedented heat wave and it got too hot for jeans, she was hands down the worst dressed among them. Her careless appearance explained Elaine Shipley's wide eyes. If Cecily's mother had been there, she would have died of shame.

But then, her mother had vegetated into a person who was incapable of understanding any choice Cecily made, especially her choice to be a veterinarian instead of a—fashion designer, maybe?

"The maid of honor," Miss Peach said with a note of triumph in her voice, "is present and accounted for."

A dark-haired beauty at the center of the group, whirled, and her eyes widened just as her mother's had. "Cecily? Cecily!" she said and pulled Cecily into a bear hug.

The bride, Sally Shipley, daughter of Elaine, was dressed even more sedately than her entourage and even more perfectly pulled together. Cecily got as far as saying, "Sally, it's been a long—" before Miss Peach, who had to be the wedding planner, interrupted.

"No time for reminiscence." Much like a gravel truck, she scooped up all of them and hustled them down the aisle, shoving them into place. "Leave a space," she said to Cecily. "The matron of honor hasn't shown up yet. Reverend Justice," she commanded the cleric who already stood facing an imaginary crowd, "go for it. I'll bring in the others when they choose to grace us with their presence." Her voice dripped annoyance.

The bride grabbed her groom by the elbow. "This is Gus," she whispered to Cecily.

Cecily held out a hand. "Nice to meet—"

"No introductions *now*." Miss Peach practically yelled the words, then sprinted up the aisle.

Sally meekly turned toward the minister, who intoned, "Dearly beloved…"

Feeling dizzy and disoriented, Cecily shifted her weight from one aching foot to the other. The rest of the wedding party might be dearly beloved by each other, but she wasn't even dearly beloved by the bride, whose maid of honor she'd foolishly agreed to be. *Barely remembered* was more like it.

But however reluctant to be in the wedding of a woman she hadn't been friends with since they were five years old, she now had a mission, one she could start on while the wedding party was…

"…gathered here today to share with Sally and Gus that most sacred moment when they join their lives in holy—"

Hell. Marriage was such a crock. It was a mistake Cecily didn't intend to make. She'd never do what her mother had done—give up a career to marry a man who largely ignored her.

Her father. He didn't understand Cecily's choices, either, the only difference being that he didn't particularly care. He loved only one thing, making…

"…that most honored of all commitments, most binding of all vows, to love, honor and cherish…"

…news in the academic world by writing brilliant papers in his field, finance. Her mother had wanted her to be a socialite. Her father had wanted her to go into marketing. No wonder she'd chosen to hang with cows.

Cecily took a deep, calming breath. She was in a bad mood because her mother had conned her into accepting Sally's maid-of-honor position. Because she'd had to get up at four this morning in the frosty cold of May in Vermont to make it to the searing heat of May in Dallas for the rehearsal. But most of all because the four-inch heels with long, witchy toes were killing her feet. Not even a mature, professional woman, a large-animal vet, for heaven's sake, could go from thirty degrees to ninety-plus, from Teva sandals to torture devices, and still stay grounded.

But as Sally's maid of honor, she had to act nice. She'd always acted nice, and this was no time for a personality change. Besides, this was merely the rehearsal. Sally, who was doing the wedding two-step for the second time around—as if the disastrous first time hadn't taught her a lesson—still had twenty-four hours to come to her senses. With any luck, Cecily might be able to kiss these shoes goodbye after one wearing.

And she had her mission to accomplish. There'd once been a boy who might have changed her mind about love and marriage, and with any luck at all, he was here right now, standing in the line of groomsmen winging out behind Gus. Through pure serendipity, this weekend might be her second chance with him. She zeroed in on the last groomsman in the line.

He had bleached light blond hair cut short and charmingly disheveled. Blue eyes. Stone-colored chinos—Hugo Boss. White polo shirt—Calvin Klein. Burgundy loafers—Gucci—no socks. She knew the designers because the logo was visible on each piece of clothing. He was cute but definitely not Will Murchison. Too bad.

It wasn't that she was hoping she and Will would fall in love and start planning their own wedding. Now that she was a sensible, career-oriented adult, she was determined never to marry, never to make the mistake her mother had made, giving up her own career in business to follow her father from one university position to a better one. All Cecily wanted was a weekend fling with a boy—a man by now— she had, for some odd reason, never quite forgotten.

The memory had come back like the crash of waves on the shore when she had finally, on the plane this morning, looked at the wedding itinerary and seen Will's name on the list of groomsmen. That boy's name was Will Murchison. She'd heard him say he was from Dallas, and until the afternoon in the groundskeeper's cottage, the most exciting thing he'd ever said to her was, "I rode her pretty hard. Give her a good rubdown, okay?"

He'd been talking about a horse. He was a senior at Exeter, the prestigious boys' school, while she was a senior at a day school in Boston and, because she was already intrigued by the idea of being a veterinarian, worked weekends at the stables where he rode.

She hadn't said more than two words to him. She might have opened a conversation by telling him she'd been born in Dallas, for heaven's sake. She might have mentioned that her parents still had friends there. She might have dropped the names of those friends, looking for a connection, and they would probably have found one. But no. She was too shy, too awed by him, to do anything but goggle and occasionally stammer, "You're welcome," because he always said, "Thanks," with a smile that shot heat through her from head to toe.

She eyed Groomsman Number Three, looking for that sexy smile. Blue eyes. Khaki chinos—Calvin Klein. Yellow polo shirt—Lacoste. Sandals—more Gucci. No socks, naturally. Was it possible his hair had blond highlights? But no sexy smile. He wasn't Will, either. The odds were diminishing.

Will had usually been surrounded by a gaggle of horse-crazy, man-crazy girls, but that stormy afternoon when she'd been sent out to find him on the trail and lead him to shelter, they'd been alone, and he'd tried to kiss her. Instead of accepting a dream come true and kissing him back, whatever the cost, she'd fled out into the storm. The school year had ended and she'd never seen him again. And nobody like him—oozing with an overabundance of adolescent testosterone and still kind and mature for his age—had come along to take his place.

She looked over the second groomsman. Dirty-blond hair and *green* eyes. The sunglasses perched on top of his head had the Gucci logo on the earpiece. He wore running gear that was covered in logos and sweat and, like her, he wasn't paying attention to the minister. He was too absorbed in his cool-down stretches.

All the groomsmen had fashion-victim facial hair, Numbers Three and Four with cheeks unshaven and Number Two with a manicured goatee.

They all looked alike, but none of them looked in the least like the Will she remembered. Murchison was an important Texas name. There might be dozens of Will Murchisons. Now disappointment washed through her. But in front of Groomsman Number Two was a wide, empty space. The wedding planner had said something about people missing. There was still hope.

Faint hope. Will had come into her life a gazillion years ago, but she hadn't been able to stop herself from thinking *what if*. What if she'd let him kiss her? The psychiatrist her mother had forced her to see had said she was using the memory of him as an excuse not to get involved with anyone else and had suggested in a most un-Freudian way that Cecily should *get over it*.

Obedient as always, she had. She was happy with her life's plan—a successful career and a succession of lovers. The career part was going fine. As for the succession of lovers, she was tanking. And that, of course, was why she'd been so excited to see Will's name on the roster of wedding attendants.

If they connected this weekend, there was always the possibility she might be able to use the opportunity to catch up on her sex life. It wasn't shoes, sleepiness or submission to her mother's will after all, she decided. It was her deprived and complaining libido that had put her in a bad mood.

But what if Will did show up among the missing? Why hadn't she spent a little time in New York checking out current fashion and then bought some of it? And some decent underwear! She shuddered just thinking about the white cotton bras and panties she bought three to a pack at the Ben Franklin store in Blue Hill, Vermont. This might be her chance to…

"...embark on that ship of love that will sail them to the shores of supreme happiness..."

...and she wasn't prepared! She cast another glance at the beautiful bridesmaids, the gorgeous groomsmen. These were Will's type of people. She sighed. She didn't have a chance.

At least the church was pretty—St. Andrews, favored for weddings by Dallas brides, Cecily's mother had told her. The early afternoon Texas sun shone through the stained-glass windows, tinting the bridesmaids' pale shoes petal pink and bathing their sharp-featured faces with a rosy glow. The scent of vetiver-scented soaps and aftershave drifted in Cecily's direction from the collection of groomsmen, while light, summery perfumes emanated from the bridesmaids, as though to compete with the flowers that would soon fill the church.

It was an exquisite scene, but not a serene one. The chaos continued, even increased in motion and volume. Miss Peach dispatched her army of minions hither and yon. A photographer fiddled with lights and tripods in the balcony overlooking the sanctuary. The good-looking man scribbling on a pad must be a reporter. Sally's mother stood at the back of the church, wringing her hands. Of course, three members of the wedding party were missing the rehearsal, and Gus— tall, broad-shouldered, as heavily muscled as an ox and at the moment, looking tense—appeared capable of murdering all of them. She hoped Sally hadn't married the Mob. Cecily supposed that was enough to make a mother of the bride wring her hands.

Listening to the minister drone on, sounding as if even he didn't believe a word he was saying, she swallowed a yawn of the most graceless magnitude.

It was too bad she'd known Sally since they were tiny, adorable babies in breathtakingly expensive dresses, Sally looking like a dark-haired devil, Cecily a blond angel—not that Cecily remembered, but her mother had sent a packet of pictures to jog her memory. It was also too bad that Sally, known to be the wild child in her group of friends—a fact sorrowfully confided by her mother to Cecily's mother—would suddenly reveal her sentimental streak and invite her *first* friend rather than her *best* friend to be her maid of honor.

Even in an unaccustomed fit of sentimentality, how could inviting Cecily to be in the wedding have crossed Sally's mind? By the time they were five their interests had taken them in different directions—Sally to ballet, Cecily to horseback riding. That, plus the fact that Cecily's father had moved from Southern Methodist University to Purdue, the first of a string of moves, meant she and Sally hadn't been close friends since they were five and hadn't seen each other since they were sixteen.

But through all those moves, Cecily's mother had never lost a friend. Thus it was embarrassingly possible she had suggested to Sally's mother that since Sally was dead set on leaving her wild reputation behind when she married Gus, inviting her first friend to be her maid of honor would convey that impression— something the wedding reporter might pick up on.

Cecily had tried saying no, that she couldn't leave Vermont during calving season. Her mother, who'd joined the Mothers in Support of Offspring Guilt Club upon moving to New York, had called to say weepily, "Don't you care about anything but cows? Can't you give a passing thought to your family and—"

"...friends are here to witness their vows and share their happiness as they embark upon..."

A dangerous sea in a rickety boat. That's what marriage was. But Cecily had capitulated, although she hadn't been happy about it.

"Do you, Gus Hargrove, take Sally Shipley to be..."

If Will appeared, if he showed even the slightest flicker of interest, she'd take him in a New York minute! As far as she could tell, an available, compatible man didn't exist in Blue Hill or points nearby. To require the services of a large-animal vet, a man apparently had to be married, preferably a long time, therefore both married and old. She worked so hard that these were the only men she came in contact with—plus Dr. Vaughn, of course, but not only was he older and more married than any of his clients, Maddie Vaughn had become Cecily's surrogate mother. So the part of the plan that involved having a string of casual lovers had reached desperation point. She hadn't had a date, much less sex, for three years.

A long, steamy twenty-four hours in Dallas stretched in front of her like an invitation to wild and uninhibited behavior. No one in Blue Hill would ever know that their own Dr. Connaught, respected veterinarian, was a tightly leashed tigress inside.

"I do," Gus said.

"Instead of the traditional vows, Sally will read a poem she wrote in honor of this, the most important event in her life."

"Your eyes delight me," Sally began in a Miss America voice, gazing passionately into Gus's eyes, which shifted away uneasily. "Your lips excite me," she continued, and Gus's mouth tightened. "Your love ignites me..."

Oh, for chrissakes. Sally's father should have hired somebody to write that poem. Maybe he had. A very bad poet. Mr. Shipley should ask for his money back, because—

"Sorry, sorry, sorry." The voice came like thunder from the back of the church, and Cecily whirled against an imminent lightning bolt.

"Will!" Sally shrieked. "You're late, you turkey. Where's Muffy?"

"She didn't make it. She's having the baby. I need help. *Fast.*"

Mrs. Shipley's moan was audible from the back of the church.

Cecily felt as if she might moan, too. Eros had shot an arrow straight to her crotch. One look at Will and her heart had dropped to the tips of her unpedicured, possibly not even clean, toenails. God help her, had he ever aged well.

Memories flooded back as he gave Sally a warm hug and Gus a manly slap on the shoulder. That hair, short and tousled now, the silky red-brown of a fine Santa Gertrudis bull. His shoulders had actually broadened and they held up a loose-fitting, short-sleeved white polo shirt that showed off muscled arms and a spectacular tan. Stone-colored pants hung casually off tight buns. The pants had a logo across one pocket. It said Ralph Lauren.

As he talked to Sally, Cecily got a profile view of his eyelashes, as long as the bridesmaids' skirts. Unlike the groomsmen, his only facial hair was his thick, glossy chestnut eyebrows. Not a fashion victim, even if he was wearing pants with a logo, which she'd forgive.

A shiver ran down her thighs. She felt hot and wet, and swayed rhythmically from a sudden attack of heavy, dreamy lethargy. Here he was, the prize bull of her dreams, and she'd lassoed him too late. He wasn't merely married, he was about to be a daddy.

She wanted to burst into loud sobs.

"Call the po-po," chirped the bridesmaid with the perfect navel. Cecily swiveled to stare at her. She'd meant 911, surely.

Will swiveled, too. "I did that already. I'm telling you the baby's coming *right now,* in my car, in the church parking lot!" He raised his voice to include everybody in the church. "Is there a doctor in the house? Anybody with medical experience or first aid—"

"Cecily," Sally said, grabbing her arm and pushing her toward this frantic Will person. "Cecily can deliver the baby."

"Cecily?" Will said in a suddenly hushed voice, and his gaze locked directly on her. "From the Green Trails Stable?" His hazel eyes glinted with gold and they were filled with some emotion Cecily didn't care to explore. She hated to think what her eyes were saying to him.

It was more than she could bear. Cecily spun away from those marvelous eyes to hiss at Sally. "No, I can't. I'm a vet, not a—"

"Don't tell Muffy," Sally snarled back.

"Cecily Connaught," Will went on in that distracted voice. "I can't believe it really is you. After all these—"

He'd remembered her name, her entire name. Cecily leaned toward Sally's ear, anything to keep from looking at Will. "It might even be illegal."

Sally practically spat into Cecily's opposite ear. "Muffy's a bitch. You're a vet. What's illegal?" Then she wheeled them both into positions flanking Will. "How nice you've already met. Get going."

Mrs. Shipley sped forward, wringing her hands even more violently. "But Sally—"

"Chill, Mama."

"So, you've become a doctor?" Will didn't seem inclined to move.

"Catch up on old times later! Have you forgotten the baby? This is an emergency!" Sally sounded a lot like Miss Peach.

"Right," Will said, taking his eyes off Cecily at last. "It *is* an emergency." Suddenly purposeful, he grabbed Cecily while Sally—the snake—slithered back up to the altar and Mrs. Shipley shrank into a pew and sank limply onto the cushion. "All of you stay here," Cecily said over her shoulder quite unnecessarily, since nobody seemed to be rushing forward to help, either from the wedding party or the mob in the foyer. "The fewer spectators, the better." Her words trailed away on the breeze she and Will made as he propelled her through the foyer crowd and out the doors of the chapel into the glaring sun. "Wait a minute, wait a minute—"

"We don't have a minute." He sounded grim.

"My bag's in the church foyer. I need it."

Cecily felt the jolt when he halted. "You brought your medical bag to the wedding rehearsal?"

"Had to come here straight from the airport. I never travel without it." She spared a second to wonder why. Had she thought a horse might turn up in first class needing a tracheotomy?

"Oh." They reversed direction and he whizzed her back into the church, where she swooped down and gripped the bag without losing speed, and then they were off again toward the parking lot, racing past limousines, the florist's van and enough BMWs to start up a dealership.

Her shoes weren't made for running. She was in agony. "Has it been a normal pregnancy?" she said, thinking ahead.

"Far as I know."

"Full term?"

"Apparently. The baby is coming."

It was clear he hadn't taken the proper interest in his wife's pregnancy. Maybe he'd grown up to be one of those men who only *looked* good. But oh, wow, did he ever look good.

"Here she is." He flung open the back door of a still-running luxurious gray sedan. A blast of icy air emerged along with a piercing scream.

"*Where have you been?* I'm about to drop a baby all by myself onto a church parking lot from the back seat of a freaking car!"

Together Cecily and Will leaned into the car. Cecily was shoulder to shoulder with the muscles, hip to hip with the tight buns, smelling the scent of a deliciously clean, very hot man. He turned to her with a desperate glance. They were nose to nose, eye to eye, and Eros was shooting arrows like a madman, zigzags that shot down through the center of her body. *Move over, Muffy, I'm the one who needs the back seat of this car.*

She felt the heat rise to her face. It had been an inappropriate thought, and fortunately no more than a thought. Will was looking at Muffy now, oblivious to anything other than the crisis at hand.

"Muffy." She could tell he was trying to be firm, but his voice wasn't totally steady. "I said let's go to the hospital, you said it was a false alarm, you said—"

Cecily whacked him on the elbow and, wonder of wonders, he got the message.

"Here's the doctor," he said, calm now and very gentle. "She'll take care of you."

Muffy raised herself up on one elbow and left off screaming long enough to puff a few times and then say, "You don't *look* like a doctor. Have you ever delivered a baby?"

"Many," Cecily said, taking a second out to put her hand on Muffy's flailing one, trying to make a connection with the woman before they got to the hard part. It worked with cows and horses in distress. Maybe it worked with bitches. "Keep up your breathing while I prep."

"Forget prep. Wash your hands and get on with it!" A long, pitiful wail emerged from a wide, carnivorous mouth as another contraction consumed her.

Cecily glanced at her big, chunky, utilitarian watch, starting to time the contractions. "Breathe, that's right, breathe. Puff, puff, puff…" She dived into her bag, wincing at the sight of the huge syringes, the Veterinary Purposes Only medications and the oversized forceps, got out the antibacterial wash, poured it over her hands and slid them into sterile gloves, then slid a sterile apron over her sundress. "I'm doing a quick exam. Don't push." In spite of herself, she'd said it pretty sharply, because Muffy was pushing like mad.

"Are…you…*insane?*" Muffy's words came out sporadically between puffs of breath. "If I don't push, how the hell am I going to get this thing out of me?"

Cecily reflected on the advantages of delivering calves. No cow had ever mooed at her in that tone of voice. Nor had she ever delivered a calf with the bull running around in tight little circles, clutching a cell phone to his ear. Nor had she ever lusted after the bull, but that was another story. Soothing, that was what she had to be. Calm and soothing. "If everything's fine, I'll tell you to push. Just hold back for a minute, okay? You," she said to the father-to-be, "hold her hand, help her with her breathing."

"Yeah, sure, that will do a lot of good, him holding my hand, helping me with my breathing. He tried to *smother* me once. Tell him to go away. He's making me dizzy."

"What do you mean *if* everything's fine?" That was Will, looking for something else to worry about.

"I want to be sure the head's coming this way, not the hooves."

"The *what?*" Muffy rose up on her elbows.

"A doctor joke," Cecily said, still struggling for calm and soothing. "I meant the feet, of course."

A loud shriek came from Muffy. A deep moan came from Will.

"The mother is often not herself during delivery," Cecily murmured to Will. "Don't take it personally."

"She *is* herself," Will said. "Muffy's a hater. Just deliver the baby, okay?"

"Righto," Cecily said, wondering if Will's marriage might be destined to end in divorce. Probably not. Men gravitated to bitches, confident in their ability to tame them. The worst of her lust attack was over, dimmed by the harrowing excitement of the impending birth as well as awareness of the futility of lusting after Will.

A sigh rose from deep inside her anyway. Oh, well, if she'd found Will too late to have his baby, she could sure as heck deliver it.

She didn't have time or the equipment to do an episiotomy. But Muffy was fully dilated and the baby was crowning, Cecily noted with great relief. "Now you can push," she told Muffy. "That's right, push, push, almost there. Come on, you're a trooper, you can do it—"

Simultaneously Muffy screamed at the top of her lungs and the baby came into the world with a healthy cry. "It's a girl!" Cecily said, swiftly clamping and cutting the umbilical cord, hoping the navel would equal the bridesmaid's in beauty and symmetry. And as the sound of sirens drowned out Muffy's shuddering sobs of relief, Cecily added, "A beautiful little girl and a fire truck, a police car…no, three police cars and—oh, wonderful—here at last are the EMTs, just when we need them least."

Cecily examined the baby while the paramedics gently lifted Muffy onto a stretcher and carried her toward the ambulance, ignoring the blistering she was giving them for taking so long to get there. Then Cecily handed over the child, explaining the conditions of the delivery as well as giving them a verbal checklist of what she had and hadn't done. At long last, the ambulance doors closed and blessed silence prevailed.

Alone in the parking lot, Cecily pulled off her gloves and apron, then wiped her forehead. She hadn't seen Will leave with Muffy, but he must have. A tear of regret dripped down her face and landed on the toe of one satin shoe, matching the splash of antiseptic on the other. Then she caught sight of another pair of shoes.

Loafers—Gucci. No socks. Her gaze traveled upward…on Will, who lay slumped against a tire.

She'd always heard this happened—new mother did fine and new father fainted—but she'd thought it was an amusing contemporary myth. Apparently not. She crouched down beside him. "Will. Will!" She grabbed his hands and began to massage his wrists with her thumbs, then took his pulse.

"What happened?" He sounded groggy, but he was apparently alive.

"The baby came."

"Oh. Good."

Cecily stifled an exasperated sound. "It's a girl."

"Mmm."

She raised her voice. "Mother and child are doing *fine*."

"I wish I were."

She'd had it. "Look," she said, thinking how wonderful it was not to need a verbal bedside manner in veterinary medicine, "your relationship with Muffy is none of my business, but this is one of those times you have to rise above your differences and support her. A woman who's just given birth feels very vulnerable. She needs you now." Cecily stood up. "So get your ass in gear. We're going to the hospital to see her, and I mean right this second."

She glared at him.

He stared at her.

"I'll drive," she said with a confidence she didn't feel. "Last thing in the world I would have expected you to be, but it seems you're a fainter."

He didn't look the least bit guilty about his disinterest, just puzzled. Still staring at her, he went around the car—Cecily noticed the distinctive Audi emblem—got in on the passenger side and maneuvered the seat so far back she couldn't see his face out of the corner of her eye.

But she could feel his eyes on her and allowed herself one sidelong glance at him as she adjusted the rearview mirror. God, he was sexy. Everything about him said male, male, *male*. His mouth was full and enticing. His eyes were hot. Suddenly feeling overwhelmed, she pushed the key into the ignition.

He settled his sunglasses into place, hiding whatever message his eyes might have been sending, so she could let herself imagine that his gaze was an approving one, could feel it wash over her like warm honey.

Honey, but no crumpet. One look at Will and she'd fallen for him again. This time she was drippily, stickily in lust with a married man.

2

WILL SETTLED INTO THE LEATHER upholstery of his new car, wondering what the hell was going on. Cecily had miraculously dropped into his life again after many, many years, and all she seemed able to think about was his and Muffy's relationship.

Maybe Sally had told her about Muffy. He'd never mentioned her at the stables, and for good reason. When they were growing up, he and Muffy had gotten along about as well as a Maine coon cat and a Yorkshire terrier, he being the terrier. It was one of the reasons their parents had sent him to Exeter. They'd thought it was time to get Will out from under her thumb.

It had worked, too. They were doing much better as adults. They hadn't sunk to physical violence since they were twenty-seven or so, although Muffy had been telling the truth when she'd said he'd tried to smother her once. When they were kindergarten age, he'd put a plastic bag over her head and attempted to tie it around her throat while she was sleeping. He'd done it because she'd sneered at him and said he'd never be popular in the neighborhood because he was about as exciting as phonics. He'd felt like killing her.

Not really. A thinking man, even at that early age,

he'd poked holes in the bag before he shoved it over her head. He'd just wanted to send the message, *Make fun of me again and you're toast*.

Muffy hadn't seen it that way.

When they were seven, their parents had taken them on a short car trip to the mountains of the Big Bend—a trial run, their mother had called it, to test whether or not the family could survive a major trip west the following year to see the Grand Canyon and Yosemite Park. Will still hadn't seen the Grand Canyon or Yosemite.

Years later, they'd made a pact to get through the holidays at their parents' house by not speaking to each other at all. Marrying Gator had softened Muffy some—at least toward Will, now that she had Gator to pick on—but they still didn't get together socially or as a family except under duress.

It was a miracle he didn't hate women.

He'd been a prince, a virtual *prince*, to pick her up in Waco and drive her to Dallas when Gator had to fly up to Fort Worth earlier in the week for a sports-equipment trade show. A less princely man would have chosen slow death by torture over being in a confined space with Muffy for a couple of hours.

He was doing it for Sally. Sally was their cousin and they'd lived through every second of her disastrous first marriage. Sure, she'd been a wild thing, a seriously dedicated playgirl, until she'd met Gus, fallen madly in love and sworn to change her ways. But she had a good heart. Which reminded Will that he had a family responsibility to make sure Gus was a man who would give Sally the happiness she deserved. And Will had reasons to feel concerned.

About the time Sally met Gus, he'd been looking

for a new tax man and Sally had recommended Will. As was customary at his accounting firm, Helpern and Ridley in Houston, since Will did the taxes for Gus's security business, he also filed Gus's personal returns. In March, looking at the numbers Gus had sent him, Will saw some discrepancies in Gus's reported income and his lifestyle. Will had put many hours of his own time into tracking down what Gus might have left out of his documentation and hadn't come up with a thing. Since Gus had done him the honor of asking him to be a groomsman, Will felt guilty as all hell accepting, knowing he'd be doing his best to pump Gus and his friends for information. But tax was his profession, damn it, and he had a professional obligation to make sure a tax return was honest and accurate before he signed his name to it.

He couldn't let Sally marry somebody engaged in something shady. He had twenty-four hours to satisfy himself about those discrepancies or he'd have to stop the wedding.

With no time to waste, Cecily was a distraction he didn't need. She was the girl from his past he'd never forgotten, the girl who wouldn't let him kiss her, a girl who *still*, after all these years had passed, didn't seem the slightest bit interested in him. Seeing her wouldn't have come as such a shock if he'd bothered to read the itinerary of events Sally and Gus had sent him. He might have prepared for it, thought up a few cool moves, a sophisticated line.

Sheltered behind his sunglasses, he gazed at her, at her straight little nose, her perfect skin, but pale now, no tan. No makeup, either. With the sun shining through her lashes, he could see they were long and light and slanted down instead of curling up. Her mouth was wide, a mouth made to smile, although she hadn't smiled much in the few minutes since she'd sprung so unexpectedly back into his life.

She still had the thick blond hair he remembered, a little darker now, more the color of honey. When she used to come down from Boston to work at the stables, it had been in a neat bob. Now it was long and sloppily tied at the nape of her neck, as if all she wanted was to get it out of the way. At the stables, her jodhpurs had been perfect, her shirts impeccable. She'd looked like the girls who attended the private schools near Exeter. But today she was wearing a shapeless flowered sundress. He liked the look. It was natural, unlike the look of most women who wandered in and out of his life these days. Cecily's dress left him wondering about the curves beneath it, let his imagination loose, and his imagination didn't fit the profile of an accountant's.

One thing hadn't changed. Her eyes were as wide and blue as they'd always been, that monitor-screen blue of a midday sky. From the first moment she'd handed him the reins of a horse, pinning him with those eyes, she'd appealed to him in some way he couldn't quite get a handle on. And she still did. So why the hell couldn't he get her to feel the same way about him?

Muffy, Muffy, Muffy. All she seemed to be able to think about. He had nothing to feel guilty about where Muffy was concerned. He'd been wallowing in his own self-righteousness until Cecily, who'd apparently become a doctor, had decided that delivering his niece, a simple act of professional mercy, gave her the right to tell him he *still hadn't done enough for Muffy*.

In fact, he hadn't. Not quite. "Which hospital are they taking her to?" he asked.

"Glen Oaks Care Center. Have you heard of it?"

"Sure," he said, already dialing Gator's cell, where he left a terse message, then dialed the number for Gator's plane. As he listened to the phone ring, he observed that while the doctor looked capable at the wheel—strong armed and steady—they still hadn't made it out of the church parking lot. "It's a small, private— Hey," he said when Gator answered, "she's at GOCC. Okay. Okay. O-kay, I'll do it. Yeah, see you."

"We need cigars," he told Cecily. "We'll stop on the way."

She did another one of those little whooshy sounds, like the one she'd done when he'd still been trying to get the blood running back to his head. "Do you happen to know where GOCC is?" she said, sounding like patience sitting on a pressure cooker.

"Yes."

"Would you consider sharing it with me?"

Uh-oh, a little steam was starting to show. She'd found the parking lot exit at last, and sat there poised, waiting for him to answer.

He saw a way to put off visiting Muffy indefinitely. "Left," he instructed her and punched the number two on his phone to direct his next call to his parents.

"Now what?" Cecily had reached an intersection.

"Take the LBJ."

"Okay." The car didn't move. "Where is it?"

"Take a right and follow the signs. I need to make these calls." When his mother answered, he said "Hi. You have a granddaughter." Interrupting the shrieks of excitement, the string of questions, he said, "Details later. She's at GOCC. Right. See you there."

Now he'd done everything anyone could have expected. Gator was about to take off from Meacham Field in Fort Worth. He'd be at Love Field in Dallas in the time it took a small plane to go straight up, then straight down. The proud Murchison grandparents, who lived in Highland Park, would beat Gator to the hospital. Muffy would soon be surrounded by people who actually liked her.

What he wanted to do now was renew his acquaintance with Cecily. What she wanted to do was take him straight to the hospital to see Muffy. Why was she so determined to make him visit the twin sister who, from the second he'd entered the world, had made his life a living hell?

CECILY HAD TO ADMIT THAT SHE was a little disappointed in the kind of man Will had apparently grown up to be. And she didn't mean a *married* man. If he had to be a married man, she wanted him to be a *good* married man. It was upsetting that he'd seemed so reluctant to follow his wife and baby to the hospital. Maybe he'd been in shock, because now, making his phone calls to family or friends, he sounded pleased and excited.

Driving Will's luxurious car made her intensely nervous. She was out of her element. Three years in the country and she'd already forgotten that in a city, even a parking lot could be hard to negotiate without a map. In Vermont, even the freeway was a gentle, comfortable, aesthetically pleasing experience. The LBJ, she feared, would be a jungle.

Seeing the first sign pointing toward it, she went

into panic mode. She'd never had a sense of direction, and she'd lost her freeway fighting skills. Those two things combined with the inappropriate feelings she had toward the man she was driving were a foolproof recipe for disaster. Still, getting Will to the hospital was a job she had to do, and she always did her job.

Uh-oh, she had to make a choice—head north and east or south and west. "Will," she said, "which direction do I go on the LBJ? Tell me quick, because northeast is the left lane and southwest is the right lane, and I don't know how the hell I'm going to change lanes."

Will sat back, folded his arms over his chest and said, "You're fine where you are."

What a relief. The traffic swarmed around her, cars cutting in front of her, sliding in behind her, but all she had to do was cling to her spot in this lane. It led her up the entrance ramp. She'd arrived. She was on the freeway. Standing still.

"Lots of traffic," she said.

"It's always like this," Will said.

"But we need to hurry!" She raised her hand to slam the heel onto the horn in the center of the steering wheel.

He grabbed her wrist. "Honking won't help."

The touch of his fingertips sent her into total meltdown. Will had turned her on to a degree she couldn't ignore. It was her own fault that she'd let it happen. If she'd only read on after she'd sighted Will's name, if she'd only noticed that a Muffy Murchison was also in the wedding party, she would have assumed the worst and accepted it with spartan stoicism. But she hadn't read on, and one look at him had her drooling on his shoes. Now she had to redirect her raging lust.

This frivolous trip to Dallas for Sally's wedding had become a landmark in her life. She'd buried herself so completely in her work that she'd forgotten the realities of life. She needed sex just as any normal woman did.

And she needed it now. She'd find somebody else to spend a hot, steamy twenty-four hours with, and Will could help her do it.

She'd delivered Will's baby. Now he, by golly, could deliver her into the arms of an *unmarried* man.

WILL WAS AFRAID HE'D MISSED his calling. He should have been a military strategist. While Cecily was hardly the enemy, his diversionary tactics had gotten her onto the LBJ going in the wrong direction, and the freeway was packed. Now that they were on it, they'd be here a while.

Which suited Will just fine because he'd be sitting beside Cecily, charming the pants off her, he hoped. It had been a long time since anybody had called him dull. In fact, from the time he'd left home for Exeter, he'd been amazed at the number of girls—now women—who wanted to go out with him. In those years away from Muffy he'd discovered he could be himself, not Muffy's stuffy twin brother, Will.

Cecily didn't know he'd *ever* been Muffy's stuffy brother. So why, when he'd tried to kiss her, had she run like a bunny out into a violent electrical storm?

It hadn't boosted his ego any. He'd eventually gotten over the ego part, so why hadn't he completely gotten over Cecily?

"We should be looking for the Glen Oaks exit." Which was actually where they'd gotten on the freeway. A full loop of Dallas in heavy traffic ought to give him time to have her eating out of his hand. Figuring it was time to set the scene for intimate conversation, he punched up a CD, turned the surround sound down low and searched for a conversation starter. "So, you came back for the wedding." *Brilliant, Will, just brilliant.*

"Under duress." The fine line of cheekbone and jaw tightened.

"You and Sally were friends somewhere along the way? I mean, obviously you were."

"When we were too young to know better."

"So, you lived in Dallas and then you moved away?" It was as if cracking a crab getting anything out of her. But that explained why he didn't know her. By junior high their group had been pretty tight, a clique that grew out of sharing a neighborhood, school and country club. Some of them didn't even like each other, but those things and family ties—their parents' friendships or business relationships—bound them together. Sally and Muffy, for example, were always at each other's throats, and yet Sally had asked Muffy to be her matron of honor.

To his surprise, Cecily suddenly got chatty. "My father's a professor of economics. I was born here while he was at SMU. We've moved numerous times. He's at New York University now. But my mother keeps up with Elaine Shipley. We lived next door to the Shipleys in Dallas. I don't know why Sally asked me to be maid of honor. Will, this traffic is impossible," she wailed. "We'll never make it to the hospital."

"Muffy'll understand. She knows what the freeway is like." *Get back to you and me.* Cecily had fallen silent. It was up to him again. "This is going to be a really big wedding." That was a good one. "As far as I can tell, everybody in Dallas will be there."

"That's what my mother told me," Cecily said. "Except she said 'the most important people in Dallas.'"

"Yep, everybody from the mayor to the Dallas Grand Opera director. Oh, and Congressman Galloway and both senators. You keep up with local politics?"

"No."

So there was no point in pursuing that tack any further. Will cleared his throat. "Where's your practice?"

It was a simple question, but it seemed to jar her a little. "Blue Hill, Vermont."

"Why Vermont?"

This time she hesitated even longer. Maybe it was just because the traffic had started to move. "It's where the big bucks are in my field."

"Yeah, you have to think about things like that." In spite of himself, he was getting interested. "You have a specialty?"

"I'm in general medicine, but...but I've gotten pretty good at high-risk deliveries."

"No kidding? What a coincidence for you to be right there in Sally's wedding party just when Muffy needed you." He considered what she'd said. "I'm surprised, though. I would have thought the big bucks would be in New York, Chicago—a big city full of career women who don't have kids until they're getting close to forty."

"Yes, but Vermont's such a beautiful place," she said, "and the pace is slower. No place is perfect, of course."

"What's the downside?"

"It gets lonely sometimes." The traffic really was moving now, not quickly but steadily, and she seemed to be concentrating on it.

"You have your patients." He gazed at her, increasingly curious about how she lived her life.

"Yes, but…"

"You don't like socializing with them?"

A corner of her mouth quirked. A tic, probably, brought on by the car that had cut so sharply in front of them it made even him nervous. "I'm very fond of my patients," she said, "but I have to admit they have certain limitations. Not big readers. Not particularly exciting to talk to. Very little interest in theater or movies or concerts. Unsophisticated tastes in food."

Damn. She was a snob. Didn't mind treating the mountain men or delivering their women's babies but looked down on them socially and intellectually. Too bad. Just looking at her, he wouldn't have thought she'd feel that way.

"What about you? What did you grow up to be?"

"A CPA. But I'm good to my mother."

She gave him an odd look. Most people, when he told them what he did, immediately told him their favorite accountant joke, which tended to illustrate the cold humorless nature of people who chose the profession. When she didn't say anything at all, he added immodestly, "I have a law degree, too. I'm with Helpern and Ridley in Houston. I'm Gus's tax man."

"Ah. But you know Sally, too?"

"Sally's my cousin."

"All in the family." She actually took her eyes off the road and gave him a smile. If she hadn't, he might have gone back to worrying about Gus's reported income.

"You can trust family," he said, hoping it was true.

"You like your work?"

He loved his work. "It's a living." He patted the

dashboard of the Audi. "Buys the toys. How about you? You like being a doctor?"

She hesitated briefly, then said, "Too much, apparently."

"Meaning?"

She sighed, then took a deep breath and seemed to be gearing up to say something important. "With no social life to speak of, I've really let myself go. Just look at my dress. And my hair. I'm a mess. I didn't realize it until I walked on to the rehearsal scene. This wedding is a fashion show!"

He didn't think she was a mess at all. She looked fresh and wholesome, and he liked it. "You look just fine to me, and I don't think patients notice what the doctor is wearing."

"Mine are more undiscriminating than most." It came out like a groan. "It doesn't bother me there, but here, with Sally and all her gorgeous bridesmaids... I mean, who'd choose me unless I..." She came to a halt. "Will," she said, "may I ask you an extremely personal question?"

He sat up a little straighter. He hoped the "extremely personal" question would turn out to be really *personal*. "Whose person?" he said. "Mine or yours?"

"Mine."

"Sure."

Her head swiveled. "What can I do to myself in the next couple of hours to make a man want to have sex with me?"

He jolted upright. His sunglasses flew off his head. The car swerved. Cecily shrieked. Will grabbed the steering wheel. He put one foot down hard on the floor of the car to keep his balance. The crunch told him that's where his sunglasses had fallen.

It was his signal to get new sunglasses.

After he'd taken this woman to bed.

NOW THAT THE CAR WAS GOING straight again and Cecily's were the only hands on the steering wheel, she had time to realize the enormity of the mistake she'd made. Earlier, when she'd had her epiphany while driving the endless highway toward the peculiarly distant hospital, she'd realized she needed help if she were to find a man to release the pressure inside her. Seeing Will again had caused the problem, but Will was married. He couldn't provide the solution.

Still, for a moment she'd let herself imagine Will as The Man, imagine him looking at her. Her clothes— limp, frumpy, with no logos anywhere. Her hair—just the way God made it, somewhere between blond and brown and tied back so she wouldn't have to look at it.

Even if he—not Will, of course, because it couldn't be Will—were undiscriminating enough, horny enough, to get to the undressing stage with her, how would he react to her severe cotton bra, her enormous white cotton panties? They weren't even snowy white. The water in Blue Hill was very hard and tended to turn white things gray.

He'd said she looked fine, but what would you expect a man to say? Truth was, she was clean—or had been that morning, which seemed like a lifetime ago—with the possible exception of her toenails and allowing for the grayness of her lingerie. It was the only positive thing she could say about herself. As for metamorphosing into the kind of woman one of the other men—not Will—would be interested in, she didn't have a clue. Eyelash batting, even with mascara added, was not enough.

It required the proper external trappings, the area in which she was most clueless, always had been. While she'd lived at home, her mother had functioned as her personal dresser, bringing home trendy outfits appropriate for every occasion, dragging her to beauty salons. She'd been thrilled to be out on her own, away from all that fussing. And look what had happened to her.

But Will fit in with these friends of Sally's, looked like them, dressed like them. He'd know. And since he was married and they weren't total strangers, she'd decided she wouldn't feel too embarrassed about consulting him. If she couldn't have him, she could pick his brains, because she wanted to look like the kind of woman Will would fall hard for—if he weren't married with a new baby. But she'd said it all wrong and she'd scared the dickens out of him.

Her face went hot with mortification. He'd thought she was asking *him* to have sex with her. He'd settled back into his seat, panting—from fear, undoubtedly—simply tossing the shards of his sunglasses from one hand to the other. Most men would have yelled at her for swerving like that. She thought he was probably too unnerved to yell.

"Sorry I jumped," he said suddenly. "You surprised me, that's all."

"I'm the one who's sorry," she said, feeling miserable. "That's another downside to being…" She'd come close to saying, "being with cows." She'd have to tell him eventually that she was a vet. When the time was right. "…being so isolated. You forget how to express yourself. I said what I said very badly."

"You didn't say it badly. It was just that—"

"You're being polite. In fact, I made you think I

was asking you to have sex with me, when nothing could have been further from my mind."

She was puzzled by his long silence, until he said, "Really."

She forged ahead. "Of course not. That would be terrible of me. What I meant was… Well, let me start at the beginning."

"Okay."

Her skin prickled when she felt his fixed gaze on her cheek. "It's just that I haven't had sex in a while. Not by choice," she added hastily. She still wasn't saying it right. She didn't want to sound sad and deprived. She wanted to sound bright and brassy, lusty and lascivious, to keep her tone breezy and confident. Most of all, she wanted to sound as if she'd planned all along to turn the wedding weekend into a sexual marathon. "What matters to me is my career. Sex is something I decided to handle with one-night stands now and then. You know, nothing serious. No strings."

"Just casual sex."

"That's me, your typical slut-puppy." *Sure I am.* "But I've hit this little snag. There aren't a lot of men available for casual sex in Blue Hill." *Like none, and if I did find someone, the whole town would be talking about it the next morning.* "So I thought this weekend would be a good time to catch up, but now that I see my competition, I can tell I don't have the—"

"The steelo to tap anybody?" He'd grown very still.

"Have the *what?*"

"Never mind. Go ahead."

"Anyway, I need to do an instant makeover, head to toe, inside and out. And since you were an old friend and married with a new baby and all that, I felt comfortable asking you where to start." She gave him a sidelong glance.

Will froze with his mouth hanging open. She thought he and Muffy were married? That he was the father of Muffy's baby? It was such a chilling thought that every atom in his body wanted to shout, *No! It's not true!*

Except for that one atom that whispered, *Maybe it's the only reason having sex with you is the furthest thing from her mind.* Because he'd felt a connection, felt a spark between them. So if he told her he wasn't married to Muffy, wasn't the father of the baby...

He couldn't tell her now. He didn't want to end this up-close-and-personal conversation. But when the right time came, he definitely wanted Cecily to know he was single. Then he'd find out if that was her only reason for rejecting him—again. Now he wanted to get to the hospital as fast as possible. As bad as her sense of direction seemed to be, she'd never figure out she was making a U-turn and going right back in the direction they'd come from. The hospital was in fact about six blocks from the church. "Start moving to the right," he said abruptly. "There's the Preston Road exit. I know a shortcut to the hospital."

"What?" Cecily yelled, then sped up and began demonically shifting lanes. Will closed his eyes, seeing his life pass before him as she shot in front of a sixteen-wheeler going eighty, honking furiously and flashing its lights. And then she had them flying down the exit ramp and coasting onto the access road without looking to see if anyone was coming.

His eyes were still closed when the car came to a stop. "Left or right on Preston Road?" Cecily said in a voice as calm as an angel's. "Will, I said left or right? Which way to the hospital? Oh, for God's sake, Will, have you fainted again?"

3

"I THOUGHT I'D LOST ALL MY hazardous driving skills," Cecily marveled, "but they came right back to me, just like riding a bicycle."

"You do excel at hazardous driving."

She shot him a glance. He hadn't fainted, apparently, but he did look stunned. "Now if only I could remember how to clean myself up, blow-dry my hair properly, do my nails, exfoliate and moisturize regularly…."

"I'm telling you, you look fine."

"I used to look fine," she corrected him. "I honestly think my mother kept me at home instead of sending me to boarding school so she could have a few more years of keeping my hair trimmed and buying my clothes, hoping it would sink in. But the minute I left home— Oh, look, Will, the hospital." Her right turn might have been a little abrupt. Will paled again. "I'm so glad we're finally here. I'm just sorry I didn't get to pick your brains a little more about specifics— you know, the clothes and underwear."

"Maybe we'll find a spare minute to discuss… clothes and underwear."

Nothing she'd love more than a spare minute with Will, but every minute that went by was more dangerous to her psyche. The sooner she was away from

him, the better. She'd take a taxi back to the hotel, go
to Sutherland's downtown and use her own best
judgment to change from ugly duckling to swan.

She looked at him again, worrying that she'd already overstepped the bounds by talking to him
about something as personal as bras and panties. "I
hope I haven't embarrassed you."

"No, no, not at all. I'm...I used to be an expert in
the field of sexy women."

She was glad she'd driven up an oak-lined drive
and not up a tree when Will put her in the category of
"sexy women." He directed her into a parking lot with
Glen Oaks Care Center signs plastered all over the
place. The neighborhood looked familiar, very like
the one in which the St. Andrews church was located.
The hospital was a pleasant-looking red-brick structure with white trim and many wings and outbuild-
ings.

Cecily felt that the moment of truth had arrived.
She couldn't lie anymore about being a veterinarian
and she wanted to come clean with Will first, ask
him if it would come as too great a shock to Muffy.
"Will," she said, "there's something I really must tell
you before we see Muffy."

He was unbuckling his seat belt, pocketing his
keys, reaching for the door handle. He turned to her,
curiosity in his gaze but something else, too, something compelling that drew her toward a promise he
could never keep.

Her heart sank. He thought she was going to confess that he'd turned her on, that she'd hoped to
lead him astray, distract him from total concentration on Muffy and the baby, and that's why she'd
been talking about sex. He couldn't be more wrong.

Her confession would probably make him mad. Maybe he'd be so ugly-mad she'd never want to see him again—although Will ugly-mad wasn't something she could conjure up in her mind. Mad, maybe. But ugly? Impossible.

But she would go straight home tomorrow and never see him again and everything would be all right.

Everything except her. He'd gotten out of the car, apparently figuring she could make her confession on the run. Or maybe he wasn't all that curious after all. So she got out, too. "Will?"

"I'm listening." He was walking too fast. She lengthened her stride to match his.

"Will, I'm not a doctor."

That slowed him down. "I mean, I am a doctor, but I'm an animal doctor. A vet. It's true that I've gotten rather adept at difficult deliveries, but my difficult deliveries aren't human babies."

He paused on the ball of one foot, carefully set down his heel and moved the other foot up to match. "You're what?" To her amazement, his eyes were dancing and a smile curved his sensuous lower lip.

"I'm a veterinarian. A large-animal vet. My patients are cows and horses, sheep and pigs, your occasional goat—"

Laughter growled in his throat. "That explains why you don't date any of them."

"Yes," she said, still waiting for the ax to fall.

"Hah!" Will yelled out the word and raised his arms high above his head in a V for victory.

"See," Cecily hurried on, "that's why rural Vermont is a good place for me to be. Lots of dairy farms, horse breeding, sheep raising. That's where my big patient base is—"

"All those deliveries you bragged about were baby farm animals! Muffy's gonna trip. Wow, oh, wow, I can't wait to see her face!"

Cecily was astounded. Astounded and upset. "Will, you're treating it like a good joke on Muffy. You should be on her side. You should be mad at me for misrepresenting myself. You should be threatening litigation. You should—"

"Muffy's gonna blow a gasket," he was chanting happily. "Muffy's gonna—"

At the hospital doors he dropped his happy act and turned to her, a new man and a suddenly dangerous one. He brought his face very close to hers, apparently oblivious to the fact that the doors had opened automatically and the women at the reception desk were staring at them. "I'm going to get you for this," he said, but he smiled.

CECILY SHRANK BACK WHILE HE spoke briskly to the receptionist. "Muffy's in Twenty-Four East," he said when he came back.

"Maybe I should take a taxi home and just let you visit with her," Cecily said. Then Will could bear the burden of Muffy's rage alone.

"No, she'll want to thank you, I'm sure." Will's smile was positively evil. "Let me have a few minutes alone with her. I'll tell her about your, um, true life's work and get her calmed down, then you come up."

"If you think it's the right thing to do."

"Definitely. Hang around down here for ten minutes, then follow me up."

Right. Glumly Cecily sat down in the lobby and

thought that if she had a choice between facing an
angry bull or a hysterical, hormonal woman, she'd
take *el toro* any day.

"WILL! YOU'RE HERE! I'M SO glad to see you. Come
look at your niece. Isn't she beautiful? You're going
to be the *greatest* uncle. She'll adore you."

The woman cradling a baby in the crook of her
arm and beaming at him from the hospital bed *looked*
like Muffy—except for the beaming and the baby—
but she didn't sound like Muffy. He was still standing in the doorway, so to make sure this was Muffy's
room, he leaned back into the hall to read the number on the door and then the name on the chart.
"Margaret Murchison Tidwell."

Yep, it was Muffy all right, but she'd been taken
over by some alien force! Where had that sweet expression come from? That affectionate voice?

Still, those were his and Muffy's parents coming
toward him, smiling as though they knew her and
him both. To get in touch with reality, he strode forward to grab them in a big hug.

"Good to see you, son," his father said, sounding
embarrassed.

"Does Muffy seem *changed* to you?" he muttered
into his mother's ear.

"Why, no, honey, she seems like the same sweetheart she's always been," his mother murmured
back. "I knew she'd make a wonderful mother. Just
as you'll make a wonderful father someday."

Will looked back at Muffy with narrowed eyes. He
didn't buy her new attitude for a minute. He did
need her help, though.

He walked over to the bed and bent down to look

at his niece. He had to admit it, this was one cute baby. He could actually feel himself swelling with pride, imagining himself taking her to the zoo, teaching her to ride a bike….

But that would come later. He had issues now. "Gator's not here yet?"

"No." Muffy smiled softly. "He calls every five minutes, though. He's on his way from Love Field right now."

"So he'll be here any minute," Will said brightly, raising his voice.

"Well…"

"Any minute," Will said, and frowned at her. "Maybe Mom and Dad should go out and wait for him, bring him right up to the room. You know Gator. He'll be so excited, he might get lost. He'd appreciate a welcoming committee."

She raised an eyebrow and contemplated Will for a long, scary moment. "Oh, yes, I know he would. Mom, Daddy, would you go outside and wait for Gator? He can't be more than a couple of minutes away."

"Gator's parents will be along pretty soon, too, I imagine," Will said, knowing perfectly well they'd have to drive up from Waco, a good hour and a half from the hospital.

"And," Muffy added, "I really need some body lotion from the gift shop. I forgot mine."

The idea of body lotion seemed to pull their mother's trigger. "Of course, darling," Mrs. Murchison said warmly. "Nothing more important than body lotion right now. We don't want stretch marks. I hope they have something nice. Come on, Bill, let's look out for Gator and his parents. Back soon, angels."

"What are you up to?" Muffy whispered when their parents were out the door.

"The doctor," Will said tersely. "I know her. I've had the hots for her since I was at Exeter. But she got the idea you and I are married."

"Oh, my God," Muffy said, sounding much more like the old Muffy.

"I want to keep it that way for a while."

"Why would you want to do that?"

Why? Because he'd just realized that as long as Cecily thought he was safely married, she'd let him advise her about sexy clothes and lingerie. He might even be able to con her into letting him come shopping with her.

The idea really turned him on.

He cleared his throat. "I have my reasons. You'll go along, right?"

Muffy gave her little daughter a lingering, loving glance. "I do have other, more important things going on in my own life right now," she began, then looked up at Will. "But twins have a sacred trust to lie for each other." She sighed.

"I sure kept you out of a hell of a lot of trouble," Will said and took another look at the baby. She was a doll. Now was the time to put Muffy through the acid test, find out how far her unprecedented loving mood stretched. "Incidentally, Muff, Cecily's actually a—"

But the door opened and Cecily's head poked tentatively into the room.

IN THE LOBBY, CECILY HAD KEPT one eye on her watch and the other on the steady stream of visitors, home-bound patients and medical personnel who flowed through the lobby. Friday must be a popular dismissal day. At last her ten minutes were up and she started for the elevator. When the doors opened, an attractive older couple stepped out. Cecily did a double take.

The woman was slim and pretty, her hair a pale shade of blonde that suggested dark hair gone gray. The man, though, was a dead ringer for Will, or the way Will would look twenty-five or thirty years from now. Either these were Will's parents or Muffy was one of those women who'd married her father. She thought about coming right out and asking them, but considered the complications if she introduced herself as "the doctor who delivered the baby." So she merely smiled, went up to Twenty-Four East and shyly stuck her head through the doorway.

"Oh, look, Will, it's the doctor!" Muffy said. "You're so sweet to come and check on me."

Cecily stumbled forward, feeling stunned. Was this the same Muffy? Everything she'd told Will at the delivery scene, those things about women not being themselves during labor, had been true. There was nothing terrible about Muffy. She'd merely been having a baby.

Muffy grabbed Cecily's hand. "You were great," she said. Her voice was warm and soft. "I can't thank you enough."

"She did a good job, didn't she?" Will said, his tone nearly as warm and soft as Muffy's, but his voice did different things to Cecily than Muffy's did. "Wasn't it amazing, finding a top-notch doctor in the wedding party? You know what she told me in the car, Muff? She says she's an expert in difficult deliveries!"

Cecily was startled. He was supposed to have told Muffy already that she was a vet.

"No kidding," Muffy said, looking wide-eyed. "What a coincidence! Gosh," she said, looking positively saintly, "I must have a guardian angel."

Cecily saw the look Will gave Muffy—a slanty-eyed, teasing glance—before he said, "She's an expert, all right, an expert at delivering calves, colts and piglets, not babies." He crossed his arms over his chest. "Your guardian angel sent you a *vet*. How about that, Muff?"

Cecily felt the tension in the air. Something was going on between Will and Muffy that had nothing to do with her or with her being a vet. Her stomach tightened.

Muffy stared wide-eyed at her for a moment, then at Will. Her face suddenly lit up in a gleeful smile. "That's the funniest thing I ever heard." She began laughing.

Will looked dumbfounded. "My God, she's for real," he murmured.

"What?" Muffy and Cecily said in unison.

"Uh, nothing, nothing. Come here, Cecily, and take a look at this baby."

Cecily took a look, feeling her heart melt at the sight of the tiny hands, the long lashes, the wispy dark curls, the button nose. "She's adorable," she said. "She's going to make you two so happy." Will couldn't be having any problems with this sweet, motherly version of Muffy, couldn't be thinking about divorce. And he couldn't under any circumstances be thinking of giving up this beautiful baby. Cecily was trying really hard to feel happy for both of them.

Muffy gave Will a smile that might even be called sappy. "We haven't decided on a name yet, *darling*, but now I think I'd like to name her Cecily. Cecily," Muffy said to the baby, "meet Cecily Connaught, the miracle woman who brought you into the world under the most terrible conditions—"

"Well, no," Cecily interrupted, made intensely nervous by the conversation and the thought of Will having a baby Cecily. "Not all dairy farmers keep their barns in—oof!" Will had grabbed her in such a strenuous hug that it took the breath out of her.

"We sure will," he said heartily. "We'll name her Cecily. Maybe," he continued as he released Cecily to give her a soulful look, "you would be her god-mother."

"Oh, yes," Muffy cried. "It would mean so much to us."

"I'm flattered," Cecily said, her nervousness reaching the panic level, "but I—"

"Thank you," Will and Muffy said together, giving her oddly similar grateful glances.

The telephone rang and Muffy reached for it. "Just a second," she said, and put her hand over the mouthpiece. "It's our friend Gator," she said to Will.

"You talk to him," Will said. "I'll take Cecily home and be back as soon as possible, *sweetheart*."

"Absolutely not," Cecily said. She'd never felt as firm about anything in her life. She couldn't stand another second in the confines of a car with Will. "I'll call a taxi."

"No way!" Muffy said with a quick glance at Will. "What kind of manners would that be? I insist that Will take you back to the hotel." She went back briefly to the phone. "Hang on, Gator. We're having a little argument here." She smiled. "I know. What else is new?"

Cecily felt confused. Maybe they did argue a lot. Maybe Muffy was just being polite because Cecily was there. She stamped on the thought. She still couldn't have Will. Period.

"One more thing," Will said. "I need to buy cigars and Cecily needs to do a little shopping, and when I take Cecily to the hotel, I'll go ahead and register. You won't mind if I'm not back for a couple of hours."

Now Cecily was having a full anxiety attack. "No, you don't need to take me shopping—"

"Take all the time you need, darling. Mom and Daddy will be along soon."

"And my mom and dad."

"Right. Your mom and dad, too."

Maybe that was the source of the tension, their parents.

"So we'll say goodbye." Will stepped up to the bed and gave Muffy a peck on the cheek, then leaned way down to give the child—who was apparently going to be baby Cecily—a soft, gentle kiss. "You and I are going to be best friends," he whispered.

A tiny finger gripped his, and something intense gripped Cecily's heart. She stepped up, too. "And I'm your godmother Cecily," she said, wondering how the hell she was going to be a decent godmother to Will's baby.

"A godmother who will reappear at just the moment you need her," Will said in a surprisingly commanding voice, "but for now is going to disappear."

"Gator," Cecily heard Muffy say, "When will you get here?" Then she yelled, "Will! Can you talk to Gator?"

Will put his head back through the door just long enough to say, "He just wants to remind me to buy cigars. Tell him I'll get them on this trip."

"I just said I'd be that precious baby's godmother," Cecily said as Will dragged her down the hall with surprising speed.

"Very kind of you."

"But we hardly know each other, and I'll be in Vermont while little Cecily's in Houston with you. Feel free to change your mind. Minds. I know Muffy's a little overemotional right now."

Will's step slowed. "She's transformed."

"Transformed?"

"Yes." He frowned deeply. "Having that baby did something to her body chemistry."

"Whatever," Cecily said. "Now you two can truly bond with each other and little Cecily."

"Believe me," Will said, "we're bonded."

"Well, good." For him anyway, and for Muffy and the other Cecily. As for this Cecily, she needed to be out of his atmosphere and fast. "You really are very nice to take me back to the hotel," she said, "but we're not going to waste any time shopping. I'll go to Sutherland's. It's just a block or so from the Courtland."

"That's right, it is."

"So you'll take me right back to the hotel?"

"If that's what you want."

It wasn't what she wanted, but it was the only alternative she could bear. The tigress, she feared, had lost her appetite for anyone but Will.

No. She couldn't let that happen. She had to remember that her persona for the next twenty-four hours was that of a skanky ho, to whom a one-night stand was as natural as delivering a baby.

WILL COULDN'T STOP MARVELING at the change in Muffy. They'd just coordinated a successful team effort to keep Cecily in the dark about his marital status. There were too many fingers on his right hand to count the number of times in their tumultuous past he and Muffy had coordinated on anything except keeping her out of trouble.

Now all he had to do was get Cecily's mind going in the direction of having sex with him and this could turn out to be one of the greatest days of his life.

"Before you go shopping, we should talk," he said. "You'd asked me about clothes." He was driving now, to his relief, and Cecily hadn't protested.

"Oh. Yes. It's not that I don't know how to be seductive," she said, and catching her slanted look, all Will could do was silently agree with her statement. "It's just that I'm out of practice. I didn't notice any of the groomsmen giving me a second glance, and a groomsman would be so...convenient. What should I wear to signal that I'm available? Um, I mean hot and horny and ready for action." She cleared her throat.

The expression jarred Will and it upset him unaccountably to hear that she was thinking about the rest of the groomsmen, though he was grateful that three of them were married and Chaz, the megajock in running clothes, was gay.

The one person he didn't know was the best man. It was odd, come to think of it, that all Gus's attendants were Sally's friends except the best man, who was an unknown just as Gus was. Will had met him at a couple of parties, and he hadn't been with a woman. It was possible he was single.

He'd have to be watched.

And so would Gus—for different reasons. The little hum of alarm that often hit him when he thought about the mysterious Gus returned in full force.

But Cecily was waiting for an answer about a…a dress. He was supposed to describe a sexy dress.

"Oh, something short," he said, slicing his hand across his legs just above the knee. "And black and low here," he said, making a big scoop on his chest. He thought about scooping that line along the tops of Cecily's breasts, and feeling a familiar heat in his groin, shifted beneath the steering wheel.

"I figured you'd suggest something like that." She paused, gazed at him. "You sure you feel like driving?"

"Positive," Will said.

"What about underwear?"

Mine are getting tight. "What about it?"

"What kind of underwear do men like?"

"Well, some like briefs but others prefer boxers." He wished he were in boxers right now.

She gave him a look. "*Women's* underwear. What kind do men like to see on *women?*"

This really got his juices going. "Uh," he said eloquently, shoving his butt back against the seat and leaning over the steering wheel, still trying to get comfortable. "Well…"

"Is it true that peekaboo lingerie actually turns a man on more than nakedness?" she persisted.

He realized she had no idea he was mentally holding a slinky nightie to her shoulders as if she were a paper doll. He had to get on the program here, had to act like a married man giving sage, *platonic* advice. He leaned back again and began, "Okay, here's what men like to see women wear." And then he actually started thinking about it.

"I don't know what other men like because guys are more apt to sit around talking about women's boobs than about their clothes, so I'll just tell you what I like. When I pick—" he caught himself just in time "—when I used to pick up a woman for a date, I wanted her to look like she cared about me, not what other women thought about her clothes. I wanted her to look pretty. Soft. Nice. Kind. Glad to see me."

Cecily was giving him her full attention as he delivered this sentiment he'd never expressed before, not even to himself. It embarrassed him to realize he'd revealed something so personal about himself. He glanced at her quickly to see how she'd taken it and saw sadness on her face.

It worried him. "You okay? Was it something I said?"

Her face cleared up. "No. I'm fine."

He couldn't help hoping that what had made her sad was thinking he was married to Muffy. Should he confess right now that he was single, available and as hot and horny as she could ever imagine being?

What if she'd really meant it when she said she didn't want to have sex with him? If it had nothing to do with her thinking he was married? He wasn't ready for that big a disappointment. The more time he spent with her—and the longer he kept her away from single men in the wedding party—the better his chances with her.

He was taking her shopping whether she liked it or not. He wondered how she'd look in a thong.

His mouth watered just thinking about it.

4

THE COURTLAND WAS A DOWNTOWN HOTEL, old, elegant and a Dallas tradition of beauty, comfort and exquisite service. Early oil millionaires had stayed there, stomping across the marble floors and Aubusson rugs in their dusty boots, heading for the dark-paneled bar and a bourbon and branch. Will pulled up in front of the hotel, wrestled Cecily's medical bag away from her and handed it and his own bag to the porter, then asked for valet parking. "We'll shop now and check in later," he said.

"No!" Cecily said, literally feeling frightened. "*I'm* shopping. *You're* going back to the hospital."

"I have to buy cigars."

"They sell cigars at Sutherland's?"

"I'm sure they do."

"Then you shop for cigars, and I'll shop for clothes. You were very helpful in the car."

"I'll be even more helpful in the store. We really didn't get into specifics about the underwear. Besides, I can show you easier than I can tell you."

"I think that would make me feel very uncomfortable." Not think, *know.* And she was already about as uncomfortable as she could stand.

"But why?" He couldn't have looked more innocent. "We're old friends. You've met Muffy. You heard Muffy say we should take as long as we needed to do your shopping. I'm only here to help you make the right choices and wow the guys."

"Well, I—" He really wasn't giving her another option. His hand gripped her elbow as he hustled her across the street, down the sidewalk and through the old-fashioned front doors of the store, then sped her past the handbags and cosmetics and onto the escalator.

"We'll try the third floor," he said.

Several minutes later, Cecily was thumbing through a rack of black cocktail dresses. This part wasn't too difficult. *Just pick one. The sexiest one.* "How about this?" she said, trying for a confident, tigress sort of tone. Just looking at it made perspiration pop out on her upper lip. Not from arousal. From fear. She'd rather treat a shark with a toothache than walk out the door in a two-and-a-half-foot length of silk jersey with spaghetti straps.

But if Sutherland's was selling it, Dallas was wearing it. Will didn't seem all that excited about it. "Wow," he said, his lips tight, thin line. "Wear that to the rehearsal dinner tonight and men will be lining up outside your room afterward. Which is the point, I guess."

No, that was going a little far. One man would be quite enough, if he was the right man. She darted a look at him, but he was still staring at the dress, so she grabbed the price tag and stared at it instead. "My God. I could make it myself with a piece of cloth and a staple gun. Explain to me why it's worth seven hundred dollars."

"Ours is not to reason why," Will said.

"But just to buy."

"Right." He folded his arms over his chest. "Wrong. It's overpriced."

"Money is no object." She slung the dress over her arm, indicating her intention to flee.

"So your practice pays well."

"Pretty well, and I don't spend a third of what I make." She shifted from one foot to the other, feeling like a kid who had to go to the bathroom, which was not her problem. Her problem was suddenly imagining Will seeing her in the dress, not out in public but in the privacy of a shared room, and the image had started her hormones flowing.

"Why?"

Damn, he was persistent. "Nowhere to spend it. Nothing to spend it on. But don't worry. I've got it all locked up in mutual funds. Look, Will, you're supposed to be buying the cigars, and I'm supposed to be buying the clothes. We don't have time for a lecture on estate planning."

"Right, right."

But did he say goodbye and leave? No.

"I still think you should do a little more looking. That dress, well, it *is* sort of...obvious." He was getting a stubborn, alpha expression on his face.

"No time to look."

"Guys scare easy," Will argued. "I'd suggest something more subtle."

She was feeling like a stubborn alpha herself. "Will, I don't need the kind of guy who gets scared by a dress. I have no time for subtlety. Obvious is what I'm after. I'm trying it on. Thanks for your help. 'Bye, and good luck finding cigars."

"But—" was the last thing she heard him say before she fled to the fitting room.

WILL HAD A FEELING HE WAS IN over his head. If he'd told her the truth, they might be lying together in a nice, soft bed right now and she wouldn't be planning to go out that night looking like a hooker. He really didn't want her to. The more he thought about it, the surer he was that Derek Stafford, the best man, was single. He was positive the man would be at the rehearsal dinner—the best man always gave a speech, didn't he? And Stafford looked like a wolf. He didn't want Cecily shaking her booty in front of any wolves.

Okay, no more getting scared. Forget the cigars. Let Gator buy his own. Will would go in search of the lingerie department so he could steer Cecily right to it before she had a chance to argue with him, and on the way…

He halted, staring at a mannequin. There it was— The Dress. It was a thin silk dress, sleeveless, just the color of Cecily's skin, with a faded-looking design of flowers that were blue like Cecily's eyes. A soft, floppy ruffle ran over one shoulder and down the front to the hem, where it went around and came up again underneath. How was a mystery, but it made the skirt open up in the front in a flirty sort of way.

It was just a soft, sweet, pale, pretty—he glanced at the price tag—*expensive* little dress, but something about it got his attention, just the way Cecily did. She might look soft and sweet, but the force of her personality reached out and grabbed him in an assertive way that knocked him off his feet.

She'd been like that with the horses at the stable— sweet, loving and firm as an orthopedic bed. Thinking about beds made him wonder if she'd be an assertive lover. He began imagining her in the dress, wearing it to have dinner with him, just the two of them at a small table in his room. No, her room—it was probably neater. She'd sit down at the table, then she'd cross her legs ever so slowly, and the dress would part in the front....

At last he'd see her legs. He couldn't wait. Until today, he'd never seen her in anything but jodhpurs and long-sleeved shirts. Today he'd glimpsed her slim, well-toned arms and her ankles, and they were pale and slim. All he could see of her was pale and slim, so she must be pale and slim all over—her calves, her thighs....

The dress, imagining Cecily in it, imagining her long, pale, slim thighs wrapped around him, was making him feel hot and jangly all over. He summoned a salesperson and demanded the dress in the same size he'd noticed on the tag hanging from the black dress Cecily had picked out, then raced back toward the fitting room he'd seen her vanish into.

A salesperson tackled him. "May I help you?"

"No, thanks. I'm looking for the woman in the flowered dress—"

"With the white satin stilettos?"

"That would be the one. She's trying on a dress." He took off.

"Wait, sir, you can't go in there...."

Yes, he could. He was already there. "Cecily," he yelled into the long bank of stalls. "Where are you?"

He listened to little shrieks from other stalls before Cecily's calm voice said, "You're not supposed to be in here, Will. You're supposed to be buying cigars." She stepped through one of the doors. "But since you're here, what do you think? I think I look like a billboard advertising sex."

A tsunami of desire swept through him. That was

exactly what she looked like—a billboard advertising sex. The dress skimmed over soft curves without hiding anything. She'd taken off her bra to try on the dress, and tight little nipples showed through the thin silk, as did the shadow of her belly button. The fabric outlined her thighs so suggestively that again he imagined them wrapped around him, the dress riding up to her waist....

Was he scared? No. Just scared to let anybody else see her in that dress. And scared to realize how much he didn't want anybody else to see her in that dress. Why should he care? What did it matter, really, in the long run?

But somehow it did. He raised his fist and shouted, "Take it off!" This simple, straightforward request seemed to set off a chain reaction in the dressing room, because the noise level shot way up.

Cecily stared at him. "Will, have you lost your mind? If I'd suspected you'd turn into a lecher, I wouldn't have asked you for help in the first place."

He realized why he couldn't make himself clear to her—he was too aroused to be coherent. "Take that dress off before anybody else sees you in it," he insisted, "and put this one on." It seemed a reasonable enough thing to ask. What was everybody getting so excited about?

At last, Cecily focused her monitor-screen-blue eyes on the dress he'd brought back with him. This was good because it meant she'd finally realized he wasn't acting like a jerk in a strip joint with his "Take it off!" It was bad because he'd figured out he really liked having them focused on him, even if it did make him dizzy.

"Oh," she said, and her voice sounded soft and

surprised. "It's so pretty. But Will," she continued, and to his disappointment, her voice firmed up, "pretty isn't what we're after. I want to look like a large-animal trap."

"What are they talking about? Animal traps?" A querulous voice came from a stall in the fitting-room area.

"Sounded like it. Lock your door, Mama."

"Try it on," Will said, ignoring the voices. "One man's animal trap is another man's turnoff. You never know."

She gave him an odd look, but she disappeared inside the stall. "I'll wait," he called out to her.

"I'm afraid not, sir," said the security guard who stepped up beside him.

Oops. He'd been busted.

Will was big, but the security officer was bigger. Will was tough, but the security officer looked as if he could take down the entire defensive line of the Dallas Cowboys single-handedly. In the absence of superior strength, skilled diplomacy was called for.

"Officer, I can explain," he said. "I expressed my-self badly. My only purpose in being here—"

"Quiet down, buddy, and come along with me. We can do this nice and polite or—"

"Daphne, are you sure this is the women's dress-ing room?" It was the querulous voice again. "It seems to be full of men."

"It's okay, Mama. That's the police. They'll be out of here in a minute."

"Officer," Cecily said breathlessly from behind her door, "please don't arrest him. We have a situa-tion here."

Will let out a grateful breath. The officer put his

hands on his hips and glared, looking like a guy who'd heard everything by now and was anticipating another whopper.

"We had to do a little shopping for me in a big hurry because he has to get back to the hospital to his wife and new baby. He's only here to buy cigars, but I needed a little help picking out a dress, so— Oh! This feels *so good.*"

Her voice had been coming and going as she reasoned with the security man. Will could have guessed when the dress went over her head, when she wriggled it down over her hips, when she angled her arms around to reach the zipper, when she felt the silk slithering against her skin.

If the security officer noticed his erection, Will would find himself in prison for life. Swiftly he shut out the image of Cecily combined with slithering silk.

The officer had indeed tensed up again. "Doesn't make much sense," he said, but he seemed to be weakening a little at the cries of "A new daddy!" "How sweet!" "Congratulations, Daddy" that were coming from stalls up and down the length of the dressing room.

"No, it doesn't make much sense," Cecily said. She sounded dreamy now, and Will was forced into another fight against his testosterone level. "That's what I'm telling you. We have a situation. Okay, I'm taking this dress. It's a—" her voice faltered a little "—twelve-hundred-dollar dress." It grew stronger. "You want Sutherland's to make this sale, don't you? If you take Will away, I'll have to focus on finding him a lawyer. I wouldn't dream of doing anything as trivial as buy-

ing a dress. But if you'll release him into my custody,
I promise he won't get into any more trouble."

There was a whooshing sound, which meant she
was taking off the dress. "Does Sutherland's have a
cigar department? Because Will needs some *really
good* ones, don't you, Will?" Another whoosh, and
Will could almost see the flowered sundress she'd
been wearing earlier settling down over her body.

"The Humidor, behind gentlemen's loungewear,"
said the querulous voice. "They have a small but *very
special* selection. Harold always went there while I
shopped."

"Now, Mama, don't start grievin'."

"I'm not grieving. I'm getting mad at him all over
again. The money he burned on cigars. Enough to
put me in sable instead of mink."

Will couldn't imagine how much cigars would
cost at Sutherland's. Not that Sutherland's would
charge more, just that they would stock nothing
but the best. He saw his savings slipping away, saw
himself selling stocks and bonds, dipping into his
401K. Gator would want to pay him back, but he'd
pay for them himself rather than bring it up with
Gator, who was one of those thrifty rich guys. Then
he saw Cecily slipping out of the dressing room,
the dress over her arm, her heavy, honey-blond
hair escaping from its ponytail to make wisps
around her face, her blue eyes sparkling with fighting spirit and he thought, *What the hell*. It was
worth it.

The officer took one look at her and crumpled like
a toasted marshmallow. "Is it always this exciting
being around you?" she asked Will as they stepped
away from the fitting room.

Will smiled. "Yes," he said, thinking things were going really well.

"No wonder Muffy gets a bit testy at times," she grumbled. "Well, thanks and goodbye again—"

"You owe me," Will said swiftly. "I helped you with clothes. You have to help me with cigars."

"Will!" She glared at him and looked like a woman who'd like to stamp her foot. Then she just flung her arms out in a gesture of defeat. "Why am I arguing? Give me a minute to pay for the dress." She began muttering to herself. "This dress costs more than I've spent on clothes in the last three years, *including* parkas and mittens and barn boots and balaclavas and sock liners." But seconds later she was engaged in complex negotiations with the salesperson. By the time she'd finished, she had the woman's promise that appropriate size-seven-narrow shoes and a small, dressy bag would be waiting with the dress thirty minutes from now, and she'd pay for the whole package when she left the store.

"Okay, now the cigars," she said. "It's really silly for me to be going with you, because what I know about cigars you could put on the tip of a cigarette, but if you truly feel I owe you…"

"I do," Will said. "I faced arrest and professional ruin to find you that dress," he said while steering her onto an escalator going up.

"Where's The Humidor?"

"You heard the lady. Behind gentlemen's loungewear."

"Which is?"

"Behind ladies' lingerie, I'm sure," Will lied. "That's the logical conclusion, and here we are in ladies' lingerie. What a coincidence," he marveled. "Didn't you want my advice on lingerie?"

Yes, she had mentioned wanting his advice on lingerie and she deeply regretted it. She was already in deep internal trouble. Will had unwittingly picked out a seductress of a dress, the kind that seduced the wearer as well as the viewer. The silk moving over her had felt like the caress of fingertips, making her moist and heavy between her thighs, and she'd thought about a man—not Will, of course, because he was married—but *some* man—putting his arms around her and sliding that silk against her bare breasts, her buttocks. In short, she was already wasted. The last thing she needed was to see Will fingering the lace at the waistband of a pair of cream-colored panties and eyeing her speculatively.

5

"I LIKE THESE PANTIES," WILL said, looking thoughtful. "I'll tell you some basic things to look for in a pair of panties. First of all, this lace isn't scratchy." He smoothed the front of the panties with his hand and her knees buckled. "How panties feel is just as important as how they look, because you know men—they like to touch. Second, these panties leave something to the imagination. Guys don't have a whole lot of imagination, but all they have is focused on women, and there they let their imaginations run wild." He spoke slowly and he sounded dreamy, as if his own imagination was already running wild. He turned the panties over. "See, they're cut low, but they'll still cover, well, almost cover... You don't mind my talking so frankly, do you?" he asked interrupting himself. He gave her an earnest look. "It's just technical stuff, really."

"Rules one and two," Cecily said briskly, her hands closing on the edge of the display table for support. "Not scratchy, not too revealing. Very helpful. Thank you." If he said the word *panties* again, particularly if he said it the way he'd been saying it, like an addict saying *chocolate*, she'd come right here in the store.

Will held up the panties. "These are all you'll need under that dress."

"No bra?" She squeaked the words.

His voice had thickened to maple syrup. "You don't need one. Just these. And bare legs. Or the stockings that just come up to the thighs."

"With lace at the top." Now she'd resorted to moaning.

"If you insist on stockings at all. Men like to grab the lace and sliiide—" he stretched out the word

"—the stockings down one at a time. It's a real turn-on."

"Maybe no stockings." Her fingers shaking, Cecily found the panties in her size and moved on. "What about this?" She showed him a pale apricot camisole and matching French pants with lace trim. The outfit looked...sweet. She needed sweet right now, needed to get away from sexy quick as a bunny.

"Very nice." He cocked his head to one side and contemplated the outfit. "The camisole lets a woman's breasts go free, shows the nipples."

Ah-h-h-h.

"Panties like these are good, too. Lots of room in the legs for a man to run his fingers up—"

He'd said the word again. Cecily grabbed the ensemble. "Fine. Let's go."

"You're getting the idea," he said admiringly. "See, while that set just looks pretty and feminine, it's actually sexier than the more revealing stuff because the woman's body is freer inside it, so the man is more aware of the motion of her—"

"Right. I'll find a sales—"

"And in that color, you'll look nearly naked."

"—person." Cecily wiped sweat off her forehead and was on the run when he caught her by one elbow.

"On the other hand, this has its own kind of sexiness."

Uneasily, Cecily looked back. He was holding a bra, studying it intensely.

He dropped his grip on her elbow. "The way the front of this bra dips down to here, where it opens, is really sexy. And the fastener's good, too. No hooks, nothing hard or sharp, just this plastic thing that slides in and out, in and out, in and out…" He demonstrated. Repeatedly.

She snatched the bra away from him. "Get me three of these," she said, "in different colors."

"Size?"

She sent him a withering glance. "I take it back. I'll find them."

"Panties to match?"

She gritted her teeth. "Panties to match." Gritting wasn't enough. She ground her teeth and then said, "Size five."

"We shouldn't forget thongs."

"Why not?"

"Because a thong's sort of basic to the whole idea of looking sexy, isn't it?" he said. "I'll look for thongs." He wandered away. She bent over, her head to her knees, hoping it would help her start breathing again.

"I like this outfit," he called to her much too soon and in a louder voice than she would have wished. She straightened up, spotted him and rushed over just to keep him from yelling again. He was holding a black lace thong by the crotch—or what would have been the crotch if it had had enough crotch to warrant calling it one. At the same time, he was gazing at a mannequin, just a torso in a tiny, baby-blue bra of sheer lace with bikini panties to match. He turned to face her. "There's something really different about this. Don't know what it is, but I like it. Better see if it's scratchy." He ran his hand over one mannequin breast. "Nope, not scratchy."

The lace was unlined. Everything would show through it.

"Maybe it's because your eyes are that same blue. On you they'll look, you know, subtle, but wow." His voice dropped a full octave.

"Wow, huh?" Cecily could hardly breathe.

"Yeah."

"Okay." A salesperson hovered, but something about them made her back away as if she were intruding.

"Where—Here they are." She picked up a set. Her legs were trembling now. She felt as if the lower half of her body weighed a thousand pounds as she tried once again to escape to the safety of that salesperson and the closest cash register.

"You'll need something to sleep in." Will handed her the thong he was still holding and gave her a long, slow smile. "Or not sleep in."

"Something like this, I suppose." She brandished a teddy, black, trimmed with lace and red bows.

Will slouched toward the night wear. "I know men are supposed to be turned on by teddies, but personally I like something with a little more freedom. You know, the teddy has to be unsnapped or unzipped or unbuttoned, maybe it's Velcro, I don't know. Kind of spoils the—"

This time Cecily forced herself to stifle the moan. "So what do you as a man prefer, because there must be many other men who feel the same way you—"

"Nothing," Will said. "Nothing is best."

"Good," Cecily said briskly. "Look at the money I've saved. I'm all finished now, so I'll pay and we'll get on to the cigars."

"But…" Will grabbed her again. "Nothing comes later. First you have to *get* to the part where nothing is best." His voice rose slightly. "That's what you asked me, remember? How you could make the man in question want to strip off everything you're—"

"That isn't what I said!"

"It's what you meant." He gave her a serious, psychiatrist-like look of understanding.

Cecily did a little more damage to the enamel of her teeth. "You've grasped the general idea." She was getting pretty damned tired of his reminding her that this surrealistic scene was all her fault. With one simple little question she'd kidnapped a man who should have been buying cigars and cooing over his new daughter, forcing him instead into consulting with her on the matter of provocative feminine attire.

But at this point, who was forcing whom? If she'd said *cigars* once, she'd said it more times than Will had said *panties*, yet here they were in lingerie, the most dangerous place she could possibly be with Will. Of course, he was an accountant. He saw life as a matrix of horizontal and vertical columns. Once he'd started filling in a column with data related to her question—how to look desirable to a man—everything else would fly out of his head until he'd filled out the column and totaled it up. But when the "everything else" included a wife and new baby, that's when it got surreal.

How could he possibly be here with her, saying

these provocative things to her, if he loved Muffy enough to marry her and give her a child?

His voice had gone all deep and rumbly again. "I like to see a woman in something...accessible, something that says, 'Here I am. Take me.'"

"Here I am. Take me," Cecily repeated in a whisper. She couldn't help herself. Her conscience was yelling at her, but Will's voice was having a stronger effect on her.

"Yes." His gaze melted into hers. The gold in his hazel eyes glittered.

Irresistibly drawn toward the idea of starting her own personal gold rush, she leaned toward him, stepped back, leaned again—then heard a warning bell from deep in her mind. "Show me an example," she croaked.

He cleared his throat, sent all that glittering gold in another direction, looking, apparently, for examples. Cecily felt relieved and bereft at the same time.

"May I help you?"

They both whirled, Cecily feeling as guilty as a child caught misbehaving. But Will lavished a smile on the salesperson who'd appeared at his elbow and was eyeing the pile of wispy lingerie draped over Cecily's arm. "I'm looking for one of those short gown-and-robe combinations."

"It's for his wife," Cecily improvised, scurrying along behind the two of them as the saleswoman led the way. "She just had a baby, and—"

A thought struck her in midsentence. It was Muffy Will had been thinking about as they'd cruised through the lingerie. The birth of their daughter had changed Muffy from shrew to seductress. Thoughts of the new Muffy had brought the glitter to his eyes, not a dangerous attraction to Cecily. She'd heard that couples were encouraged not to make love in the last weeks of the pregnancy and couldn't for another six weeks after. Will was merely sex-starved, not contemplating infidelity.

Or was he? What if Will resented having six more long, loveless weeks ahead of him? Did he see her as his ticket to a little no-strings sex?

She would never allow Will to be unfaithful to Muffy with her. She'd never get that desperate.

Just close to that desperate.

She turned her back on Will and the saleswoman, afraid the woman would take one good look at her face and know she was a good-for-nothing liar. Across the room she saw a familiar face, one she couldn't quite place. He was in the section politely referred to as Sexy Plus, ducking around a rack of gown-and-negligee sets suitable for the bigger woman.

"Oh, look, there's Congressman Galloway," the saleswoman said.

Bingo! "Shouldn't you go over and speak to him, Will?" Anything to get him away from shorty gowns.

"Oh, yes, do," burbled the salesperson. "He must be buying something pretty for his wife." She paused. "She's a skinny little thing, though. I'd better help him find the right size. Women get real mad when their husbands bring home things that are too big."

"Right," Will said briskly. "You can help him right after you help me. I'm looking for a sheer, *very* sheer—"

"You should introduce yourself and tell him you have a new baby," Cecily insisted, the words *very sheer*, shaking her up even more than *panties*. "Politicians love to be recognized. He'll probably issue a proclamation declaring it Cecily Murchison Day. It will be a memento she'll cherish forever."

"I'm not a groupie," Will said in a voice that didn't invite her to go on babbling. "Let the poor guy shop in peace."

"In peace, but in Sexy Plus" the saleswoman said pointedly, "when he should be in Petites."

"As I said," Will said, his voice rising a little, "after we find this very sheer…"

While Will selected something the salesperson showed him, Cecily gave in to total despair. She'd never in her life felt so turned on, so obsessed by desire, but she was starting to feel certain she wouldn't find a man to relieve her need. Without even turning around, she fished out her credit card and held it out behind her. "Whatever he picks out," she said over her shoulder to the saleswoman, "it's my baby gift to the happy couple." She looked down at the panties and bras dangling over her arm. "These are for me." She held them out behind her, too, and felt them being taken from her cold, dead fingers.

In the last few minutes, a terrible truth had become crystal clear to her. It didn't matter how attractive she made herself to the available men who might appear on the wedding scene. The only man she could possibly have sex with this weekend was standing behind her, chatting happily with the salesperson about the joys of parenthood and the treatment of colic.

She couldn't have him, even though she felt hotter, needier, readier than ever before in her life. So what was she going to do about it?

Help him buy cigars. And maybe he'd give her one. A cigar sounded really sexy right now.

"WOW, THESE CIGARS SMELL GOOD."

"Feel free to smoke one as soon as we leave the store."

"Can't afford to. I'm hanging on to a thousand dollars' worth of something that will eventually go up in smoke. Why couldn't Muffy's friends just get together and set fire to a thousand-dollar bill?"

"My dress cost more than that. And the shoes! Four hundred for a spike heel and a strap across the toe?" She sounded tense and nervous.

"Four hundred for those little words *Jimmy Choo* nobody will ever see because you'll be standing on them."

"She did a nice job picking out those two skirts and tops, though," Cecily said. "Nice for Sutherland's, anyway. How was I to know those little skirts cost so much? And whoever heard of a cotton T-shirt costing two hundred dollars? Sally's friends must all be gazillionaires."

Will realized he should have said earlier, "our friends," not "Muffy's friends." He couldn't keep up the game of being Muffy's husband a minute longer. The lingerie shopping had been the last straw.

He hadn't made up the thing about men's imaginations being focused on women. Imagining those little pieces of silk and lace on Cecily had sent his testosterone sky-high, and he was pretty sure he was getting signals from her that she'd be amenable to reducing his hormone levels if only he weren't a married man. He was dying to tell her he was single, available and hotter than a car seat in July, then whiz back to the hotel with all due speed to watch her model her new underwear.

So where could he tell her and how? He chewed

his lip. It was important to tell her before they checked into the hotel.

"Would you mind a quick trip up the elevator to the infants' department?" he improvised. "Muffy's not happy with little Cecily's diaper bag. You might do a better job of picking out one she'd like."

The expression on her face filled him with hope. He was pretty sure that the last thing in the world she wanted to do was help him buy a diaper bag.

But she was nice enough to agree. In fact, there was something despairing about the way she agreed, her "Why not?" delivered with a sigh, which he also took as good news. The fates were with him. The elevator—old, slow and less popular than the escalator—was empty.

"You're all set to bring some guy to his knees," he said by way of getting the conversation started.

"Oh, Will, I'm not so sure."

"Why?" He moved a step closer.

She moved a step away. "The probability of finding someone I'm hot for who's hot for me…"

"Earlier you sounded like you'd be hot for any man who was in your bed." As he said it, a flicker of doubt lit up a few of his brain cells. Was she really like that?

At the moment, he should be hoping she was, right? Because that gave him a chance with her, and he was getting hotter every second he spent with her. So why had he suddenly hoped she wasn't up for letting any Tom, Dick or Harry into her bed?

Forget it. There was only so much you could figure out in an elevator. He regained his proximity to Cecily and rested a hand against the wood-paneled wall, which put his arm right behind her shoulders.

When she stepped back, trying to get away, she got herself hugged instead.

She looked truly agitated. "I'm beginning to think it does matter. Let's not talk about it, Will, really."

"Okay," he said agreeably. "What would you like to talk about?" He didn't have to figure out what to say or how to say it. Cecily was setting herself up for a big surprise. What could be better?

HE DIDN'T MOVE HIS ARM. In fact, he leaned in a little closer. Cecily frantically groped for a neutral topic. "Let's talk about Muffy."

"Oh. Okay. What do you want to know about her?"

The elevator stopped on each floor. Shoppers got on, shoppers got off. "Well..." Cecily hesitated. "How long have you known each other?"

"All our lives," Will said, and his face was so close to her hair, she could feel his breath ruffle through it.

"All your lives. So your differences, your tensions, didn't come as any surprise to you?"

"Oh, no. We never got along. That's why my folks sent me to Exeter."

"To get you away from Muffy?" All this sounded very strange. Maybe Will was dumber than he looked—had to be to marry a woman he'd never gotten along with. Maybe she had a lot of money. Maybe she was really great in bed. *Don't go there.*

"Yep."

"But you got together again?"

"No way to avoid it."

"Yes, there is," Cecily cried. "You have to be strong! It's kinder to tell a woman the truth than to marry her and make her miserable with constant fighting."

"I know that," Will said.

She felt his smile against her hair. His mouth was much too close to her cheek. How many trips had they made up and down in this elevator? She felt as if she'd been stuck in there with him for most of her adult life.

"But it's too late now," she said miserably. "She's just had the baby, and as I've told you over and over, you need to be at the hospital with her, giving her your full support."

"But I'd rather be the man who gets to see you in that black thong."

Thank God the elevator was temporarily empty when he uttered those dire words. The thing she'd most dreaded had happened. She'd caught a man at a vulnerable moment and, because of her own selfish need to question him about attracting *other* men, had made him think she might be willing to satisfy his starved libido.

She felt sick inside. She'd made things worse by implying that she wasn't looking for anything lasting. He might be a bit on edge right now, but he was a good man inside. She could just feel it. And what he was thinking was that a temporary-fling type of woman wouldn't disturb the already uneven equilibrium of his marriage.

She felt like a piece of trash, but now she had to rise to the level of at least something worth recycling. "Will!" She flung his arm away and faced him, her eyes both hot and tearing up at the same time. "I was afraid something like this would happen. I'm horrified at myself, I'm ashamed and so, so, so sorry. I'm ashamed of you, too, but it's all my fault. And to answer your question, I absolutely will not go to bed—"

She stopped abruptly when the elevator doors

opened on five and two very pregnant women got on. The women gave them curious looks. Cecily wondered just how far her voice had carried.

"—until after the eleven o'clock news. So you can call me up to eleven-thirty—"

She paused again and spoke directly to the women. "I forgot. I'm in Dallas, in central standard time. That would be the ten o'clock news, so he can call me until ten-thirty." Even in her overemotional state, she could see the pregnant women were starting to look frightened. The world was whirling around her, and now the elevator was going down.

"Cecily…" Will said.

The women turned away. Cecily was sure they felt as comforted by the calm, deep voice as she was, sensing that even if they had a crazy lady on their elevator, they also had a man who could handle her.

She'd show them *she* could handle *him*. She tugged Will to the back of the elevator. "I mean it," she implored him, barely moving her lips. "Back off, now, while you're still clean. You can trust me. You never said it. It never happened."

"I don't want to back off," he whispered into her ear, setting off a fire alarm in her nervous system. "I don't need to back off. I'm not—"

They'd reached the first floor again. Cecily tried to leap out of the elevator, but Will had a firm hold on her. The pregnant women got off, whispering agitatedly to each other. Two elegantly dressed women stepped in and pushed the button for the third floor. Cecily looked them up and down and decided they were too self-absorbed to notice a warring couple at the back of an elevator. "You're not the man I thought you'd grow up to be," she fired at him. "I thought I could trust you, or I would never have laid out my personal problems in front of you."

"You should never trust a person you know as little about as you know about me."

"How right you are," she mourned.

They'd reached the third floor. The doors opened, but the two women didn't get off. Instead they whispered something to each other and pushed one of the elevator buttons.

Will lowered his voice. "So, let's get acquainted."

"On the elevator?"

"It won't take long."

"Will, this is very silly. I want to go to my room and—"

"Just follow my lead. Cecily, do you have brothers and sisters?"

"No."

"Pets?"

"Yes."

"Names?"

"Skip the names. Too many of them."

"Your turn now."

"Will, do you have brothers and sisters?" Cecily intoned.

"Yes."

"What kind? Brothers or sisters?"

"A sister. A *twin* sister."

"Name?"

"Margaret."

A little bell dinged in Cecily's head. "Margaret. Do you call her Margaret? Maggie? Or Marge?"

"Muffy," Will said and put his hands on either side of her head, turning her to face him.

Dumbstruck, she stared at him. "What are you saying to me?"

"Read my lips. Muffy…is…my…twin…sister."

The elevator doors opened and two more women got on. Cecily saw one of them eye Will and her speculatively before she faced front.

"Well, that's just sick," Cecily snapped.

"It's not sick. I'm not the father of my sister's baby. You thought I was, so I let you think it, and when you said you'd lied about what kind of doctor you were, I decided you deserved to think it. I pulled Muffy in on the job, but we knew we couldn't trust Mom and Dad to keep their mouths shut, so we got rid of them." With every word he drew her closer and her heart beat faster.

A couple of the shoppers turned around, looking startled. The others began to shift nervously. One quickly pushed a button. The elevator stopped on the next floor, and as a single unit, all of them got out.

In a shocked flash of memory, Cecily remembered the couple who'd exited the elevator at the hospital as she was getting on, the man's resemblance to Will and, she now realized, the woman's resemblance to Muffy. "Are you saying…?"

"I'm saying—" his arms went around her, both of them leaning against the back of the blessedly empty elevator "—that I'm free as a bird and ready for whatever you have in mind for the next twenty-four hours. If you'll have me."

She could hardly breathe. "You're not married to Muffy, and the child I so unwisely agreed to godmother is not your baby." Her heart pounded furiously as the elevator reached the top floor, halted and began its descent again.

"We can negotiate the godmother thing if you really don't want it, but not until the weekend's over." His gaze mesmerized her, and she closed her eyes. His hands caressed her shoulders, drew her closer, as his mouth hovered over hers then brushed her cheek, her forehead. At last his arms were around her, pulling her tightly to him, and Cecily melted in his embrace, flowing like liquid with the power of his desire. "We have to forget little Cecily and move on to big Cecily, wonderful Cecily, Cecily who needs exactly what I'd love to give her."

The elevator doors opened on the first floor and the security officer loomed in the doorway. This time he had backup, two more officers as burly as he, and behind them, the women who'd been their elevator companions formed a solid wall. "Hands above your head, sir, and get off the elevator."

"What's this all about?" Will said, letting go of Cecily and putting his hands in the air.

"We've received a complaint that you are molesting this woman."

"He may be a murderer!" said one of the women.

"He might even be the father of his sister's baby!"

The officer shook his head sadly. "What is the world coming to? I have to ask you, sir, to come along quietly."

"YOU OWE ME," CECILY SAID when she'd convinced the officer once again that Will was merely mentally disturbed—in a benign way, of course.

"I can't wait for you to call in your chits," Will said as they jaywalked across the street to the hotel.

She only hoped her legs would hold her up a few minutes longer. A miracle had happened. Will was hers for the weekend.

6

"CECILY CONNAUGHT," CECILY said to the man beneath the Courtland's brass Registration sign, then sent a sidelong glance toward Will, who'd gone to the other end of the gleaming black marble counter to check in.

"Will Murchison," Will said to the woman behind the counter, then sent a sidelong glance toward Cecily.

"The Shipley-Hargrove wedding party," Cecily said in unison with Will, then whipped her head back to stare at the nattily uniformed man behind the counter.

The registration man and woman sent sidelong glances toward each other.

"Your luggage arrived," the man said to Cecily, eyeing the many Sutherland's bags dangling from her hands, "and we've sent it up to your room. With your…shoes."

"Oh, thank heavens, somebody sent my sandals along," Cecily said. "I was afraid they were lost to me forever. You can burn the suitcase, for all I care."

"Good plan," Will said from his end of the counter.

"And we'll send your luggage up in a minute," the woman said to Will, giving him a sharp glance. "Warm day, isn't it?" she added, apparently reacting to Will's flushed face and tousled hair.

"Humid outside, isn't it?" Cecily's man said to her. She'd been gazing at Will. Now, looking down at herself, she realized he was referring to her dress—wrinkled, damp and sticking to her. Not that anything showed beneath her cotton bra. Which was a good thing. Her condition resulted from the heat and humidity of Will, not Dallas, and her body still zinged from his touch. "Uh-huh," she said, hearing Will say something quite similar.

"You've received a call," Cecily's man said to her as Will's woman said the same thing to him. They looked at each other.

"You both have voice-mail messages waiting," the woman said, taking over.

"Thank you," Will answered in unison with Cecily.

The clerks handed over keycards in little folders and wished them a pleasant stay at the Courtland. Cecily felt their eyes boring into her and Will's backs as they stepped briskly toward the bank of elevators.

"What's your room number?"

Cecily looked at the card. "Seven-oh-nine."

"I'm seven-seventeen."

"I'm sure Sally booked a block of rooms together," Cecily said.

But Will had halted in his tracks. "Not close enough," he muttered and started back to the desk.

"But Will, they'll know…"

He wrapped his arm around her waist, pulled her close and lightly touched his lips to hers. "Why should a slut-puppy like you care?" He smiled.

It was a slow, lingering, teasing smile. What did it mean? Had he figured out that this was her debut at being a slut-puppy?

He gave her a quick kiss. "Go to your room and start taking off price tags." He kissed her again. "Then put on your favorite new thing."

HER ROOM WAS DECORATED IN English-country style, pretty and feminine, with a king-sized four-poster bed covered in a floral print trimmed in eyelet. She peeked out the window. The hotel, which from its exterior appeared to be a solid block, actually consisted of three wings around a kidney-shaped black pool. Now, in midafternoon, bronzed bodies filled the white chaises that surrounded the pool.

She backed away from the window and caught a glimpse of her familiar self in the full-length mirrors that covered the closet doors. Slowly she tugged her dress off over her head, then undid her clumsy bra and peeled it away from her damp skin. The cool air of the room washed over her like a caress, and she breathed a deep sigh of relief. She slid her panties down into a puddle at her feet, then picked them up. Holding the underwear that represented the utterly practical nature of her current life, she thought it would give her a clean-break sort of feeling to toss them out the window, then imagined them landing on the head of one of those bronzed bodies.

Would he look at the underwear with distaste, and say, "What are these? Orthopedic undies?"

Alas, the windows probably didn't open.

She let down her hair, brushed it out, then went to the bathroom to sponge her body with cool water. The soap was lemon-scented and refreshing as she dragged the cloth across her skin. She thought about how it would feel for Will to be holding the cloth, sliding it down her throat, her arms, her breasts, between her legs. It was an arousing image, one that made her long for Will's return.

Naked, she stretched out luxuriously on the bed, dragged one of her shopping bags close beside her and began taking the new underthings out of their tissue-paper wrappings. They felt wispy and featherlight in her hands, filling her with a tingly sense of anticipation.

Several minutes later, she faced the mirror wearing the pale blue lace ensemble Will had picked out for her, had said she'd look good in, the bra and panties no more than a web of soft, silky, slightly stretchy lace exactly the color of a robin's egg. The woman staring back at her was an unfamiliar person, a new person. She raised her arms over her head, spread her feet apart, let her hips sway from side to side. She felt free. She felt…sexy.

A new, free, sexy woman who would soon be in the arms of the man she'd never stopped wanting, a man who had awakened her desires from their long, long sleep. Still stretched out, she tightened her hands into fists and held them aloft in a victory sign. "I am tigress," she growled. "Hear me roar."

Her suitcase still lay open, and she pounced on it tigerlike. "Die," she shouted at her white underwear as she tossed dingy bras and panties into the wastebasket near the desk. She dug a little farther and pulled out a somewhat ragged sleep shirt. "You, too." She gave it a toss.

Her suitcase was a mess. She'd packed in ten minutes, as usual, and everything she took out of it from now on would be a surprise. A bad surprise. But that untidy tangle of clothes belonged to her past—her extremely recent past, admittedly, but nonetheless over. Her future lay on the bed, all silk and lace. Pure femininity.

Feeling better already, she made a snarly face at the mirror and then gazed at herself again, suddenly not quite satisfied with what she saw. Tigresses had more color than she did. She did own makeup—not that she ever wore anything but Bert's Bees lip balm. Knowing this, her mother had apparently spent hours and a fortune at a cosmetics counter in Saks— carrying pictures of Cecily, for heaven's sake—and had mailed Cecily a whole new face, complete with instructions on how to apply each of the numerous potions and powders and which of the numerous brushes to use for each. There was a typical note in the box that said, "Please, darling, for me, use this during the wedding festivities. You could be so pretty if you'd just try."

So Cecily made up her face, maybe for the first time since undergraduate school. Stroking on the pale pink lip gloss, she had to admit she looked more like a woman a man might want to make love with. Shivering with growing impatience, she carefully put away the rest of her new treasures and stretched out on the bed to wriggle against the soft cotton of the coverlet.

She was wriggling, increasingly hot and frustrated as she let her imagination take her into the near future, when two things distracted her. She had a voice mail waiting, and where the hell was Will?

WILL WAS STEPPING PURPOSEFULLY across the lobby, clutching the plastic key to his hard-won room— seven-eleven, which connected with Cecily's—when he recognized the man already waiting for the elevator. Sneaking up behind him, Will nudged the large Sutherland's shopping bag he held. "Congressman," he said. "Gotcha."

A low, desperate sound came from Congressman

Galloway's throat as he whirled to face Will. His face was as white as an arctic hare's. God, the man was goosey. Both Will's and Sally's parents were among his big supporters, financial and otherwise, and frequently entertained him in their homes. Even Muffy liked him. Will had never seen him get this nervous, even in an election year.

"Will," Galloway said weakly. "You're a man I haven't seen in a while." Slowly his face got a little color back.

Donald Galloway was twenty-five or so years Will's senior, but he'd laughed and joked with Will when he was a kid, and Will thought a little teasing wouldn't be out of order. "Yeah, but I saw you thirty minutes ago." Will gave him a sly smile. "Find something pretty for Nora in the lingerie department?" Hell, the man's face was going pale again. Will felt he'd misjudged and was presuming a camaraderie between them that didn't exist.

He suddenly felt like a naive fool. Maybe the lingerie hadn't been for Nora.

If Galloway was fooling around, Will didn't like the idea much, because Nora was a nice lady and her husband's biggest fan, but he sure wasn't going to tell. If he did, Nora would be the person he'd hurt the most. He thought he knew how to make the congressman feel more relaxed. "Tell you the truth," he said conspiratorially, "I would have spoken to you, but I was with a lady who preferred not to be seen shopping for underwear with me. Know what I mean?"

"Uh, sure, Will, sure."

He didn't seem to feel a whole lot better. His eyes had gone glassy. Will decided to be even more direct. "So I won't tell if you don't."

"Yeah, yeah," Galloway muttered. "Hey, I forgot. I need to buy shaving cream in the gift shop. See you later, Will."

He slunk away, a big change from his usual confident stride. Will was puzzled, but only one thing was on his mind right now. Not even Gus's finances could distract him, and certainly not the possibility that Congressman Don Galloway had a girlfriend on the side.

PACING THE ROOM IN HER BRA and panties, Cecily began to feel plagued by the blinking message light on the desk telephone. She knew the voice-mail message was from her mother. Her mother hadn't been completely convinced Cecily wouldn't find a plausible reason to skip out on the wedding.

Admittedly, her worry was justified. Cecily had indeed sinned in her heart when she'd told herself that if Vermont were to have an outbreak of mad cow disease, this would be an excellent time for it. Her father, at least, would understand that his daughter couldn't be in a wedding when her duty was to protect the meat-producing industry from financial ruin and thereby protect the very core of democracy—the GNP.

But no crisis had arisen and here she was. At the moment, she was extremely pleased she had come. *Elated* wouldn't be too strong a word. But the last thing in the world she wanted to do was talk to her mother. So she couldn't pick up the phone. If she picked up the phone and heard the message, she wouldn't be able to say, "Oh, sorry, I didn't get your call."

Which is what she planned to say. As she congratulated herself again on her irrefutable logic, she heard a knock on the door. And in her frantic dash to slip her dress back over her head, she realized the knock wasn't coming from the door to the hall but from the locked door that led to the next room.

"Cecily, unlock your door."

She let the dress fall to the floor. He had scored the connecting room. A thrill of heat passed through her. She stepped over to her door. "Say 'Rapunzel, let down your hair.'"

"I'm going to say 'Open, sesame' and kick the door in if you don't open it."

She smiled at the laughter in his voice and unlocked the door on her side. His boyish, gleeful smile faded. He stepped through the open door and slowly, like a man in a dream, rested his hands lightly at her waist, caressing the bare skin, devouring her with his gold-flecked gaze. "Lady," he said in a voice made thick from desire, as thick as sorghum molasses, "you have knocked me flat on my ass."

SHE WAS TOTALLY BOWLED OVER herself, and the man still had his clothes on. She put her hands on his shoulders and stroked the underside of his chin with her thumbs, watching his eyes darken. "None too romantic, but we're not really talking about romance here, are—"

His mouth swallowed the end of her sentence. His kiss was hard and deep, filled with need as consuming as hers. She kissed him back, claiming him as her prey, devouring the sweetness of his lips, the warmth of his skin.

His hands slipped up under her hair to caress her neck, trailed down her bare back to her waist, where he pressed her tightly against him. She felt the power and promise of his erection, and the ache inside her built explosively. Abruptly he broke off the kiss and relaxed his hold on her, his hands moving to the front closure of her bra. With excruciating slowness, he opened it, and her breasts fell free into his hands. Holding them, caressing them, his thumbs circling her peaked, throbbing nipples, he lowered his mouth to take hers. She opened to him, meeting the thrusts of his tongue, dizzy with desire.

"You're so beautiful." He backed her to the bed, where she collapsed with her arms stretched out to him. He yanked off his shirt and then covered her with his body, stroking her thighs, moving his hand between them.

Her breasts moved against crisp, chestnut hair and her hips instinctively thrust upward to meet his caress. The years fell away as if they'd never happened, and in her mind she was back in the groundskeeper's cottage, realizing a dream come true as their adolescent passions crashed around them more thunderously than the storm that raged outside.

He was everything she'd imagined he would be, a beautiful man, a warm man, her man—for now. She spread her legs, wanting more, hearing his gasp of pleasure as he slid his fingers inside her panties to touch her, found her wetness, knew the depth of her need.

He took his time, exploring, caressing, dipping down to kiss her mouth, her throat, her breasts, to run his tongue over the taut nipples, slipping off her panties to bury his face between her thighs. In a sudden agonized need for immediate release, she knew she wanted more of him. She wanted that hardness she'd felt, wanted him inside her. She was on the edge, falling, falling, falling....

"Does it feel good?" His voice was a murmur, gritty with arousal.

"Oh, yes." It was hard to get out the words.

"Am I doing what you like?"

"You're doing things...I didn't know how much I liked."

His laugh was low and soft. "Are we going too fast?"

"I want you inside me." She said it on a sob. She wanted him now, wanted him there for a long time, wanted to feel his pleasure as well as her own. He raised himself on one elbow and reached for his zipper, and in a few swift movements lay beside her, splendidly male, infinitely desirable.

Holding her breath, she touched him, heard him groan. He laved her with kisses—her face, her ears, her throat—while she stroked him lightly, tantalizingly, until she felt his impatience and knew she would soon possess all of him.

"You came prepared," she whispered as he protected himself and her.

He raised himself over her and stayed there for a moment, poised, gazing down at her with hunger in his eyes. "The Boy Scout type," he whispered back. "We are always prepared." And slowly, tormentingly, he entered her while, consumed by her own impatience, she lifted her hips to pull him in more deeply.

He filled her and surrounded her. She had thought she would possess him but instead was completely possessed by him. No one had ever made her feel this way, so totally embraced and cherished. He withdrew and thrust again and again, and with each thrust she felt more complete. It seemed they were beyond reality, locked in a world that was theirs alone.

The thrusts deepened, came faster, and she jousted with him in a battle both would win, until the aching pressure and heat built up feverishly and she was unable to hold back. With a cry she arched up to him and exploded in a tide of spasms that rocked her body, feeling the groan come from deep in his body as he, too, gave in to the pure pleasure of release.

Hot, panting and wet with sweat, they lay together in a tangle of sheets, separate, though, in their thoughts. At last he sighed deeply and stroked his hand between her breasts and down her belly. "You are some doctor, Cecily Connaught," he said, each word a warm stroke of its own.

She smiled at him. "Your condition requires many treatments, I'm afraid."

"That's good news. Because I was just thinking…"

He was fully erect again, throbbing against her thigh and tucking his arm beneath her to pull her over onto the length of his body when someone knocked none too discreetly on the door of his room.

"Don't answer it," Cecily said in a breathless whisper.

"It's the porter with my bag," he groaned.

"Clothes are the last thing you need right now." She got a determined grip on him.

"If I don't answer it, he'll come in. That's what porters do. They're supposed to walk right in and not notice us in the next room buck naked and rolling in the hay. It's your call, lady. I answer the door, or we give him the thrill of his life." His words puffed hotly against her skin.

The knock came again, even louder this time.

"Can you get the connecting door closed before he comes in?"

"No." He was already moving, rolling away from her, sliding out of bed, reaching for his pants, struggling into his shirt, and she could hear an ominous sound coming from the next room—the sound of a door opening.

She gave up. She couldn't quite face having sex in front of an audience. "Put a large bill in his hand and tell him you know how to work the air-conditioning and you're as happy to be here at the Courtland as he is happy to be your host."

He drowned out this sensible advice with a shout that might possibly have carried to a keen-eared Fort Worth resident. "Just a minute. Be right there." And he leaped toward the connecting door and closed it behind him.

FOR A MAN WHO'D BEEN YANKED straight from a dream come true—a dream of long, silky thighs, skin like heavy cream flavored with a drop of vanilla—to hideous reality, Will thought he was behaving pretty well.

It was particularly annoying to recall that all he had was one bag—a suit bag, and a *rolling* one at that. He hadn't needed a porter to bring it up. He could have managed with a duffle if he hadn't had to bring a dark suit for the party tonight and his monkey suit for the wedding.

The monkey suit was white. The whole wedding was white. "White on white," Sally had told him with a romantic sigh, which seemed to mean the whites didn't have to match, because his tux was very white and the satin lapels were—not very white and the pants were very white with a not-very-white stripe and the shirt was blindingly white—with ruffles that had some kind of stitch at the edges in the white of the lapels and stripes. He growled.

"Sir? Is anything wrong?"

"Oh. No." While these random thoughts had been running scattershot through his head, he'd been try-ing to remember where the hell he'd put his billfold, because in his haste to get to Cecily he recalled giving it a Frisbee kind of throw onto or into something or other. When he found it on the floor in one of his loafers, it took him another embarrassing minute to fumble out a ten-dollar bill—a ridiculous tip for one bag, but he'd read somewhere that guys did that when they were embarrassed. While he'd thought he was an exception to the rule, apparently he wasn't. At last the bill was in his fingertips, and he handed it to the porter.

"Thank you, sir. We're delighted to have you here at the Courtland. I hope you enjoy your stay."

Hadn't he heard that somewhere recently?

"May I show you the amenities of the room? This thermostat controls the—"

"Air-conditioning. I know. I'm sure I can figure out all the...amenities." He made an encouraging gesture toward the door. *Thank you. Now leave.*

"Perhaps you haven't noticed that you have a voice-mail message." Now the man looked more re-proving than a man should look when he'd just got-ten a ten-dollar tip.

"Yes, I know," Will muttered. *Leave, dammit, leave.*

"They told you at the desk, I think. You haven't checked it yet."

"But I will," Will said in a firmer, more forceful tone. "When I have time."

"I can show you how to access it if you—"

"All right!" He'd had it. "If I listen to the message, will you *leave?*"

"Of course, sir. I don't want to intrude on your privacy."

True to his word, he closed the door behind himself at last, but not until he'd watched Will pick up the phone. Will shook his head. Was there any business that didn't have some crazies in it?

Madder than hell, he pushed the message button.

"Will? Gator. Sorry I missed you at the hospital, but I wanted to ask you… Well, I know this sounds dumb, but when I was leaving Love Field, I thought I saw Gus getting on a private plane. Since I'm getting to the scene late and you know him a little better than the rest of us, I wondered if you knew what he might have been doing. Has anything gone wrong between him and Sally? Call me back in Muffy's hospital room." He repeated the number slowly. Twice. "Can't use my cell in here."

Shaken, Will put down the phone, consumed with guilt that he had managed to put Gus completely out of his mind and let Cecily completely fill it. He wanted the day to go on that way—filled with Cecily—and he gazed longingly at the door that separated him from her. Then with a muttered curse he returned Gator's call.

Gator answered with a cheerful, "I'll go outside and call you back on my cell. Stay put." Time passed while Will stayed put, shifting his weight from one foot to the other because he didn't want to be there, he wanted to be on the other side of the door where

Cecily was. But at last the phone rang and he snatched it up before it had done more than peep at him.

"You saw Gus getting on a plane?" Will asked, skipping the formalities, keeping his voice low and his back to the door.

"I thought it was Gus. I don't know the guy except for meeting him at a couple of parties. I guess nobody does except you, maybe. And it wasn't his plane, it was another one, a Learjet, so maybe I was wrong."

Will devoutly hoped so. The combination of possible tax fraud and Gus skipping town was making him crazy. "He was at the rehearsal. I don't think anything's wrong between him and Sally."

"That's good news."

Good news for Sally. Not necessarily good news for Will.

"You must know the guy better than I do," Gator said. "What's he like?"

"I don't know anything about him but his numbers." And those weren't adding up. "When we talk, he sounds like he's rapping with me, but when I look back, it turns out he hasn't told me a thing about himself. Whose plane was he getting on?"

"Well, I was in my car and thinking about Muffy and the baby, but the plane had a black-and-silver logo…let me think…something International. Shepherd. No, that's not it…."

"Think, Gator, *think*."

Gator thought. "It reminded me of wedding presents, that I'd forgotten to ask Muffy what we bought Sally and Gus. China, crystal, sterling. That's it— Sterling International."

Will sat down at the desk, reached for the phone pad and pen and scribbled down the name. Nothing in Gus's tax information had included a company named Sterling International. What the hell was it? And what was so important about it that it had drawn Gus away from Sally on the eve of their wedding?

STILL NAKED, HOT, FRUSTRATED and impatient, Cecily couldn't imagine what was keeping Will. Surely the porter had left long ago. Had Will forgotten what he'd been doing when he was interrupted?

She was finally impatient enough to go to the door and open it just an inch, and what she saw made her temper flare. With one touch he'd managed to turn her on again, and now he was talking on the phone!

She marched straight to the desk and snatched up the phone pad he'd been writing on. He jumped sky-high. She stared at him, then wrote, "You still have business with me."

She wrote it under the words Sterling International. He was working! What kind of one-night stand was he, anyway?

He wrote on the pad: "Sorry, just a second." Into the phone, he said, "Yeah, well, let me know if you find out, um, anything, ummmm, about, uh, him or it."

"What's this?" she wrote and drew an arrow up to the company name.

"Nothing important," he wrote. "Just another minute, promise."

"E-mail me, okay? I'll get the computer set up. Right," he told the receiver.

Cecily was grabbing for the pad, intending to write exactly what she thought about his setting up his computer and e-mailing at a time like this, but he snatched it back. "Model your new nightgown for me and wait for me in bed," he wrote. "I'll be right there." He added a slow, sexy smile and a caress that started at her shoulder and ran all the way down to her thigh. How could she say no?

She marched back into her room and, feeling more grumpy than sexy, put on the gown and robe. They were pale blue, like the lace lingerie, very sheer and very short. The gown was nothing more than a shapely little slip, and the robe was the same length, with satin trim down the front and at the hem of the kimono-style sleeves. It tied at the waist, but it didn't stay tied. It kept slipping open, silk sliding against silk…

She shivered. Silk sliding against skin, stroking her breasts, hardening her nipples, tickling her pubic hair, turning her on like a lover's caress.

Wow, Will really knew his undies.

She slid onto the bed and tried out several poses, then settled for sitting up against the pillows, one leg stretched out, the other drawn up in a way that wasn't blatant flashing but showed a bit of her bottom—quite accidentally, of course. This involved a good bit of thighs-rubbing-together action, which only intensified her impatience as she waited for Will.

Waited and waited and waited…

"Damn," she said and got off the bed. She opened her door and then Will's door. Will was off the phone—and on the computer!

"You are out here doing business instead of in there doing me?" she yelled at him.

He whirled away from the screen and leaped out of his chair. "Uh…I'm sorry. I mean I really do apologize. It's just this little situation that's come up…."

Fuming, she crossed her arms over her chest, then realized the effect was to shorten the gown and robe and dropped them back to her sides. "Seems to me your little situation has gone down rather than up."

He held out his arms imploringly. "Look, this is urgent. Not just important. Immediate. Believe me, this is not what I want to be doing right now."

She gazed at him. As much as she wanted to have a really big fight with him, what she wanted much, much more was to have sex with him right up until the rehearsal dinner.

She would simply have to seduce him.

7

WHEN HE SAID HE DIDN'T WANT to be doing this right now, that was God's own truth. She was almost edible in all that sheer blue stuff, and his hunger for her was nowhere close to being satisfied. Just his luck to find her again at the same time he was finding all kinds of reasons to worry about Gus's financial situation.

Not only was his professional reputation at stake, he also had a personal obligation to Sally. She was family. Their mothers were sisters. He couldn't sit by silently and let her marry a man whose financial situation was suspicious, nor could he let Gus break her heart by skipping the country with unreported, possibly illegal gains.

What he was doing was searching for information about Sterling International. Gus ran a security business. If Sterling International was a client, they might have summoned Gus because of an emergency, such as debugging the plane or checking out a bomb threat. Will just needed to know what the man was up to.

But even if he were engaged in something perfectly legal this afternoon, it still didn't explain the discrepancy between Gus's lifestyle and his reported income.

First things first, though. Will had found several

dozen companies with Sterling in their names and
three called Sterling International. Gator might have
misread or imagined the International part, so Will
wouldn't restrict his search to those. He'd been going
to one Web site after the other looking for clues and
was anxious to get back to it.

But now Cecily was coming toward him, giving
him a slow, meaningful smile, and her robe was coming open at the waist, giving him a full view through
one layer of sheer blue silk of her small, perfect
breasts with their tiny pink nipples hardened to
points, her flat tummy centered by a neat little navel,
the swell of her hips and, between her thighs, the
mound of honey-blond hair that had tickled his
mouth and tasted so sweet....

To his relief and gratitude, she slid her hands
around his neck and gave him a light, off-center kiss.
"I've been too selfish," she murmured into one corner of his mouth, which set everything stirring in his
body that shouldn't be stirring when he was in the
midst of a professional crisis. "If you have an emergency, of course it's more important than having fun
with me."

"I like having fun with you," Will croaked, not
letting himself touch her.

"Well, sometimes we just have to make sacrifices,
don't we?" She moved up a little closer and the tight
nipples brushed against him. "I know you want to
take off your clothes and carry me back to that bed
as much as I want you to." Her hips swayed forward,
almost but not quite touching him. "But people have
to take work seriously, don't you think?"

Oh, God, she was even closer, and with her arms
around his neck, the gown and robe were riding up

higher and higher. Will tried as hard as he could not to put his arms around her, but he failed. He settled his hands lightly on her back. The silk must be slippery, because his hands kept sliding down toward her delicious bottom when he'd intended to keep them high on her shoulder blades.

"Don't you worry. When you think you can take a little break from your work, I'll be ready and waiting for you." She punctuated the word *ready* by taking that last fatal step forward and wriggling ever so lightly against his aching erection. The last drop of blood left in his brain cells flew south like a Canada goose. "I'll snuggle up against you, and then I want to kiss you all over your body—and I mean all over."

His hands took the last fatal slide and his fingers closed over taut, silky-skinned, bare buttocks.

He actually gasped aloud.

And then he thought about Gus and he thought about Sally. He thought about Sally's failed first marriage and his aunt Elaine's grief when it had ended.

And then Cecily moved against him again, a little more suggestively.

Gus, he thought desperately. *Sally, my job, my family's peace of mind are all at stake here.*

"I…" he said, "I…have to do just a little bit more work." And he managed to let go of her delicious bottom, spin himself around and sit back down at the desk, throbbing uncomfortably, to bring up his e-mail.

He felt an electrical storm brewing behind him, but she surprised him. "I understand," she said, all kindness. "I have things to do, too. I haven't tried on even half of my new underwear. You go ahead and work." She slid her arms around his neck, tucked her hands inside his shirt and splayed them across his chest, almost but not quite touching his nipples, playing in his hair.

He gritted his teeth and entered his password.

"I especially want to try that pretty little apricot-colored set," she purred, dropping a kiss on his ear. "I'll be back in a few minutes."

She left. Will thought about locking his door, but that seemed childish. Gator hadn't sent an e-mail message, so he went back to the Internet, returning to a Web site for Sterling, Inc. This company was located in Montana, was owned by a man named Sterling and made things out of sheepskin.

Who'd want to steal a sheepskin?

"Where to look next?" he muttered.

"At me," Cecily said from a spot too close behind him.

It rattled him, but he turned around to see her in the camisole and panties that were the pinkish color of salmon, the camisole doing nothing to conceal her breasts and the panties so narrow that a few strands of crisp, curly, dark gold hair peeked out above them.

"How do I look in this?" she said, her eyes glittering.

"Very nice," he managed to say. Even his throat felt swollen. He was hit by a brilliant thought. "But I haven't seen you in that black thong yet. Try it on for me."

She slithered back into her room. He closed his eyes and moaned, then opened his e-mail again.

Still nothing from Gator. He e-mailed a friend who was a professor at the business school at New York University, and revealing as little as possible, asked him how to go about finding out if a company owned a plane and employed a security agency. Just as he clicked the Send button, he felt Cecily's hands cover his eyes.

"Surprise," she said into his ear, vibrating every nerve ending in his body.

Those were her naked breasts brushing his shoulders. He could tell without looking. He leaned back against them, then turned to sneak a peek at her.

"You didn't say which bra I should model."

"No," Will groaned. "No, I didn't."

"So I didn't wear one. What do you think?"

Reluctantly he turned around, and so did she, and his gaze was suddenly filled with the ultimate butt, round but with well-toned firmness, like the butt of a woman who worked out regularly.

Or delivered calves regularly.

Or a woman who was often in the arms of a man, lifting to meet his thrusts, her legs spread to draw him in deeply, twisting, turning, struggling in an agony of desire…

He was wasted. He gave up. His hands closed on those creamy cheeks, kneading them, lifting them— and from his laptop came a little ping.

His hands stilled, then dropped away from her, and he clenched the back of the chair. Like a man in a dream, he turned back to the laptop. The ping meant he had a new message, maybe from Gator.

His hand was on the mouse, bringing up Mail and Newsgroups, when in one fluid motion Cecily poured herself over him, straddling him, her hair loose and flowing, hiding the screen, her breasts crushed against his chest, making him suddenly uninterested in the screen, the e-mail, Gator or Gus.

She felt hot, aflame with a need too intense to play games anymore. She was desperate for the sex—even more desperate than he was. He could feel it in the way she sought out his swelling erection and moved against him, slow and languid but purposeful. He had to satisfy her, at least cool the flames inside her with one moment of relief.

And so he held her, moving with her, his face buried in her throat and his hands on her bottom, lifting her, stroking her, raking her with his fingernails. He felt her come in a series of violent shudders, with a moan from low in her throat, just as he glimpsed over her shoulder the e-mail address at the top of the screen.

While she clung to him, he snaked a hand out to the mouse and opened the e-mail from Gator. It was a short, simple, chilling statement.

Gus was missing.

IT WAS A PECULIAR POSITION to be in—Cecily sitting on an erection that was still the size of the Chrysler Building and him with a professional problem the size of a small civil war.

He couldn't talk to her about the problem. She'd learn soon enough that Gus was missing, but discretion forbade him to tell her what Gus's disappearance meant to him.

She stopped moving against him and gave him a little shake. "Will, still here?" Her mouth was swollen, her eyes heavy-lidded, her voice smoky. She was irresistible—nearly.

"Sure." He tried for a wide, sexy smile, but his eyes kept drifting toward his laptop screen.

"So maybe you'd like to continue this activity instead of *staring at your e-mail?*" Her eyes were starting to flash and her voice rose with every word. He was in big trouble.

He tucked her head against his shoulder and ran his fingertips down her back. He could see the screen better with her hair out of the way. "Oh, yeah. That was just a sample. In just a minute, right after I look at this one little thing, we'll do some more sampling, and then…"

Gus was missing. Had Gator asked all the right questions? Had he tracked down the best man, that Derek guy, and asked him where he thought Gus might have gone?

Derek Stafford's connection to Gus was a professional one. Will had inferred that they'd worked together in the past, which was why Gus had asked him to be best man, and maybe Derek still served as a consultant in Gus's new security business. Other than those assumptions, none of their mutual friends knew any more about Stafford than they knew about Gus.

His lap was suddenly, sadly, empty, and Cecily was standing behind him. He could tell she was madder than hell without even turning around to look at her. "Sure we will," she said. "I know your definition of 'a minute.'" She flounced away, opened his door, opened her door, slammed his, slammed hers, and Will was left with an empty lap, a classic case of blue balls and a whole lot of silence.

His door flew open. She was back. "I have never, *never* known a man so attached to his clothes and his computer as you." She huffed for a second. "In fact, you're so boring, I'm going to find out who my voice-mail message is from and call her back, *even though I know it's my mother!*"

Muffy's words came back to him as if she'd yelled them at him only yesterday: "You're about as much fun as phonics!"

But he didn't feel as though he could kill Cecily as

he had Muffy. He wanted to drag her off to bed and make love with her until she screamed.

CECILY GAVE WILL'S DOOR AN especially emphatic slam and then did the same thing with her own. The moment of relief had given way to suddenly building desire to be skin to skin with him, to have him inside her again, deep inside her, thrusting inside her while she writhed against him. He wasn't having the same vivid, arousing image. He wasn't interested in anything but his work.

It had always made her a little uneasy to think of her parents having sex, but now she realized she didn't need to feel uneasy, because her father probably did this same thing to her mother all the time.

And really, what right did she have to complain? Didn't she put work before everything else? The only reason she was free this weekend was that it was difficult to impossible to bring her patients with her.

If she could have, she would have brought Bertha the sow, who would soon give birth to the biggest litter she'd ever had, and Cecily had predicted complications. With Bertha's condition to monitor, she had to admit sex with Will would have been second on the list in order of importance.

She unclenched her fists, anger giving way to disappointment and frustration. Also, the thong was a torture device, undoubtedly invented by men. She took it off, then looked through her new lingerie again and put on the lace panties like the blue ones, but in white. From her suitcase she took a shirt she liked, a long-sleeved blue-and-white stripe—well, more blue and grayish by now—and put it on, relaxed by its much-washed softness.

Still reluctant to face the real world, she picked up the phone, pushed the message button and lay down on the rumpled bed, resigned to the sound of her mother's voice.

"Cecily, we don't really know each other yet, but—"

She sat bolt upright. True, her mother didn't really know her, but this was not her mother.

"—this is Gus, and I need your help."

Something was wrong. Her heart pounded. She slung her legs over the side of the bed and slid them into her Teva sandals, ready to run if she needed to, reminding herself she would need to put on pants first. But something in Gus's voice told her he wasn't sending her out to buy eye-makeup remover for Sally.

"I had to leave town for the afternoon. I didn't tell Sally, didn't have time for an argument, so she'll go ballistic when she finds out I wasn't at the golf course with the rest of the guys. I thought maybe since you were the maid of honor and her oldest friend, you'd be the right person to call her. Tell her I'm fine, this is just a little job I had to do, and I'll be back in time for the rehearsal dinner, okay? And tell her I love her more than ever. It's not like I'm leaving her at the altar. Thanks. See you tonight."

Cecily began to relax. It wasn't a crisis after all. Sally would be royally ticked off for sure—the very idea of a man working on the day before his wedding—

The similarity between Sally's situation and her own was striking, come to think of it. Gus had a higher priority than his imminent marriage, and Will had a higher priority than Cecily's sex life.

Men.

Just for the heck of it, Cecily went through her

suitcase, her medical bag and her purse looking for the schedule of events for the weekend, but couldn't find it. Seeing Will's name in the wedding party roster had rattled her badly. She must have left it on the plane. She'd immediately decided not to join the bridesmaids for the spa afternoon—a spa afternoon ranked right up there with a root canal—had memorized the times and places for the rehearsal, rehearsal dinner and wedding and had promptly forgotten the name of the spa.

But it wasn't that important. She was just letting Sally know Gus wasn't jilting her. So she'd leave a message for Sally in her room, the honeymoon suite, where Sally's mother was forcing Sally to stay alone tonight.

Mothers.

The hotel operator connected her to Sally's voice-mail, where she quoted Gus's message verbatim. Then she went back to her tangled suitcase to get the book she'd brought to read—*Syngamus Trachea, Recent Strides in Prevention*—by a famous veterinary professor.

The room was cool, the bed was comfortable and a study of parasites wasn't something destined to turn a person on, but she couldn't focus on worms— at least not those of the parasitic variety. Gus and Will both qualified as worms of the *Homo sapiens* sort. She had reasons to be mad at Will, but didn't know why she suddenly felt uneasy about Gus.

Of course, with her attitude toward marriage, she was just looking for something to go wrong. He might be buying something beautiful for Sally—diamonds or a new car. He hadn't sounded scared or worried. But had his lazy drawl sounded a bit rushed? That was understandable, wasn't it? He had to do what he had to do and get back for the rehearsal dinner.

She read another page. Then she decided she'd feel better if she spoke to Sally personally. Maybe Will had brought the itinerary. Accounting, lawyerly types did that kind of neat, organized thing. Clutching the book, she opened both connecting doors and stepped into Will's room. "Gus called," she said.

She certainly wasn't prepared for Will's reaction. He levitated straight up from the desk chair, whirled, rushed over to her and grabbed both her arms. "You should have told me. I need to talk to him."

She was too startled to answer for a second or two. "It was just a message on the voice mail," Cecily said. "The one I was so sure was from my mother. Why are you so—"

"What did he say? Where is he?"

"I don't know where he is," she said, trying to calm Will, "but he's fine. He wanted me to tell Sally not to worry about him, that he'd be back for the rehearsal dinner."

"Did he say why he left?"

"He said he had a little job to do. Really, Will, you're overreacting, especially for a man who seems to have a few little jobs of his own to do." She glared at him.

"Sorry," he said hurriedly, dropping his grip on her arms. "How did he sound?"

What an exasperating man. "He sounded like an airline pilot, you know, that fake good-old-boy voice they use when they're saying the plane's encountering some turbulence and would we please fasten our seat belts and pray."

"But did he sound like the pilots do when they're telling the truth or the way they sound when they're lying and the plane's about to crash?"

Cecily gritted her teeth. "I can't really answer that penetrating question, Will. I've never been on a plane that was about to crash."

"In the movies," he said, ignoring her sarcasm. "You know what I mean."

She tightened up her mouth, but she did think about it. "Marginally more like a pilot who's lying and trying to sound soothing."

Will snapped his fingers. "Just as I thought."

Cecily simply snapped. "Thought what? And by the way, I resent that even half-naked I can't drag you away from your job, while Gus has you forgetting all about your work simply by leaving town fully dressed."

He held out his arms in a gesture of appeal. "Cecily, Gus *is* my work."

HE WAS BREAKING EVERY RULE in the book by telling Cecily why he was more than worried about Gus. But even when she was glaring at him, she looked so sweet and friendly in her blue-and-white striped shirt that he couldn't help himself. Somewhere inside him he knew he could trust her, and he'd been worrying alone as long as he could handle it.

"Whew," Cecily said when he'd finished his short, blunt statement that he suspected Gus had income from some source other than his security company and that Muffy's husband, Gator, had seen him at the airport, apparently flying somewhere. "That puts a different spin on his leaving town the day before his wedding."

"Doesn't it, though." He didn't protest when Cecily dragged him down to the sofa, sat close beside him, crossed her long, slim, bare legs and reached for another pad and pencil that lay on the coffee table beside another telephone.

"Start at the beginning," she said. "What worried you about Gus's tax return?"

He observed with some surprise that in this mode, no longer brazenly seductive but simply supportive, Cecily was for some mysterious reason even more desirable. An enveloping warmth and a strength that made her seem Amazonian emanated from her. This was a woman who'd back him up if he had to trade a friendship for professional ethics. He let himself snuggle shoulder to shoulder with her, reminded himself that business had top priority over pleasure and then came out with everything.

"He sent me his tax information. He pays himself a salary from the security company proceeds, and it's right in line with the reported profits—decent but not exorbitant. He has the middle-class person's stock portfolio, also decent, but he's not quite a millionaire."

"Sounds fine so far."

"So what about the Lamborghini? And the classic Citroën? And the house in Highland Park? And the country club memberships. Skiing time-shares, travel, Rolex watches and Armani suits. The clues I've gotten from my mother and Muffy go on and on."

"He's spending a lot more than that decent income could pay for?"

"Looks like it. Then there's his plane…"

"But he deducts that from the security company grosses."

The woman was sharp, but he had the numbers.

"More than the company could afford with those grosses."

"Sally's loaded," Cecily said without the slightest indication of envy. "She has trust funds out the wazoo."

"Mr. Shipley insisted on a prenup. Gus thought it was great. Sally was embarrassed."

The way Cecily's perfect forehead creased when she was puzzled began to entrance him. They were alike in some ways. He was sure his forehead creased in the same way and his eyes squinted up in the same way when he was working out a problem. When a problem arose, she seemed to care about solving it as much as he did. And this was a really big problem.

"Did he leave in *his* plane?" she asked him, pencil poised.

"No." His conscience bleeped at him like a pager. Should he tell her absolutely everything or not? At this point, why the hell not? "The plane had a Sterling International logo. I've never heard of the company, so I've been looking at companies called Sterling on the Internet."

"That's a start," Cecily said. "But how will you know when you find the right one? There must be dozens."

"I have no idea," Will said, feeling pretty glum.

"My first responsibility is to Sally. I have to talk to her in person," Cecily said with an air that said "don't mess with my priorities." "In fact, that's why I came out here—to see if you knew where the bridesmaids were going this afternoon."

"You didn't get the schedule of events?" Why Sally hadn't included Cecily in the luxurious spa afternoon distracted him briefly from his big problems.

"Of course Sally sent me a schedule of events," Cecily said crossly. "It grossed me out. It was a chatty little letter from her and Gus telling the wedding party what their perks were. Like members of a wedding party deserve perks. And what fun everyone was going to have. How do they know what they think is fun will be fun for everybody else? Anyway, I had no intention of going to the spa, so I didn't bother remembering its name." She paused. "The name of a spa isn't the kind of thing that sticks in my mind. Ask me to remember the names of twenty-five known stomach parasites—that I can do."

"As enlightening as that sounds, we'll do it some other time," Will said. Now he was thoroughly distracted. Cecily, who'd sounded like a woman who'd been exiled from the bridesmaids' treats of facials, hair coloring, manicures and pedicures, was telling him she'd excluded herself on purpose because she didn't need all that stuff.

He also noticed that she'd glanced guiltily at her toes. He couldn't see anything wrong with her toes. The nails weren't polished, but the toes looked as long, slim and suckable as the rest of her.

Forget the toes, he said firmly to the lower half of his body. Gus was his top priority right now.

"I didn't read the itinerary," he confessed. "The first sentence put me off. Something like, 'Hey, Dudes and Divas, we're gonna have us a hell of a wedding weekend.'"

"I found it annoying, too," Cecily said primly.

"So I just wrote down the times for the rehearsal, the dinner and the wedding."

Cecily gave him a focused gaze that almost wiped out all his good intentions of making sure Sally would be marrying a decent man—and he, Will, would be signing an honest tax return. "I saw your name and stopped there," she said.

It rocked him to the core. It was the time to say something significant, something that would change the whole atmosphere of their time together. But he couldn't come up with it fast enough. Cecily was already on to the task at hand.

"I'll look up spas in the Yellow Pages," she said.

Will made a dive for the drawer that held phone books. He was infused with an urgency to get the problem to a reasonable stopping point—stopping for the thing he really wanted, which was Cecily naked in his bed or hers and the other parts of their lives moving smoothly along without them.

No, he wanted a little more. He wanted to establish her back in his life. The next twenty-four hours would do nothing more than whet his appetite.

With the phone books, he sat on the sofa, just a little too close to her. He was gratified when she moved a little closer to him, too, and thrilled when she slipped off her sandals and tugged her feet up under her thighs, the Yellow Pages resting on her lap and her head resting on his shoulder.

Cozy. He slid an arm around her.

"Spas," she said, but her voice was rich and dreamy, and again he experienced that sense of animal strength in her. Animal in that she focused intently on what she wanted at any given moment— and at this moment, she wanted to help him while feeling close to him. Watching her thumb through the pages for the S section and begin to browse through an endless list of spa entries heated him up even more than the black thong had.

It was as if they were a team. A couple. A couple

who had sex and a whole lot of other things keeping them together.

And he'd lost his head and was thinking way out of the box, which as everybody knew was not the kind of thing an accountant—especially an accountant whose client might be cheating on his tax return—should be doing.

Didn't mean he had to stop cuddling Cecily. Awareness of all aspects of the situation—that was the ticket. List the tasks, then prioritize them.

That was his current problem—prioritizing them.

"What are you looking for?" he asked her, tightening his hold on her such a little bit he hoped she wouldn't notice.

"Something that rings a bell." Her profile told him she was drawing her light brown, arched brows closer together as she studied the phone book.

He felt too warm again. She was working on *his* problem, was willing to help *him* solve it, and he wasn't helping *her* at all.

"I read the whole agenda," she said, "so the name of the spa would have made some sort of impression in my mind. I'm hoping I'll see it and think 'that's the one.'"

"Is there anything that might jog your memory?" He was thinking about Gator saying, "Wedding presents...sterling." Seeing the puzzled look on her face, he added, "Did the name remind you of something else? A book? A movie?"

She looked up at him so suddenly that their mouths hovered together like butterflies in flight. "America the Beautiful," she whispered in a smoky voice, her breath warm and sweet against his lips, then quickly looked down at the phone book.

Will took it off her thighs, cuddled her a little closer and found he needed to clear his throat before he spoke. "American Spa," he said, starting off at the top of the list.

"No."

"Beautiful You Day Spa."

"No."

"Spacious Skies Day Spa."

"There can't be a Spacious Skies Day Spa."

"No, there isn't," he said, checking the S listings. "There is a Big Sky Day Spa."

"That's not it."

He went back to the A listings. "What about Amber's Salon?"

"No. Why Amber?"

"Amber waves of grain."

"Of course. And purple mountains' majesty above the fruited—"

"Purple Plains Day Spa. No mountains."

"Maybe we should sing the song all the way through. I know the words. I can't carry a tune, though."

Singing hadn't been part of the weekend culture at Green Trails Stable. "That's what everybody says. I'm sure you have a great voice. Oh, beautiful…" Will began.

"For spacious skies…" Cecily chimed in.

She was right. She really couldn't carry a tune. How could someone with such a beautiful, sultry speaking voice sound so terrible when she was singing?

"For amber waves of…"

The first stanza failed to awaken the memory of the name of the spa, and Will's eardrums were aching. "Maybe we should bite the bullet and go down the list one name at a time," he suggested.

"Did you see how many spas are on that list? I remember the words to the next stanza. I'll sing it. Oh, beautiful, for patriots' dreams that see beyond…"

Listening to Cecily's rendition of the second stanza was a painful experience. Why did it make him hug her a little tighter?

"…the years. Thine…Alabaster Day Spa!" she shrieked so suddenly they both almost fell off the sofa. Righting herself she grabbed the phone book out of his hands and frantically punched in the number.

"I understand your promise to your guests is to protect them from their everyday interruptions," Cecily said a few minutes later, after she'd asked for Sally and stressed the importance of reaching her. "But this isn't an everyday interruption. In fact, it's something of an emergency, so I'd appreciate it very much if you'd get her off the warm-oil-massage table and put her on the phone."

Will was worried about how pink her face was getting and even more concerned when her knuckles on the phone began to turn white.

"I can see your point there, too," she said with a sweetness that wasn't backed up by anything in her body language, "that if Sally were expecting an emergency call from me she'd have given me her cell number…."

Apparently she was repeating the conversation for his benefit, because she turned to him, rolling her eyes.

"But you see—" her voice started to rise "—how the hell was she supposed to guess she'd have an emergency, know what I mean? That's what an emergency is, isn't it? Something that happens suddenly and without warning? That needs to be handled quickly? So get the woman on the phone. Now!"

Will knew that would have done it for him, and apparently it did it for the Alabaster Day Spa receptionist. While she waited, Cecily muttered imprecations to herself, but her skin tone was returning to normal and she'd switched the phone to her other hand and was flexing her fingers.

She abruptly stopped flexing. "She what? She did. How long ago? Can you catch the limo?" She drooped all over. "Okay, well…" She gritted her teeth. "Thanks so much for trying."

She slammed the phone down. "While that…that airhead argued with me, Sally and her bridesmaids walked right past her and out to the limo."

"Undisturbed by everyday interruptions," Will said. He went horizontal on the sofa, arms and legs stretched out.

Cecily stayed at the desk, her forehead resting on one hand.

Her hands, when she'd touched him, had the same controlled strength he saw in the rest of her. Those hands had delivered baby lambs and piglets, lifted sick and wounded animals. She was different from anyone he knew. She was a special person. Special and especially sexy. And he'd recognized it even when he was an adolescent, testosterone-driven, mindless organism.

He opened his eyes and looked at her at the same moment she lifted her head and looked at him. "I was just thinking," he said, slowly getting into a more upright position.

"So was I," Cecily said, uncrossing her legs, clearly planning to stand up.

"That we've done all we can for now," Will said, getting up to meet her.

"Right, we've done all we can. We have to wait for Sally to get the message in her room," Cecily said.

"And Gus will be back for the rehearsal dinner, so I can ask him right up front instead of nosing around behind his back, just a simple, 'Hey, Gus, what's Sterling International?'"

Cecily glanced at her watch. "You'll have to wait a while to do that. Are you sure you can handle it?"

Will put his hands on her shoulders and brushed his lips across hers. "I have never," he said, pulling her a little closer and sliding his arms around her, "been so sure," he continued, giving her a more purposeful kiss, "of anything in my life."

AT LAST SHE LAY BESIDE HIM again, the warmth of his skin and the prickle of the crisp hair on his chest and legs exciting her to near madness. She was getting exactly what she'd wanted but not what she'd expected. She'd expected to prance around in sexy underwear and be excited, then satisfied, by erotic words, technical competence and her own deprived libido. Instead she was being stroked by a real man, excited by his desire and her own—a man who seemed to like her body, maybe even liked her.

The way he caressed her breasts—circling her nipples with his tongue, moaning softly as if every second of the delight he was giving her pleased him just as much—stirred both her body and her heart. He made her feel not merely desired as any man might desire a woman but cherished.

That feeling of being cherished collapsed every defense against personal involvement she had at her disposal, and she gave herself completely to the sensations and emotions that were taking over. Heat and moisture flooded to the apex of her thighs, and she trusted him enough to let those reactions carry her away, let her mind go free in his arms.

His hands, his mouth on the most secret, private parts of her, inflamed her, and when at last, having driven her over the peak again and again, he entered her to give himself release at last, the flames burst even higher, and she came with him in a glorious burst of fireworks.

The entire concept of a one-night stand fled in the explosion, and Cecily accepted the terrible truth that she needed Will for much more than twenty-four hours. She might even be in love.

8

"LET'S NOT GO."

"Okay," Will said.

"You can call Gus. You don't have to see him."

"Right."

"Just say, 'Gus, what are you up to?' Not like a fickle, faithless friend who's trying to mess up the wedding but like an outraged cousin who'd rather mess up a wedding than let Gus mess up Sally's life."

"Um."

"Or we could tell Sally's father we're worried. He wouldn't have to pretend to be an outraged father. He does outrage naturally, my mother tells me."

"Uh-huh."

"Besides, so many people will be at that rehearsal dinner, they won't even miss us," Cecily said.

"Never miss us," Will said.

Cecily rose up on one elbow to gaze at him. He was supine, lying on his back with his eyes closed. She ran her fingertips down his chest, tangling them in the crisp, curly chestnut hair, then drew little circles around his navel.

He moaned.

She paused, fingertips poised over the flat plane of his stomach. "You okay?"

"Where are you getting all this energy?"

She resumed her stroking. "Oh, this takes hardly any energy at all. Now this—" she slid over him "—this takes effort."

He yawned. Not encouraging.

"Food," she said. "That's what you need. We can order from room service." Her mouth suddenly watered for real Texas nachos loaded with beef and cheese, sour cream, guacamole and salsa. "I could handle a nacho or two." She sat up, still straddling him, and reached for the hotel directory of services in hopes of finding a room-service menu. Thumbing through the pages, she glanced down at him. "Ah. I see the nachos got your attention."

His eyes still closed, he smiled. It was the most action she'd gotten out of him in the last fifteen minutes.

"Oh, look, a menu at last. Okay, how about nachos and an order of fajitas with all the trimmings?"

"Two orders. Each."

"Three words," she said. "I can tell you're in a state of hysterical excitement. What do you want to drink?"

"Beer. Goes well with Tex-Mex."

"Beer it is."

She reached for the phone just as it rang. "You don't suppose room service is calling *us*, do you?" And then she said, "Mother! Hi!" She scrambled off Will, who said, "Oof," almost loudly enough for her mother to hear, retreated to the other side of the bed with the telephone and pulled the sheet up to her chin. Will turned on his side to face her. He looked amused. She switched to the speaker phone. Let Will see for himself how amusing it was to talk to her mother.

"At last. I can rest easy tonight. My daughter is

alive and speaking to me. You might have called when you got there."

"I've been busy."

"For all I knew," her mother said, "you might have backed out at the last minute. Your father wouldn't let me call any earlier. He said, 'Samantha, of course she'll go, so don't bug her.' But I said, 'Fred, I'm her mother. I have to hear her voice to be sure—'"

"You've heard it, so you know I came."

"About fifty times," Will said.

Cecily rolled over and clapped her free hand across his mouth. "See, you worried for no reason at all."

"Is there a man in your room, Cecily?"

"Just Dan Rather."

"Oh." Instead of relieved, her mother sounded disappointed. "He's already married, isn't he?" Now a wistful note entered in. "Is Sally glowing with happiness?"

Cecily frowned at the phone. Instead of parenting methods, her mother had mastered method acting. "Utterly radiant," she said. "The perfect bride." *Absent a groom for the moment.*

"Just as you will be one day," her mother said. "I hope."

"Never, Mother. You can delete your folder of wedding ideas."

Will gave her an odd look.

"Did you have a productive afternoon at the spa?"

Cecily winced and crossed her fingers. "I had a great afternoon." At least it made Will smile again.

"I hope so." Now the motherly mood was one of worry. "I hope you had your hair done and a manicure and a pedicure. I know you can't get those things done properly in Vermont."

"No," Cecily said patiently, "up there I just cut my hair with a scythe and my nails with pruning shears."

"That's what I thought the last time I saw you." She let out the resigned sigh of a martyr. "Well, darling, now that we've talked I feel much better. Have a lovely evening, and I hope we can spend a minute with you before the wedding tomorrow. We're taking the earliest plane. I'm so sorry we couldn't come today, but there was the matter of the paper Daddy had to give."

"Yes. Daddy's paper." Cecily said goodbye, and pushed the speaker phone off.

Will was gazing at her, looking curious and thoughtful. "You told your mother you were never going to get married."

"As I have told her repeatedly."

"What makes you so sure?"

Cecily tugged the sheet up a little farther. "Living with them. With my parents. Watching them."

"They don't get along?"

"They don't fight like you and Muffy do. Or did. They just move along parallel lines. They don't connect."

"But they stay together. They must have something going."

"I don't know what it is. Except plenty of money. There's family money on both sides, but Daddy pursues his academic career as if it were the only thing standing between him and welfare. He makes money, Mother spends it and he doesn't pay the slightest attention to her, ever. He communicates with his colleagues and his students but mostly with his own brain, and she communicates with her women friends, her hairdresser and her decorator. They never communicate with each other. As I said, parallel lives."

"I guess lots of marriages drift like that," Will said.

"When one person has sacrificed a career for the marriage, yes, I think they do. Okay, enough sociology, let's order food before anything else happens."

Right on cue, the phone rang again. With a disgusted snort, Will got out of bed. "You take your call, I'll order from my room."

Cecily took a second to admire his magnificent naked backside before she picked up the phone. She wished she'd taken another second to sigh and drool, because the voice on the phone came at her like an electrical shock.

"Thanks for the call, but he's not back and the rehearsal dinner starts in fifteen minutes! What the hell am I supposed to do? Go to my own rehearsal dinner without a date?" And with that, Sally burst into tears.

WILL WALKED BACK INTO CECILY'S room no longer exhausted. He'd added a few more things to their room-service order, and the evening seemed filled with promise. He stopped short at the door, though, because he could see that Cecily was in the midst of a disaster. As if it would help, he got a towel from the bathroom and wrapped it around his waist, a prehistoric warrior girding himself for battle and protecting his only truly essential body part.

"Sally," Cecily was saying soothingly, "all I know is what Gus told me. He said he loved you more than ever. Things happen, you know? Maybe he's in a traffic jam in a no-service area, so he can't call you on his cell. This is the eve of your wedding. You have to have faith in him."

"Bull," Will said, and Cecily shushed him with a finger on her lips.

"He definitely said it was a job he had to do," she said after a long silence at her end of the line. Then her voice faltered a little. "Yes, he did say out of town—"

Another long silence. "The security business isn't a nine-to-five job, Sally, and something came up—" The phone nearly leaped out of her hand from the decibel level of Sally's response.

"Of course I will. Absolutely." She was speaking into the receiver, but she finished the sentence looking straight at Will. "Wouldn't miss it for the world, especially not now when you need all the support you can get. We'll…I'll be a little late. My hair's not cooperating. Now calm down, Sally. Remember what a gracious and charming person you are, and you'll get through this dinner like the lady your mother taught you to be." She stuck her finger in her mouth and pretended to be gagging.

Will threw both arms in the air—so much for the nachos and fajitas, because she was obviously talking about the rehearsal dinner—and the towel fell off, revealing how ready he was to make love with Cecily some more, much more and as quickly as possible. He grabbed the towel off the floor, went briefly into his own room and returned with a shaving kit. Marching into Cecily's bathroom with as much dignity as he could muster under the circumstances, he turned on the shower.

She joined him in mere seconds. "I can't believe I just said exactly what my mother would have said under the same circumstances," she said, not even noticing the magnitude of his manly pride. "Is that shower for me?"

"For both of us. Separation anxiety."

She gave him a look that said things might be happening elsewhere but they couldn't change what had happened between them. "I'll shower with you if you'll wash my hair."

"It's a deal. I'll wash every hair on your body."

While he gently massaged shampoo into Cecily's thick mane, he thought regretfully of how much fun this would be if he could take it slowly, lather every inch of her and then slide against her while she was wet and soapy. But Cecily, in spite of that look, seemed hell-bent on speed.

"Conditioner," she said tersely, and when he'd put it on and rinsed it out, she leaped out of the shower. Through the frosted glass he could see her body in motion, rapidly making progress toward getting ready.

More slowly than the situation warranted, Will rinsed off the last of Cecily's shampoo that clung to his body, thinking about her focus on the task at hand—in this case, her maid-of-honor responsibility to Sally—and wondering if that focus, that sense of responsibility, had any connection to her decision never to get married.

Could he ever convince her that he was the same kind of person and that two people with massive senses of responsibility were people who could love and understand each other and would do anything in their power to make the relationship work? Because a relationship was a big responsibility, too.

Could he do that? Did he want to?

Before he explored the internal mysteries of Cecily,

he had to deal with Gus, Sally and this fiasco of a wedding.

He stepped out of the shower to find Cecily's face hidden under a curtain of hair. Wearing the tiny cream-colored panties he'd picked out for her, with one foot propped up on the bathroom counter, she was peering out from under the curtain, polishing her toenails with her right hand and wielding the hair dryer with her left.

"A multitasker," he said approvingly, whipping out a razor and shaving cream.

"Damn. I don't know how anybody gets this stuff on without dribbling it over the edges," Cecily said grimly. "How likely is it anybody will look closely at my toes?"

"I will. In fact, I may give them some fairly close attention after dinner."

"Then you can repaint them when we get home if they offend your aesthetic sensibilities. I don't dare do more than one coat or they won't get dry." She put her feet on the floor and attacked her fingernails with polish.

Even Will—because he'd grown up with Muffy—knew things were getting dicey when Cecily attempted to polish her fingernails and dry her hair at the same time. "Let me help," he said, attempting to wrench the dryer out of her hand.

She struggled to hang on to it. "You have to get yourself ready."

"Hey, you're looking at Transformation Man. I can make myself acceptable in five minutes flat." He finally had a grip on the hair dryer, which he applied to the back of Cecily's head while she studiously, although not skillfully, applied polish to her fingernails.

"Sally said something interesting," she said from under her hair-shield. "She said, 'He promised me no more dangerous work. That's what the security company is all about—no more dangerous work.' That's why she's so hysterical. But what dangerous work? That's what you're looking for, Will. What was he doing before he set up his security company? Will! My hair needs drying, not my boobs."

Too stunned to aim properly, Will was hung up on the two words *dangerous work.* He'd seen Gus's bio— the neat, straight bio of a neat, straight man. So had Sally's father. This was a fact he had to keep secret forever. Mr. Shipley had had Gus investigated all the way back to his kindergarten days and had come up with the American dream of young and successful manhood. Nothing dangerous about the guy.

Except that this dream man had disappeared the day before his wedding.

On the bright side, Cecily had appeared the day before the wedding.

Will reaimed the hair dryer, tossing Cecily's hair with his fingertips, loving the heavy, silky feel of it. The bad always came along with the good. It meant he had to keep his brain compartmentalized, and thinking about it, he realized that compartmentalization was what people expected of accountants. If only accountants' private parts could be trained to get the message.

While he ruminated, Cecily had disappeared, then returned to the bathroom in the silk dress he'd picked out for her. Seeing it on her for the first time, he gave up his regret for the nachos. She was all he wanted to eat for as long as he could see into the future.

"You look fantastic," was the best he could manage. "I need my five minutes, and we're off to the rehearsal dinner."

"Separately," Cecily said. She put down the makeup brush she'd been wielding and looked at him, her gaze sliding over him in his black briefs, resulting in a disastrous effect on the fit of those briefs.

"Right. Of course. We'll reintroduce ourselves during the cocktail hour." *And I'll fall in lust all over again right there in front of everybody.* He thought about the two of them on the sofa mangling "America the Beautiful," how he'd relaxed into the strength he felt inside her. *So maybe there's a little more to this than lust.* "Right," he said again, quickly, grabbing for his dress shirt, turning away from her distracting eyes.

"GATOR, OLD MAN! SHE LET YOU come tonight. Here, I brought enough cigars to stink up the whole hotel." Will handed over a Sutherland's bag and shook Gator's hand vigorously. When that didn't feel as if it were enough to express his feelings, he put a hand on Gator's shoulder and gave it a squeeze.

He loved Gator. Redheaded, freckled, homely as a lizard, Gator was brilliant at business and adored Muffy. Will couldn't be happier that Muffy had made a good marriage—and moved to Waco.

"Thanks," Gator said, accepting the cigars. "I'll pay you back."

Will waved his hand dismissively, then moved in close. "We have problems," he said. "Gus is still AWOL."

"Oh, God," Gator groaned. "That explains why Sally's on her third martini."

Will checked his watch. "It's only eight-fifteen."

"Right. She's holding up great so far, though. Look

at her over there, smiling and blowing little air kisses. But I can imagine what she's thinking—that if this wedding falls through, everybody's going to say she shouldn't have given marriage a second go, especially with somebody she doesn't know anything about." Gator shook his head, then lifted it to gaze around the room. "Look at the money the Shipleys have poured into this wedding."

The smaller of the Courtland's two ballrooms was the venue for the rehearsal dinner. Round tables for eight were arranged toward the back of the room, sporting arrangements of white flowers that reached up toward the many crystal chandeliers. The men in their dark suits and the heavily iced women in their designer cocktail dresses were having drinks on the dance floor, while waitstaff wove among them with cold shrimp, smoked salmon canapés and small peppers stuffed with cream cheese.

Will snagged a pepper. "Whatever happens, it's an event Dallas won't ever forget. I know I won't."

The door to the banquet room opened, and it was as if a sudden breeze had wafted through the room. Cecily stepped in, ruffles dancing around her knees, her hair full and glorious, her face lightly made up, her legs bare and her sandals sexy. Every eye in the room was on her as she made her graceful way toward Sally, who was standing on a chair, apparently planning to climb up on a table, while Mrs. Shipley stood beneath her, obviously pleading.

"Oops," Gator said, "looks like Sally's cracked."

Everybody's looking at Cecily, but I'm the only one who knows her toenail polish is sloppy. Will had to clear his throat before he could speak. "Hey, Gator, that's the doctor who delivered your baby."

"My baby's godmother. Cecily," Gator said, going teary eyed and apparently forgetting all about Gus.

"Come on," Will said, thinking he'd better claim Cecily immediately, before some other guy took her away from him. "I'll introduce you."

"OH, CECILY, MY DEAR, YOU LOOK stunning." Looking and sounding surprised, Elaine Shipley fled the spectacle of Sally and rushed to Cecily's side, wringing her hands. "Sugar, would you please see if you can do something with Sally? She's crazy mad at Gus and about to make a fool of herself, and her Daddy's threatening murder. Not to murder Sally," she added unnecessarily, with more hand-wringing, "to murder Gus."

Cecily saw Jim Bob Shipley out of the corner of her eye. A gentleman rancher, Texas-tall, he was wearing an elegant, Italian-cut suit with cowboy boots, and while he'd taken off his Stetson, as was proper, he was hanging on to it tightly. That's how mad he was.

"Of course," Cecily said soothingly. "Really, Elaine, I'm sure Gus will show up any minute and everything will be fine. You and Jim Bob mingle, you know, keep down the rumors among the guests, and let me try to get Sally in order."

"Good luck," Elaine moaned as she skittered off to grab Jim Bob by the arm.

"Hi, Sally," Cecily said, looking up. "Sorry I'm late. Come down and let's talk."

Sally gave her a hard, wild look, then took her foot off the table she was about to climb onto and got down from the chair she was using as a ladder.

"What were you about to do on the table?" Cecily said. "Dance? Strip?"

"No, my dancing-on-tables-and-stripping days are over. I was about to make an announcement," Sally said.

"Announcing what?"

"That Gus hasn't jilted me. He's just late." Sally waved an unsteady hand around the room. "Look at this. Everybody's afraid to come over and say hello because they're so embarrassed for me that Gus isn't here." She turned to Cecily, tears in her eyes. "My own party, and nobody will talk to me."

"I'm talking to you," Cecily said, "and I know you're right. Gus hasn't jilted you." She put an arm around Sally. Sally's shoulders were tight with tension. "But if he has—"

"You think he has?"

"Of course not. I know he hasn't, but if he did…"

She was going to tell Sally this much—that if Gus had bolted, he wasn't worth marrying anyway. But her voice faded away, as did the room and everyone in it, at the sight of Will walking across the floor in his dark suit, crisp shirt and black tie. He looked strong and solid, and the remembered warmth of his skin, the erotic thrill of his caresses, the memory of him drying her hair and the way he'd run his fingers through it, sent heat flooding to her face even as the tenderness of that moment made her uneasy in her heart.

"Hey, Gator," Sally said to the red-haired man with Will. "Congratulations, Daddy. Thank God there are a few good men left in the world."

Gator gave Sally a quick kiss. "Have a cigar," he said. "I have a message for you from Muffy. The doctor says she can be in the wedding if she feels like it. Isn't that fantastic?"

With a quick spin he grabbed Cecily in a bear hug.

"And it's all because of this woman. How can I ever thank you?" he burbled onto the top of her head, going teary eyed again. "I'm so grateful you were there."

"It's my pleasure," Cecily puffed into Gator's suit jacket.

Will gently peeled Gator off Cecily. "I guess I don't need to do introductions after all. Lucky me." He took her hand and smiled at her, an earthquake-producing smile—the earthquake taking place in Cecily's knees. "Thanks again."

She couldn't stop looking at him.

Sally's attention had been momentarily distracted from her missing groom, but now she was focused again. "You two knew each other a long time ago, right? Crazy you got together again here. Will, have you heard from Gus recently?"

"No," Will said, still smiling at Cecily. But then he seemed to shake himself loose. He turned to Sally. "Gus is here, isn't he?" He was the very picture of innocence.

"No, he's not here," Sally said, bitterness showing up in her voice. "Why should he be? It's only his rehearsal dinner."

"Oh, my," Gator said, equally innocent.

"Where is he, Sally, and what is he doing?" Will said.

Cecily sent him a glance. He was wearing an interrogator's intense expression. She gave him a surreptitious poke with her elbow. "He called me," she said as if all three of them didn't know it already, "and said he had to go out of town this afternoon and please give Sally the message, but he didn't tell me where he was."

"Are his parents here?" Will said. "Or family members or friends? They might know." He clearly hadn't gotten the point of her elbow in his ribs.

"Gus has no parents. He has no family members. He has no friends as far as I can tell, except that scum-bag pirate Derek who isn't here yet, either." Sally's voice rose. "Who have you ever known in your life who didn't have any family or friends? The topic never came up until we started on the wedding invitations. How was I to know? I need another drink." She snagged a member of the waitstaff. "Get me a vodka martini, straight up. No fruit. Fast."

Sally's tentative grip on composure was slipping fast, and Will wasn't making things better.

"What's up with that Derek, anyway?" she continued. "I thought the best man was supposed to look after the groom, make sure things like this didn't happen." She hiccuped.

If Sally didn't shape up, she wouldn't make her own wedding. On the other hand, it was possible she wouldn't have a wedding to make.

"We all need to remain calm," Gator said nervously.

"I am calm," Sally muttered. "It's the rest of you who're getting your panties in a twist."

"I'm going to have a glass of wine," Cecily said quickly. "Anybody else?"

"I'll get the wine," Will said. Cecily observed that Will looked conscience stricken for having tried to pump poor Sally for info in her time of trial. "White or red?"

"White," Cecily said.

"I'll help," Gator said.

"Wine drinkers," Sally said, slurring the words. "Whatever happened to real men?"

"THIS IS BIZARRE," GATOR muttered to Will while they waited at the bar. "Feels more like a wake than a rehearsal dinner." He grabbed a handful of mixed nuts, ate the cashews and offered Will the rest. Will took them. Anything for Gator.

"The doctor's a pretty little thing," Gator said next.

"Competent, too," Will said, wondering if Muffy had told him Cecily was in fact a veterinarian.

"She single?"

"Yes," Will said.

"Hmm," Gator said.

"Shut up," Will said. "I have enough problems already." And in fact he had a new one. A big one. Somebody had a killer grip on his elbow, right at the funny bone. He turned to see who it was. "Uncle Jim Bob," he said, trying not to squeak from the pain.

"What the hell's goin' on here, Will?" Jim Bob Shipley growled. "I'm sick of actin' like everything's fine when that sumbitch has gotten my baby all upset and turned Elaine into a blithering idiot."

"Have a drink, sir." Will extricated his elbow and discreetly rubbed it.

"Just what I was after. Bourbon and branch," Shipley said, interrupting Gator's order. "No, skip the water and make it a double. Congratulations, Gator. Good thing somebody here's happy."

"Have a cigar," Gator said.

Shipley took it and sniffed it. "Good cigar. Wish I could say the same thing about that sumbitch—"

"Your drink." Will handed it to him.

"I'm gonna kill him when I see him," Shipley said. "I'm really gonna kill him if I *don't* see him. I told Sally, I told her a million times, don't hook up with a man until you've met his family. That's what tells you about a man—his family." He upended the glass of bourbon and drank the two shots in one massive gulp, then handed the glass back to the bartender for a refill.

"I'll take Cecily's wine to her," Gator said, deserting Will.

Shipley grabbed Will's shoulders, squished them together and hissed into his ear. "There's something else, too."

"What?" Will said with the last breath in his collapsing lungs.

"Don Galloway. Somebody burglarized his room this afternoon."

"Congressman Galloway? Oh, my God," Will said. "What got stolen?"

Shipley frowned. "I don't know. But the whole thing was kinda strange. He went up to his room, and—"

"Jim Bob, darling, Mayor Watkins is here. Come say hello." Elaine Shipley tugged at her husband's elbow, and he followed her, as docile as a bull with a ring in his nose.

Will straightened his shoulders, took several deep breaths, then glanced at Cecily. This was his chance to get back to her. He wanted all these distractions to go away so he could get back to making love to her, do it right this time, give her a night she'd remember forever. He started in her direction, where she was still talking to Sally.

"Hey," Sally said, making a sloshy turn toward Cecily, "you and Will seem to be getting reacquainted pretty fast. Y'like the way he turned out?"

"He seems very nice," Cecily said.

"Will is nice," Sally said. "I wish he'd been my brother. Muffy doesn't deserve him. Now Will, wine drinker or not, is a real man. I thought Gus was one, too," she said grimly.

"Muffy's changed," Cecily said, steering the subject away from the groom. "I mean, not that I knew her before, but according to Will—and now you—she must have been…" She halted because Sally wasn't listening.

Her gaze had suddenly zeroed in on someone who'd just come through the ballroom doors. "Speaking of real men, there's Derek."

She was on the move, streaming across the room like a heat-seeking missile aimed at a darkly handsome man. As Cecily watched, Sally grabbed him by the arm and yelled loudly enough to carry halfway across the ballroom, "Where the hell is Gus?"

9

"IT'S UP TO US, BUDDY," WILL said to Gator, seeing Sally near the door yelling at Derek Stafford, Gus's best man. He set down his wineglass.

"To rescue Derek from Sally? I hardly know the guy." But Gator put his wineglass down, too.

"Nobody knows him. So nobody is going to rescue him but us."

"Does he deserve rescuing?"

"Well, I don't know," Will said. "It's Gus who deserted Sally. Derek's here."

"You have a point," Gator said. "But think how Sally's feeling. One husband gone already, public humiliation when that marriage ended, now Gus has disappeared. Even when Sally's feeling good about life I would pity the guy facing her wrath."

Will wondered if it were possible that Gator had never faced Muffy's wrath, or if he'd faced it and just hadn't noticed. "So we might just two-step over…"

"Real slow…" Gator added.

"…and run interference if we need to."

They were already on their way, cowboys to the rescue of a guy who looked as if he could take care of himself—with anybody except Sally on the warpath.

Will observed that Cecily had set off toward Sally.

The room was humming nervously. Elaine Shipley had her feet braced against the floor and was hanging on to Jim Bob, probably to keep him from turning a gracious and elegant rehearsal dinner into a barroom brawl.

As they crossed the room, they saw Derek put his hand on Sally's arm, saw that Sally had stopped yelling, saw her engaged in earnest conversation with the man.

"He must have said the magic word," Cecily said, suddenly at Will's side.

They sauntered up beside Sally and Derek. Sally said, smooth as cheesecake, "Derek, remember Will? And Gator? This is Cecily, my oldest friend and maid of honor."

Will shook hands, did and said the right things but was increasingly troubled for two reasons. One was his certainty that Derek and Sally knew where Gus was and were keeping it a secret. The other was the way Derek's hand reached out to Cecily, who took it and shook it. He knew that's what everybody did— proffered a hand and the other person took it—but in this case it was Cecily and a man who was way too good-looking. Plus, he had a dark and dangerous air about him that Will knew for a fact women just loved. No wonder Sally had called him a pirate.

Derek's smile was as thin and tense as his handshake was warm and lingering—at least, Will thought it was warm and lingering—when he was shaking hands with Cecily. "Sally and I were talking about Gus," he said. "I know I was supposed to keep him captive until we made it through the wedding, but who can control a guy like Gus?"

"Right. Who?" Sally said. She seemed to be listening intently to every word coming from Derek's mouth.

"Anyway, I just heard from him. Everything's fine, but he can't take off in this weather."

"There is no weather." Will narrowed his eyes. "It's just hot."

"The weather where he is," Sally said, schoolteacher patient.

"Which is?"

Sally looked at Derek. "I guess it's okay to tell, isn't it?"

"Sure," Derek said. "One of the companies Gus does security for had a break-in. Gus had to investigate."

"But where—" Will said.

"While the crime scene was fresh," Sally cut in. "That's the kind of guy Gus is. Responsible. Thanks, Derek, for coming by to tell me."

"What company did you say he—" Gator said.

"Gus said he'd kill me if I didn't," Derek said. "Excuse me. I'm going to speak to a few people before dinner."

"Me, too," Sally said. "I want everyone to know Gus is all right."

"We can calm down and have a great dinner, with or without the groom," Derek added. "A few years from now, we'll all be laughing about this."

Left alone, Will and Gator gazed at each other for a long moment. "Did you believe him?" Gator said.

"Believe what? He didn't tell us anything."

Gator nodded. "Something fishy's going on."

"You have no idea," Will muttered. He couldn't confide in Gator, either, no matter how much he wanted to.

"I gotta leave you with it for a while, Will. I need to call Muffy and see if her milk's coming in all right."

Yeah, Gator wouldn't want to sit through the

evening without knowing that. Will hoped he'd understand a concern about breast milk one day. "Okay." He felt dull and tired. "I'll hold down the fort, but if you hear gunfire, cut the call short. And say hi to Muff for me. By the way, Gator…"

"Ummm?" Gator's mind was clearly on his baby's milk supply.

"Do you think Muffy's changed?"

"Oh, yeah. She's gained a lot of weight. Maybe, she'll lose it, maybe not. I'll still love her no matter what." With a wave, looking happy at the thought that he'd soon be talking to Muffy, Gator left Will alone with his thoughts.

Derek Stafford was smooth. Too smooth. Even now he was moving smoothly through the crowd with Cecily on one side and Sally on the other, acting like a man who thought he was all that.

Will glanced around the back of the room where the tables were and observed place cards at each table setting. He scanned the names on the cards, located his own name, then went looking for Cecily's. The wedding planner's staff had put her next to Derek. The maid of honor next to the best man. Well, to hell with that. He didn't care if the wedding planner had a stroke. He switched Cecily's card with the one to the right of his own spot.

Then he realized Derek wasn't even sitting by a bridesmaid anymore and someone might notice the error. So he looked around for another bridesmaid's card and put it beside Derek's, then went back to the spot where he'd picked up the bridesmaid's card and found she'd been sitting beside her husband. He went on a search for a different bridesmaid to sit beside Derek.

In no more than five minutes he'd pretty well messed up the tables. So be it. All that mattered to him was to have Cecily sitting beside him, and he'd achieved it.

A gong sounded, inviting the guests to sit down for dinner, so he began looking for Cecily. He couldn't find her. He moved through the crowd, trying not to look as frantic as he felt, sighting all the people she might have chosen to chat with—the Shipleys, the other bridesmaids now surrounding Sally, undoubtedly hearing the excellent news about Gus—without finding her.

Worse, he didn't see Derek, either. He became increasingly certain that she was somewhere with Stafford. A man with a mission, he strode out of the room and into the hallway, past sitting rooms and meeting rooms, checking each of them. A few people looked up, startled, but none of them was Cecily.

He started back the way he'd come and caught a glimpse of pale silk coming around a corner. "Cecily!"

"Will? Is something else wrong?"

"Where have you been?"

She gave him a look. "I went to the powder room."

"You were in the powder room with Stafford?" He'd have the man arrested.

"Of course not. Why would I be in the powder room with him?"

"That's what I'd like to know." He folded his arms over his chest. Inside, he was fuming, angry, hurt. Face it. He was jealous as all get out.

She moved closer to him. He could smell the soft scents of citrus soap, shampoo, baby powder, lotion—the simple scents of Cecily. They only made him feel worse.

"I haven't been anywhere with Derek Stafford." She looked up at him. "What made you think so? Have you lost your mind?"

He uncrossed his arms. "Maybe." He wrapped an arm around her shoulders, spun her away from the ballroom and into an empty sitting room, then kicked the door shut with his foot. "I've lost my cool, that's for sure."

He wanted her more than a man had a right to want a woman, wanted and needed her to ease the weight on his shoulders. It had tripped him, this burden of feeling responsible for fixing the crises swirling around him—Gus detained on some mysterious mission, Derek too smooth with his explanations, Sally too quick to believe whatever it was Derek had told her, Elaine Shipley with a wedding threatening to turn into a disaster. Tripped him so badly that thinking Cecily had left the room for a quick tête-à-tête with Derek Stafford had set off an explosion inside him.

She'd warned him, hadn't she, that sex for her was a series of one-night stands? The longer he saw her in action, the less he was able to believe her, but if it were true, he realized he wanted to be her entire series of one-night stands. He could do it. He was up to it. And he intended to demonstrate it.

His mouth closed over hers. It was like honeycomb against his, meltingly sweet, opening to him, inviting the invasion of his tongue. And he accepted the invitation, exploring, teasing, melding with her in a dance of deepening passion.

Her body felt wonderful against his, long and slim, all woman and filled with an energy that buzzed through him, stirring him to pull her closer, feel all of her melt against him. Her breasts moved against his chest and his hands slid downward, feeling the narrow waist yield to his pressure.

Her mouth slid away from his, making him feel sad. "Will..." She was breathless. "We have a rehearsal dinner still to get through."

"They can get through it without us." He slid his hands down her back, pressing her hard against him, relishing the feel of her moving against his erection. He didn't give a damn about Gus or Sally. He just wanted Cecily, wanted her desperately, wanted her now.

His fingers tugged at her dress, scrunching it up in his hands until he could feel the lace of her panties and closed his fingers over them instead, stroking her, sliding his hands under her. And then he lifted her off the floor. It was his private fantasy—and his chance to make it come true.

She gasped, then locked her thighs around him, just as he'd dreamed she would, rocking with him, meeting his thrusts, her head flung back in ecstasy. Until, very quickly, she cried out, collapsing against him, shuddering, her hair shrouding him in its silky strands.

He held her there for a moment, agonized by desire, wanting nothing more than to take her upstairs and reach that same peak, have that same release himself.

But...regretfully, he lowered Cecily to the floor and tucked her head against his cheek. Even aching with frustration, so hot he itched to get out of his skin, he remembered that he did indeed have a few little responsibilities in there—responsibilities to his family and a responsibility to learn as much about Gus as he could from anyone who might know the slightest detail about the man's life, especially about his business. He sighed.

"Will…" Cecily sounded as if she could be talked into shirking her responsibilities. But then she sighed, too. "You're terrific," she said simply and made things much worse by reaching up to kiss him lightly. "You've made me feel so good, and now I want to make you feel good, too. But…"

"Just what I was thinking. *But.*" He smoothed down her dress, stroked her hair back into submission, wiped a little smear of eye makeup off her cheek, then slowly, painfully, escorted her out the door and toward the ballroom.

He hoped he'd still fit under the table.

THEY WALKED IN TO A MILD level of chaos at the back of the ballroom. Guests darted about, bumping into waiters who were attempting to deliver first-course plates and pour wine. "I left my Judith Leiber bag where my place card was before," a bridesmaid said, "and it's not there anymore. Has anybody found a sparkly little frog on his plate?"

"Dr. Connaught!" The wedding planner, wearing peach again, flagged her down. "We've had a little mix-up. My assistant is certain she seated you beside Mr. Stafford, but it seems she accidentally put another bridesmaid there. She's already sitting down, I'm afraid. I could ask her to move…." Her eyes said she *so* didn't want to.

Will choked on a cough. "I'll find our seats," he said, moving swiftly away.

"I don't mind at all," Cecily said. "Don't worry about it."

"Hello, there, Paula Perry." A woman in a stunning black dress stalked up to the wedding planner brandishing a place card, her eyes blazing. "Well, you finally found a way to pay me back for not asking you to plan my wedding."

"What's the problem?" Paula Perry rolled her eyes.

"You seated me at the same table with my ex-husband and his twenty-two-year-old spandex bimbo, Kimmy, the Pilates instructor. Thanks *ever* so much. I'm sure we'll have a lovely talk about my flabby abs."

"Meredith, I would never do something so childish. I can't even keep track of your weddings." Ms. Perry seemed to be holding her own. "Someone did mention seeing a man back here looking at the place cards during the cocktail hour."

"Don't give me the suspicious-stranger-changing-the-placecards story. I know you—"

"I'll trade seats with you," Cecily interrupted her.

The woman gave her a not particularly friendly glance, and instead of "Thank you," said, "Where are you sitting?"

"I don't know yet."

"I'd better find your place and check out the table." She got Cecily's name, then, teetering on her four-inch heels, the woman stalked away.

"She's had several husbands," Ms. Perry explained, "and they're probably all here. If you'll excuse me, I see another crisis developing at table five."

The woman in black returned. "Okay," she said to Cecily, handing her a place card with Cecily's name written on it in calligraphy. "It's just Muffy's stuffy brother I'll have to sit by. Not the most exciting company in the world, but I don't mind him."

"Muffy's what?" Cecily was floored. She'd lucked into a seat beside Will and had given her rights away to this terrible judge of male flesh? No wonder Meredith's marriages hadn't lasted. She turned around to see Will several tables distant, standing behind his chair and looking shell shocked.

She marched over to the table, whisked up the Meredith Winslow place card and firmly stood her own in its place. "Sorry," she said, "I've changed my mind. I'll help you find another place."

The woman didn't seem to mind sitting beside Congressman Galloway, whose wife was on his other side. Galloway and his wife looked less than happy about the situation, but you couldn't please everybody. Feeling she'd done her best, she returned to Will.

"Sit down, Florence Nightingale," he said through his teeth.

She sat. He pushed in her chair and sat down beside her. While he spoke to an older woman on his left and the man to her right was talking with the woman on his right, Cecily watched Paula Perry soothing the guests, straightening things out, and knew she herself would have made a terrible wedding planner. She didn't even want a wedding of her own.

No, this was just the way she wanted it—sex with attractive men when she found them, and nothing more. She just needed to find them a little more often. No, a lot more often. She really needed to get serious about it. Finding Will again had been the purest stroke of luck. She thought about finding her next man and felt an unpleasant little ripple of distaste run through her stomach.

She turned to Will and found him gazing at her. She looked deep into his eyes. "It is sort of coincidental, isn't it, that we're sitting together?"

"As coincidences go," Will said, "it's a great one."

"Uh-huh," Cecily said. "You did it. You are the 'suspicious stranger' seen loitering around the tables."

"What?"

"Just a little gossip I heard."

"Want to know what the suspicious stranger was thinking?" His voice, deep and very soft, stroked her like a feather.

"I'm endlessly fascinated by the motives of suspicious strangers."

"That if you were sitting beside him, he could do this," Will said and put his hand on her knee, then ran it straight up her thigh to the cream-colored panties.

Cecily shifted in her chair, feeling her eyes close, stifling a moan. What did that woman Meredith mean, "Muffy's stuffy brother"? Will had behaved outrageously, if not downright lawlessly, since the minute he charged into St. Andrews. Could that have been mere hours ago? It seemed like a lifetime.

A waiter set a first course in front of her. It was an elaborate tower of endive, pears, walnuts and diced bits of crispy bacon. A salad erection. The thought brought a nervous giggle to her throat.

Will had been chatting politely with the woman to his left, and now that everyone at the table had been served, he dived into his erection—or rather his salad—with gusto.

He was left-handed. Had to be, although his right hand, still resting on Cecily's thigh, was equally skillful. Just when she'd forked a bite of salad into her mouth, she felt his fingers spread around the circumference, then felt his thumb on the most sensitive part of her.

"Ah-ahh," she said, half rising from her chair. "Great salad."

"WILL."

Will heard his name coming from across the table and decided he'd better get his hand off Cecily's leg, which he did as furtively as possible.

"Did you hear about Congressman Galloway's room being trashed?"

The question came from Max Mitchell, a college friend of Will's, who was sitting across the table with his pretty wife, Maggie.

"I heard it happened," Will said. "That's all. Did Don lose anything valuable?"

Max patted his mouth with his napkin, stood up and came around the table, where he hunkered down between Will and Cecily, making Will exceptionally glad he had both hands in full view. "It's a weird story," he said sotto voce to Will. "It'll probably be in the newspaper tomorrow, but can we keep it private for now? You know I'm one of Don's supporters, like your folks. I wouldn't tell anybody but you."

"Absolutely," Will said. He had to smother an inappropriate smile when he saw Cecily had stopped chewing, probably in order to eavesdrop.

"Well—" Max moved in even closer and lowered his voice even more. "Don checked into his room this morning. Nora wasn't going to join him until tonight, so he went out for lunch and did some errands, I guess, and when he got back to his room, his door was wide open and a housekeeper was in there screaming."

"My God. What had happened?" Will was getting an uneasy feeling.

"I heard—"

If Max tucked himself in any closer, he'd have his head in Will's lap like a large and affectionate dog.

"—that clothes were tossed all over the place. Not

his clothes, his sister's. I don't know why he had his sister's suitcase. Maybe she's coming in for the wedding and sent her suitcase ahead for Don to hang on to until she got here."

Will's heart skipped a few beats. "How do you know they were his sister's?"

"He told hotel security they were and then the police when they got there. The clothes were plus sizes for big women. You know Nora. She's about the size of a parking meter."

Will's gaze met Cecily's. She wasn't even pretending not to be listening. Her eyes were wide and her sexy mouth was open. She was thinking exactly what he was thinking, and she didn't even know Don Galloway. And he knew in his heart that she, like him, would never reveal what she suspected.

"Will?"

Will whipped his attention from Cecily back to Max.

"What do you think? Don's been a congressman for—what—six terms? You think somebody vandalized his room to see if they could find anything interesting for his next opponent to use against him?"

"Sounds like it," Will said. "Politics is nasty. And all the vandal managed was to mess up Don's sister's clothes."

"You know his sister?" Max sounded both interested and a little bit competitive. He knew Will's folks were on intimate terms with Galloway, and in politics this was a status symbol.

"Y'know, I'm not sure I've ever met her."

"One of those invisible political siblings," Max said. He gave Will a friendly jab to the shoulder and went back to Maggie.

Will went back to Cecily, feeling purposeful, and found the soft, sweet nub wet and waiting for his touch.

CECILY ENJOYED THE SALAD while her lower half enjoyed Will's artful thumb moving against it, keeping up the happy-diner-relishing-the-cuisine facade while she relished his touch. His thumb moved gently, rhythmically against her, and when he slipped his fingers inside her, she stifled her gasp.

She couldn't get enough of him. He'd just sent her sky-high in the sitting room, but she didn't seem to be coming down. It was unbearable, the pleasure of it, the heat and heaviness spiking to every nerve in her body. Her face felt hot, her lips swollen, and it became more and more difficult to keep up the pretense.

The sensations that threatened to take control of her demanded relief. So she moved with him while he stroked her, a wiggly sort of happy diner, while a torrential flood built up inside her, higher and higher....

"Ummm!" Conversation at their table ceased as all eyes focused on her, including Will's, which sparkled wickedly. "A chocolate tower," she breathed, gazing adoringly at the dessert the waiter had just placed in front of her while patting the mist of perspiration off her forehead. "My favorite."

She was looking at the second erection of the evening—no, the third. She attacked this one with a fork and sneaked her left hand onto Will's lap. Now it was her turn.

"You're right," he was saying to the woman on his left. "Dallas has to be constantly vigilant about reserving green spa-aces!" he said suddenly and a little too loudly when her fingers made contact with his swollen heat.

"Oh, look," she said sweetly. "It's time for the speeches, and, my goodness, Sally's up on the stage."

Sally was indeed on the stage, looking beautiful, her dark hair gleaming, her ivory sheath perfectly fitted, her pearl jewelry elegant and classic. Someone clinked a knife against a wineglass, and the hum of the room died down.

"Hi, everybody," Sally said with a big, wide smile. Her audience clapped, and she waved them regally into silence. "I know it's not the usual thing for the bride to make the first rehearsal-dinner speech, but these aren't the usual circumstances."

For a moment, the hum rose again, as if people were asking each other whether something embarrassing might be about to happen.

"I want to say a special thank you to everyone who *did* show up, unlike a *very* important member of the wedding party who did *not* show up." She said it with a giggle in her voice, and generated a nervous laugh from her guests. "In fact, what you're apt to remember about this wedding is the list of primary players who didn't show."

She mentioned Muffy and congratulated Gator's and Will's parents. "This special baby was delivered by none other than my very first friend and my maid of honor, Cecily Connaught, who is actually…" she paused, building up the interest, then said, "…who is actually a large-animal vet in Blue Hill, Vermont."

"What?"

Gator's cry of alarm rose above the laughter of the audience and had Cecily snatching her hand from Will's lap. He leaped up from his seat several tables away to stare at Cecily, his freckled face bright pink.

"Muffy didn't tell him," Cecily whispered to a

dazed-looking Will. Gator looked really mad. She wondered if he ever got violent. Or litigious. She'd prefer violent.

"I guess she didn't want to worry him." Will looked thoughtful as he gazed back at her, and she wondered what he was thinking about.

She looked back at Gator to find he'd joined in the laughter. What a relief.

Sally took back the floor. "The bride's father usually makes the first speech, but this bride's father is madder than a coon in a cage at this bride's groom, so I'm not letting him up here on this stage. Y'all know my daddy and what he's like when he's mad, and here he is, Jim Bob Shipley. Stand up, Daddy. And Mama, you stand up, too. My mama, folks, Elaine Shipley. Let's lift our glasses in a toast to Mama and Daddy for giving us a beautiful party tonight."

"Hear, hear," chorused the audience, standing for the toast.

Sally's speech went on and on. She introduced everyone in the room by name without making a single mistake and mentioned something personal about each of them. She smiled, she laughed and soon had everyone relaxed and in good humor. Cecily felt so proud of her.

At last, she brought out the pièce de résistance. "Now we're going to hear from Gus," she said, "and about time, don't you think?"

She waited for the laughter to die down, then said, "Gus dictated this to me on the phone." She slowly pulled out a piece of paper. "And asked me to read it to you tonight if he didn't make it." She paused, looking innocently around the room. "Gus, you here?

Guess not. Okay, here goes. 'You're gathered together, I'm stuck in the weather, you're wondering whether I'll make it at all. But I'll put on that tether if I have to burn leather, if it takes my last breath, or die trying. 'Bye, y'all."

The poem had a familiar ring about it, imperfectly rhythmed and perfectly dreadful. Just like the poem Sally would read to Gus in lieu of the traditional vows—if Gus made it to the wedding. In the midst of the applause, Cecily turned to Will and found, as she always did, that he was already looking at her. "Gus didn't write that poem, Sally did," she whispered.

"She's lying about everything," he whispered back. "But I have to say this for her, she's a trooper."

He reached for his wineglass. Cecily reached for hers. "Let's do it," she said, realizing she was once again about to do exactly what her mother would have done in these same circumstances.

"We'd like to make a toast," she called out, "to Sally!"

10

"IT WAS A PLEASURE SITTING with you," Cecily said, holding out her hand to Will.

"For me, too." With a smile, he took her hand, stroking the back of it with his thumb and not letting go.

The man should patent his thumbs. That gentle caress and the gold gleam of his eyes were a dangerous combination. But soon they'd be alone and she could handle all the danger he wanted to get her into.

"I'm sorry to see the evening end," he said.

Revelers surrounded them, and Cecily was unwilling to share their secret with anyone. "It does seem a shame. So," she said, extricating her hand before she lost her cool and jumped him, "I'll just say my goodbyes and thank-yous. I look forward to seeing you tomorrow at the wedding."

"If not sooner." His eyes flickered at her.

"I look forward to that." She fled while it was still possible.

She looked around for Gator, hoping to give him a chance to bawl her out for being a veterinarian, and found him in a corner talking on his cell with a finger stuck in his other ear. He was laughing. Good sign. When he saw her, he took his finger out of his ear, blew her a kiss and gave her a thumbs-up sign.

She smiled back and went in search of Elaine and Jim Bob Shipley.

On the way she saw Sally surrounded by the rest of her bridesmaids. She didn't look as perky as she had while giving her uplifting speech. Her mood seemed to be darkening. She'd put on a terrific public show, but she wasn't happy about what Gus was doing. Cecily bit her lip, wishing the wedding weekend were going more smoothly.

Spying Jim Bob, she thanked his scowly face for a lovely evening, apologized again that her parents couldn't arrive until the next day, then found Mrs. Shipley.

"Oh, Cecily, honey, I just wanted to make sure you'd hung up your dress for the wedding. If it's wrinkled, you'll want to send it out for pressing." She patted Cecily's arm. "Your mama would never forgive me if I let you come down the aisle wrinkled, but I must say, seeing you tonight, I think she greatly exaggerates your tendency to ignore your appearance."

Prickles shot up Cecily's neck, and they had nothing to do with this latest shot from her mother. The problem was that she hadn't given the slightest thought to her maid-of-honor outfit. "Don't worry about a thing," she said as her heart began to thud. What she knew for a fact was that her suitcase was a mess. And as for the dress—it was in the suitcase, wasn't it? She'd covered it in plastic and then…

It was the *and then* part that was giving her neck the prickles.

"Samantha, of course, is one of those never-a-hair-out-of-place people," Elaine Shipley went on. "When you were a baby, she kept you the same way—always perfect, never a spot of dirt on you."

No wonder I chose to fill my life with cow dung. "Thank you again, Elaine," she said as she fled, panicky, to the elevators.

WILL SMILED AS HE WATCHED Cecily take off at a run. She was as excited about the night they'd spend together as he was. He'd take his time going up, let her pretty herself up, get into that skimpy gown—

Maybe he wouldn't take his time.

Still, there were people to speak to, an alarming number of whom had heard the story about Congressman Don Galloway. He didn't know what was going on, but damn it, Galloway was an old friend and he didn't want him libeled or Nora hurt.

He'd corroborate Don's story about his sister's plus-size clothes no matter what Don was up to.

He sought out Max Mitchell first. "I just remembered, I may have met Don's sister once," he told him. "She lives in…Australia, I think. Owns a sheep ranch in the outback, so she's rarely here. A big woman, almost as big as Don."

"Somebody told me she wasn't coming for the wedding," Will told another friend, who shared the story in absolute confidence. "She came back to Dallas to attend to some legal matters, so when she got to the hotel, she asked Don to hang on to her suitcase while she saw lawyers. That's what I heard, anyway."

He'd almost reached the doors of the ballroom when Elaine Shipley rushed up to him. "Will, I feel so sorry for Don's sister, Wilma, having all her things messed with. If I can do anything for her… I have a special saleslady at Sutherland's and I bet they'd open up for her early tomorrow morning…."

Ah. The congressman's sister had a name now, and it sounded as if one of the gossips along the way had named her after him. No one would remember that the rest of the information about Wilma had come from Will Murchison.

Congratulating himself, Will started for the elevator bank. He hoped he had enough condoms. A practical man—and a hopeful one—he never traveled without them, but Cecily might test the number he'd arrived at based on his earlier experiences.

Not Cecily herself, but the way he felt about Cecily. It was a warming thought, and when he reached the seventh floor, he sped like a rescuing knight to his room.

He walked in to find a covered tray loaded with cold nachos and fajitas, the grease congealing over them, and not two but four bottles of warm beer. Lovely. A midnight snack. He put the tray under lamplight, which would at least melt the visible grease, then went back out and down to the ice machine, dumped the ice in the bathroom sink, buried the beer in the cubes and laid a bath towel over the arrangement. It wasn't champagne and caviar, but he was a man in a hurry and the last thing he wanted was a waiter coming to the door.

And while he'd been engaged in his culinary preparations, he'd dreamed up another little surprise for Cecily. A few minutes later, he opened both doors with a flourish and delivered a vocal rendition of the trumpet signal that the walls of Jericho were falling. What he saw stopped him cold.

Cecily was circling the room, fully dressed, with clothing littering the bed. Her suitcase was there, too, upside down. She'd even dumped her medical bag.

When she looked at him, her eyes were enormous, intensely blue and wild.

"I can't find it," she wailed.

Will had to push his left brain to the max to come up with an adequate response. "Your diaphragm? Your sponges? Not to worry. I have condoms, and the firm requires a blood test every three months. Until further notice I'm free of all known diseases—"

"Not birth control. My dress. I can't find my dress."

"You're wearing it." She'd flipped out. Was she allergic to something they'd had for dinner? Nuts? Chocolate?

"Not this dress." She grabbed a handful of the silky, ruffled dress he'd picked out for her, lifted it and shook it at him like a flamenco dancer, then dropped it. "My maid-of-honor dress." She sank down on the bed and buried her head in her hands, her hair flowing forward to cover her face. Then she looked up and her eyes widened. "Will, you're buck naked."

True. He was. That had been his surprise for Cecily—to go to her room without the clothes she'd accused him of being neurotically attached to, indicating that he'd put Gus on the back burner and was ready to give her a night of quality time. Now it seemed it hadn't been such a great idea. "Hang on," he said, went back to his room and returned in the wildly printed boxer shorts he liked to sleep in. "Let's start over," he said. "What do you mean you can't find the dress? A long white dress—" he was sure it was white, and furthermore, several different kinds of white "—isn't the kind of thing you can lose. The earrings, maybe, or the little white gloves—"

"It's not lost. I know exactly where it is," she moaned, hiding her face again.

"And…"

"It's in Vermont. I forgot to pack it."

"Oh, God," Will said, sat down beside her and buried *his* head in his hands. They sat there in silence for a minute or so.

"How can we fix it?" Will finally roused himself to say. He also had the presence of mind to put his arm around Cecily. Just because he obviously wasn't getting laid until he found Cecily's dress didn't mean he couldn't try to comfort her in her crisis.

"There…is…no…way…to…fix…it." She sounded like an old-fashioned record on the wrong speed.

"There is always a way." He gave her a little squeeze, then got up to pace the room, which was supposed to help you think. "Somebody could FedEx it to you."

"The last FedEx pickup at the general store was at seven o'clock. Josh Miller's our FedEx man and he's so dependable. I know because I send out specimens to—"

"You could wear my tux shirt and tights. Sometimes the maid of honor has a different getup from the bridesmaids, doesn't she?"

She looked at him. "Not *that* different."

"Where'd the dress come from? Maybe the store has a spare."

"They're Vera Wang, custom made. Mrs. Ogletree in the Ben Franklin fabric department measured me and I sent the measurements to Sally and Sally shipped the dress to me for a final fitting, but it felt okay to me just as it was, maybe a little loose in the waist, and Mrs. Ogletree offered to take it in, but I said loose was better than tight and it was fine as it was and now it's in my closet in Blue Hill." Another wail rose from low in her throat.

"Somebody could fly down with it tomorrow morning."

"I can't ask Moira to do that. Besides, she has to take care of my cats."

"Who's Moira?"

"Dr. Vaughn's and my new resident. Just out of the Iowa State vet school, excellent credentials and she's turned out to be even better than we'd hoped. She offered to stay over while I was gone. She's also a very nice and cooperative person who has a real grasp of what it means to work as a team—"

"How many cats?"

"Eleven, but I've only been working there three years."

Will's depression was deepening, but he forced himself to concentrate on Cecily's problem. One of them had to. She was finding her solace in stream-of-consciousness babbling.

"Some of the dairy farmers don't treat their barn cats right. They don't do anything to keep them from having babies, but when they do, they…destroy the litter." Her voice broke in a sob. "Dr. Vaughn and his wife had the full responsibility for taking in the kittens until I got there and volunteered to take half."

"How many cats do the Vaughns have?" Will whispered and realized with a not unpleasant little shock that he was imagining himself living with a squadron of killer cats.

"The number holds pretty steady at around thirty," Cecily said. "But it's okay. The Vaughns built the cats their own house."

"Built the cats their own—" Will stopped himself. The information coming in was more than he could process when he had so many other things on his mind. "Cecily, try to focus on the dress. We can talk about feline rights later." *And about us.*

"Oh. Right. The dress." She flung herself backward against the pile of clothes on the bedspread. "All is lost. Sally should never have asked me to be her maid of honor. My mother should have known better than to make me accept. Maid of honoring isn't one of my skill sets. Packing isn't one of my skill sets, either."

"Didn't you say your parents were flying down here early tomorrow morning?" She looked so accessible, stretched out on the bed, it took all the practicality he could muster to get the question out.

"Break of dawn. How else could they get here by noon?" She got up and began to unload the bed. Will observed that she put some things in dresser drawers and others in the trash can. He hoped she'd be happy with her choices later. "Mother's in a bad mood about it, I can tell you that, and it's all because of the paper Daddy had to give in Chicago that she'll probably have to put on her makeup in the limousine and dress for the wedding at four in the morning, but do you think she'd come without him? No-oh. Ohhhh." She was back to wailing again. "She's going to be so mad at me."

Feeling dizzy, Will closed his eyes tight and opened them again. A family dynamic, one for which he was sadly lacking in data, was going on here, so he'd have to look at the bottom line and hope he'd guessed right. "I was wondering if she'd bring you the dress."

Cecily's body went very still and she opened her eyes. "How's she going to get it?"

"Well…" How the hell did he know? "Somehow we have to get the dress from Vermont to New York. Where in New York?"

"Manhattan. Greenwich Village."

Will felt another wail coming and didn't know what had set Cecily off this time but felt certain he'd find out. "Could they drive up to get the dress?"

"It's a six-hour drive from the Village to Blue Hill. It would be five if Daddy had gone to Columbia instead of NYU, but we can't base our professional choices on my ultimate convenience, can we? Especially not the convenience of a daughter who was dumb enough to forget her maid-of-honor dress. Anyway, how could he have known that he needed to work somewhere closer to northern Vermont?"

Will stuck to the point. "Six hours down, six hours back." She was right. All was lost. He decided he'd go ahead and order champagne and brandy and they could both get schnockered to forget their sorrows, but when he looked back at her, she'd sat up and she had a weird light in her eyes.

She stared into space for a moment. "I can't do it," she said. She'd emptied the bed, and she flung herself down on it again.

"What?"

"Ask my mother."

"Sure you can." He wasn't sure where this was going. The wedding was in thirteen hours. It wasn't possible to make a twelve-hour drive and make the wedding in thirteen.

"No, I can't." She sat up again. "But I have to. And I have to ask Moira if she'd be willing to meet them halfway. She'd be within her rights to file suit with the, the…oh, whatever the agency is that protects employees from having to drive through the night on errands that have nothing to do with their job descriptions."

As Will started to answer, the phone rang in his room. He was weighing his choices—answer it, don't answer it—when Cecily said, "Answer it. I'll keep thinking."

About what, he wondered, *your cats?* But he went into his room and picked up the phone.

"Will. Gator."

"Hey, Gator." Will picked up a cold nacho and took a bite. Not bad. "Everything okay?" he said with his mouth full.

"I just wanted to know if you heard the news about Don Galloway. He was holding a suitcase for his sister—you know, Wilma? With the safari operation in Ghana? And—"

"I heard," Will said, smiling to himself. "Tough, huh? Listen, Gator, I've been talking to Cecily—"

"You have?" A curious note crept into Gator's voice.

"Yes," Will said firmly. "She's on the other line and I need to get back to her. She has a big problem. She forgot her dress for the wedding. It's in Vermont, a million miles away from here, so we have to figure out—"

"Hang on," Gator said. In a minute he came back to the phone. "Muffy says Cecily can wear her dress and she'll skip the wedding. It'll be too big, but Muffy says there's a way to pin it so it'll fit."

Muffy? Willing to miss being in the wedding, and all because she wanted to help Cecily out? "I'm touched," Will said. And he really was. "Muffy would do something like that for Cecily?"

"There's nothing we wouldn't do for that woman."

"Hold the phone a minute and I'll tell Cecily," Will said, rushing it before Gator could get emotional again.

He crept across the floor and into Cecily's room, where he found her sitting on the bed, staring into space.

"Good news," he whispered, pointing to his room and putting an imaginary phone to his ear to indicate that the phone was still live. "You can wear Muffy's dress."

He expected excitement. Instead Cecily said, "I wouldn't dream of doing that to Muffy. You're Sally's cousins, and it sounds to me as if you two have always been close to her. Muffy was willing to haul herself up out of bed twenty-four hours after having a baby—that's how important Sally's wedding is to her. She has to be there."

"But—"

"I'm not backing down. Far better for Muffy to be in the wedding."

Defeated, Will slunk back into his own room.

"She won't do it," he told Gator. "She insists it's more important to Muffy than to her."

"Well, okay then," Gator said cheerfully, "we move on to plan B."

"Which is?" Will frowned.

"She can take my plane to Vermont and get the dress."

"Gator!"

"Why not? Like I said, we'd do anything for that woman. It's a matter of a couple of phone calls. I'll get back to you in a few minutes."

"Cecily," Will yelled when he'd hung up, "deliverance is on the way."

"Oh, good," came a listless voice from the next room.

He stepped in. "Something about the situation is upsetting you a lot more than it should. I mean, it's upsetting you to the point of making you dysfunctional. I mean that in a nice way," he added quickly.

"That's me. Dysfunctional Cecily."

"No, no, no, what I meant was…"

"It's true. I've reached the point that I can only function in one area—veterinary medicine. I'm an *idiot savant.*" Already slumped, she slumped even more.

Will took off his tie. "We'll talk about it on the plane."

"What plane?"

The phone rang. Will went for it.

"It's all set," Gator said. "The pilot's on his way to the field to file a flight plan. They're gassing up the plane and doing the inspections. He says be there in an hour."

"Gator, have I ever told you that the day you became my brother-in-law was the happiest day of my life?" Will said, and rang off.

He was afraid the blunt statement that they were flying to Vermont to get her dress would put her over the edge. He'd better lead up to it slowly. "Cecily," he said, "Gator has thought of a way to get your dress."

She looked up at him. It was progress.

"He has a plane."

Her eyes flickered slightly.

"He's loaning it to us."

Her face lit up. "I can flee the country and escape total humiliation and my mother's scorn."

"No, we can go to Vermont to get your dress. He says the plane will be ready to leave in an hour."

It finally registered. He could tell because she leaped up. "I can't believe this," she said. "I can't believe Gator's doing this wonderful thing." Then after a second or two of glowing, she got down to business. "Let's see, it's eleven-fifteen. An hour to the airport, four hours to Vermont, an hour to Blue Hill, an hour back, four hours back to Dallas—what time will that be?"

"Ten-fifteen tomorrow morning."

She drooped a little. "That's cutting it pretty close. And things happen, delays…" She lit up again. "But if Moira would meet us at the Burlington airport with the dress, that would cut off two hours."

"I wanted to see where you live. I wanted to count cats."

"But what if—"

He gave in. "You're right. Call her. I'll pack a couple of toothbrushes for us."

"Will, you don't have to go with me. You shouldn't go with me. In fact, I'll have to insist you let me go alone. What if something happens and you miss the wedding, too?"

SHE GAZED AT HIM, wondering what she'd done right in her life to be given a second chance to know him. She'd offered him a one-night stand and had mainly delivered frustration and chaos, in return for which he'd given her passion, affection and one-hundred-percent support.

"You should be here, trying to figure out what Gus is up to."

"I'll take my laptop along. I'm going with you." His eyes darkened and his face showed an unexpected bit of uncertainty. "Unless you don't want me to."

"I want you to," she whispered. Then she burst out, "This isn't fair to you, not any of it. We were supposed to be in bed, me being as good to you as you've been to me, and instead we'll be on a plane—"

The uncertainty on his face was gone. "In the back of the plane is a berthable sofa—it turns into a three-quarter bed. There's a double-lined privacy curtain between the bed and the cockpit, and the bathroom's in the front of the plane. Pilot and copilot in the front, us in the back behind curtains." He gave her a slow, suggestive smile. "For the first time since my beloved sister Muffy went into labor I'll have you alone. I wouldn't miss this flight for anything in the world." He licked his lips.

Cecily was close to drooling, and had been since he mentioned the bed. "We'll be killing two birds with one stone."

He pulled her into his arms and gave her a promising kiss. "Speak for yourself. I'm not all that easy to kill."

She threw her arms around him. "When should we leave for Love Field?"

He consulted his watch. "Twenty minutes."

"I'll call Moira." She dialed her home phone number.

Moira picked up right away. "Cecily. Hey, are you having a good time? The babies are doing great. We had tuna fish for dinner."

Moira was so nice. She was smart *and* nice and clearly wide awake, probably studying. "I would be having a good time if I hadn't forgotten my maid-of-honor dress. Moira, could you, would you…"

Moira could and would. Except…

"Of course. Bring the usual cats with you. Will

wanted to see them anyway," Cecily assured her. "You'll find a stack of carriers in the basement next to the boiler."

"Who's Will?"

"That's a long story. For later."

The arrangement made, Cecily gazed at the phone for a while, then picked it up and phoned her parents' apartment.

"Cecily! Are you all right?" Her mother's voice was sleep-clogged.

"No. I have something to tell you."

"You're in the hospital. You're fatally wounded. You're—"

"No, just feeling humble."

The silence began to alarm her. "You really aren't all right," her mother said at last. "Sugar pie, I'll call our psychiatrist friend in Dallas—"

"No need, Mother. I called to tell you I understand at last why you were always after me to keep my clothes in order and to think about events I'd be attending while I was packing for a trip. I apologize for slamming my door in your face when you came to my room to ask if I'd packed skin toner to take to the university. I'm sorry I yelled at you when you sent the box of nude pantyhose after your one visit to me in Blue Hill. I deeply regret the call I made after you sent the makeup. I've used it twice already today."

There was another silence and then her mother said, "Something is terribly wrong."

"Or terribly right."

"Don't do anything foolish until I get there tomorrow."

"Have I ever done anything foolish? 'Bye, Mother."

Had she ever done anything foolish? Not until now.

Feeling good about the call, Cecily looked around to see what Will was doing. He'd assembled a little pile of things he thought they'd need and was staring at the pile, eating a nacho. "Have one," he said.

"Thanks. They're cold," she said after taking a bite.

"I noticed. I've got your toothbrush here and some other stuff, like shampoo, just in case."

"I have to take my medical bag."

"Of course. We'll pack this stuff in it." He roused himself. "Let's go."

THE ENGINES THROBBED BENEATH them, matching the throbbing of Cecily's heart. Several minutes to takeoff, Will motioned her into the rear of the plane, where he'd already pulled out the sofa. "This is what I dreamed of doing when I saw this dress on the mannequin," he said, sliding his arms around her.

"What?" She didn't have to ask. She could feel the answer in the way his hands slid across the thin silk, caressing her skin with the fabric, sliding down her spine, sending a shiver of pure pleasure straight through the center of her body.

His hands cupped her buttocks, bunching up the silk, then smoothing it out, sliding under her to lift her up to him. He teased the ruffle down the front with his knee, opening the dress, tugging her tightly against him. She moaned against his shoulder, feeling the strength of his need, reveling in the sheer largeness of him, imagining him encompassing her with his arms, imagining herself encompassing him with her thighs and at last taking that pulsing part of him inside her.

"Ready for takeoff." The voice that came over the intercom system was dry—no Hollywood training here—and the message was unwelcome. Slowly Ce-

cily disentangled herself from Will's embrace and
led him back to the seats in the front of the plane,
where they sat side by side on luxurious leather and
dutifully buckled up.

They sat in silence, then Cecily met Will's sidelong
glance with her own. "I have plans for you," Will said
and stretched out his legs.

"What plans?"

"When that seat-belt sign goes off, I'm going to
jump you."

Cecily giggled. "Surely you can be a little more inventive than that."

"Um. Maybe I can." He took her hand, threaded
his fingers through hers and slid them back and forth.

It hit Cecily that they'd never held hands before.
There was so much she didn't know, hadn't experienced with Will. They'd never gone to a movie, dis-
cussed a book, cooked something together. This
realization forced her to face up to how short a time
they'd spent together. So why did she feel so close to
him? Was it because of their history in the long-dis-
tant past?

The sensitive skin between her fingers tingled at
his touch. She felt like a teenager again, recognizing
that first flush of desire. "Tell me what inventive
things you're going to do."

"I'm going to nibble on your earlobes," he said
and fastened his teeth on the one nearest him. "And
then I'm going to blow in your ear, like this…."

A flash of heat went spinning from that small caress to the tips of Cecily's toes. With a roar, the plane
took off—or was she the one who was taking off?

"And then," he said, "I'll chew your arm like a
drumstick." His mouth settled on her bare shoulder.

She leaned into him, breathless, when his teeth barely grazed her skin, and then slid down the inside of her arm. When he reached the inside of her elbow, she moaned and slid down in her seat, her legs apart.

She felt his face buried between her breasts, felt his hand begin the slow trip from her knee to her thigh and simply put her arms around him and held on. His hair, silky against her skin, smelled clean and woodsy. She closed her eyes and rubbed her cheeks against it while he touched her in her most secret place. He nuzzled her breasts, his mouth open and wet against them, moving with excruciating slowness, tantalizing her, arousing every nerve ending in her body.

"We're cruising at twenty-four-thousand feet. You guys can relax now."

Cecily moved just in time to keep Will's head from decking her jaw.

"Come on," he said. His voice was low and husky. Together they returned to the back of the plane, and Will gazed at her as he closed the curtains tightly.

He came toward her slowly, touched her shoulders, her arms, ran his hands down her sides all the way to the hem of her dress, pulling it up an inch at a time until it covered her face, and holding it there, he brushed kisses down her breasts, her waist, her stomach, before pulling it off entirely. Gently he placed her on the berth and gazed at her while he unbuttoned his shirt, unzipped his trousers and at last was as naked as she.

For the first time she could have more than a glimpse of him, and she drank in his beauty and strength, his darkly glistening skin, the gold in his eyes glowing in the dim light of the cabin. Carefully he lay down beside her and stroked her, kissed her lips, her cheeks, her forehead. She had to touch him, and so she did, the skin of his penis satiny under her fingertips, the shaft rigid and ready.

His kisses deepened and a new urgency infused his caresses. Her desire exploded, matching his suddenly frantic need. He spread her legs and buried his face between them, flaming her with more of his generous kisses, his moisture mingling with the wetness of her. One touch of his tongue to her tiny, aching nub and she was already coming in deep, even spasms, each one an earthquake shattering her body. "Please," she begged him. "Please…"

He lifted himself above her and deftly applied a condom. Poised over her, hot, breathing hard and obviously at the end of his self-control, he hesitated.

She couldn't let it happen. "Will…" she said, tugging at his waist. "What's wrong? Why…"

He relaxed a little beneath her desperate hands and she heard his soft laugh, almost a sob. "I can't believe it," he said, smiling into her hair. "I keep waiting for the phone, the knock on the door, the pilots to tell us to go back to our seats, buckle up and put our heads between our knees…."

"Then hurry," she demanded. "It might happen." And she tugged at him with all her strength.

And then he was inside her, the massive length and breadth of him thrusting deeply, bringing with each thrust such exquisite pleasure that she cried out, her folds blossoming in his heat, opening up to him. She lifted her hips and wrapped her legs around him to pull him in even tighter. He gasped with pleasure, his thrusts growing more forceful, withdrawing only to plunge into her again ever more powerfully, until he drew her into a dream that was nothing but sensation, a sensation that ebbed and flowed, built and relaxed only to climb even higher.

At last the pleasure was too great and there was no holding back. With one last desperate thrust, he groaned and collapsed against her, carrying her along with him in wave after wave of shuddering delight, sliding his arms beneath her to hold her sweat-slicked body tight against his while she trembled in the aftermath of the most momentous, most fulfilling event of her life.

Tears of relief streamed down her face. It was not the right time to make a sensible decision. Even in her uplifted state she knew that. But what went through her head was that she didn't want to do this ever again with anyone but Will.

The thought terrified her.

11

"THAT WAS AS GOOD AS IT GETS." Lying by her side, Will ran a fingertip down Cecily's cheek.

They'd made love again, but this time she wasn't crying. This time they'd taken it more slowly, more deliberately, and it had felt dangerously more like love than sex. Looking up into his eyes, she wished she hadn't come to the wedding after all. Meeting Will had rattled the foundations of her life goals. A one-night stand had turned into a lifetime problem. *Keep it light.* "Where do you suppose we are?" Wanting to touch him, too, she traced his smile.

"We've crossed the Mississippi and we're over—" he squinted "—Tennessee. We're about halfway there."

"How do you know?"

"I'm looking at that little television screen behind you."

"Do you wear contacts?"

"No."

"Glasses?"

"No. You?"

"Not yet."

"Why did you ask?"

"You squinted to see the screen." Cecily yawned and stretched her arms over her head. The bed was barely big enough for the two of them—barely big enough for Will—and her hip overlapped with his, a nice feeling.

"Your hair was in the way."

"My hair is always in the way. Maybe I should cut it."

"Touch it and die."

She rested her head on her arm to gaze at him. Feeling very shy, she said, "I guess the real reason I asked is that now I know one more thing about you. I think—" she hesitated, wondering if this was a good idea "—we've sort of gotten to be friends again, don't you?"

He smoothed her tangled hair back from her face. "More than friends. We've been through a lot together since noon yesterday."

"It hasn't been the usual one-night stand," Cecily agreed. It might have been her imagination, but she felt him draw away from her a little—not his body, not his hands that still touched her, but something inside him. She wished she hadn't said it. It wasn't as if she'd had any one-night stands. How did she know what the usual one was like?

"A little more time and we might be best friends," was all he said.

"We have a little more time now," she said, stroking his chest, tangling her fingertips in the crisp, curly hair, tracing the triangle down to his waist and below. *Just not enough,* she thought.

"Hey, folks, time to wake up. We're thirty minutes from landing. We'll be asking you to get back into those seat belts in fifteen."

"Better timing than we've had in the past," Will

said. Reluctant to move at all, he untangled his and Cecily's arms and legs, got up and started pulling on his clothes. "I'm making a trip to the head. We have a small disposal problem."

"Not so small," Cecily said, gathering up condom wrappers from the floor. "You go first. I'll get dressed and straighten up the bed."

"Wonder what you do with these things on a plane?"

"Your guess is as good as mine. I've never done this on a plane."

He was glad to hear it. More or less dressed, he went forward to the rest room behind the cockpit. Once there, he saw a discreet, handwritten sign on the trash bin. Condom Disposal, it said.

Will stared at it for a long moment. Busted. The pilots knew exactly what he and Cecily had been up to beyond those drawn curtains. Gator must have tipped them off to the possibility.

He splashed his face with water. He never got away with anything. Muffy? She got away with everything—sometimes with his help, of course. He thought about other friends and acquaintances who seemed to have some magic going for them, something that let them come out on top, whatever happened. Not him.

He drew a line of toothpaste on his brush. Wasn't that the thing that kept him honest? The sure and certain knowledge that if he ever stepped out of line he'd end up in jail without passing Go and without collecting two hundred dollars?

And then he thought, *It's not the worst neurosis a guy could have.*

Except now, when it seemed likely that Gus's situation would force him to choose between professional ethics and family obligations.

On the way back, he'd talk to Cecily about it. He finished up in the rest room and returned to the back of the plane, where he found her dressed and sitting on the neatly made berth with her long, beautiful legs crossed and one sandal swinging. As soon as she glimpsed him coming back, she scampered forward toward the bathroom. "Don't let the plane go down without me," she said.

"MOIRA!" CECILY RAN ACROSS the tarmac and threw her arms around a plump, pretty, dark-haired woman dressed in jeans and a plaid shirt.

"Aren't you freezing?" Moira said.

"Yes. Thanks for asking." Cecily smiled at her.

"Here's a sweater." Moira draped a fuzzy blue one over her shoulders.

"Oh, fabulous. This is Will, Moira."

"Will Murchison." He shook her hand. "It was great of you to bring the dress."

"It was great of you to fly up with Cecily." Her smile was sweet and genuine, but it contained a certain speculative quality, too. Will knew that look. He'd seen it a million times. It was a woman-thinking-wedding kind of look.

"How's everything at the clinic?" Cecily asked Moira.

"Oh, just fine, except—"

"The pilots said they needed thirty minutes on the ground," Will said. "You two talk. I'll get the dress out of the car and put it on the plane."

"Thanks," Cecily said. "Now, Moira, what's the 'except'?"

Will walked toward a Subaru station wagon, the only car on the tarmac in the private section of the Burlington airport, and peered through the windows. On the back seat were three animal carriers but no dress. It must be in the trunk.

His curiosity got the best of him. He opened the back door and looked inside the window of one of the carriers.

"Mrrr." A small black paw touched his nose through the window.

Will thought that was really cute. "Hey, kitten. Got some friends in those other nylon palaces?" It was cold here, a sharp contrast to the heat of May in Dallas. He'd be warmer in the car, so he climbed in, pushed the cases over to make room and sat down before he looked through the window of the second carrier, where an enormous yellow tabby was sitting up with its tail curling around its feet, purring at him. In the third case was another kitten, a calico. In a few minutes, the entire car seemed to be purring.

It was a comfortable sound. Will opened the two kittens' cases, then let out the big tabby. An outraged "Meow" came from the front seat, where, upon investigating, Will found another case and opened it. A fluffy gray-and-white cat got out, stretched and leaped straight over the seat and onto his shoulder.

He was covered with cats. They not only purred, they snuggled, climbed, kneaded him with their soft paws and very sharp claws. He leaned back and closed his eyes.

"Will." Will jolted awake. It was Cecily, looking at him through the car window, which he rolled down an inch. "What are you doing?" Her voice softened.

"Hey, Buster. Look, Mommy's back for a minute. Come on, Rags, give me a snuzzle." Both cat and woman put their faces to the crack.

Will yawned. "I thought there were eleven of them."

"These four love to ride in the car. They would have been heartbroken if Moira had left them at home."

"Thirteen," Moira said from behind Cecily. "You have thirteen cats."

"Don't be silly, Moira. I only have eleven."

"Thirteen. I counted."

"When I left at four this morning," Cecily said pointedly, "I had eleven."

"When I got to your house at seven," Moira said firmly, "you had thirteen."

Cecily stared at her. "Somebody brought home friends?"

"Apparently."

"Huh," Cecily said, then turned back to Will. "Have you had a good time here in the car with four of my *thirteen* cats?"

"Yes." It surprised him, too. "They almost put me to sleep."

"So I noticed. We have to put them back in the cases so Moira can take off. The pilots are calling us. You got the dress, right?"

"Wrong," Will said, struggling to convince the calico it wanted back in its case.

"Will! What if we'd let Moira drive away with it because you decided to organize a little predawn playgroup?"

"I don't know. We'd have to come back, I guess." He'd put everyone away now, and while they weren't happy about it, they seemed to be settling down. He got out of the car, opened the trunk and got the dress. "Back to our chariot. Thanks again, Moira. Glad I got to meet you."

He got the same speculative look in return, but this one was a little more positive. "Great to meet you, too." She smiled. "Safe trip."

"I DIDN'T KNOW CATS WERE SO...relaxing," Will said.

The sun was coming up and the sky was streaked with pink as the plane took off to wing them back to Dallas. The mountains were a hazy blue, the trees bare-limbed with a few touches of bright, new green at the tips.

"You folks want some coffee when we level out, there's a carafe in the kitchen area with some cinnamon rolls. Water, soft drinks, snacks—help yourselves."

The voice came over the intercom. The pilots had apparently decided invisibility was the safest route with these two passengers.

"Coffee?" Cecily said.

"I was thinking about a little more, um, sleep," Will said, putting his hand on her knee and caressing it.

An hour and a half later, bone-tired and satisfied, Cecily fell asleep, then woke up to an odd clicking sound. She rolled over. Will wasn't in sight. He must have moved to the front of the cabin. She slipped her dress over her head and peeked through the curtains.

Will sat in a booth composed of two long, leather-covered benches with a table between them. He'd plugged his laptop into the airplane's phone line and was frowning deeply and scrolling madly down a Web page. A cup of coffee and a huge cinnamon roll sat on the table. He was up for the night.

With a deep sigh, she faced up to the truth. She'd

hoped Will was a playboy who'd take her out of herself, and instead he was a workaholic just like herself.

Barefoot, she snuggled in beside him on one of the padded benches and put her head on his shoulder. "Okay," she said, "let's see what we can learn about Gus."

"IF HE'S TELLING THE TRUTH—that the weather is keeping him away—he must be in the D.C. area," Will said a while later. "I talked to the pilot just before you woke up. He said we took a half circle around the area to avoid the storm, and according to the Internet, Dulles and Reagan airports are the only ones showing canceled flights due to inability to take off. The other airports, like O'Hare, are just suffering the consequences, waiting for planes out of D.C., people missing connections, that kind of thing."

"What could he be doing there?" Cecily wondered aloud. "Planning to blow up something?"

Will leaned back and shrugged. "Steal something? Make a big drug delivery?"

"Now we're catastrophizing."

"He has income coming from somewhere."

"What are you going to do?"

"I don't know. I don't have enough evidence to stop the wedding. I don't have any evidence, just suspicions."

"You have to make your suspicions known sometime, though, don't you?"

"I was hoping I could just ask Gus outright and tell him he has to prove anything he tells me before I can file his tax return. I'd rather do it after the wedding—if there is a wedding."

"And let Sally marry a dangerous man?"

Will hesitated. "Didn't you get the feeling that Sally and Derek were in on whatever Gus is doing?"

"I did," Cecily admitted.

"So I'm not that worried about Sally anymore, unless Gus doesn't turn up for the wedding. I just wonder what I'm supposed to do." He laid his head back and closed his eyes. "Pursue Gus's sources of income down to the last dime, even if it means ruining him? And by doing that, making Sally unhappy, being resented by my aunt and uncle, damaging my mother's relationship with her sister, not to mention causing tension among our friends? Or just drop it, take Gus's facts as he gave them to me and sign the return?"

Cecily thought about it and knew it would be a hard choice and that the choice he made would reveal the kind of man Will really was. "The important thing," she said slowly, "is to make a choice. Whatever you do, do it all the way."

"Black-and-white. Family and friends on one hand, my profession on the other."

"I know. Hardest choice in the world." She paused, thinking. "Back in the old days, doctors often had to choose between saving the mother or the baby. There wasn't a halfway measure. There were so many things to take into consideration, like which one had the best chance of survival after the choice was made. Sometimes," she added, caressing him with her gaze, "they chose wrong, but they had to make a decision."

He sighed. "You're right. So do I."

"The sooner the better."

He turned to her, then picked up her hand. "Thank you. It won't be easy, whatever I do. But it would be easier," he said, looking deep into her eyes, "if I had you to help me through it."

"I'll be happy to talk to you anytime," she assured him. Inside, tension was building. She knew tomorrow couldn't end just like that with her going away and never seeing him again. They'd made too strong a connection—exactly what she hadn't intended to let happen.

"As you said, we've gotten to be friends. I want to be more than that."

"We barely know each other." She wanted to plead with him to go back to bed and stop all the serious talk. It would be a cop-out, but that's exactly what she wanted to do. Cop out. "There are all sorts of things you don't know about me. You might hate me when you got to know me better."

"I doubt that. But we'll never know if we're not together." He smiled a warm, sweet smile, that almost made her want to throw her arms around him and shout, "Marry me!"

But she didn't intend to marry. She was doing well in her field. She might practice a few more years and then start teaching in one of the schools of veterinary medicine. That would mean moving. To keep her options open, she had to stay free and unencumbered.

Even as all these sensible thoughts went through her head, she was getting drawn into the green-and-gold pools of Will's eyes. Her body was beginning to tingle. She was beginning to want him.

Oh, so much more than that. She was beginning to want to settle down with him and eleven—no, thirteen—cats. She had to shake the image and shake it fast. So she said the coldest thing she could think of. "Now, Will," she said with a bright smile and a sad heart, "you know this is just a little fling we're having, making up for the fling we didn't have when we were teenagers. It turned out to be more stressful than we'd planned, but we can't let our emotions run away with us and try to turn it into something it isn't."

He stroked her hand, started to speak a couple of times, then finally said, "Cecily, why wouldn't you let me kiss you that afternoon in the groundskeeper's cottage?"

She gazed at him for a long moment. "Because the staff were absolutely forbidden to become involved with the riders. The job at the stables meant a lot to me. If you'd kissed me, I would have been fired."

"The job meant more to you than kissing me?" She felt he was trying for a teasing tone, but he failed. He was asking her something deeper and more important.

"Whether it did or not, I'd taken the job and made the commitment," she said.

"But did it matter more?"

She couldn't look him in the eyes anymore. Gazing at the tabletop, she said, "I guess it did."

"Do you still feel the same way—that the job is more important than a personal relationship?"

"I don't know," she whispered. "I'm asking myself the same question."

She could tell he didn't like her answer, but he didn't let go of her hand.

HE UNDERSTOOD WHAT SHE WAS saying and instinctively he felt pain. In the few hours they'd spent together, exploring the physical side of their youthful friendship at last, he'd found something both gentle and tough as steel, sensitive and creative but smart and practical, as well. He wanted to do more exploring, wanted to give this relationship a chance.

Look at her—thirteen cats, four of who came to meet her at the airport. It amused him, but it also said something important about her. She was serious about her profession and he appreciated that. He was serious about his profession, too, but he wanted more than that one thing in his life. She had more love to give than casual sex would ever allow her to demonstrate. Their brief time together hadn't been one of many one-night stands for her, it had been a one-time thing. He was sure of it.

He surely felt like a man in love, and it was possible, of course, that she hadn't fallen for him the way he'd apparently fallen for her. That would hurt. Even if it hurt, he didn't intend to let her slip away from him without finding out.

"I didn't mean to scare you," he said, realizing he had. "I just think we ought to work out ways to see each other."

"Maybe we could do that," Cecily said, but her eyes were still round and worried. "Like a trip now and then. I do stay awfully busy, even on weekends…."

He waved that away. "So do I, especially in personal and corporate tax seasons, but let's say we manage it. After a few visits back and forth, if we're still liking each other—" he paused to smile tentatively "—you could look around at some of the cattle operations here, find out what veterinarians they use, see if you might like to work in Texas."

It alarmed him when her eyes narrowed. "You could see what accounting firms have offices in Burlington, too," she said.

"Yes, of course," he said in a hurry, then realized he should point out the negatives of his being the one to move. "In the accounting business, you usually do better in the long run by staying with the same firm."

"And you want to make as much money as you possibly can, for the cars and the clothes with logos."

"The what?"

"Nothing."

"I'll investigate Burlington, of course," he said, wondering what he'd said wrong.

SO THAT WAS THE BOTTOM line. Will wasn't impulsive enough to ask her this soon to give up her job for him, but he was suggesting that she would be the one to adjust to his job. She had no doubt she could find a position near Houston—one with a long commute, probably, but people adjusted to those long commutes. The closest veterinary school, though, if she followed through on her desire to teach, was in College Station, some distance from Houston. So she had a hard choice to make, too—stick with her career plans or do whatever it took to continue this thing she'd found with Will, whatever it turned out to be. It wasn't life and death, but it wasn't an easy choice, either.

If she let up on her career in order to spend time with Will and the relationship didn't live up to its promise, she'd have to work hard to regain her position in the veterinary world. If she stuck to her current attitude of total commitment to career and gave up the possibility of exploring a long-term relationship with Will she might regret it for the rest of her life. Her career was highly satisfying, but it wouldn't keep her warm at night or give her children or someone with whom to grow old. If she wanted those things, she'd have to reconsider her bias against marriage.

"We're tired and strung out, and I've given up on Gus for now," Will said. "We can talk some more tomorrow." He broke the awkward mood entirely by moving his mouth slowly down to hers and brushing it back and forth. "We're still more than an hour away from Dallas. Why waste a second of the time worrying about the future?"

No, not an easy choice. She opted for the physical delight of making love with Will, storing up for the dry season to come, and the plane roared on toward Dallas, the wedding and the time she would have to make that choice.

12

"GO UP TO YOUR ROOM and start ironing your dress," Will said when the taxi pulled up in front of the hotel. "I'll take care of the driver." Cecily draped the dress over her arm and started toward the entrance, but he tugged her back. "After I check with Gator, see if Gus has turned up, we can shower together—" he dropped a kiss on her nose "—for old times' sake."

This was nothing like the old times. Looking back at the way she'd yearned for Will, too shy to speak to him, the way she'd run from her one chance to kiss him, those times seemed a lot simpler. In her room, she got out of her rumpled silk dress and gave it one last pat before she stuffed it into her suitcase. How, she wondered, did you get something dry-cleaned in Blue Hill? She put on her blue-striped shirt and went to the closet for the iron and ironing board. The dress would challenge her domestic skills to the max.

She was already challenged long before getting to the ironing part. It seemed that setting up an ironing board was far more complicated than setting an equine bone. It didn't surprise her to hear a knock on the door to the hall just when she'd gotten herself obscenely tangled up with the thing. As Will had said, everything they set out to do seemed to be interrupted by a knock or a ring.

"Mother!" Samantha Connaught was the last person she'd expected to see when she opened the door. But there she was, standing in the hall, slim as always and beautifully clothed as always—but her hair was untidy, she wasn't wearing any makeup and she was leaning on a contraption that looked like a stand from which an intravenous liquid dripped into the vein of a hospital patient. "What happened to you?"

"What happened to me? After you called, I stayed awake the rest of the night wondering what had gone wrong. And now that I've seen you, I know my premonitions were right. You haven't even started getting ready, and you're supposed to be downstairs at eleven. Oh, dear, were you getting ready to *iron* your bridesmaid's dress?"

She bustled into the room in her pale blue silk suit and a second later she screamed. "Look at it!" She was staring at the dress that Cecily had laid out on the bed—the bed she hadn't slept in last night. "It's a wreck. It's supposed to be on the van going to the church at ten-thirty! Thank goodness I'm here. I'll get you ready and then see what I can do about my own appearance."

To Cecily's relief, her mother disengaged herself from the device she'd been hanging on to. No bags of fluid hung from it. There were no needles in her mother's still-shapely arm. "What the hell is that thing?" Cecily asked.

"Don't swear. It's my clothes steamer."

"You brought a steamer on the plane?"

"I called the hotel," Samantha Connaught said, sounding defensive, "and asked if the cleaning service worked on weekends. The very nice lady I spoke with said no, but there were irons in the room. Then

I started having nightmares about you ironing your dress, so I got Fred and me an even earlier flight on another airline and put us in first class. They were happy to put the steamer in the coat compartment."

"Mo-ther," Cecily groaned.

"You sound like your daddy. I ordered coffee and pastries for us. They should be up in a minute," Samantha went on briskly. "I was desperate for more coffee, and I know we shouldn't be eating pastries, but to heck with it, we are. I'll start steaming your dress. Get in the shower. You look like you've been up all night."

"That's what a wedding weekend is—party, party, party," Cecily said limply.

"Seems more like a funeral from what I've heard," Samantha said, unpacking equipment and examining the dress she'd laid out on the bed.

Cecily's eyes widened. "You know about Gus?"

"Elaine called me right after you did. She's hysterical. Jim Bob didn't buy the story Sally was telling at the rehearsal dinner, so he was storming around the house, calling private eyes on his cell while she and I talked. He won't have his little girl humiliated. He's decided to find the man and force him to go through with the wedding even if they have to do a quiet annulment in a week or two. She did tell me how pretty you looked last night. That was a relief. But the two of you left me wide awake and thinking I'd better get down here fast."

"So forget me and go to Elaine's rescue."

"Like you don't need rescuing? You have bags under your eyes. Thirty, with bags under your eyes." Samantha shook her head, then began searching for an electrical outlet for the steamer. "Go on, dear, take your shower. Why are you dancing around in circles?"

She was dancing around in circles in an attempt to keep her mother's back turned toward Will's room. For good reason. While her mother was bent double, her trim, blue-silk rear end jutting up into the air as she plugged in the steamer, the connecting door opened. Will stood there for a split second, the doorway framing him in all his naked glory, while Cecily pointed desperately toward the prominent rear end. He stared at her, frozen with shock, then silently closed the door.

She was thirty years old and realizing that nothing had changed since they were teenagers—he still made her want what she couldn't, wouldn't have. Their last chance to be alone together, to resolve the things they'd talked about in the night, had been stolen from them by an overzealous mother and a full-size professional clothes steamer.

She could think of only one thing to do—take her shower, and keep it cool.

"Now we'll do your hair," her mother said when Cecily had emerged from the bathroom wrapped in a towel. She frowned. "And your makeup."

"Mother, I can do—"

"Put something on first. Something cute and casual to wear in the limo."

"Yes, ma'am. Is that the coffee?" She pointed toward a napkin-covered silver tray.

"Get dressed. I'll pour."

Cecily cut the tags off one of the skirt-and-top combinations the Sutherland's salesperson had selected for her and went back to the bathroom with the outfit and the lingerie she'd wear under her dress. She slipped into the skirt. The top was a shelf-bra camisole. "Do I need a bra with the bridesmaid dress?" she called out to her mother.

Ominous hissing sounds came from steamer in the bedroom. "Of course you need a...well, no, I guess you don't. This thing has bones."

Cecily smiled and struggled into the camisole. It was pale blue. The skirt fit snugly over her tummy, then exploded into pleats, not too full, just flirty. It was cream with blue flowers. Why were people always picking out blue for her? It was pretty, though, and resembled the outfits the other bridesmaids had been wearing yesterday. She'd feel anonymous, and found the idea comforting. She felt that if anyone took a moment to look at her, they'd be able to read her like a book and know she was a woman reluctantly and despairingly in love.

Combing out her hair, she went back into the bedroom. Her mother had poured two cups of coffee, and Cecily picked one up. It was hot and fragrant. A frosted roll caught her eye, and she balanced it on the saucer. If only she could dispel the image of Will in her doorway, the memory of his hands on her in the night, she might actually feel faintly happy. All she could think about was that she'd never experience those moments again.

"I'll let this hang a while," Samantha was saying, "and then touch it up. Vera Wang was such a good choice for the bridesmaids' dresses. Now, let's get started on your hair."

Cecily suddenly felt tired enough to give in. She collapsed into the chair that pulled up to the desk while Samantha unplugged the steamer and plugged in her own hair dryer. When the warm air from the dryer hit her scalp and her mother began lifting strands of hair with a large, round bristle brush, Cecily felt a calm descend over her.

It made her feel like a little girl again, being dressed up for a birthday party. Her hair had been silvery-blond then, and everyone told her how pretty she was. Samantha had been a good mother in those days, tender and caring. It was Cecily herself who'd caused the problems between them. The very fact that her mother had named her Cecily indicated certain expectations, and they didn't include horses, gymnastics and veterinary medicine. Samantha had wanted a doll to dress.

Cecily pondered this and decided she could be a doll to dress for a few minutes, as long as it didn't impact the rest of her life.

"Your hair is so lovely. Will you wear it up or down?" Samantha's voice had softened, as if she, too, were reliving those days long ago.

"Sally has hairdressers coming to the church to do some kind of messy ponytail thing."

"I know the style."

"Mother…" Cecily had wanted to ask the question for years, and had a feeling the time was now—or wait for her own wedding day, which she was still fairly certain would be never. "What made you stick with Daddy instead of your career?"

Samantha aimed the dryer at the hairbrush wound with Cecily's hair. "I guess you're old enough for us to talk about these things."

Cecily hoped she was. She steeled herself against some terrible revelation that would change her perception of her parents forever. She took a sip of coffee, fortifying herself.

"The truth is…" Samantha said hesitantly, then she sighed. "The truth is, well, he's just fantastic in bed."

Cecily choked on the coffee, which went up her

nose. "Are we still talking about Daddy?" she spluttered.

"Of course," Samantha said, patting drops of coffee off Cecily's camisole with a damp cloth. "Who else would I be talking about?"

"But he's so quiet and reserved. He doesn't listen to you, he doesn't answer you...."

"That's when he's working." Samantha's smile was positively smug. "He's different at night. And in the morning. Sometimes at noon. We wanted more children, but I think the reason I didn't get pregnant again was that we made love so often that his sperm count was always low, so..."

"Mother," Cecily said faintly, "can we wait until I'm ten years older to expand on the details?"

"Of course. I don't want to embarrass you."

"It's too late. You have."

Samantha sighed. "I worried about you all through high school, looking for signs of nymphomania. Coming from the two of us, it seemed likely, but you didn't seem to inherit—"

"Yes," Cecily said distinctly, "I did."

It startled her mother, who would obviously have loved to ask for clarification, so while she was still looking gobsmacked, Cecily went into the bathroom and began putting on her makeup. Alone. She felt pretty gobsmacked herself. Her mother, *her mother,* had married for love and sex, had given up a career for love and sex. That was more amazing than learning that her reserved, studious father was in fact a rampaging tiger in the bedroom.

Amazing and in fact, just what she'd needed to hear at this important moment in her life.

Ten minutes later she was still working on her

eyes. She was doing it by the book—concealer, shadow, dark stuff beneath the bone, liner above and below, mascara and eyebrow pencil, resenting every instruction on that list the makeup salesperson had made for her mother. She looked at herself in a mirror and decided she'd met clowns who were made up more subtly.

But the worst was over. She checked the list for what she still had to do. Foundation, powder, blusher, lip fix, lip liner, lipstick, blotted, with lip gloss on top. She gritted her teeth. Maybe the worst wasn't quite over yet.

She was examining the row of brushes, looking for the one suitable for applying foundation, when she heard voices coming from the bedroom. Recognizing Will's, she went right out.

"Oh. Will. Hello," she said in a bright, unnatural voice. "Mother, this is…"

"We've been talking," Samantha said. Her eyes were gleaming almost lustfully. Not lusting for Will, lusting for this highly desirable male to be interested in her daughter. "I remember Will's mom and dad from long ago. We were just discussing the cruise through Alaska they're planning this summer."

"Yes, we were," Will said. His eyes were glinting with restrained mischief as he stood there in perfectly pressed khaki trousers and a black shirt with the sleeves rolled up, holding the hanger of a plastic-covered white suit, his groomsman gear. The suit would have done Elvis proud. "I was just telling your mother that Sally asked me to come by and see if you were ready. And also to carry your dress down for you."

Damn him, he was enjoying himself.

"Aren't you an *angel*," Samantha cooed. Cecily could hear her thinking, *What a well-brought-up young man*.

"Is Gus back?" she asked abruptly.

The fun went out of Will's eyes as his gaze slid from her to her mother. "Mother knows he left," she explained. "Elaine Shipley called her. Jim Bob didn't buy the weather story. He was calling private eyes, Elaine was calling Mother." That was interesting, too—that Elaine Shipley, with all her Dallas friends, would call Samantha instead, who she actually saw about twice a year.

"Last Gator heard, which was five minutes ago, he hadn't shown up yet."

Cecily groaned. "Sally must be at the end of her rope."

"Well, we all have to go on to the last possible second as though nothing were wrong," Samantha said firmly. "Stay positive for Sally's sake. And Elaine's. Cecily…"

When Samantha turned back to Cecily, Will's gaze skimmed up and down Cecily's skirt and camisole and he gave her a thumbs-up. Her mother was looking at her, but Cecily couldn't take her eyes off Will. Sally's wedding was falling apart, and she still couldn't think about anything but Will.

"…you're almost ready, aren't you, darling?" Samantha persisted. "Need any help with the rest of your face?"

"No," she stammered, trying hard to meet her mother's eyes, "I think I've got the hang of it. Go on downstairs, Will. I can carry my dress. It weighs about eight inches. I mean ounces." Heat rose to her face.

"Her dress is ready," Samantha said, "but why don't you wait for Cecily? You and I can visit while she does those last few little things."

"I need a bag with pantyhose and my shoes…."

"I've put that together for you. I'm sorry I didn't think to bring you a pretty little tote to carry, but…"

"Not to worry. Put everything in my medical bag."

"Your medical bag!"

"She never travels without it," Will said. His eyes were glimmering a little again.

"Yes, in my medical bag," Cecily said, giving Will a sharp look. "I'll hurry."

"And what happened to your shoes, young lady? I cleaned them up as well as I could, but…

"I delivered a baby in them," Cecily said, whisking off to the bathroom.

"You what?"

"Let Will tell you," she yelled back. "It was his baby."

That ought to keep her mother from inquiring about inherited diseases or scandalous behavior in Will's family history—at least in the time it would take Cecily to finish giving herself the perfect maid-of-honor face, whatever that was. The wedding photos would be beautiful, even if the groom didn't appear in any of them.

"ALL RIGHT, DARLING, YOU LOOK wonderful and I'm off to do something with my face and hair." Samantha gave Cecily an excessively careful kiss and Will a little hug. "I'm so glad we met," she told him. "I'll make a point of seeing your mom and dad and congratulating Gator. Cecily, don't you dare leave the reception without telling us, okay?"

Will felt a stab in the pit of his stomach at this reminder that Cecily would be leaving soon, leaving without him, leaving without their having a moment alone together. "'Bye, Mother," Cecily was saying. "Thanks." A serious look came over her face. "You gave me something to think about." Then she was herself again. "Come on, Will. I've made us five minutes late. Sally's already upset enough. We shouldn't make it worse."

After his near miss, almost walking in naked on Samantha Connaught, Will had had a brainstorm. He'd thought of a solution to both his problems—Gus and Cecily. It would take some maneuvering. He might have to play hardball. But first he had to know if she wanted more of him than a few weekend visits.

They got on the elevator with several members of the wedding party, making it impossible for him to say anything with the bridesmaids making eyes at him, telling Cecily how gorgeous she looked and then lapsing back to the only topic of interest currently circulating through the Courtland—whether Gus had gotten back yet.

They got off the elevator to find Paula Perry, the wedding planner, hopping up and down on one stiletto heel and then the other. "Come on, wedding party, we need those outfits for the van. We have to load the limos." She was hustling them along, a dynamo in the same dress she'd been wearing the night before—the same color, anyway. A color a lot like Cecily's little top and bikini panties. *Dangerous thought. Drop it now.* "We have to get there early for the photographs. Move, move…that's it, suits and dresses to the van, then the men to the black limo and the women to the white."

They wouldn't be talking on the way to the church, either.

"Have you heard if Gus is back?" the chirpy bridesmaid asked Paula.

"He will be," she said, her lips set in a grim line.

Will fumed. He could rebel. He could accuse the wedding planner of sexist attitudes and demand to ride with the women. No, that wouldn't work. They wouldn't be alone. They'd be with all those women. Including Muffy, and then it would all be out in the open and his folks would be naming his and Cecily's first baby. So he'd demand to take Cecily in his car, no matter what anybody thought….

Unfortunately, while he planned his strategy, he'd somehow lined up with everyone at the van and then gone with the herd to the black car. By the time he'd decided what to do, he was sitting in the middle seat of the stretch limo, hot, frustrated and already missing Cecily.

He tried to imagine how much he'd be missing her tomorrow or a week from now. It was not a pretty thought.

13

AFTER A LOOK AROUND FOR WILL, Cecily got into the white limo. The three bridesmaids filled the back seat, so Cecily slid into the middle seat. Sally sat in the front, pale but beautiful, calm but not cheerful. Once Cecily was settled, she put her arms around her. "It's going to be all right. I'm sure of it," she lied.

"Of course it will," Sally said, sounding like a robot.

The limo door opened and Muffy got in. Cecily scooted over. Muffy said, "Cecily, you look beautiful!" and then threw her arms around Sally. "Don't worry, sugar, Gus will get here in time."

"Everybody stop hugging me and telling me everything's going to be fine," Sally burst out. "You're doing it because you know it won't be fine. Well, I know it will."

Her outburst was startling and they rode silently to the church. From the limo they went to a classroom-turned-dressing room, accompanied by the wedding planner. Mrs. Shipley waited for them there, wringing her hands, naturally. A hairdresser stood poised behind a chair, armed with combs, brushes and hair spray. Where there should have been laughter and joy, Cecily expected someone to say, "Scalpel, Nurse."

"YOU GUYS LOOK GREAT." THE speaker, a male assistant to the wedding planner, made a small adjustment to one of Will's shirt ruffles. "Just hang here until we call you."

"Why?" Will said.

The man blinked. "Well, the men are supposed to stay in here and the ladies in their own dressing room. Those are my instructions. We don't want anybody disappearing. Anybody *else* disappearing," he amended himself.

"I need to speak with one of the ladies," Will said.

"You can't go in there." The man was very firm. "No peeking."

"You're thinking about the bride and groom," Will argued. "The groom's not supposed to see the bride in her wedding gown until the wedding." He wondered if Gus would get to see Sally in her wedding gown at all. "Doesn't mean the rest of the wedding party can't see each other."

"All I know is—"

"Besides..." Will knew he was getting wound up, but he couldn't stop himself. "Besides, we're doing group photos before the wedding and we'll be peeking then. Why not now?"

He had the guy looking pretty nervous. Mutiny in the groomsmen's dressing room. Big stuff. "I'll find out," he said and scurried out.

Will left right behind him, bolting out into the hall of what appeared to be the educational wing of the church. He threw open every closed door in the vicinity and finally just bellowed, "Cecily."

No one answered.

A prim-looking woman passed by. "Happen to know where the bridesmaids are?" he asked her.

"No peeking," she scolded him.

So he followed her. The woman held a bag and had what looked like a pincushion around her wrist, and he knew for a fact that Muffy's matron-of-honor dress needed to be pinned. Will Murchison, sleuth.

Her path led him to the second floor of the wing, where he did his bellowing act again. "Cecily!"

A door popped open and Cecily's head popped out. "Will! They're holding us prisoner in here."

She stopped him dead in his tracks. "Cecily," he said in a hushed voice, "you look great in that dress." The way it hugged her breasts, she had no business being in a church. "Rapunzel, let down your hair?" he said hopefully.

"I would if I could, but I can't. The woman over there—" she cocked a thumb at the busy hairdresser "—just put it up and she'd kill me if I took it down. She used so much hair spray, I'm not sure it will ever come down," she muttered to herself. "But..." She came all the way out of the room and said, "I can escape."

She floated over to him, a butterfly in the white dress, elegant in long white gloves. He opened his arms to her. She came slowly toward him. His heart thudded in his chest.

Commotion suddenly filled the hall. "Okay, we're starting the photo shoot. Ladies, down to the chapel."

"Will, what are you doing here?" Muffy said as the bridesmaids exploded from their dressing room. Will swam with the sea of white as it trooped down the stairs and along a corridor that connected the wing to the church. He tried to stick close to Cecily, but in the corridor, Muffy tackled him.

"Will, I have something to say to you."

"Later, Muff."

"No, now."

They'd reached the chapel and apparently had a moment of free time while the photographer adjusted his equipment. "Now" was his time to talk to Cecily, maybe his only chance. Frustrated and impatient, Will tried to give Muffy his full attention.

"Thank you," she said, putting her hand on his arm, "for taking care of me yesterday. No one could have a more wonderful twin brother than you."

At last she had his attention. "Well, that's a first."

She smiled at him. "I know I was bad to you when we were kids, but…" Her smile faded. "I was always so jealous of you." She sighed. "I was the oldest twin, but you turned out to be the smartest and the nicest and the cutest and the most athletic—well, just *everything*."

He stared at her. Damn, were those tears stinging his eyes? He was falling apart!

"I wish I hadn't been such a bitch," she said, and her eyes shone as if she were about to cry, too. "I feel as if I missed out on the best friendship I could ever have had. Can we be friends now?"

Can we do it quickly? went through Will's mind as he hugged her carefully, mindful of the dress. This wedding, someone else's wedding, was turning out to be the beginning of the rest of his life.

As soon as Muffy had turned away, giving him one last smile and pat on the arm, he spun and found Cecily gazing wistfully at him. He went straight to her. "Cecily, we need to—"

"We're ready, folks. Okay, we want to start with a shot of all the bridesmaids…."

Damn! Will fidgeted and fumed while the photographer took a mile of film, snapping and snapping at the row of bridesmaids. Will just stared at one of them—Cecily, with her hair up in a casual knot, strands falling around her face and sprayed so they'd stay there. He'd like to see her without the spray, would like to take her hair down, brush it, run his fingers through it.

She was spectacular in the white dress, holding a bouquet of white flowers—too stunning for words. He wanted to touch her, to kiss her, to tell her that whatever else went wrong with this wedding, they'd be all right.

What he really wanted to do was take the dress off.

She was gazing at him, too, and her lips parted as if she'd read his mind.

It almost did him in. He took a step toward her.

"Groomsmen."

Will froze.

"The best man isn't with us yet, so we'll skip the group photo and start pairing you guys up with bridesmaids for individual photos."

Will literally snatched Cecily out of the line of bridesmaids. It might be his only chance.

"That's right, Will and Cecily, you'll be opposite each other in the line. Muffy, you'll have to wait for a photo with Derek because he's late getting here. Will, stand beside Cecily, but a little behind her…"

And speak directly into her left ear. "Cecily, we'll have to say our goodbyes now."

"…hand on her elbow, Will, not around her shoulders…good, good…"

"I have a plan, sort of," she said out of the side of her mouth. "Can you come up to Vermont next weekend?"

"No," he said. "I have to work. But…"

"Would you be free for the Memorial Day week-

end?" She was starting to sound sad, while his ela-
tion was growing by leaps and bounds. She didn't
want to tell him goodbye.

"I don't know exactly where I'll be on Memorial
Day, but…"

"Fourth of July?"

He yawned. "It's hard to travel over the Fourth
of July."

"Labor Day?" She was starting to sound desperate. That was good.

"It's a little far ahead to schedule Labor Day."

"So I suppose it's way too far ahead to schedule
Thanksgiving."

"Straighten up, you two. Smile, Cecily. You look
like you've seen a ghost. That's right. Nice smile…"

"Are you telling me goodbye—for good?" Cecily
asked him, smiling maniacally.

"No, I was thinking how much easier it would
be if I—"

"Look at the camera, please, Will, and stop moving your lips, both of you."

Will hissed through closed, curved lips. "—if I
moved to Vermont. Then I wouldn't have to do all
that traveling."

"What?" She spun to face him.

The photographer heaved an exasperated sigh.
"Can we have a little cooperation here?"

Cecily turned toward the camera again, and Will
decided not to keep her dangling. "I've decided to re-
sign from the firm. I'll set up my own office. In Vermont, if you'll have me. You may have to support me
financially while I get the business up and running."
He was exaggerating here, but he thought it sounded good.

"But Will, is that what you want? A small office instead of a high-powered, well-staffed one?" she spoke with her mouth skewed to one side.

"Is she having a stroke?" the photographer moaned.

"That's the choice I'm making," Will said, soft and low. "I can't lie and I can't do damage to the people I love. It will take me a month or so to wrap things up, but I'm going to hand over Gus's tax business to a colleague and welcome Gus into the family, whoever, whatever, he is. If Sally loves him, that's enough for me." He moved in a little closer. "And if you think you could learn to love me, I'll move anywhere."

"Oh, Will." Cecily seemed to forget they weren't alone. She turned and gazed into his eyes. "I think there's a strong chance, a very strong chance, I might." Her eyes shone. "You would really do this to be close to me?"

"Come on, people, let me get one decent shot before you…"

"Can't help myself," Will said. "You're just too great in bed. Gotta have you." He smiled as he folded his arms around her and she came to him, face upturned, lips parted.

"I give up," the photographer said disgustedly. "I'll shoot somebody else first."

"This wedding is nuts." That was Paula Perry, getting dramatic. "Everybody's missing or late or mad or falling in love. Does *anybody* know if Gus is back yet?"

"Gus who?" Will said. His mouth moved down toward Cecily's waiting one, and in front of the entire wedding party, he kissed her.

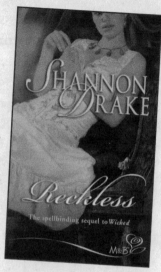

From the elite circles of Victorian London society to the golden sands of Egypt

When Kat Adair plunges into the waves to rescue a drowning man, it is the beginning of an odyssey that will sweep her on an adventure of danger and desire. Convinced she is in love with the man she saved, Egyptologist David Turnberry, she plots to linger among the highborn, hoping to win David's heart. The only problem is Hunter MacDonald – rugged archaeologist, bold adventurer, and a man who is wise to her charade.

On sale 18th August 2006

Also available by Shannon Drake
Wicked – *A novel steeped in darkness, danger and desire*

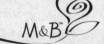

1923,
the village of Kingshampton, Berkshire...

Sophie and Lydia Westlake have always been
close, thinking of themselves more like sisters than
cousins. Sophie has always been the prettier and
more light-hearted one, leaving the shy and
retiring Lydia to grow up happily in her shadow.
But everything changes the moment dashing
young architect Christian Mellor arrives at the
village summer fête...

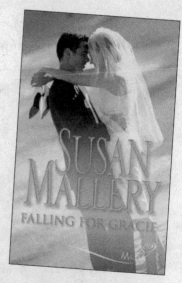

First comes love, then comes marriage...

That was Gracie's plan, anyway, at the ripe old age of fourteen. She loved eighteen-year-old heart throb Riley with a legendary desperation. Even now that she's all grown up, the locals in her sleepy town won't let her forget her youthful crush.

...but it's not as easy as it looks.
And now she's face-to-face with Riley at every turn. The one-time bad boy has come back seeking respectability – but the sparks that fly between them are anything but respectable! Gracie's determined to keep her distance, but when someone sets out to ruin both their reputations, the two discover that first love sometimes is better the second time around.

On sale 1st September 2006

0906/51 V2

SILHOUETTE®
Desire™ 2 in 1

BOSS MAN by Diana Palmer

Stubborn, smart Blake Kemp, the town's tough lawyer, hadn't looked twice at his dedicated, gentle assistant Violet before but, when she left him, Blake mounted a campaign to win her back!

TANNER TIES by Peggy Moreland

Estranged from her family, Lauren Tanner was getting her life back on track. But she hadn't counted on Luke Jordan, who was determined to bring her back to the fold by any means possible —even seduction...

THE MILLIONAIRE'S CLUB

BLACK-TIE SEDUCTION by Cindy Gerard

Christine Travers had no time for flirtatious millionaire Jacob Thorne. But he was confident that only he could satisfy her needs. So he decided to show her just how good he could be...

LESS-THAN-INNOCENT INVITATION
by Shirley Rogers

Years had passed since Melissa Mason had thrown Logan's marriage proposal back in his face and left town. But the burning anger and desire he felt seeing her again made him demand answers...

APACHE NIGHTS by Sheri WhiteFeather

Though Joyce Riggs and combat trainer Kyle Prescott were as different as night and day, they entered into a no-strings affair... But what would happen if Joyce confessed her secret hope?

BEYOND BUSINESS by Rochelle Alers

One look at sultry secretary Renee and Sheldon Blackstone knew he would make her his mistress. But he hadn't bargained on her vulnerability and charm chipping away at the shell that encased his heart.

On sale from 15th September 2006

Visit our website at www.silhouette.co.uk